THE NEW MAGDALEN

WILKIE COLLINS

THE NEW MAGDALEN

ALAN SUTTON

First published in 1873

First published in this edition in the United Kingdom in 1993
Alan Sutton Publishing Ltd
Phoenix Mill • Far Thrupp • Stroud • Gloucestershire • GL5 2BU

First published in this edition in the United States of America in 1993
Alan Sutton Publishing Inc • 83 Washington Street • Dover • NH 03820

British Library Cataloguing in Publication Data

Collins, Wilkie
New Magdalen. – New ed. – (Pocket Classics)
I. Title II. Series
823.8 [F]

ISBN 0-7509-0455-0

Library of Congress Cataloging in Publication Data applied for

Cover picture: The Thank You Letter *by Louie Marie de Schryver (1862–1942). (Photograph
courtesy of the Fine Art Photographic Library Ltd, London)*

Typeset in 9/10 pt Bembo.
Typesetting and origination by
Alan Sutton Publishing Limited.
Printed in Great Britain by
The Guernsey Press Company Limited,
Guernsey, Channel Islands.

To the Memory
of
CHARLES ALLSTON COLLINS

April 9, 1873

'LEAD US NOT INTO TEMPTATION.'

CONTENTS

FIRST SCENE

THE COTTAGE ON THE FRONTIER

SECOND SCENE

MABLETHORPE HOUSE

EPILOGUE

BIOGRAPHICAL NOTE

WILLIAM WILKIE COLLINS was born on 8 January 1824, in New Cavendish Street, London, the elder son of William Collins, a fashionable and successful painter of the early nineteenth century, who counted among his friends Wordsworth and Coleridge. William Collins was a religious man, and in his strict observances may have been a repressive influence on his son, who appears to have inherited his mother Harriet Geddes' attractive and friendly personality. Wilkie was named after his godfather, Sir David Wilkie, RA, a bachelor and close friend of the family.

Little is known of Wilkie's early life. His brother, Charles, was born in 1828, and the family lived comfortably, first in Hampstead, then in Bayswater, where Wilkie attended Maida Hill Academy. The following year the whole family left for Italy, where they spent two years, visiting the major art collections and learning Italian. On their return, Wilkie attended a private boarding school in Highbury, where his story-telling talent was recognized and exploited by a senior prefect who demanded, with the threat of physical violence, to be entertained. 'Thus', wrote Collins, 'I learnt to be amusing on a short notice and have derived benefit from those early lessons.'

When he left school in 1840, he showed no inclination to enter the Church, as his father wished, and chose, without enthusiasm, the world of commerce, accepting a post with Antrobus & Co., tea importers. He was totally unsuited to the regularity of business life, preferring to escape to the vibrant atmosphere of Paris. He started to write articles and short stories, which were accepted for publication, albeit anonymously, and in 1846 his father agreed that he should leave commerce and take up law, which would, in theory, provide him with a regular income. He studied at Lincoln's Inn Fields, and was finally called to the bar, but his legal knowledge was to be applied creatively in his novels, rather than practically in the law courts.

In his early twenties Collins painted as well as wrote. He had many friends who were artists, and he supported the new Pre-Raphaelite movement. In 1848 he had a picture exhibited in the Royal Academy. In the same year his first book was published: the memoirs of his father, who had died the previous year. These were diligently researched and provided a training ground for the emerging writer, developing his thorough methodical approach to compilation and exercising his descriptive ability. His first novel, *Antonia,* was published by Bentley's two years later. Although of no great literary merit, it was written in the then popular mode of historical romance, and so enjoyed instant success. The following year Bentley's published *Rambles beyond Railways*, an account of a holiday in Cornwall, which reflected Collins' life-long love of wild and remote places.

It was in the same year, 1851, that Wilkie Collins first met Charles Dickens, an introduction effected by their mutual friend, the artist, Augustus Egg. The meeting was significant for both, leading to a close friendship and working partnership from which both benefited. Dickens had found a friend of more stable temperament than himself, affable and tolerant, responsive to his restless demanding nature. From Collins he acquired the skill of economic and taut plotting, as evidenced in a *Tale of Two Cities* (which may be interestingly compared with Collins' story of the French Revolution, *Sister Rose*, 1855), and in his later novels. Collins was welcomed by the Dickens family, and spent many holidays with them in England and France. He was encouraged and guided in his writing by Dickens, and he must have been stimulated by the latter's enthusiasm and vitality. The two authors worked together on Dickens' magazines, *Household Words*, and *All the Year Round*. Collins was employed as an editor, and many of his works appeared first in these publications, while both writers collaborated on several short stories.

A Terribly Strange Bed – Collins' first work in the macabre genre – was the first of his short stories to appear in *Household Words*, in 1852. The following year the magazine saw the publication of *Gabriel's Marriage*, a story of a Breton fishing community. In the interim, Dickens had turned down *Mad Monkton*, a study of inherited insanity, as unsuitable subject matter, and this was later published by *Fraser's Magazine* in 1855. These, along with *Sister Rose, The Yellow Mask,* and *A Stolen Letter*, originally published in *Household Words*, were reprinted in *After Dark*, 1855, for which anthology Collins wrote the successfully economic and melodramatic *Lady of Glenwith Grange* (an inspiration for Miss Haversham?). *A Rogue's Life*, Collins' venture into the picaresque, was serialized in 1856. This was followed in 1857 by *The Dead Secret*, a full length novel, which in its complexity suggests the author's technical potential. *The Biter Bit*, which was published in 1858 and is commonly held to be the first humorous detective story, shows Collins' development of the epistolary form. Both of his two greatest novels, *A Woman in White* and *The Moonstone*, appeared first as serializations in *All the Year Round* – as did the less well known *No Name*. This unconventional study of illegitimacy was published in its full form in 1862, two years after the masterpiece of suspense and drama *A Woman in White* and six years before his original detective story, *The Moonstone*, appeared as complete books.

Another interest shared by Collins and Dickens was a love of the theatre. *The Frozen Deep*, 1857, written by Collins and starring Dickens, was inspired by an interest in the Arctic exploration of the time. It was followed by a series of minor productions, the stage version of *No Thoroughfare* (with combined authorship), enjoying a record run of two hundred nights in 1867.

Anyone meeting Collins in those days would have seen:

A neat figure of a cheerful plumpness, very small feet and hands, a full brown beard, a high and rounded forehead, a small nose not naturally intended to support a pair of large spectacles behind which his eyes shone with humour and friendship.

R.C. Lehmann, *Memories of Half a Century*

But how many would have glimpsed, as did the young artist, Rudolf Lehmann, the strange far-off look in his eyes, which gave the impression of investing 'almost everything with an air of mystery and romance'? It was suggestive of a depth of personality not accessible to many, but demonstrated by the author's expressed unconventional views of the class and social *mores* of the day; which were further borne out by what is known of his personal life. During the 1860s, Collins met and fell in love with Caroline Graves, who had a daughter by a previous marriage. He never married her, but lived with mother and daughter for most of the remainder of his life. In 1868, Caroline mysteriously married another, and Collins entered into a relationship with Martha Judd, by whom he had three children. However, by the early 1870s, he was once more living with Caroline, who was still known as Mrs Graves. It has been suggested that Martha Judd may have been employed originally by Collins as an amanuensis. Over the years Collins' health had been deteriorating. He was a victim of gout, which attacked his whole body, including his eyes. He suffered a particularly severe attack in 1868, when his mother died, and he was working on *The Moonstone*. A dedicated woman, capable of disregarding his suffering and attending only to his words was employed, to whom Collins dictated the rest of the work, but she has never been named.

In 1870 Charles Dickens died. During the previous ten years Collins had produced his best work: the three novels serialized in *All the Year Round; Armadale,* 1866, in the *Cornhill Magazine,* and *Man and Wife,* 1870, in *Cassell's Magazine.* But with Dickens' death , something in Collins seemed to die too, although his popularity remained undiminished. His novels, produced regularly until his death, were widely read, and his was some of the first fiction to appear in cheap editions. In the 1870s he enjoyed some success with the stage versions of his novels, which were produced both in London and the provinces. Two of Collins' novels were published in the early '70s; *Miss or Mrs?* in 1872, and *The New Magdalen* in 1873. Not only was Collins' work popular in England; his novels and plays were translated and produced in most European countries, including Russia, and were widely available in America. In 1873 Collins was invited to give readings in the eastern United States and Canada. Although his readings lacked the vitality of Dickens', the Americans were charmed by him.

Of course, it was not only Dickens' death which adversely affected Collins' work. His gout was becoming persistent, and he relied increasingly on laudenum to relieve the pain. However, he never lost his mental clarity, taking care to be properly informed about medicine, drugs and chemistry, as is clearly shown in *Heart and Science*, 1883, and the detailed notes he left for his last novel, *Blind Love*, 1890 – completed, posthumously, at his request, by Walter Besant. His novel *Legacy of Cain* was published in 1888, the year before he died. During his later years, his social life was restricted by poor health, but he did not become a recluse as has been suggested. He maintained close friendships with Charles Reade, Holman Hunt, the Beard and Lehmann families, and theatrical people, including Ada Cavendish and Mary Anderson. In 1889, after being involved in a cab accident, Collins' health rapidly declined, and he died while suffering from bronchitis on 23 September. He was buried at Kensal Green Cemetery.

SHEILA MICHELL

FIRST SCENE

THE COTTAGE ON THE FRONTIER

PREAMBLE

The place is France.

The time is autumn, in the year eighteen hundred and seventy – the year of the war between France and Germany.

The persons are: Captain Arnault, of the French army; Surgeon Surville, of the French ambulance; Surgeon Wetzel, of the German army; Mercy Merrick, attached as nurse to the French ambulance; and Grace Roseberry, a travelling lady on her way to England.

CHAPTER THE FIRST

THE TWO WOMEN

It was a dark night. The rain was pouring in torrents.

Late in the evening a skirmishing party of the French, and a skirmishing party of the Germans, had met by accident, near the little village of Lagrange, close to the German frontier. In the struggle that followed, the French had (for once) got the better of the enemy. For the time, at least, a few hundreds out of the host of the invaders had been forced back over the frontier. It was a trifling affair, occurring not long after the great German victory of Weissenbourg and the newspapers took little or no notice of it.

Captain Arnault, commanding on the French side, sat alone in one of the cottages of the village, inhabited by the miller of the district. The captain was reading, by the light of a solitary tallow candle, some intercepted despatches taken from the Germans. He had suffered the wood fire, scattered over the large open grate, to burn low; the red embers only faintly illuminated a part of the room. On the floor behind him lay some of the miller's empty sacks. In a corner opposite to him was the miller's solid walnut-wood bed. On the walls all round him were the miller's coloured prints, representing a happy mixture of devotional and domestic subjects. A door of communication leading into the kitchen of the cottage had been torn from its hinges, and used to carry the men wounded in the skirmish from the field. They were now comfortably laid at rest in the kitchen, under the care of the French surgeon and the English nurse attached to the ambulance. A piece of coarse canvas screened the opening between the two rooms, in place of the door. A second door, leading from the bedchamber into

the yard, was locked; and the wooden shutter protecting the
one window of the room was carefully barred. Sentinels,
doubled in number, were placed at all the outposts. The French
commander had neglected no precaution which could
reasonably insure for himself and for his men a quiet and
comfortable night.

Still absorbed in his perusal of the despatches, and now and
then making notes of what he read by the help of writing
materials placed at his side, Captain Arnault was interrupted by
the appearance of an intruder in the room. Surgeon Surville,
entering from the kitchen, drew aside the canvas screen, and
approached the little round table at which his superior officer
was sitting.

'What is it?' said the captain sharply.

'A question to ask,' replied the surgeon. 'Are we safe for the
night?'

'Why do you want to know?' enquired the captain,
suspiciously.

The surgeon pointed to the kitchen – now the hospital
devoted to the wounded men.

'The poor fellows are anxious about the next few hours,' he
replied. 'They dread a surprise; and they ask me if there is any
reasonable hope of their having one night's rest. What do you
think of the chances?'

The captain shrugged his shoulders. The surgeon persisted.
'Surely you ought to know?' he said.

'I know that we are in possession of the village for the
present,' retorted Captain Arnault, 'and I know no more. Here
are the papers of the enemy.' He held them up, and shook
them impatiently as he spoke. 'They give me no information
that I can rely on. For all I can tell to the contrary, the main
body of the Germans, outnumbering us ten to one, may be
nearer this cottage than the main body of the French. Draw
your own conclusions. I have nothing more to say.'

Having answered in those discouraging terms, Captain
Arnault got on his feet, drew the hood of his great-coat over his
head, and lit a cigar at the candle.

'Where are you going?' asked the surgeon.

'To visit the outposts.'

'Do you want this room for a little while?'

'Not for some hours to come. Are you thinking of moving any of your wounded men in here?'

'I was thinking of the English lady,' answered the surgeon. 'The kitchen is not quite the place for her. She would be more comfortable here; and the English nurse might keep her company.'

Captain Arnault smiled, not very pleasantly. 'They are two fine women,' he said, 'and Surgeon Surville is a ladies' man. Let them come in, if they are rash enough to trust themselves in here with you.' He checked himself on the point of going out, and looked back distrustfully at the lighted candle. 'Caution the women,' he said, 'to limit the exercise of their curiosity to the inside of this room.'

'What do you mean?'

The captain's forefinger pointed significantly to the closed window-shutter.

'Did you ever know a woman who could resist looking out of a window?' he asked. 'Dark as it is, sooner or later these ladies of yours will feel tempted to open that shutter. Tell them I don't want the light of the candle to betray my head-quarters to the German scouts. How is the weather? Still raining?'

'Pouring.'

'So much the better. The Germans won't see us.' With that consolatory remark he unlocked the door leading into the yard, and walked out.

The surgeon lifted the canvas screen, and called into the kitchen:

'Miss Merrick, have you time to take a little rest?'

'Plenty of time,' answered a soft voice, with an underlying melancholy in it, plainly distinguishable though it had only spoken three words.

'Come in then,' continued the surgeon, 'and bring the English lady with you. Here is a quiet room, all to yourselves.'

He held back the canvas, and the two women appeared.

The nurse led the way – tall, lithe, and graceful – attired in her uniform dress of neat black stuff, with plain linen collar and cuffs, and with the scarlet cross of the Geneva Convention embroidered on her left shoulder. Pale and sad, her expression and her manner both eloquently suggestive of suppressed suffering and sorrow, there was an innate nobility in the carriage of this woman's head, an innate grandeur in the gaze of her large grey eyes, and in the lines of her finely-proportioned face, which made her irresistibly striking and beautiful, seen under any circumstances and clad in any dress. Her companion, darker in complexion and smaller in stature, possessed attractions which were quite marked enough to account for the surgeon's polite anxiety to shelter her in the captain's room. The common consent of mankind would have declared her to be an unusually pretty woman. She wore the large grey cloak that covered her from head to foot with a grace that lent its own attractions to a plain and even shabby article of dress. The languor in her movements, and the uncertainty of tone in her voice as she thanked the surgeon, suggested that she was suffering from fatigue. Her dark eyes searched the dimly-lighted room timidly, and she held fast by the nurse's arm with the air of a woman whose nerves had been severely shaken by some recent alarm.

'You have one thing to remember, ladies,' said the surgeon. 'Beware of opening the shutter, for fear of the light being seen through the window. For the rest, we are free to make ourselves as comfortable as we can. Compose yourself, dear madam, and rely on the protection of a Frenchman who is devoted to you!' He gallantly emphasised his last words by raising the hand of the English lady to his lips. At the moment when he kissed it, the canvas screen was again drawn aside. A person in the service of the ambulance appeared, announcing that a bandage had slipped, and that one of the wounded men was to all appearance bleeding to death. The surgeon, submitting to destiny with the worst possible grace, dropped the charming Englishwoman's hand, and returned to his duties in the kitchen. The two ladies were left together in the room.

'Will you take a chair, madam?' asked the nurse.

'Don't call me "madam," ' returned the young lady cordially. 'My name is Grace Roseberry. What is your name?'

The nurse hesitated. 'Not a pretty name like yours,' she said, and hesitated again. 'Call me "Mercy Merrick," ' she added, after a moment's consideration.

Had she given an assumed name? Was there some unhappy celebrity attached to her own name? Miss Roseberry did not wait to ask herself those questions: 'How can I thank you,' she exclaimed gratefully, 'for your sisterly kindness to a stranger like me?'

'I have only done my duty,' said Mercy Merrick, a little coldly. 'Don't speak of it.'

'I must speak of it. What a situation you found me in when the French soldiers had driven the Germans away! My travelling carriage stopped; the horses seized; I myself in a strange country at nightfall, robbed of my money and my luggage, and drenched to the skin by the pouring rain! I am indebted to you for shelter in this place – I am wearing your clothes – I should have died of the fright and the exposure but for you. What return can I make for such services as these?'

Mercy placed a chair for her guest near the captain's table, and seated herself at some little distance, on an old chest in a corner of the room. 'May I ask you a question about yourself?' she said, abruptly.

Under ordinary circumstances, it was not in Grace's character to receive the advances of a stranger unreservedly. But she and the nurse had met, in a strange country, under those circumstances of common peril and common trial which especially predispose two women of the same nation to open their hearts to one another. She answered cordially, without a moment's hesitation.

'A hundred questions,' she cried, 'if you like.' She looked at the expiring fire, and at the dimly visible figure of her companion seated in the obscurest corner of the room. 'That wretched candle hardly gives any light,' she said impatiently. 'It won't last much longer. Can't we make the place more cheerful? Come out of your corner. Call for more wood and more lights.'

Mercy remained in her corner and shook her head. 'Candles and wood are scarce things here,' she answered. 'We must be patient, even if we are left in the dark. Tell me,' she went on, raising her quiet voice a little, 'how came you to risk crossing the frontier in war time?'

Grace's voice dropped when she answered the question. Grace's momentary gaiety of manner suddenly left her.

'I had urgent reasons,' she said, 'for returning to England.'

'Alone?' rejoined the other. 'Without anyone to protect you?'

Grace's head sank on her bosom. 'I have left my only protector – my father – in the English burial-ground at Rome,' she answered simply. 'My mother died, years since, in Canada.'

The shadowy figure of the nurse suddenly changed its position on the chest. She had started as the last word passed Miss Roseberry's lips.

'Do you know Canada?' asked Grace.

'Well,' was the brief answer – reluctantly given, short as it was.

'Were you ever near Port Logan?'

'I once lived within a few miles of Port Logan.'

'When?'

'Some time since.' With those words Mercy Merrick shrank back into her corner and changed the subject. 'Your relatives in England must be very anxious about you,' she said.

Grace sighed. 'I have no relatives in England. You can hardly imagine a person more friendless than I am. We went away from Canada, when my father's health failed, to try the climate of Italy, by the doctor's advice. His death has left me not only friendless, but poor.' She paused, and took a leather letter-case from the pocket of the large grey cloak which the nurse had lent to her. 'My prospects in life,' she resumed, 'are all contained in this little case. Here is the one treasure I contrived to conceal when I was robbed of my other things.'

Mercy could just see the letter-case as Grace held it up in the deepening obscurity of the room. 'Have you got money in it?' she asked.

'No; only a few family papers, and a letter from my father, introducing me to an elderly lady in England – a connection of his by marriage, whom I have never seen. The lady has consented to receive me as her companion and reader. If I don't return to England soon, some other person may get the place.'

'Have you no other resource?'

'None. My education has been neglected – we led a wild life in the far West. I am quite unfit to go out as a governess. I am absolutely dependent on this stranger who receives me for my father's sake.' She put the letter-case back in the pocket of her cloak, and ended her little narrative as unaffectedly as she had begun it. 'Mine is a sad story, is it not?' she said.

The voice of the nurse answered her suddenly and bitterly in these strange words:

'There are sadder stories than yours. There are thousands of miserable women who would ask for no greater blessing than to change places with you.'

Grace started.

'What can there possibly be to envy in such a lot as mine?'

'Your unblemished character, and your prospect of being established honourably in a respectable house.'

Grace turned in her chair, and looked wonderingly into the dim corner of the room.

'How strangely you say that!' she exclaimed. There was no answer; the shadowy figure on the chest never moved. Grace rose impulsively, and drawing her chair after her, approached the nurse. 'Is there some romance in your life?' she asked. 'Why have you sacrificed yourself to the terrible duties which I find you performing here? You interest me indescribably. Give me your hand.'

Mercy shrank back, and refused the offered hand.

'Are we not friends?' Grace asked in astonishment.

'We never can be friends.'

'Why not?'

The nurse was dumb. She had shown a marked hesitation when she had mentioned her name. Remembering this, Grace openly avowed the conclusion at which she had arrived. 'Should I be guessing right,' she asked, 'if I guessed you to be some great lady in disguise?'

Mercy laughed to herself – low and bitterly. 'I a great lady!'

she said contemptuously. 'For heaven's sake let us talk of
something else!'

Grace's curiosity was thoroughly roused. She persisted. 'Once
more,' she whispered persuasively, 'let us be friends.' She gently
laid her arm as she spoke on Mercy's shoulder. Mercy roughly
shook it off. There was a rudeness in the action which would
have offended the most patient woman living. Grace drew back
indignantly. 'Ah!' she cried, 'you are cruel.'

'I am kind,' answered the nurse, speaking more sternly than
ever.

'Is it kind to keep me at a distance? I have told you *my* story.'

The nurse's voice rose excitedly. 'Don't tempt me to speak
out,' she said; 'you will regret it.'

Grace declined to accept the warning. 'I have placed
confidence in you,' she went on. 'It is ungenerous to lay me
under an obligation and then to shut me out of your confidence
in return.'

'You *will* have it?' said Mercy Merrick. 'You *shall* have it! Sit
down again.' Grace's heart began to quicken its beat in
expectation of the disclosure that was to come. She drew her
chair closer to the chest on which the nurse was sitting. With a
firm hand Mercy put the chair back to a distance from her.
'Not so near me!' she said harshly.

'Why not?'

'Not so near,' repeated the sternly resolute voice. 'Wait till
you have heard what I have to say.'

Grace obeyed without a word more. There was a momentary
silence. A faint flash of light leapt up from the expiring candle,
and showed Mercy crouching on the chest, with her elbows on
her knees, and her face hidden in her hands. The next instant
the room was buried in obscurity. As the darkness fell on the
two women the nurse spoke.

CHAPTER THE SECOND

MAGDALEN – IN MODERN TIMES

'When your mother was alive were you ever out with her after nightfall in the streets of a great city?'

In those extraordinary terms Mercy Merrick opened the confidential interview which Grace Roseberry had forced on her. Grace answered simply, 'I don't understand you.'

'I will put it another way,' said the nurse. Its unnatural hardness and sternness of tone passed away from her voice, and its native gentleness and sadness returned, as she made that reply. 'You read the newspapers like the rest of the world,' she went on; 'have you ever read of your unhappy fellow-creatures (the starving outcasts of the population) whom Want has betrayed to Sin?'

Still wondering, Grace answered that she had read of such things in newspapers and in books.

'Have you heard – when those starving and sinning fellow-creatures happen to be women – of Refuges established to protect and reclaim them?'

The wonder in Grace's mind passed away, and a vague suspicion of something painful to come took its place. 'These are extraordinary questions,' she said, nervously. 'What do you mean?'

'Answer me,' the nurse insisted. 'Have you heard of the Refuges? Have you heard of the Women?'

'Yes.'

'Move your chair a little farther away from me.' She paused. Her voice, without losing its steadiness, fell to its lowest tones. '*I* was once one of those women,' she said quietly.

Grace sprang to her feet with a faint cry. She stood petrified – incapable of uttering a word.

'*I* have been in a Refuge,' pursued the sweet sad voice of the other woman. '*I* have been in a Prison. Do you still wish to be my friend? Do you still insist on sitting close to me and taking my hand?' She waited for a reply, and no reply came. 'You see you were wrong,' she went on gently, 'when you called me cruel – and I was right when I told you I was kind.'

At that appeal, Grace composed herself, and spoke. 'I don't wish to offend you,' she began coldly.

Mercy Merrick stopped her there.

'You don't offend me,' she said, without the faintest note of displeasure in her tone. 'I am accustomed to stand in the pillory of my own past life. I sometimes ask myself if it was all my fault. I sometimes wonder if Society had no duties towards me when I was a child selling matches in the street – when I was a hard-working girl, fainting at my needle for want of food.' Her voice faltered a little for the first time as it pronounced those words; she waited a moment and recovered herself. 'It's too late to dwell on these things, now,' she said resignedly. 'Society can subscribe to reclaim me – but Society can't take me back. You see me here in a place of trust – patiently, humbly, doing all the good I can. It doesn't matter! Here, or elsewhere, what I *am* can never alter what I *was*. For three years past all that a sincerely penitent woman can do I have done. It doesn't matter. Once let my past story be known, and the shadow of it covers me; the kindest people shrink.'

She waited again. Would a word of sympathy come to comfort her from the other woman's lips? No! Miss Roseberry was shocked; Miss Roseberry was confused. 'I am very sorry for you,' was all that Miss Roseberry could say.

'Everybody is sorry for me,' answered the nurse, as patiently as ever; 'everybody is kind to me. But the lost place is not to be regained. I can't get back! I can't get back,' she cried, with a passionate outburst of despair – checked instantly, the moment it had escaped her. 'Shall I tell you what my experience has been?' she resumed. 'Will you hear the story of Magdalen – in modern times?'

Grace drew back a step; Mercy instantly understood her.

'I am going to tell you nothing that you need shrink from hearing,' she said. 'A lady in your position would not have understood the trials and the struggles that I have passed through. My story shall begin at the Refuge. The matron sent me out to service with the character that I had honestly earned – the character of a reclaimed woman. I justified the confidence placed in me; I was a faithful servant. One day, my mistress sent for me – a kind mistress, if ever there was one yet. "Mercy, I am sorry for you; it has come out that I took you from a Refuge; I shall lose every servant in the house; you must go." I went back to the matron – another kind woman. She received me like a mother. "We will try again, Mercy; don't be cast down." I told you I had been in Canada?'

Grace began to feel interested in spite of herself. She answered with something like warmth in her tone. She returned to her chair – placed at its safe and significant distance from the chest.

The nurse went on.

'My next place was in Canada, with an officer's wife: gentlefolks who had emigrated. More kindness; and, this time, a pleasant peaceful life for me. I said to myself, "Is the lost place regained? *Have* I got back?" My mistress died. New people came into our neighbourhood. There was a young lady among them – my master began to think of another wife. I have the misfortune (in my situation) to be what is called a handsome woman; I rouse the curiosity of strangers. The new people asked questions about me; my master's answers did not satisfy them. In a word they found me out. The old story again! "Mercy, I am very sorry; scandal is busy with you and with me; we are innocent, but there is no help for it – we must part." I left the place; having gained one advantage during my stay in Canada, which I find of use to me here.'

'What is it?'

'Our nearest neighbours were French Canadians. I had daily practice in speaking the French language.'

'Did you return to London?'

'Where else could I go, without a character?' said Mercy, sadly. 'I went back again to the matron. Sickness had broken out in the Refuge; I made myself useful as a nurse. One of the doctors was struck with me – "fell in love" with me as the phrase is. He would have married me. The nurse, as an honest woman, was bound to tell him the truth. He never appeared again. The old story! I began to be weary of saying to myself, "I can't get back! I can't get back!" Despair got hold of me, the despair that hardens the heart. I might have committed suicide;

I might even have drifted back into my old life – but for one man.'

At those last words, her voice – quiet and even through the earlier parts of her sad story – began to falter once more. She stopped; following silently the memories and associations roused in her by what she had just said. Had she forgotten the presence of another person in the room? Grace's curiosity left Grace no resource but to say a word on her side.

'Who was the man?' she asked. 'How did he befriend you?'

'Befriend me? He doesn't even know that such a person as I am is in existence.'

That strange answer, naturally enough, only strengthened the anxiety of Grace to hear more. 'You said just now——' she began.

'I said just now that he saved me. He did save me; you shall hear how. One Sunday our regular clergyman at the Refuge was not able to officiate. His place was taken by a stranger, quite a young man. The matron told us the stranger's name was Julian Gray. I sat in the back row of seats, under the shadow of the gallery, where I could see him without his seeing me. His text was from the words, "Joy shall be in Heaven over one sinner that repenteth, more than over ninety and nine just persons which need no repentance." What happier women might have thought of his sermon I cannot say; there was not a dry eye among us at the Refuge. As for me, he touched my heart as no man has touched it before or since. The hard despair melted in me at the sound of his voice; the weary round of my life showed its nobler side again while he spoke. From that time I have accepted my hard lot, I have been a patient woman. I might have been something more, I might have been a happy woman, if I could have prevailed on myself to speak to Julian Gray.'

'What hindered you from speaking to him?'

'I was afraid.'

'Afraid of what?'

'Afraid of making my hard life harder still.'

A woman who could have sympathised with her would perhaps have guessed what those words meant. Grace was simply embarrassed by her; and Grace failed to guess.

'I don't understand you,' she said.

There was no alternative for Mercy but to own the truth in plain words. She sighed, and said the words. 'I was afraid I might interest him in my sorrows, and might set my heart on him in return.'

The utter absence of any fellow-feeling with her on Grace's side expressed itself unconsciously in the plainest terms.

'You!' she exclaimed, in a tone of blank astonishment.

The nurse rose slowly to her feet. Grace's expression of surprise told her plainly – almost brutally – that her confession had gone far enough.

'I astonish you,' she said. 'Ah, my young lady, you don't know what rough usage a woman's heart can bear, and still beat truly! Before I saw Julian Gray I only knew men as objects of horror to me. Let us drop the subject. The preacher at the Refuge is nothing but a remembrance now – the one welcome remembrance of my life! I have nothing more to tell you. You insisted on hearing my story – you have heard it.'

'I have not heard how you found employment here,' said Grace; continuing the conversation with uneasy politeness, as she best might.

Mercy crossed the room, and slowly raked together the last living embers of the fire.

'The matron has friends in France,' she answered, 'who are connected with the military hospitals. It was not difficult to get me the place, under those circumstances. Society can find a use for me here. My hand is as light, my words of comfort are as welcome, among those suffering wretches' (she pointed to the room in which the wounded men were lying) 'as if I was the most reputable woman breathing. And if a stray shot comes my way before the war is over – well! Society will be rid of me on easy terms.'

She stood looking thoughtfully into the wreck of the fire – as if she saw in it the wreck of her own life. Common humanity made it an act of necessity to say something to her. Grace considered – advanced a step towards her – stopped – and took refuge in the most trivial of all the commonplace phrases which one human being can address to another.

'If there is anything I can do for you——,' she began. The sentence, halting there, was never finished. Miss Roseberry was just merciful enough towards the lost woman who had rescued and sheltered her to feel that it was needless to say more.

The nurse lifted her noble head, and advanced slowly towards the canvas screen to return to her duties. 'Miss Roseberry might have taken my hand!' she thought to herself, bitterly. No! Miss Roseberry stood there at a distance, at a loss what to say next. 'What can *you* do for me?' Mercy asked, stung by the cold courtesy of her companion into a momentary outbreak of contempt. 'Can you change my identity? Can you give me the name and the place of an innocent woman? If I only had your chance! If I only had your reputation and your prospects!' She laid one hand over her bosom, and controlled herself. 'Stay here,' she resumed, 'while I go back to my work. I will see that your clothes are dried. You shall wear my clothes as short a time as possible.'

With those melancholy words – touchingly, not bitterly spoken – she moved to pass into the kitchen. She had just reached the canvas screen, when Grace stopped her by a question.

'Is the weather changing?' Grace asked. 'I don't hear the rain against the window.'

Before Mercy could check her, she had crossed the room, and had unfastened the window shutter.

'Close the shutter!' cried Mercy. 'You were warned not to open it when we came into the room.'

Grace persisted in looking out.

The moon was rising dimly in the watery sky; the rain had ceased; the friendly darkness which had hidden the French position from the German scouts was lessening every moment. In a few hours more (if nothing happened) Miss Roseberry might resume her journey. In a few hours more the morning would dawn.

Hurriedly retracing her steps, Mercy closed the shutter with her own hands. Before she could fasten it, the report of a rifle-shot reached the cottage from one of the distant posts. It was followed almost instantly by a second report, nearer and louder than the first. Mercy paused, and listened intently for the next sound.

CHAPTER THE THIRD

THE GERMAN SHELL

A third rifle-shot rang through the night air, close to the cottage. Grace started and drew back from the window in alarm.

'What does that firing mean?' she asked.

'Signals from the outposts,' the nurse quietly replied.

'Is there any danger? Have the Germans come back?'

Surgeon Surville answered the question. He lifted the canvas screen, and looked into the room as Miss Roseberry spoke.

'The Germans are advancing on us,' he said. 'Their vanguard is in sight.'

Grace sank on the chair near her, trembling from head to foot. Mercy advanced to the surgeon, and put the decisive question to him:

'Do we defend the position?' she enquired.

Surgeon Surville ominously shook his head.

'Impossible! We are outnumbered as usual – ten to one.'

The shrill roll of the French drums was heard outside.

'There is the retreat sounded!' said the surgeon. 'The captain is not a man to think twice about what he does. We are left to take care of ourselves. In five minutes we must be out of this place.'

A volley of rifle-shots rang out as he spoke. The German vanguard was attacking the French at the outposts. Grace caught the surgeon entreatingly by the arm. 'Take me with you,' she cried. 'Oh, sir, I have suffered from the Germans already! Don't forsake me, if they come back!' The surgeon was equal to the occasion; he placed the hand of the pretty Englishwoman on his breast. 'Fear nothing, madam,' he said, looking as if he could have annihilated the whole German force with his own invincible arm. 'A Frenchman's heart beats under your hand. A Frenchman's devotion protects you.' Grace's head sank on his shoulder. Monsieur Surville felt that he had asserted himself; he looked round invitingly at Mercy. She, too, was an attractive woman. The Frenchman had another shoulder at *her*

service. Unhappily, the room was dark – the look was lost on
Mercy. She was thinking of the helpless men in the inner
chamber, and she quietly recalled the surgeon to a sense of his
professional duties.

'What is to become of the sick and wounded?' she asked.

Monsieur Surville shrugged one shoulder – the shoulder that
was free.

'The strongest among them we can take away with us,' he
said. 'The others must be left here. Fear nothing for yourself,
dear lady. There will be a place for you in the baggage-
waggon.'

'And for me, too?' Grace pleaded eagerly.

The surgeon's invincible arm stole round the young lady's
waist, and answered mutely with a squeeze.

'Take her with you,' said Mercy. 'My place is with the men
whom you leave behind.'

Grace listened in amazement. 'Think what you risk,' she said,
'if you stop here.'

Mercy pointed to her left shoulder.

'Don't alarm yourself on my account,' she answered, 'the red
cross will protect me.'

Another roll of the drum warned the susceptible surgeon to
take his place as director-general of the ambulance without any
further delay. He conducted Grace to a chair and placed both
her hands on his heart this time, to reconcile her to the
misfortune of his absence. 'Wait here till I return for you,' he
whispered. 'Fear nothing, my charming friend. Say to yourself,
"Surville is the soul of honour! Surville is devoted to me!" ' He
struck his breast; he again forgot the obscurity in the room, and
cast one look of unutterable homage at his charming friend. 'A
bientôt!' he cried, and kissed his hand and disappeared.

As the canvas screen fell over him, the sharp report of the
rifle-firing was suddenly and grandly dominated by the roar of
cannon. The instant after, a shell exploded in the garden
outside, within a few yards of the window.

Grace sank on her knees with a shriek of terror. Mercy –
without losing her self-possession – advanced to the window,
and looked out.

'The moon has risen,' she said. 'The Germans are shelling the village.'

Grace rose, and ran to her for protection.

'Take me away!' she cried. 'We shall be killed if we stay here.' She stopped, looking in astonishment at the tall black figure of the nurse, standing immovably by the window. 'Are you made of iron?' she exclaimed. 'Will nothing frighten you?'

Mercy smiled sadly. 'Why should I be afraid of losing my life?' she answered. 'I have nothing worth living for.'

The roar of the cannon shook the cottage for the second time. A second shell exploded in the courtyard, on the opposite side of the building.

Bewildered by the noise, panic-stricken as the danger from the shells threatened the cottage more and more nearly, Grace threw her arms round the nurse, and clung, in the abject familiarity of terror, to the woman whose hand she had shrunk from touching, not five minutes since. 'Where is it safest?' she cried. 'Where can I hide myself?'

'How can I tell where the next shell will fall?' Mercy answered quietly.

The steady composure of the one woman seemed to madden the other. Releasing the nurse, Grace looked wildly round for a way of escape from the cottage. Making first for the kitchen she was driven back by the clamour and confusion attending the removal of those among the wounded who were strong enough to be placed in the waggon. A second look round showed her the door leading into the yard. She rushed to it, with a cry of relief. She had just laid her hand on the lock when the third report of cannon burst over the place.

Starting back a step, Grace lifted her hands mechanically to her ears. At the same moment, the third shell burst through the roof of the cottage, and exploded in the room, just inside the door. Mercy sprang forward, unhurt, from her place by the window. The burning fragments of the shell were already firing the dry wooden floor, and, in the midst of them, dimly seen through the smoke, lay the insensible body of her companion in the room. Even at that dreadful moment the nurse's presence of mind did not fail her. Hurrying back to the place that she had just left, near which she had already noticed the miller's empty sacks lying in a heap, she seized two of them, and, throwing them on the smouldering floor, trampled out the fire. That done, she knelt by the senseless woman, and lifted her head.

Was she wounded? or dead?

Mercy raised one helpless hand, and laid her fingers on the wrist. While she was still vainly trying to feel for the beating of the pulse, Surgeon Surville (alarmed for the ladies) hurried to enquire if any harm had been done.

Mercy called him to approach. 'I am afraid the shell has struck her,' she said, yielding her place to him. 'See if she is mortally wounded.'

The surgeon's anxiety for his charming patient expressed itself briefly in an oath, with a prodigious emphasis laid on one of the letters in it – the letter R. 'Take off her cloak,' he cried, raising his hand to her neck. 'Poor angel! She has turned in falling; the string is twisted round her throat.'

Mercy removed the cloak. It dropped on the floor as the surgeon lifted Grace in his arms. 'Get a candle,' he said, impatiently; 'they will give you one in the kitchen.' He tried to feel the pulse: his hand trembled, the noise and confusion in the kitchen bewildered him. 'Just heaven!' he exclaimed. 'My emotions overpower me!' Mercy approached him with the candle. The light disclosed the frightful injury which a fragment of the shell had inflicted on the Englishwoman's head. Surgeon Surville's manner altered on the instant. The expression of anxiety left his face; its professional composure covered it suddenly like a mask. What was the object of his admiration now? An inert burden in his arms – nothing more.

The change in his face was not lost on Mercy. Her large grey eyes watched him attentively.

'Mortally wounded?' she asked.

'Don't trouble yourself to hold the light any longer,' was the cool reply. 'It's all over – I can do nothing for her.'

'Dead?'

Surgeon Surville nodded, and shook his fist in the direction of the outposts. 'Accursed Germans,' he cried, and looked down at the dead face on his arm, and shrugged his shoulders resignedly. 'The fortune of war!' he said, as he lifted the body and placed it on the bed in one corner of the room. 'Next time, nurse, it may be you or me. Who knows? Bah! the problem of human destiny disgusts me.' He turned from the bed, and illustrated his disgust by spitting on the fragments of the exploded shell. 'We must leave her there,' he resumed. 'She was once a charming person – she is nothing now. Come away, Miss Mercy, before it is too late.'

He offered his arm to the nurse. The creaking of the baggage-waggon, starting on its journey, was heard outside, and the shrill roll of the drums was renewed in the distance. The retreat had begun.

Mercy drew aside the canvas, and saw the badly-wounded men left helpless at the mercy of the enemy, on their straw beds. She refused the offer of Surgeon Surville's arm.

'I have already told you that I shall stay here,' she answered.

Monsieur Surville lifted his hands in polite remonstrance. Mercy held back the curtain, and pointed to the cottage door.

'Go,' she said. 'My mind is made up.'

Even at that final moment the Frenchman asserted himself. He made his exit with unimpaired grace and dignity. 'Madam,' he said, 'you are sublime!' With that parting compliment the man of gallantry – true to the last to his admiration of the sex – bowed, with his hand on his heart, and left the cottage.

Mercy dropped the canvas over the doorway. She was alone with the dead woman.

The last tramp of footsteps, the last rumbling of the waggon-wheels died away in the distance. No renewal of firing from the position occupied by the enemy disturbed the silence that followed. The Germans knew that the French were in retreat. A few minutes more and they would take possession of the abandoned village: the tumult of their approach would become audible at the cottage. In the meantime the stillness was terrible. Even the wounded wretches who were left in the kitchen waited their fate in silence.

Alone in the room, Mercy's first look was directed to the bed.

The two women had met in the confusion of the first

skirmish at the close of twilight. Separated, on their arrival at the cottage, by the duties required of the nurse, they had only met again in the captain's room. The acquaintance between them had been a short one; and it had given no promise of ripening into friendship. But the fatal accident had roused Mercy's interest in the stranger. She took the candle, and approached the corpse of the woman who had been literally killed at her side.

She stood by the bed, looking down in the silence of the night at the stillness of the dead face.

It was a striking face – once seen (in life or in death) not to be forgotten afterwards. The forehead was unusually low and broad; the eyes unusually far apart; the mouth and chin remarkably small. With tender hands Mercy smoothed the dishevelled hair, and arranged the crumpled dress. 'Not five minutes since,' she thought to herself, 'I was longing to change places with *you!*' She turned from the bed with a sigh: 'I wish I could change places now!'

The silence began to oppress her. She walked slowly to the other end of the room.

The cloak on the floor – her own cloak, which she had lent to Miss Roseberry – attracted her attention as she passed it. She picked it up and brushed the dust from it, and laid it across a chair. This done, she put the light back on the table, and, going to the window, listened for the first sounds of the German advance. The faint passage of the wind through some trees near at hand was the only sound that caught her ears. She turned from the window, and seated herself at the table, thinking. Was there any duty still left undone that Christian charity owed to the dead? Was there any further service that pressed for performance in the interval before the Germans appeared?

Mercy recalled the conversation that had passed between her ill-fated companion and herself. Miss Roseberry had spoken of her object in returning to England. She had mentioned a lady – a connection by marriage, to whom she was personally a stranger – who was waiting to receive her. Someone capable of stating how the poor creature had met her death ought to write to her only friend. Who was to do it? There was nobody to do it but the one witness of the catastrophe now left in the cottage – Mercy herself.

She lifted the cloak from the chair on which she had placed it, and took from the pocket the leather letter-case which Grace had shown to her. The only way of discovering the address to write to in England was to open the case and examine the papers inside. Mercy opened the case – and stopped, feeling a strange reluctance to carry the investigation any further.

A moment's consideration satisfied her that her scruples were misplaced. If she respected the case as inviolable, the Germans would certainly not hesitate to examine it, and the Germans would hardly trouble themselves to write to England. Which were the fittest eyes to inspect the papers of the deceased lady – the eyes of men and foreigners, or the eyes of her own countrywoman? Mercy's hesitation left her. She emptied the contents of the case on the table.

That trifling action decided the whole future course of her life.

CHAPTER THE FOURTH

THE TEMPTATION

Some letters, tied together with a ribbon, attracted Mercy's attention first. The ink in which the addresses were written had faded with age. The letters, directed alternately to Colonel Roseberry and to the Honourable Mrs Roseberry, contained a correspondence between the husband and wife at a time when the Colonel's military duties had obliged him to be absent from home. Mercy tied the letters up again, and passed on to the papers that lay next in order under her hand.

These consisted of a few leaves pinned together, and headed (in a woman's handwriting), 'My Journal at Rome.' A brief examination showed that the journal had been written by Miss

Roseberry, and that it was mainly devoted to a record of the last days of her father's life.

After replacing the journal and the correspondence in the case, the one paper left on the table was a letter. The envelope – which was unclosed – bore this address: 'Lady Janet Roy, Mablethorpe House, Kensington, London.' Mercy took the enclosure from the open envelope. The first lines she read informed her that she had found the Colonel's letter of introduction, presenting his daughter to her protectress on her arrival in England.

Mercy read the letter through. It was described by the writer as the last effort of a dying man. Colonel Roseberry wrote affectionately of his daughter's merits, and regretfully of her neglected education – ascribing the latter to the pecuniary losses which had forced him to emigrate to Canada in the character of a poor man. Fervent expressions of gratitude followed, addressed to Lady Janet. 'I owe it to you,' the letter concluded, 'that I am dying with my mind at ease about the future of my darling girl. To your generous protection I commit the one treasure I have left to me on earth. Through your long lifetime you have nobly used your high rank and your great fortune as a means of doing good. I believe it will not be counted among the least of your virtues hereafter that you comforted the last hours of an old soldier by opening your heart and your home to his friendless child.'

So the letter ended. Mercy laid it down with a heavy heart. What a chance the poor girl had lost! A woman of rank and fortune waiting to receive her – a woman so merciful and so generous that the father's mind had been easy about the daughter on his death-bed – and there the daughter lay, beyond the reach of Lady Janet's kindness, beyond the need of Lady Janet's help!

The French captain's writing materials were left on the table. Mercy turned the letter over so that she might write the news of Miss Roseberry's daeth on the blank page at the end. She was still considering what expressions she should use, when the sound of complaining voices from the next room caught her ear. The wounded men left behind were moaning for help – the deserted soldiers were losing their fortitude at last.

She entered the kitchen. A cry of delight welcomed her appearance – the mere sight of her composed the men. From one straw bed to another she passed, with comforting words that gave them hope, with skilled and tender hands that soothed their pain. They kissed the hem of her black dress; they called her their guardian angel, as the beautiful creature moved among them, and bent over their hard pillows her gentle compassionate face. 'I will be with you when the Germans come,' she said, as she left them to return to her unwritten letter. 'Courage, my poor fellows! You are not deserted by your nurse.'

'Courage, madam!' the men replied, 'and God bless you!'

If the firing had been resumed at that moment – if a shell had struck her dead in the act of succouring the afflicted – what Christian judgment would have hesitated to declare that there was a place for this woman in heaven? But, if the war ended and left her still living, where was the place for her on earth? Where were her prospects? Where was her home?

She returned to the letter. Instead, however, of seating herself to write, she stood by the table, absently looking down at the morsel of paper.

A strange fancy had sprung to life in her mind on re-entering the room; she herself smiled faintly at the extravagance of it. What if she were to ask Lady Janet Roy to let her supply Miss Roseberry's place? She had met with Miss Roseberry under critical circumstances: and she had done for her all that one woman could do to help another. There was in this circumstance some little claim to notice, perhaps, if Lady Janet had no other companion and reader in view. Suppose she ventured to plead her own cause – what would the noble and merciful lady do? She would write back, and say, 'Send me references to your character, and I will see what can be done.' Her character ! Her references! Mercy laughed bitterly, and sat down to write in the fewest words all that was needed from her – a plain statement of the facts.

No! Not a line could she put on the paper. That fancy of hers was not to be dismissed at will. Her mind was perversely busy now with an imaginary picture of the beauty of Mablethorpe

House and the comfort and elegance of the life that was led there. Once more she thought of the chance which Miss Roseberry had lost. Unhappy creature! what a home would have been open to her if the shell had only fallen on the side of the window instead of on the side of the yard!

Mercy pushed the letter away from her, and walked impatiently to and fro in the room.

The perversity in her thoughts was not to be mastered in that way. Her mind only abandoned one useless train of reflection to occupy itself with another. She was now looking by anticipation at her own future. What were her prospects (if she lived through it) when the war was over? The experience of the past delineated with pitiless fidelity the dreary scene. Go where she might, do what she might, it would end always in the same way. Curiosity and admiration excited by her beauty; enquiries made about her; the story of the past discovered; Society charitably sorry for her; Society generously subscribing for her; and still, through all years of her life, the same result in the end – the shadow of the old disgrace surrounding her as with a pestilence; isolating her among other women; branding her, even when she had earned her pardon in the sight of God, with the mark of an indelible disgrace in the sight of man: there was the prospect! And she was only five-and-twenty last birthday; she was in the prime of her health and her strength; she might live, in the course of nature, fifty years more!

She stopped again at the bedside; she looked again at the face of the corpse.

To what end had the shell struck the woman who had some hope in her life, and spared the woman who had none? The words she had herself spoken to Grace Roseberry came back to her as she thought of it. 'If I only had your chance! If I only had your reputation and your prospects!' And there was the chance wasted! there were the enviable prospects thrown away! It was almost maddening to contemplate that result, feeling her own position as she felt it. In the bitter mockery of despair, she bent over the lifeless figure, and spoke to it as if it had ears to hear her. 'Oh!' she said, longingly, ' if you could be Mercy Merrick, and if I could be Grace Roseberry, *now!*'

The instant the words passed her lips she started into an erect position. She stood by the bed, with her eyes staring wildly into empty space; with her brain in a flame; with her heart beating as if it would stifle her. 'If you could be Mercy Merrick and if I could be Grace Roseberry, now!' In one breathless moment, the thought assumed a new development in her mind. In one breathless moment, the conviction struck her like an electric shock. *She might be Grace Roseberry if she dared!* There was absolutely nothing to stop her from presenting herself to Lady Janet Roy under Grace's name and in Grace's place!

What were the risks? Where was the weak point in the scheme?

Grace had said it herself in so many words – she and Lady Janet had never seen each other. Her friends were in Canada; her relations in England were dead. Mercy knew the place in which she had lived – the place called Port Logan – as well as she had known it herself. Mercy had only to read the manuscript journal to be able to answer any questions relating to the visit to Rome and to Colonel Roseberry's death. She had no accomplished lady to personate: Grace had spoken herself – her father's letter spoke also in the plainest terms – of her neglected education. Everything, literally everything, was in the lost woman's favour. The people with whom she had been connected in the ambulance had gone, to return no more. Her own clothes were on Miss Roseberry at that moment – marked with her own name. Miss Roseberry's clothes, marked with *her* name, were drying, at Mercy's disposal, in the next room. The way of escape from the unendurable humiliation of her present life lay open before her at last. What a prospect it was! A new identity, which she might own anywhere! a new name, which was beyond reproach! a new past life, into which all the world might search, and be welcome! Her colour rose, her eyes sparkled; she had never been so irresistibly beautiful as she looked at the moment when the new future disclosed itself, radiant with new hope.

She waited a minute, until she could think over her own daring project from another point of view. Where was the harm of it? what did her conscience say?

As to Grace, in the first place. What injury was she doing to a

woman who was dead? The question answered itself. No injury
to the woman. No injury to her relations. Her relations were
dead also.

As to Lady Janet, in the second place. If she served her new
mistress faithfully; if she filled her new sphere honourably; if she
was diligent under instruction, and grateful for kindness – if, in
one word, she was all that she might be and would be in the
heavenly peace and security of that new life – what injury was
she doing to Lady Janet? Once more, the question answered
itself. She might, and would, give Lady Janet cause to bless the
day when she first entered the house.

She snatched up Colonel Roseberry's letter, and put it into
the case with the other papers. The opportunity was before her;
the chances were all in her favour; her conscience said nothing
against trying the daring scheme. She decided, then and there –
'I'll do it!'

Something jarred on her finer sense, something offended her
better nature, as she put the case into the pocket of her dress. She
had decided, and yet she was not at ease; she was not quite sure
of having fairly questioned her conscience yet. What if she laid
the letter-case on the table again, and waited until her excitement
had all cooled down, and then put the contemplated project
soberly on its trial before her own sense of right and wrong?

She thought once – and hesitated. Before she could think
twice, the distant tramp of marching footsteps, and the distant
clatter of horses' hoofs were wafted to her on the night air. The
Germans were entering the village! In a few minutes more they
would appear in the cottage; they would summon her to give
an account of herself. There was no time for waiting until she
was composed again. Which should it be – the new life, as
Grace Roseberry? or the old life, as Mercy Merrick?

She looked for the last time at the bed. Grace's course was
run; Grace's future was at her disposal. Her resolute nature,
forced to a choice on the instant, held by the daring alternative.
She persisted in the determination to take Grace's place.

The tramping footsteps of the Germans came nearer and
nearer. The voices of the officers were audible, giving the
words of command.

She seated herself at the table, waiting steadily for what was to come.

The ineradicable instinct of the sex directed her eyes to her dress before the Germans appeared. Looking it over to see that it was in perfect order, her eyes fell upon the red cross on her left shoulder. In a moment it struck her that her nurse's costume might involve her in a needless risk. It associated her with a public position: it might lead to enquiries at a later time, and those enquiries might betray her.

She looked round. The grey cloak which she had lent to Grace attracted her attention. She took it up, and covered herself with it from head to foot.

The cloak was just arranged round her, when she heard the outer door thrust open, and voices speaking in a strange tongue, and arms grounded in the room behind her. Should she wait to be discovered? or should she show herself of her own accord? It was less trying to such a nature as hers to show herself than to wait. She advanced to enter the kitchen. The canvas curtain, as she stretched out her hand to it, was suddenly drawn back from the other side, and three men confronted her in the open doorway.

CHAPTER THE FIFTH

THE GERMAN SURGEON

The youngest of the three strangers — judging by features, complexion, and manner — was apparently an Englishman. He wore a military cap and military boots, but was otherwise dressed as a civilian. Next to him stood an officer in Prussian uniform, and next to the officer was the third and the oldest of the party. He was also dressed in uniform, but his appearance was far from being suggestive of the appearance of a military man. He halted on one foot, he stooped at the shoulders, and instead of a sword at his side he carried a stick in his hand. After looking sharply through a large pair of tortoise-shell spectacles, first at Mercy, then at the bed, then all around the room, he turned with a cynical composure of manner to the Prussian officer, and broke the silence in these words:

'A woman ill on the bed; another woman in attendance on her, and no one else in the room. Any necessity, major, for setting a guard here?'

'No necessity,' answered the major. He wheeled round on his heel and returned to the kitchen. The German surgeon advanced a little, led by his professional instinct, in the direction of the bedside. The young Englishman, whose eyes had remained riveted in admiration on Mercy, drew the canvas screen over the doorway, and respectfully addressed her in the French language.

'May I ask if I am speaking to a French lady?' he said.

'I am an Englishwoman,' Mercy replied.

The surgeon heard the answer. Stopping short on his way to the bed, he pointed to the recumbent figure on it, and said to Mercy, in good English, spoken with a strong German accent –

'Can I be of any use there?'

His manner was ironically courteous; his harsh voice was pitched in one sardonic monotony of tone. Mercy took an instantaneous dislike to this hobbling, ugly old man, staring at her rudely through his great tortoise-shell spectacles.

'You can be of no use, sir,' she said, shortly. 'The lady was killed when your troops shelled this cottage.'

The Englishman started, and looked compassionately towards the bed. The German refreshed himself with a pinch of snuff, and put another question:

'Has the body been examined by a medical man?' he asked. Mercy ungraciously limited her reply to the one necessary word 'Yes.'

The present surgeon was not a man to be daunted by a lady's disapproval of him. He went on with his questions.

'Who has examined the body?' he enquired next.

Mercy answered, 'The doctor attached to the French ambulance.'

The German grunted in contemptuous disapproval of all French men and all French institutions. The Englishman seized his first opportunity of addressing himself to Mercy once more.

'Is the lady a countrywoman of ours?' he asked gently.

Mercy considered before she answered him. With the object she had in view, there might be serious reasons for speaking with extreme caution when she spoke of Grace.

'I believe so,' she said. 'We met here by accident. I know nothing of her.'

'Not even her name?' enquired the German surgeon.

Mercy's resolution was hardly equal yet to giving her own name openly as the name of Grace. She took refuge in flat denial.

'Not even her name,' she repeated obstinately.

The old man stared at her more rudely than ever — considered with himself — and took the candle from the table. He hobbled back to the bed, and examined the figure laid on it in silence. The Englishman continued the conversation, no longer concealing the interest that he felt in the beautiful woman who stood before him.

'Pardon me,' he said; 'you are very young to be alone in war-time in such a place as this.'

The sudden outbreak of a disturbance in the kitchen relieved Mercy from any immediate necessity for answering him. She heard the voices of the wounded men raised in feeble remonstrance, and the harsh command of the foreign officers, bidding them be silent. The generous instincts of the woman instantly prevailed over every personal consideration imposed on her by the position which she had assumed. Reckless whether she betrayed herself or not as nurse in the French ambulance, she instantly drew aside the canvas to enter the kitchen. A German sentinel barred the way to her, and announced, in his own language, that no strangers were admitted. The Englishman, politely interposing, asked if she had any special object in wishing to enter the room.

'The poor Frenchmen!' she said earnestly, her heart upbraiding her for having forgotten them. 'The poor wounded Frenchmen!'

The German surgeon advanced from the bedside, and took
the matter up before the Englishman could say a word more.

'You have nothing to do with the wounded Frenchmen,' he
croaked, in the harshest notes of his voice. 'The wounded
Frenchmen are my business, and not yours. They are *our*
prisoners, and they are being moved to *our* ambulance. I am
Ignatius Wetzel, chief of the medical staff – and I tell you this.
Hold your tongue.' He turned to the sentinel, and added in
German, 'Draw the curtain again; and if the woman persists,
put her back into this room with your own hand.'

Mercy attempted to remonstrate. The Englishman
respectfully took her arm, and drew her out of the sentinel's
reach.

'It is useless to resist,' he said. 'The German discipline never
gives way. There is not the least need to be uneasy about the
Frenchmen. The ambulance, under Surgeon Wetzel, is
admirably administered. I answer for it, the men will be well
treated.' He saw the tears in her eyes as he spoke; his admiration
for her rose higher and higher. 'Kind as well as beautiful,' he
thought. 'What a charming creature!'

'Well!' said Ignatius Wetzel, eyeing Mercy sternly through his
spectacles. 'Are you satisfied? And will you hold your tongue?'

She yielded: it was plainly useless to persist. But for the
surgeon's resistance, her devotion to the wounded men might
have stopped her on the downward way that she was going. If
she could only have been absorbed again, mind and body, in
her good work as a nurse, the temptation might even yet have
found her strong enough to resist it. The fatal severity of the
German discipline had snapped asunder the last tie that bound
her to her better self. Her face hardened as she walked away
proudly from Surgeon Wetzel, and took a chair.

The Englishman followed her, and reverted to the question
of her present situation in the cottage.

'Don't suppose that I want to alarm you,' he said. 'There is, I
repeat, no need to be anxious about the Frenchmen, but there
is serious reason for anxiety on your own account. The action
will be renewed round this village by daylight; you ought really
to be in a place of safety. I am an officer in the English army –

my name is Horace Holmcroft. I shall be delighted to be of use to you, and I *can* be of use if you will let me. May I ask if you are travelling?'

Mercy gathered the cloak which concealed her nurse's dress more closely round her, and committed herself silently to her first overt act of deception. She bowed her head in the affirmative.

'Are you on your way to England?'

'Yes.'

'In that case, I can pass you through the German lines, and forward you at once on your journey.'

Mercy looked at him in unconcealed surprise. His strongly-felt interest in her was restrained within the strictest limits of good breeding: he was unmistakably a gentleman. Did he really mean what he had just said?

'You can pass me through the German lines?' she repeated. 'You must possess extraordinary influence, sir, to be able to do that.'

Mr Horace Holmcroft smiled.

'I possess the influence that no one can resist,' he answered – 'the influence of the Press. I am serving here as war-correspondent of one of our great English newspapers. If I ask him, the commanding officer will grant you a pass. He is close to this cottage. What do you say?'

She summoned her resolution – not without difficulty, even now – and took him at his word.

'I gratefully accept your offer, sir.'

He advanced a step towards the kitchen, and stopped.

'It may be well to make the application as privately as possible,' he said. 'I shall be questioned if I pass through that room. Is there no other way out of the cottage?'

Mercy showed him the door leading into the yard. He bowed – and left her.

She looked furtively towards the German surgeon. Ignatius Wetzel was again at the bed, bending over the body, and apparently absorbed in examining the wound which had been inflicted by the shell. Mercy's instinctive aversion to the old man increased tenfold now that she was left alone with him.

She withdrew uneasily to the window, and looked out at the moonlight.

Had she committed herself to the fraud? Hardly, yet. She had committed herself to returning to England – nothing more. There was no necessity, thus far, which forced her to present herself at Mablethorpe House, in Grace's place. There was still time to reconsider her resolution – still time to write the account of the accident, as she had proposed, and to send it with the letter-case to Lady Janet Roy. Suppose she finally decided on taking this course, what was to become of her when she found herself in England again? There was no alternative open but to apply once more to her friend the Matron. There was nothing for her to do but to return to the Refuge!

The Refuge! The Matron! What past association with these two was now presenting itself uninvited, and taking the foremost place in her mind? Of whom was she now thinking, in that strange place, and at that crisis in her life? Of the man whose words had found their way to her heart, whose influence had strengthened and comforted her, in the chapel of the Refuge. One of the finest passages in his sermon had been especially devoted by Julian Gray to warning the congregation whom he addressed against the degrading influences of falsehood and deceit. The terms in which he had appealed to the miserable women round him – terms of sympathy and encouragement never addressed to them before – came back to Mercy Merrick as if she had heard them an hour since. She turned deadly pale as they now pleaded with her once more. 'Oh!' she whispered to herself, as she thought of what she had purposed and planned; 'what have I done? what have I done?'

She turned from the window with some vague idea in her mind of following Mr Holmcroft and calling him back. As she faced the bed again, she also confronted Ignatius Wetzel. He was just stepping forward to speak to her, with a white handkerchief – the handkerchief which she had lent to Grace – held up in his hand.

'I have found this in her pocket,' he said. 'Here is her name written on it. She must be a country-woman of yours.' He read the letters marked on the handkerchief with some difficulty. 'Her name is – Mercy Merrick.'

His lips had said it – not hers! *He* had given Grace Roseberry the name.

'"Mercy Merrick" is an English name?' pursued Ignatius Wetzel, with his eyes steadily fixed on her. 'Is it not so?'

The hold on her mind of the past association with Julian Gray began to relax. One present and pressing question now possessed itself of the foremost place in her thoughts. Should she correct the error into which the German had fallen? The time had come – to speak, and assert her own identity; or to be silent, and commit herself to the fraud.

Horace Holmcroft entered the room again, at the moment when Surgeon Wetzel's staring eyes were still fastened on her, waiting for her reply.

'I have not overrated my interest,' he said, pointing to a little slip of paper in his hand. 'Here is the pass. Have you got pen and ink? I must fill up the form.'

Mercy pointed to the writing materials on the table. Horace seated himself, and dipped the pen in the ink.

'Pray don't think that I wish to intrude myself into your affairs,' he said. 'I am obliged to ask you one or two plain questions. What is your name?'

A sudden trembling seized her. She supported herself against the foot of the bed. Her whole future existence depended on her answer. She was incapable of uttering a word.

Ignatius Wetzel stood her friend once more. His croaking voice filled the empty gap of silence exactly at the right time. He doggedly held the handkerchief under her eyes. He obstinately repeated,'Mercy Merrick is an English name. Is it not so?'

Horace Holmcroft looked up from the table. 'Mercy Merrick?' he said. 'Who is Mercy Merrick?'

Surgeon Wetzel pointed to the corpse on the bed.

'I have found the name on the handkerchief,' he said. 'This lady, it seems, had not the curiosity to look for the name of her own countrywoman.' He made that mocking allusion to Mercy with a tone which was almost a tone of suspicion, and a look which was almost a look of contempt. Her quick temper instantly resented the discourtesy of which she had been made the object. The irritation of the moment – so often do the most trifling motives determine the most serious human actions – decided her on the course that she should pursue. She turned her back scornfully on the rude old man, and left him in the delusion that he had discovered the dead woman's name.

Horace returned to the business of filling up the form.

'Pardon me for pressing the question,' he said. 'You know what German discipline is by this time. What is your name?'

She answered him recklessly, defiantly, without fairly realising what she was doing, until it was done.

'Grace Roseberry,' she said.

The words were hardly out of her mouth before she would have given everything she possessed in the world to recall them.

'Miss?' asked Horace, smiling.

She could only answer him by bowing her head.

He wrote, 'Miss Grace Roseberry' – reflected for a moment – and then added interrogatively, 'Returning to her friends in England?' Her friends in England! Mercy's heart swelled: she silently replied by another sign. He wrote the words after the name, and shook the sand-box over the wet ink. 'That will be enough,' he said, rising and presenting the pass to Mercy; 'I will see you through the lines myself, and arrange for your being sent on by the railway. Where is your luggage?'

Mercy pointed towards the front door of the building. 'In a shed outside the cottage,' she answered. 'It is not much; I can do everything for myself if the sentinel will let me pass through the kitchen.'

Horace pointed to the paper in her hand. 'You can go where you like now,' he said. 'Shall I wait for you here, or outside?'

Mercy glanced distrustfully at Ignatius Wetzel. He had resumed his endless examination of the body on the bed. If she left him alone with Mr Holmcroft, there was no knowing what the hateful old man might not say of her. She answered, 'Wait for me outside, if you please.'

The sentinel drew back with a military salute at the sight of the pass. All the French prisoners had been removed; there were not more than half-a-dozen Germans in the kitchen, and the greater part of them were asleep. Mercy took Grace Roseberry's clothes from the corner in which they had been left to dry, and made for the shed, a rough structure of wood, built out from the cottage wall. At the front door she encountered a second sentinel, and showed her pass for the second time. She spoke to this man, asking him if he understood French. He answered that he understood a little. Mercy gave him a piece of money and said, ' I am going to pack up my luggage in the shed. Be kind enough to see that nobody disturbs me.' The sentinel saluted, in token that he understood. Mercy disappeared in the dark interior of the shed.

Left alone with Surgeon Wetzel, Horace noticed the strange old man still bending intently over the English lady who had been killed by the shell.

'Anything remarkable,' he asked, 'in the manner of that poor creature's death?'

'Nothing to put in a newspaper,' retorted the cynic, pursuing his investigations as attentively as ever.

'Interesting to a doctor – eh?' said Horace.

'Yes. Interesting to a doctor,' was the gruff reply.

Horace good-humouredly accepted the hint implied in those words. He quitted the room by the door leading into the yard, and waited for the charming Englishwoman as he had been instructed, outside the cottage.

Left by himself, Ignatius Wetzel, after a first cautious look all round him, opened the upper part of Grace's dress, and laid his left hand on her heart. Taking a little steel instrument from his waistcoat pocket with the other hand, he applied it carefully to the wound – raised a morsel of the broken and depressed bone of the skull, and waited for the result. 'Aha!' he cried, addressing with a terrible gaiety the senseless creature under his hands. 'The Frenchman says you are dead, my dear – does he? The Frenchman is a Quack! The Frenchman is an Ass!' He lifted his head, and called into the kitchen. 'Max!' A sleepy young German, covered with a dresser's apron from his chin to his feet, drew the curtain and waited for his instructions. 'Bring me my black bag,' said Ignatius Wetzel. Having given that order, he rubbed his hands cheerfully, and shook himself like a dog. 'Now I am quite happy,' croaked the terrible old man, with his fierce eyes leering sidelong at the bed. 'My dear dead Englishwoman, I would not have missed this meeting with you for all the money I have in the world. Ha! you infernal French Quack, you call it death, do you? I call it suspended animation from pressure on the brain!'

Max appeared with the black bag.

Ignatius Wetzel selected two fearful instruments, bright and new, and hugged them to his bosom. 'My little boys,' he said tenderly, as if they were two children; 'my blessed little boys, come to work!' He turned to the assistant. 'Do you remember the battle of Solferino, Max – and the Austrian soldier I operated on for a wound to the head?'

The assistant's sleepy eyes opened wide; he was evidently interested. 'I remember,' he said. 'I held the candle.'

The master led the way to the bed.

'I am not satisfied with the result of that operation at Solferino,' he said; 'I have wanted to try again ever since. It's true that I saved the man's life but I failed to give him back his reason along with it. It might have been something wrong in the operation, or it might have been something wrong in the man. Whichever it was, he will live and die, mad. Now look here, my little Max, at this dear young lady on the bed. She gives me just what I wanted; here is the case at Solferino, once more. You shall hold the candle again, my good boy; stand there, and look with all your eyes. I am going to try if I can save the life and the reason too, this time.'

He tucked up the cuffs of his coat, and began the operation. As his fearful instruments touched Grace's head, the voice of the sentinel at the nearest outpost was heard, giving the word in German which permitted Mercy to take the first step on her journey to England:

'Pass the English lady!'

The operation proceeded. The voice of the sentinel at the next post was heard more faintly, in its turn:

'Pass the English lady!'

The operation ended. Ignatius Wetzel held up his hand for

silence, and put his ear close to the patient's mouth.

The first trembling breath of returning life fluttered over Grace Roseberry's lips, and touched the old man's wrinkled cheek. 'Aha!' he cried. 'Good girl! you breathe – you live!' As he spoke, the voice of the sentinel at the final limit of the German lines (barely audible in the distance) gave the word for the last time:

'Pass the English lady!'

THE END OF THE FIRST SCENE

SECOND SCENE

MABLETHORPE HOUSE

PREAMBLE

The place is England.

The time is winter, in the year eighteen hundred and seventy.

The persons are: Julian Gray, Horace Holmcroft, Lady Janet Roy, Grace Roseberry and Mercy Merrick.

CHAPTER THE SIXTH

LADY JANET'S COMPANION

It is a glorious winter's day. The sky is clear, the frost is hard, the ice bears for skating.

The dining-room of the ancient mansion, called Mablethorpe House, situated in the London suburb of Kensington, is famous among artists and other persons of taste for the carved wood-work, of Italian origin, which covers the walls on three sides. On the fourth side, the march of modern improvement has broken in, and has varied and brightened the scene by means of a conservatory, forming an entrance to the room, through a winter garden of rare plants and flowers. On your right hand, as you stand fronting the conservatory, the monotony of the panelled wall is relieved by a quaintly-patterned door of old inlaid wood, leading into the library, and thence, across the great hall, to the other reception rooms of the house. A corresponding door on the left hand gives access to the billiard-room, to the smoking-room next to it, and to a smaller hall commanding one of the secondary entrances to the building. On the left side also is the ample fire-place, surmounted by its marble mantelpiece, carved in the profusely and confusedly ornate style of eighty years since. To the educated eye, the dining-room, with its modern furniture and conservatory, its ancient walls and doors, and its lofty mantelpiece (neither very old nor very new) presents a startling, almost a revolutionary mixture of the decorative workmanship of widely-differing schools. To the ignorant eye, the one result produced is an impression of perfect luxury and comfort, united in the friendliest combination, and developed on the largest scale.

The clock has just struck two. The table is spread for luncheon.

The persons seated at the table are three in number. First, Lady Janet Roy. Second, a young lady who is her reader and companion. Third, a guest staying in the house, who has already appeared in these pages under the name of Horace Holmcroft — attached to the German army as war-correspondent of an English newspaper.

Lady Janet Roy needs but little introduction. Everybody with the slightest pretension to experience in London society knows Lady Janet Roy.

Who has not heard of her old lace and her priceless rubies? Who has not admired her commanding figure, her beautifully-dressed white hair, her wonderful black eyes, which still preserve their youthful brightness, after first opening on the world seventy years since? Who has not felt the charm of her frank easily-flowing talk, her inexhaustible spirits, her good-humoured gracious sociability of manner? Where is the modern hermit who is not familiarly acquainted, by hearsay at least, with the fantastic novelty and humour of her opinions; with her generous encouragement of rising merit of any sort, in all ranks, high or low; with her charities, which know no distinction between abroad and at home; with her large indulgence, which no ingratitude can discourage and no servility pervert? Everybody has heard of the popular old lady — the childless widow of a long-forgotten lord. Everybody knows Lady Janet Roy.

But who knows the handsome young woman sitting on her right hand, playing with her luncheon instead of eating it? Nobody really knows her.

She is prettily dressed in grey poplin, trimmed with grey velvet, and set off by a ribbon of deep red tied in a bow at the throat. She is nearly as tall as Lady Janet herself, and possesses a grace and beauty of figure not always seen in women who rise above the medium height. Judging by a certain innate grandeur in the carriage of her head, and in the expression of her large melancholy grey eyes, believers in blood and breeding will be apt to guess that this is another noble lady. Alas! she is nothing but Lady Janet's companion and reader. Her head, crowned with its lovely light brown hair, bends with a gentle respect when Lady Janet speaks. Her fine firm hand is easily and incessantly watchful to supply Lady Janet's slightest wants. The old lady – affectionately familiar with her – speaks to her as she might speak to an adopted child. But the gratitude of the beautiful companion has always the same restraint in its acknowledgement of kindness; the smile of the beautiful companion has always the same underlying sadness when it responds to Lady Janet's hearty laugh. Is there something wrong here, under the surface? Is she suffering in mind, or suffering in body? What is the matter with her?

The matter with her is secret remorse. This delicate and beautiful creature pines under the slow torment of constant self-reproach.

To the mistress of the house, and to all who inhabit it or enter it, she is known as Grace Roseberry, the orphan relative by marriage of Lady Janet Roy. To herself alone she is known as the outcast of the London streets; the inmate of the London refuge; the lost woman who has stolen her way back – after vainly trying to fight her way back – to Home and Name. There she sits in the grim shadow of her own terrible secret, disguised in another person's identity, and established in another person's place. Mercy Merrick had only to dare, and to become Grace Roseberry if she pleased. She has dared; and she has been Grace Roseberry for nearly four months past.

At this moment, while Lady Janet is talking to Horace Holmcroft, something that has passed between them has set her thinking of the day when she took the first fatal step which committed her to the fraud.

How marvellously easy of accomplishment the act of personation had been! At first sight, Lady Janet had yielded to the fascination of the noble and interesting face. No need to present the stolen letter; no need to repeat the ready-made story. The old lady had put the letter aside unopened, and had stopped the story at the first words. 'Your face is your introduction, my dear; your father can say nothing for you which you have not already said for yourself.' There was the

welcome which established her firmly in her false identity at the
outset. Thanks to her own experience, and thanks to the
'Journal' of events at Rome, questions about her life in Canada,
and questions about Colonel Roseberry's illness, found her
ready with answers which (even if suspicion had existed) would
have disarmed suspicion on the spot. While the true Grace was
slowly and painfully winning her way back to life on her bed in
a German hospital, the false Grace was presented to Lady Janet's
friends as the relative by marriage of the mistress of
Mablethorpe House. From that time forward nothing had
happened to rouse in Mercy the faintest suspicion that Grace
Roseberry was other than a dead, and buried, woman. So far as
she now knew – so far as anyone now knew – she might live
out her life in perfect security (if her conscience would let her),
respected, distinguished, and beloved, in the position which she
had usurped.

She rose abruptly from the table. The effort of her life was to
shake herself free of the remembrances which haunted her
perpetually as they were haunting her now. Her memory was
her worst enemy; her one refuge from it was in change of
occupation and change of scene.

'May I go into the conservatory, Lady Janet?' she asked.

'Certainly, my dear.'

She bent her head to her protectress – looked for a moment,
with a steady compassionate attention, at Horace Holmcroft –
and, slowly crossing the room, entered the winter garden. The
eyes of Horace followed her, as long as she was in view, with a
curious, contradictory expression of admiration and disapproval.
When she had passed out of sight, the admiration vanished, but
the disapproval remained. The face of the young man
contracted into a frown: he sat silent, with his fork in his hand,
playing absently with the fragments on his plate.

'Take some French pie, Horace,' said Lady Janet.

'No, thank you.'

'Some more chicken, then?'

'No more chicken.'

'Will nothing tempt you?'

'I will take some more wine, if you will allow me.'

He filled his glass (for the fifth or sixth time) with claret, and emptied it sullenly at a draught. Lady Janet's bright eyes watched him with sardonic attention, Lady Janet's ready tongue spoke out as freely as usual what was passing in her mind at the time.

'The air of Kensington doesn't seem to suit you, my young friend,' she said. 'The longer you have been my guest, the oftener you fill your glass and empty your cigar-case. Those are bad signs in a young man. When you first came here, you arrived invalided by a wound. In your place, I should not have exposed myself to be shot, with no other object in view than describing a battle in a newspaper. I suppose tastes differ. Are you ill? Does your wound still plague you?'

'Not in the least.'

'Are you out of spirits?'

Horace Holmcroft dropped his fork, rested his elbows on the table, and answered, 'Awfully.'

Even Lady Janet's large toleration had its limits. It embraced every human offence, except a breach of good manners. She snatched up the nearest weapon of correction at hand – a table-spoon – and rapped her young friend smartly with it on the arm that was nearest to her.

'My table is not the club table,' said the old lady. 'Hold up your head. Don't look at your fork – look at me. I allow nobody to be out of spirits in My house. I consider it to be a reflection on Me. If our quiet life here doesn't suit you, say so plainly, and find something else to do. There is employment to be had, I suppose – if you choose to apply for it? You needn't smile. I don't want to see your teeth – I want an answer.'

Horace admitted, with all needful gravity, that there was employment to be had. The war between France and Germany, he remarked, was still going on: the newspaper had offered to employ him again in the capacity of correspondent.

'Don't speak of the newspapers and the war!' cried Lady Janet, with a sudden explosion of anger, which was genuine anger this time. 'I detest the newspapers! I won't allow the newspapers to enter this house. I lay the whole blame of the blood shed between France and Germany at their door.'

Horace's eyes opened wide in amazement. The old lady was
evidently in earnest. 'What can you possibly mean?' he asked.
'Are the newspapers responsible for the war?'

'Entirely responsible,' answered Lady Janet. 'Why, you don't
understand the age you live in! Does anybody do anything
nowadays (fighting included) without wishing to see it in the
newspapers? *I* subscribe to a charity; *thou* art presented with a
testimonial; *he* preaches a sermon; *we* suffer a grievance; *you*
make a discovery; *they* go to church and get married. And I,
thou, he; we, you, they, all want one and the same thing – we
want to see it in the papers. Are kings, soldiers, and diplomatists
exceptions to the general rule of humanity? Not they! I tell you
seriously, if the newspapers of Europe had one and all decided
not to take the smallest notice in print of the war between
France and Germany, it is my firm conviction the war would
have come to an end for want of encouragement long since. Let
the pen cease to advertise the sword, and I, for one, can see the
result. No report – no fighting.'

'Your views have the merit of perfect novelty, ma'am,' said
Horace. 'Would you object to see them in the newspapers?'

Lady Janet worsted her young friend with his own weapons.

'Don't I live in the latter part of the nineteenth century?' she
asked. 'In the newspapers, did you say? In large print, Horace, if
you love me!'

Horace changed the subject.

'You blame me for being out of spirits,' he said; 'and you
seem to think it is because I am tired of my pleasant life at
Mablethorpe House. I am not in the least tired, Lady Janet.' He
looked towards the conservatory: the frown showed itself on his
face once more. 'The truth is,' he resumed, 'I am not satisfied
with Grace Roseberry.'

'What has Grace done?'

'She persists in prolonging our engagement. Nothing will
persuade her to fix the day for our marriage.'

It was true! Mercy had been mad enough to listen to him,
and to love him. But Mercy was not vile enough to marry him
under her false character, and in her false name. Between three
and four months had elapsed since Horace had been sent home

from the war, wounded, and had found the beautiful English-woman whom he had befriended in France established at Mablethorpe House. Invited to become Lady Janet's guest (he had passed his holidays as a schoolboy under Lady Janet's roof) — free to spend the idle time of his convalescence from morning to night in Mercy's society — the impression originally produced on him in the French cottage soon strengthened into love. Before the month was out, Horace had declared himself, and had discovered that he spoke to willing ears. From that moment it was only a question of persisting long enough in the resolution to gain his point. The marriage engagement was ratified — most reluctantly on the lady's side — and there the further progress of Horace Holmcroft's suit came to an end. Try as he might, he failed to persuade his betrothed wife to fix the day for the marriage. There were no obstacles in her way. She had no near relations of her own to consult. As a connection of Lady Janet's by marriage, Horace's mother and sisters were ready to receive her with all the honours due to a new member of the family. No pecuniary considerations made it necessary, in this case, to wait for a favourable time. Horace was an only son; and he had succeeded to his father's estate with an ample income to support it. On both sides alike, there was absolutely nothing to prevent the two young people from being married as soon as the settlements could be drawn. And yet, to all appearance, here was a long engagement in prospect, with no better reason than the lady's incomprehensible perversity to explain the delay.

'Can you account for Grace's conduct?' asked Lady Janet. Her manner changed as she put the question. She looked and spoke like a person who was perplexed and annoyed.

'I hardly like to own it,' Horace answered, 'but I am afraid she has some motive for deferring our marriage which she cannot confide either to you or to me.'

Lady Janet started.

'What makes you think that?' she asked.

'I have once or twice caught her in tears. Every now and then — sometimes when she is talking quite gaily — she suddenly changes colour, and becomes silent and depressed. Just now, when she left the table (didn't you notice it?), she looked at me in the strangest way – almost as if she was sorry for me. What do these things mean?'

Horace's reply, instead of increasing Lady Janet's anxiety, seemed to relieve it. He had observed nothing which she had not noticed herself. 'You foolish boy!' she said, 'the meaning is plain enough. Grace has been out of health for some time past. The doctor recommends change of air. I shall take her away with me.'

'It would be more to the purpose,' Horace rejoined, 'if *I* took her away with me. She might consent, if you would only use your influence. Is it asking too much to ask you to persuade her? My mother and my sisters have written to her, and have produced no effect. Do me the greatest of all kindnesses – speak to her to-day!' He paused, and, possessing himself of Lady Janet's hand, pressed it entreatingly. 'You have always been so good to me,' he said softly, and pressed it again.

The old lady looked at him. It was impossible to dispute that there were attractions in Horace Holmcroft's face which made it well worth looking at. Many a woman might have envied him his clear complexion, his bright blue eyes, and the warm amber tint in his light Saxon hair. Men – especially men skilled in observing physiognomy – might have noticed in the shape of his forehead, and in the line of his upper lip, the signs indicative of a moral nature deficient in largeness and breadth – of a mind easily accessible to strong prejudices, and obstinate in maintaining those prejudices in the face of conviction itself. To the observation of women, these remote defects were too far below the surface to be visible. He charmed the sex in general by his rare personal advantages, and by the graceful deference of his manner. To Lady Janet he was endeared, not by his own merits only, but by old associations that were connected with him. His father had been one of her many admirers in her young days. Circumstances had parted them. Her marriage to another man had been a childless marriage. In past times, when the boy Horace had come to her from school, she cherished a secret fancy (too absurd to be communicated to any living creature) that he ought to have been *her* son, and might have been her son, if she had married his father! She smiled charmingly, old as she was – she yielded as his mother might have yielded – when the young man took her hand, and entreated her to interest herself in his marriage.

'Must I really speak to Grace?' she asked, with a gentleness of tone and manner far from characteristic, on ordinary occasions, of the lady of Mablethorpe House. Horace saw that he had gained his point. He sprang to his feet; his eyes turned eagerly in the direction of the conservatory; his handsome face was radiant with hope. Lady Janet (with her mind full of his father) stole a last look at him – sighed as she thought of the vanished days – and recovered herself.

'Go to the smoking-room,' she said, giving him a push towards the door. 'Away with you, and cultivate the favourite vice of the nineteenth century.' Horace attempted to express his gratitude. 'Go and smoke!' was all she said, pushing him out. 'Go and smoke!'

Left by herself, Lady Janet took a turn in the room, and considered a little.

Horace's discontent was not unreasonable. There was really no excuse for the delay of which he complained. Whether the young lady had a special motive for hanging back, or whether she was merely fretting because she did not know her own mind, it was, in either case, necessary to come to a distinct understanding, sooner or later, on the serious question of the marriage. The difficulty was, how to approach the subject without giving offence. 'I don't understand the young women of the present generation,' thought Lady Janet. 'In my time, when we were fond of a man, we were ready to marry him at a moment's notice. And this is an age of progress! They ought to be readier still.'

Arriving, by her own process of induction, at this inevitable conclusion, she decided to try what her influence could accomplish, and to trust to the inspiration of the moment for exerting it in the right way. 'Grace!' she called out, approaching the conservatory door.

The tall lithe figure in its grey dress glided into view, and stood relieved against the green background of the winter garden.

'Did your ladyship call me?'

'Yes; I want to speak to you. Come and sit down by me.'

With those words, Lady Janet led the way to the sofa, and placed her companion by her side.

CHAPTER THE SEVENTH

THE MAN IS COMING

'You look very pale this morning, my child.'

Mercy sighed wearily. 'I am not well,' she answered. 'The slightest noises startle me. I feel tired if only I walk across the room.'

Lady Janet patted her kindly on the shoulder. 'We must try what a change will do for you. Which shall it be? the Continent, or the sea-side?'

'Your ladyship is too kind to me.'

'It is impossible to be too kind to you.'

Mercy started. The colour flowed charmingly over her pale face. 'Oh!' she exclaimed impulsively. 'Say that again!'

'Say it again?' repeated Lady Janet, with a look of surprise.

'Yes! Don't think me presuming; only think me vain. I can't hear you say too often that you have learnt to like me. Is it really a pleasure to you to have me in the house? Have I always behaved well since I have been with you?'

(The one excuse for the act of personation – if excuse there could be – lay in the affirmative answer to those questions. It would be something, surely, to say of the false Grace that the true Grace could not have been worthier of her welcome, if the true Grace had been recieved at Mablethorpe House!)

Lady Janet was partly touched, partly amused, by the extraordinary earnestness of the appeal that had been made to her.

'Have you behaved well?' she repeated. 'My dear, you talk as if you were a child!' She laid her hand caressingly on Mercy's arm, and continued, in a graver tone: 'It is hardly too much to say, Grace, that I bless the day when you first came to me. I do believe I could be hardly fonder of you if you were my own daughter.'

Mercy suddenly turned her head aside, so as to hide her face. Lady Janet, still touching her arm, felt it tremble. 'What is the matter with you?' she asked, in her abrupt, downright manner.

'I am only very grateful to your ladyship – that is all.'

The words were spoken faintly in broken tones. The face was still averted from Lady Janet's view. 'What have I said to provoke this?' wondered the old lady. 'Is she in the melting mood to-day. If she is, now is the time to say a word for Horace.' Keeping that excellent object in view, Lady Janet approached the delicate topic with all needful caution at starting.

'We have got on so well together,' she resumed, 'that it will not be easy for either of us to feel reconciled to a change in our lives. At my age it will fall hardest on me. What shall I do, Grace, when the day comes for parting with my adopted daughter?'

Mercy started, and showed her face again. The traces of tears were in her eyes. 'Why should I leave you?' she asked, in a tone of alarm.

'Surely you know!' exclaimed Lady Janet.

'Indeed I don't. Tell me why.'

'Ask Horace to tell you.'

The last allusion was too plain to be misunderstood. Mercy's head drooped. She began to tremble again. Lady Janet looked at her in blank amazement.

'Is there anything wrong between Horace and you?' she asked.

'No.'

'You know your own heart, my dear child? You have surely not encouraged Horace without loving him?'

'Oh, no!'

'And yet——'

For the first time in their experience of each other, Mercy ventured to interrupt her benefactress. 'Dear Lady Janet,' she

interposed, gently, 'I am in no hurry to be married. There will
be plenty of time in the future to talk of that. You had
something you wished to say to me. What is it?'

It was no easy matter to disconcert Lady Janet Roy. But that
last question fairly reduced her to silence. After all that had
passed, there sat her young companion, innocent of the faintest
suspicion of the subject that was to be discussed between them!
'What are the young women of the present time made of?'
thought the old lady, utterly at a loss to know what to say next.
Mercy waited, on her side, with an impenetrable patience
which only aggravated the difficulties of the position. The
silence was fast threatening to bring the interview to a sudden
and untimely end – when the door from the library opened,
and a man-servant, bearing a little silver salver, entered the
room.

Lady Janet's rising sense of annoyance instantly seized on the
servant as a victim. 'What do you want?' she asked sharply. 'I
never rang for you.'

'A letter, my lady. The messenger waits for an answer.'

The man presented his salver, with the letter on it, and
withdrew.

Lady Janet recognised the handwriting on the address with a
look of surprise. 'Excuse me, my dear,' she said, pausing, with
her old-fashioned courtesy, before she opened the envelope.
Mercy made the necessary acknowledgement, and moved
away to the other end of the room; little thinking that the
arrival of the letter marked a crisis in her life. Lady Janet put
on her spectacles. 'Odd, that he should have come back
already!' she said to herself, as she threw the empty envelope
on the table.

The letter contained these lines; the writer of them being no
other than the man who had preached in the chapel of the
Refuge:–

'DEAR AUNT

'I am back again in London, before my time. My friend the
rector has shortened his holiday, and has resumed his duties in
the country. I am afraid you will blame me when you hear of

the reasons which have hastened his return. The sooner I make my confession, the easier I shall feel. Besides, I have a special object in wishing to see you as soon as possible. May I follow my letter to Mablethorpe House? And may I present a lady to you – a perfect stranger – in whom I am interested? Pray say Yes, by the bearer, and oblige your affectionate nephew,

'JULIAN GRAY.'

Lady Janet referred again suspiciously to the sentence in the letter which alluded to the 'lady.'

Julian Gray was her only surviving nephew, the son of a favourite sister whom she had lost. He would have held no very exalted position in the estimation of his aunt – who regarded his views in politics and religion with the strongest aversion – but for his marked resemblance to his mother. This pleaded for him with the old lady; aided, as it was, by the pride that she secretly felt in the early celebrity which the young clergyman had achieved as a writer and a preacher. Thanks to these mitigating circumstances, and to Julian's inexhaustible good humour, the aunt and the nephew generally met on friendly terms. Apart from what she called 'his detestable opinions,' Lady Janet was sufficiently interested in Julian to feel some curiosity about the mysterious 'lady' mentioned in the letter. Was his choice already made? And if so, would it prove to be a choice acceptable to the family. Lady Janet's bright face showed signs of doubt as she asked herself that last question. Julian's liberal views were capable of leading him to dangerous extremes. His aunt shook her head ominously as she rose from the sofa, and advanced to the library door.

'Grace', she said, pausing and turning round, 'I have a note to write to my nephew. I shall be back directly.'

Mercy approached her, from the opposite extremity of the room, with an exclamation of surprise.

'Your nephew?' she repeated. 'Your ladyship never told me you had a nephew.'

Lady Janet laughed. 'I must have had it on the tip of my tongue to tell you, over and over again,' she said. 'But we have so many things to talk about – and, to own the truth, my

nephew is not one of my favourite subjects of conversation. I
don't mean that I dislike him; I detest his principles, my dear,
that's all. However, you shall form your own opinion of him;
he is coming to see me to-day. Wait here till I return; I have
something more to say about Horace.'

Mercy opened the library door for her, closed it again, and
walked slowly to and fro alone in the room, thinking.

Was her mind running on Lady Janet's nephew? No. Lady
Janet's brief allusion to her relative had not led her into alluding
to him by his name. Mercy was still as ignorant as ever that the
preacher at the Refuge and the nephew of her benefactress
were one and the same man. Her memory was busy, now, with
the tribute which Lady Janet had paid to her at the outset of the
interview between them: 'It is hardly too much to say, Grace,
that I bless the day when you first came to me.' For the
moment, there was balm for her wounded spirit in the
remembrance of those words. Grace Roseberry herself could
surely have earned no sweeter praise than the praise that she had
won. The next instant she was seized with a sudden horror of
her own successful fraud. The sense of her degradation had
never been so bitterly present to her as at that moment. If she
could only confess the truth – if she could innocently enjoy her
harmless life at Mablethorpe House – what a grateful, happy
woman she might be! Was it possible (if she made the
confession) to trust to her own good conduct to plead her
excuse? No! Her calmer sense warned her that it was hopeless.
The place she had won – honestly won – in Lady Janet's
estimation, had been obtained by a trick. Nothing could alter,
nothing could excuse *that*. She took out her handkerchief, and
dashed away the useless tears that had gathered in her eyes, and
tried to turn her thoughts some other way. What was it Lady
Janet had said on going into the library? She had said she was
coming back to speak about Horace. Mercy guessed what the
object was; she knew but too well what Horace wanted of her.
How was she to meet the emergency? In the name of Heaven
what was to be done? Could she let the man who loved her –
the man whom *she* loved – drift blindfold into marriage with
such a woman as she had been? No! it was her duty to warn

him. How? Could she break his heart, could she lay his life waste, by speaking the cruel words which might part them for ever? 'I won't tell him!' she burst out passionately. 'The disgrace of it would kill me!' Her varying mood changed as the words escaped her. A reckless defiance of her own better nature – that saddest of all the forms in which a woman's misery can express itself – filled her heart with its poisoning bitterness. She sat down again on the sofa, with eyes that glittered, and cheeks suffused with an angry red. 'I am no worse than another woman!' she thought. 'Another woman might have married him for his money.' The next moment the miserable insufficiency of her own excuse for deceiving him showed its hollowness, self-exposed. She covered her face with her hands, and found refuge – where she had often found refuge before – in the helpless resignation of despair. 'Oh, that I had died before I entered this house! Oh, that I could die and have done with it, at this moment!' So the struggle had ended with her hundreds of times already. So it ended now.

The door leading into the billiard-room opened softly. Horace Holmcroft had waited to hear the result of Lady Janet's interference in his favour until he could wait no longer.

He looked in cautiously; ready to withdraw again unnoticed, if the two were still talking together. The absence of Lady Janet suggested that the interview had come to an end. Was his betrothed wife, waiting alone to speak to him on his return to the room? He advanced a few steps. She never moved – she sat heedless, absorbed in her thoughts. Were they thoughts of *him?* He advanced a little nearer, and called to her.

'Grace!'

She sprang to her feet, with a faint cry. 'I wish you wouldn't startle me,' she said, irritably, sinking back on the sofa. 'Any sudden alarm sets my heart beating as if it would choke me.'

Horace pleaded for pardon with a lover's humility. In her present state of nervous irritation, she was not to be appeased. She looked away from him in silence. Entirely ignorant of the paroxysm of mental suffering through which she had just passed, he seated himself by her side, and asked her gently if she

had seen Lady Janet. She made an affirmative answer with an
unreasonable impatience of tone and manner which would have
warned an older and more experienced man to give her time
before he spoke again. Horace was young, and weary of the
suspense that he had endured in the other room. He unwisely
pressed her with another question.

'Has Lady Janet mentioned my name in speaking to you?'

She turned on him angrily before he could add a word more.
'You have tried to make her hurry me into marrying you,' she
burst out. 'I see it in your face!'

Plain as the warning was this time, Horace still failed to
interpret it in the right way. 'Don't be angry!' he said, good-
humouredly. 'Is it so very inexcusable to ask Lady Janet to
intercede for me? *I* have tried to persuade you in vain. My
mother and my sisters have pleaded for me, and you turn a deaf
ear——'

She could endure it no longer. She stamped her foot on the
floor with hysterical vehemence. 'I am weary of hearing of your
mother and your sisters!' she broke in violently. 'You talk of
nothing else.'

It was just possible to make one more mistake in dealing with
her – and Horace made it. He took offence on his side, and rose
from the sofa. His mother and sisters were high authorities in
his estimation; they variously represented his ideal of perfection
in women. He withdrew to the opposite extremity of the
room, and administered the severest reproof that he could think
of on the spur of the moment.

'It would be well, Grace, if you followed the example set you
by my mother and sisters,' he said. '*They* are not in the habit of
speaking cruelly to those who love them.'

To all appearance, the rebuke failed to produce the slightest
effect. She seemed to be as indifferent to it as if it had not
reached her ears. There was a spirit in her – a miserable spirit,
born of her own bitter experience – which rose in revolt against
Horace's habitual glorification of the ladies of his family. 'It
sickens me,' she thought to herself, 'to hear of the virtues of
women who have never been tempted! Where is the merit of
living reputably when your life is one course of prosperity and

enjoyment? Has his mother known starvation? Have his sisters been left forsaken in the street?' It hardened her heart – it almost reconciled her to deceiving him – when he set his relatives up as patterns for her. Would he never understand that women detested having other women exhibited as examples to -them? She looked round at him with a sense of impatient wonder. He was sitting at the luncheon-table, with his back turned on her, and his head resting on his hands. If he had attempted to rejoin her, she would have repelled him; if he had spoken, she would have met him with a sharp reply. He sat apart from her without uttering a word. In a man's hands silence is the most terrible of all protests, to the woman who loves him. Violence she can endure. Words she is always ready to meet by words on her side. Silence conquers her. After a moment's hesitation, Mercy left the sofa, and advanced submissively towards the table. She had offended him – and she alone was in fault. How should he know it, poor fellow, when he innocently mortified her? Step by step, she drew closer and closer. He never looked round; he never moved. She laid her hand timidly on his shoulder. 'Forgive me, Horace,' she whispered in his ear. 'I am suffering this morning; I am not myself. I didn't mean what I said. Pray forgive me.' There was no resisting the caressing tenderness of voice and manner which accompanied those words. He looked up; he took her hand. She bent over him, and touched his forehead with her lips. 'Am I forgiven?' she asked.

'Oh, my darling,' he said, 'if you only knew how I loved you!'

'I do know it,' she answered gently, twining his hair round her finger, and arranging it over his forehead where his hand had ruffled it.

They were completely absorbed in each other, or they must, at that moment, have heard the library door open at the other end of the room.

Lady Janet had written the necessary reply to her nephew, and had returned, faithful to her engagement, to plead the cause of Horace. The first object that met her view was her client pleading, with conspicuous success, for himself! 'I am not

wanted, evidently,' thought the old lady. She noiselessly closed
the door again, and left the lovers by themselves.

Horace returned, with unwise persistency, to the question of
the deferred marriage. At the first words that he spoke, she
drew back directly – sadly, not angrily.

'Don't press me to-day,' she said; ' I am not well to-day.'

He rose, and looked at her anxiously. 'May I speak about it
to-morrow.'

'Yes, to-morrow.' She returned to the sofa, and changed the
subject. 'What a time Lady Janet is away,' she said. 'What can
be keeping her so long?'

Horace did his best to appear interested in the question of
Lady Janet's prolonged absence. 'What made her leave you?' he
asked, standing at the back of the sofa and leaning over her.

'She went into the library to write a note to her nephew. By-
the-by, who *is* her nephew?'

'Is it possible you don't know?'

'Indeed I don't.'

'You have heard of him, no doubt,' said Horace. 'Lady
Janet's nephew is a celebrated man.' He paused, and stooping
nearer to her, lifted a love-lock that lay over her shoulder, and
pressed it to his lips. 'Lady Janet's nephew,' he resumed, 'is
Julian Gray.'

She suddenly looked round at him in blank, bewildered
terror, as if she doubted the evidence of her own senses.

Horace was completely taken by surprise. 'My dear Grace!'
he exclaimed; 'what have I said or done to startle you this
time?'

She held her hand for silence. 'Lady Janet's nephew is Julian
Gray,' she repeated slowly; 'and I only know it now!'

Horace's perplexity increased. 'My darling, now you do
know it, what is there to alarm you?' he asked.

(There was enough to alarm the boldest woman living – in
such a position, and with such a temperament as hers. To her
mind the personation of Grace Roseberry had assumed the
aspect of a fatality. What lesser influence could have led her
blindfold to the house in which she and the preacher at the
Refuge were to meet? He was coming – the man who had

reached her inmost heart, who had influenced her whole life! Was the day of reckoning coming with him?)

'Don't notice me,' she said, faintly. 'I have been ill all morning. You saw it yourself when you came in here; even the sound of your voice alarmed me. I shall be better directly. I am afraid I startled you?'

'My dear Grace, it almost looked as if you were terrifed at the sound of Julian's name! He is a public celebrity, I know; and I have seen ladies start and stare at him when he entered a room. But *you* looked perfectly panic-stricken.'

She rallied her courage by a desperate effort; she laughed — a harsh, uneasy laugh — and stopped him by putting her hand over his mouth. 'Absurd!' she said lightly. 'As if Mr Julian Gray had anything to do with my looks! I am better already. See for yourself!' She looked round at him again with a ghastly gaiety; and returned, with a desperate assumption of indifference, to the subject of Lady Janet's nephew. 'Of course I have heard of him,' she said. 'Do you know that he is expected here to-day? Don't stand there behind me — it's so hard to talk to you. Come and sit down?'

He obeyed — but she had not quite satisfied him yet. His face had not lost its expression of anxiety and surprise. She persisted in playing her part; determined to set at rest in him any possible suspicion that she had reasons of her own for being afraid of Julian Gray. 'Tell me about this famous man of yours,' she said, putting her arm familiarly through his arm. 'What is he like?'

The caressing action and the easy tone had their effect on Horace. His face began to clear; he answered her lightly on his side.

'Prepare yourself to meet the most unclerical of clergymen,' he said. 'Julian is a lost sheep among the parsons, and a thorn in the side of his bishop. Preaches, if they ask him, in Dissenters' chapels. Declines to set up any pretensions to priestly authority and priestly power. Goes about doing good on a plan of his own. Is quite resigned never to rise to the high places in his profession. Says it's rising high enough for *him* to be the Archdeacon of the afflicted, the Dean of the hungry, and the Bishop of the poor. With all his oddities, as good a fellow as ever lived. Immensely popular with the women. They all go to him for advice. I wish you would go too.'

Mercy changed colour. 'What do you mean?' she asked sharply.

'Julian is famous for his powers of persuasion,' said Horace, smiling. 'If *he* spoke to you, Grace, he would prevail on you to fix the day. Suppose I ask Julian to plead for me?'

He made the proposal in jest. Mercy's unquiet mind accepted it as addressed to her in earnest. 'He will do it,' she thought, with a sense of indescribable terror, 'if I don't stop him!' There was but one chance for her. The only certain way to prevent Horace from appealing to his friend was to grant what Horace wished for before his friend entered the house. She laid her hand on his shoulder; she hid the terrible anxieties that were devouring her, under an assumption of coquetry painful and pitiable to see.

'Don't talk nonsense!' she said, gaily. 'What were we saying just now — before we began to speak of Mr Julian Gray?'

'We were wondering what had become of Lady Janet,' Horace replied.

She tapped him impatiently on the shoulder. 'No! no! It was something you said before that.'

Her eyes completed what her words had left unspoken. Horace's arm stole round her waist.

'I was saying that I loved you,' he answered, in a whisper.

'Only that?'

'Are you tired of hearing it?'

She smiled charmingly. 'Are you so very much in earnest about — about——?' She stopped, and looked away from him.

'About our marriage?'

'Yes.'

'It is the one dearest wish of my life.'

'Really?'

'Really!'

There was a pause. Mercy's fingers toyed nervously with the trinkets at her watch-chain. 'When would you like it to be?' she said very softly, with her whole attention fixed on the watch-chain.

She had never spoken, she had never looked, as she spoke and looked now. Horace was afraid to believe in his own good fortune. 'Oh, Grace!' he exclaimed, 'you are not trifling with me?'

'What makes you think I am trifling with you?'

Horace was innocent enough to answer her seriously. 'You would not even let me speak of our marriage just now,' he said.

'Never mind what I did just now,' she retorted, petulantly. 'They say women are changeable. It is one of the defects of the sex.'

'Heaven be praised for the defects of the sex!' cried Horace, with devout sincerity. 'Do you really leave me to decide?'

'If you insist on it.'

Horace considered for a moment – the subject being the law of marriage. 'We may be married by licence in a fortnight,' he said. ' I fix this day fortnight.'

She held up her hands in protest.

'Why not? My lawyer is ready. There are no preparations to make. You said when you accepted me that it was to be a private marriage.'

Mercy was obliged to own that she had certainly said that.

'We might be married at once – if the law would only let us. This day fortnight! Say – yes!' He drew her closer to him. There was a pause. The mask of coquetry – badly worn from the first – dropped from her. Her sad grey eyes rested compassionately on his eager face. 'Don't look so serious!' he said. 'Only one little word, Grace! Only Yes.'

She sighed, and said it. He kissed her passionately. It was only by a resolute effort that she released herself. 'Leave me!' she said, faintly. 'Pray leave me by myself!'

She was in earnest – strangely in earnest. She was trembling from head to foot. Horace rose to leave her. 'I will find Lady Janet,' he said; 'I long to show the dear old lady that I have recovered my spirits, and to tell her why.' He turned round at the library door. 'You won't go away? You will let me see you again when you are more composed?'

'I will wait here,' said Mercy.

Satisfied with that reply, he left the room.

Her hands dropped on her lap; her head sank back wearily on the cushions at the head of the sofa. There was a dazed sensation in her; her mind felt stunned. She wondered vacantly whether she was awake or dreaming. Had she really said the word which pledged her to marry Horace Holmcroft in a fortnight? A fortnight! Something might happen in that time to prevent it: she might find her way in a fortnight out of the terrible position in which she stood. Anyway, come what might of it, she had chosen the preferable alternative to a private interview with Julian Gray. She raised herself from her recumbent position with a start, as the idea of the interview – dismissed for the last few minutes – possessed itself again of her mind. Her excited imagination figured Julian Gray as present in the room at that moment, speaking to her as Horace had proposed. She saw him seated close at her side – this man who had shaken her to the soul when he was in the pulpit, and when she was listening to him (unseen) at the other end of the chapel – she saw him close by her, looking her searchingly in the face; seeing her shameful secret in her eyes; hearing it in her voice; feeling it in her trembling hands; forcing it out of her word by word, till she fell prostrate at his feet with the confession of the fraud. Her head dropped again on the cushions; she hid her face in horror of the scene which her excited fancy had conjured up. Even now, when she had made that dreaded interview needless, could she feel sure (meeting him only on the most distant terms) of not betraying herself? She could *not* feel sure. Something in her shuddered and shrank at the bare idea of finding herself in the same room with him. She felt it, she knew it; her guilty conscience owned and feared its master in Julian Gray!

The minutes passed. The violence of her agitation began to tell physically on her weakened frame.

She found herself crying silently without knowing why. A weight was on her head, a weariness was in all her limbs.

She sank lower on the cushions – her eyes closed – the monotonous ticking of the clock on the mantlepiece grew drowsily fainter and fainter on her ear. Little by little she dropped into slumber; slumber so light that she started when a morsel of coal fell into the grate, or when the birds chirped and twittered in their aviary in the winter garden.

Lady Janet and Horace came in. She was faintly conscious of the persons in the room. After an interval she opened her eyes, and half rose to speak to them. The room was empty again. They had stolen out softly and left her to repose. Her eyes closed once more. She dropped back into slumber, and from slumber, in the favouring warmth and quiet of the place, into deep and dreamless sleep.

CHAPTER THE EIGHTH

THE MAN APPEARS

After an interval of rest, Mercy was roused by the shutting of a glass door at the far end of the conservatory. This door, leading into the garden, was used only by the inmates of the house, or by old friends privileged to enter the reception rooms by that way. Assuming that either Horace or Lady Janet were returning to the dining-room, Mercy raised herself a little on the sofa and listened.

The voice of one of the men-servants caught her ear. It was answered by another voice, which instantly set her trembling in every limb.

She started up, and listened again in breathless terror. Yes! there was no mistaking it. The voice that was answering the servant was the unforgotten voice which she had heard at the Refuge. The visitor who had come in by the glass door was – Julian Gray!

His rapid footsteps advanced nearer and nearer to the dining-room. She recovered herself sufficiently to hurry to the library door. Her hand shook so that she failed at first to open it. She had just succeeded when she heard him again – speaking to her.

'Pray don't run away! I am nothing very formidable. Only Lady Janet's nephew – Julian Gray.'

She turned slowly, spell-bound by his voice, and confronted him in silence.

He was standing, hat in hand, at the entrance to the conservatory, dressed in black, and wearing a white cravat – but with a studious avoidance of anything specially clerical in the make and form of his clothes. Young as he was, there were marks of care already on his face, and the hair was prematurely thin and scanty over his forehead. His slight active figure was of no more than the middle height. His complexion was pale. The lower part of his face, without beard or whiskers, was in no way remarkable. An average observer would have passed him by without notice – but for his eyes. These alone made a marked man of him. The unusual size of the orbits in which they were set was enough of itself to attract attention; it gave a grandeur to his head, which the head, broad and firm as it was, did not possess. As to the eyes themselves, the soft lustrous brightness of them defied analysis. No two people could agree about their colour; divided opinion declaring alternately that they were dark grey or black. Painters had tried to reproduce them, and had given up the effort in despair of seizing any one expression which they presented to view. They were eyes that could charm at one moment, and terrify at another; eyes that could set people laughing or crying almost at will. In action and in repose they were irresistible alike. When they first decried Mercy running to the door, they brightened gaily with the merriment of a child. When she turned and faced him, they changed instantly; softening and glowing as they mutely owned the interest and the admiration which the first sight of her had roused in him. His tone and manner altered at the same time. He addressed her with the deepest respect when he spoke his next words.

'Let me entreat you to favour me by resuming your seat,' he said. 'And let me ask your pardon if I have thoughtlessly intruded on you.'

He paused, waiting for her reply before he advanced into the room. Still spell-bound by his voice, she recovered self-control enough to bow to him and to resume her place on the sofa. It was impossible to leave her now. After looking at her for a moment, he entered the room without speaking to her again. She was beginning to perplex as well as to interest him. 'No common sorrow,' he thought, 'has set its mark on that woman's face; no common heart beats in that woman's breast. Who can she be?'

Mercy rallied her courage, and forced herself to speak to him.

'Lady Janet is in the library, I believe,' she said timidly. 'Shall I tell her you are here?'

'Don't disturb Lady Janet, and don't disturb yourself.' With that answer he approached the luncheon-table, delicately giving her time to feel more at her ease. He took up what Horace had left of the bottle of claret and poured it into a glass. 'My aunt's claret shall represent my aunt for the present,' he said, smiling, as he turned towards her once more. 'I have had a long walk, and I may venture to help myself in this house without invitation. Is it useless to offer you anything?'

Mercy made the necessary reply. She was beginning already, after her remarkable experience of him, to wonder at his easy manners and his light way of talking.

He emptied his glass with the air of a man who thoroughly understood and enjoyed good wine. 'My aunt's claret is worthy of my aunt,' he said, with comic gravity, as he set down the glass. 'Both are the genuine products of Nature.' He seated himself at the table and looked critically at the different dishes left on it. One dish especially attracted his attention. 'What is this?' he went on. 'A French pie! It seems grossly unfair to taste French wine, and to pass over French pie without notice.' He took up a knife and fork, and enjoyed the pie as critically as he had enjoyed the wine. 'Worthy of the Great Nation!' he exclaimed with enthusiasm. '*Vive la France!*'

Mercy listened and looked, in inexpressible astonishment. He was utterly unlike the picture which her fancy had drawn of him in everyday life. Take off his white cravat, and nobody would have discovered that this famous preacher was a clergyman!

He helped himself to another plateful of the pie, and spoke more directly to Mercy; alternately eating and talking as composedly and pleasantly as if they had known each other for years.

'I came here by way of Kensington Gardens,' he said. 'For

some time past I have been living in a flat, ugly, barren agricultural district. You can't think how pleasant I found the picture presented by the Gardens, as a contrast. The ladies in their winter dresses, the smart nursery maids, the lovely children, the ever-moving crowd skating on the ice of the Round Pond, it was all so exhilarating after what I have been used to that I actually caught myself whistling as I walked through the brilliant scene! (In my time boys used always to whistle when they were in good spirits, and I have not got over the habit yet.) Who do you think I met when I was in full song?'

As well as her amazement would let her, Mercy excused herself from guessing. She had never in all her life before spoken to any living being so confusedly and so unintelligently as she now spoke to Julian Gray!

He went on more gaily than ever, without appearing to notice the effect that he had produced on her.

'Whom did I meet,' he repeated, 'when I was in full song? My bishop! If I had been whistling a sacred melody, his lordship might perhaps have excused my vulgarity out of consideration for my music. Unfortunately, the composition I was executing at the moment (I am one of the loudest of living whistlers) was by Verdi – "*La Donna e Mobile*" – familiar, no doubt to his lordship on the street organs. He recognised the tune, poor man, and when I took off my hat to him he looked the other way. Strange, in a world that is bursting with sin and sorrow, to treat such a trifle seriously as a cheerful clergyman whistling a tune!' He pushed away his plate as he said the last words, and went on simply and earnestly in an altered tone. 'I have never been able,' he said, 'to see why we should assert ourselves among other men as belonging to a particular caste, and as being forbidden, in any harmless thing, to do as other people do. The disciples of old set us no such example; they were wiser and better than we are. I venture to say, that one of the worst obstacles in the way of our doing good among our fellow-creatures is raised by the mere assumption of the clerical manner and the clerical voice. For my part, I set up no claim to be more sacred and more reverend than any other Christian man who does what good he can.' He glanced brightly at Mercy looking at him in helpless perplexity. The spirit of fun took possession of him again. 'Are you a Radical?' he asked, with a humorous twinkle in his large lustrous eyes. 'I am !'

Mercy tried hard to understand him, and tried in vain. Could this be the preacher whose words had charmed, purified, ennobled her? Was this the man whose sermon had drawn tears from women about her whom she knew to be shameless and hardened in crime? Yes! The eyes that now rested on her humorously were the beautiful eyes which had looked into her soul. The voice that had just addressed a jesting question to her was the deep and mellow voice which had once thrilled her to the heart. In the pulpit, he was an angel of mercy; out of the pulpit, he was a boy let loose from school.

'Don't let me startle you!' he said, good-naturedly noticing her confusion. 'Public opinion has called me by harder names than the name of "Radical". I have been spending my time lately – as I told you just now – in an agricultural district. My business there was to perform the duty for the rector of the place, who wanted a holiday. How do you think the experiment has ended? The Squire of the parish calls me a Communist; the farmers denounce me as an Incendiary; my friend the rector has been recalled in a hurry; and I have now the honour of speaking to you in the character of a banished man, who has made a respectable neighbourhood too hot to hold him.'

With that frank avowal, he left the luncheon-table, and took a chair near Mercy.

'You will naturally be anxious,' he went on, 'to know what my offence was. Do you understand Political Economy and the Laws of Supply and Demand?'

Mercy owned that she did *not* understand them.

'No more do I – in a Christian country,' he said. 'That was my offence. You shall hear my confession (just as my aunt will hear it) in two words.' He paused for a little while; his variable manner changed again. Mercy, shyly looking at him, saw a new expression in his eyes – an expression which recalled her first remembrance of him as nothing had recalled it yet. 'I had no idea,' he resumed, 'of what the life of a farm-labourer really was, in some parts of England, until I undertook the rector's duties. Never before had I seen such dire wretchedness as I saw in the cottages. Never before had I met with such noble patience under suffering as I found among the people. The martyrs of old could endure, and die.-I asked myself if they could endure, and *live*, like the martyrs whom I saw round me? - live, week after week, month after month, year after year, on the brink of starvation; live, and see their pining children growing up round them, to work and want in their turn; live, with the poor man's parish-prison to look to as the end, when hunger and labour have done their worst! Was God's beautiful earth made to hold such misery as this? I can hardly think of it, I can hardly speak of it, even now, with dry eyes!'

His head sank on his breast. He waited – mastering his emotion before he spoke again. Now, at last, she knew him once more. Now he was the man, indeed, whom she had expected to see. Unconsciously, she sat listening, with her eyes fixed on his face, with her heart hanging on his words, in the very attitude of the bygone day, when she heard him for the first time!

'I did all I could to plead for the helpless ones,' he resumed. 'I went round among the holders of the land to say a word for the tillers of the land. "These patient people don't want much" (I said); "in the same of Christ, give them enough to live on!" Political Economy shrieked at the horrid proposal; the Laws of Supply and Demand veiled their majestic faces in dismay. Starvation wages were the right wages, I was told. And why? Because the labourer was obliged to accept them! I determined, so far as one man could do it, that the labourer should *not* be obliged to accept them. I collected my own resources – I wrote to my friends – and I removed some of the poor fellows to parts of England where their work was better paid. Such was the conduct which made the neighbourhood too hot to hold me. So let it be! I mean to go on. I am known in London; I can raise subscriptions. The vile Laws of Supply and Demand shall find labour scarce in that agricultural district; and pitiless Political Economy shall spend a few extra shillings on the poor, as certainly as I am that Radical, Communist, and Incendiary – Julian Gray!'

He rose – making a little gesture of apology for the warmth with which he had spoken – and took a turn in the room. Fired by *his* enthusiasm, Mercy followed him. Her purse was in her hand, when he turned and faced her.

'Pray let me offer my little tribute – such as it is !' she said, eagerly.

A momentary flush spread over his pale cheeks as he looked at the beautiful compassionate face pleading with him.

'No ! no !' he said, smiling, 'though I *am* a parson, I don't carry the begging-box everywhere' Mercy attempted to press the purse on him. The quaint humour began to twinkle again in his eyes as he abruptly drew back from it. 'Don't tempt me !' he said. 'The frailest of all human creatures is a clergyman tempted by a subscription.' Mercy persisted, and conquered; she made him prove the truth of his own profound observation of clerical human nature by taking a piece of money from the purse. 'If I must take it – I must !' he remarked. 'Thank you for setting the good example! thank you for giving the timely help! What name shall I put down on my list?'

Mercy's eyes looked confusedly away from him. 'No name,' she said, in a low voice. 'My subscription is anonymous.'

As she replied, the library door opened. To her infinite relief – to Julian's secret disappointment – Lady Janet Roy and Horace Holmcroft entered the room together.

'Julian!' exclaimed Lady Janet, holding up her hands in astonishment.

He kissed his aunt on the cheek. 'Your ladyship is looking charmingly.' He gave his hand to Horace. Horace took it, and passed on to Mercy. They walked away together slowly to the other end of the room. Julian seized on the chance which left him free to speak privately to his aunt.

'I came in through the conservatory,' he said. 'And I found that young lady in the room. Who is she?'

'Are you very much interested in her?' asked Lady Janet, in her gravely ironical way.

Julian answered in one expressive word. 'Indescribably!'

Lady Janet called to Mercy to join her.

'My dear,' she said, 'let me formally present my nephew to you. Julian, this is Miss Grace Roseberry——' she suddenly checked herself. The instant she pronounced the name, Julian started as if it was a surprise to him. 'What is it?' she asked, sharply.

'Nothing,' he answered, bowing to Mercy, with a marked absence of his former ease of manner. She returned the courtesy a little restrainedly on her side. She too had seen him start when Lady Janet mentioned the name by which she was known. The start meant something. What could it be ? Why did he turn aside, after bowing to her, and address himself to Horace, with an absent look in his face, as if his thoughts were far away from his words? A complete change had come over him; and it dated from the moment when his aunt had pronounced the name that was not *her* name – the name that she had stolen !

Lady Janet claimed Julian's attention, and left Horace free to return to Mercy. 'Your room is ready for you,' she said. 'You will stay here, of course?' Julian accepted the invitation – still with the air of a man whose mind was preoccupied. Instead of looking at his aunt when he made his reply, he looked round at Mercy, with a troubled curiosity in his face, very strange to see. Lady Janet tapped him impatiently on the shoulder. 'I expect people to look at me when people speak to me,' she said. 'What are you staring at my adopted daughter for?'

'Your adopted daughter?' Julian repeated – looking at his aunt this time, and looking very earnestly.

'Certainly! As Colonel Roseberry's daughter, she is connected with me by marriage already. Did you think I had picked up a foundling?'

Julian's face cleared; he looked relieved. 'I had forgotten the Colonel,' he answered. 'Of course the young lady is related to us, as you say.'

'Charmed, I am sure, to have satisfied you that Grace is not an imposter,' said Lady Janet, with satirical humility. She took Julian's arm, and drew him out of hearing of Horace and Mercy. 'About that letter of yours?' she proceeded. 'There is one line in it that rouses my curiosity. Who is the mysterious "lady" whom you wish to present to me?'

Julian started, and changed colour.

'I can't tell you now,' he said, in a whisper.

'Why not?'

To Lady Janet's unutterable astonishment, instead of replying, Julian looked round at her adopted daughter once more.

'What has *she* got to do with it?' asked the old lady, out of all patience with him.

'It is impossible for me to tell you,' he answered gravely, 'while Miss Roseberry is in the room.'

CHAPTER THE NINTH

NEWS FROM MANNHEIM

Lady Janet's curiosity was by this time thoroughly aroused. Summoned to explain who the nameless lady mentioned in his letter could possibly be, Julian had looked at her adopted daughter. Asked next to explain what her adopted daughter had to do with it, he had declared that he could not answer while Miss Roseberry was in the room.

What did he mean? Lady Janet determined to find out.

'I hate all mysteries,' she said to Julian. 'And as for secrets, I consider them to be one of the forms of ill-breeding. People in our rank of life ought to be above whispering in corners. If you *must* have your mystery, I can offer you a corner in the library. Come with me.'

Julian followed his aunt very reluctantly. Whatever the mystery might be, he was plainly embarrassed by being called upon to reveal it at a moment's notice. Lady Janet settled herself in her chair, prepared to question and cross-question her nephew – when an obstacle appeared at the other end of the library, in the shape of a man-servant with a message. One of

Lady Janet's neighbours had called by appointment to take her to the meeting of a certain committee which assembled that day. The servant announced that the neighbour – an elderly lady – was then waiting in her carriage at the door.

Lady Janet's ready invention set the obstacle aside without a moment's delay. She directed the servant to show her visitor into the drawing-room, and say that she was unexpectedly engaged, but that Miss Roseberry would see the lady immediately. She then turned to Julian, and said, with her most satirical emphasis of tone and manner, 'Would it be an additional convenience if Miss Roseberry was not only out of the room before you disclose your secret, but out of the house?'

Julian gravely answered, 'It may possibly be quite as well if Miss Roseberry is out of the house.'

Lady Janet led the way back to the dining-room.

'My dear Grace,' she said, 'you looked flushed and feverish when I saw you asleep on the sofa a little while since. It will do you no harm to have a drive in the fresh air. Our friend has called to take me to the committee meeting. I have sent to tell her that I am engaged – and I shall be much obliged if you will go in my place.'

Mercy looked a little alarmed. 'Does your ladyship mean the committee meeting of the Samaritan Convalescent Home? The members, as I understand it, are to decide to-day which of the plans for the new building they are to adopt. I cannot surely presume to vote in your place?'

'You can vote, my dear child, just as well as I can,' replied the old lady. 'Architecture is one of the lost arts. You know nothing about it; I know nothing about it; the architects themselves know nothing about it. One plan is no doubt just as bad as the other. Vote, as I should vote, with the majority. Or as poor dear Dr Johnson said, "Shout with the loudest mob." Away with you – and don't keep the committee waiting.'

Horace hastened to open the door for Mercy.

'How long shall you be away?' he whispered confidentially. 'I had a thousand things to say to you, and they have interrupted us.'

'I shall be back in an hour.'

'We shall have the room to ourselves by that time. Come here when you return. You will find me waiting for you.'

Mercy pressed his hand significantly and went out. Lady Janet turned to Julian, who had thus far remained in the background, still, to all appearance, as unwilling as ever to enlighten his aunt.

'Well?' she said. 'What is tying your tongue now? Grace is out of the room; why don't you begin? Is Horace in the way?'

'Not in the least. I am only a little uneasy——'

'Uneasy about what?'

'I am afraid you have put that charming creature to some inconvenience in sending her away just at this time.'

Horace looked up suddenly with a flush on his face.

'When you say "that charming creature,"' he asked sharply, 'I suppose you mean Miss Roseberry?'

'Certainly,' answered Julian. 'Why not?'

Lady Janet interposed. 'Gently, Julian,' she said. 'Grace has only been introduced to you hitherto in the character of my adopted daughter——'

'And it seems to be high time,' Horace added haughtily, 'that I should present her next in the character of my engaged wife.'

Julian looked at Horace as if he could hardly credit the evidence of his own ears. 'Your wife!' he exclaimed, with an irrepressible outburst of disappointment and surprise.

'Yes. My wife,' returned Horace. 'We are to be married in a fortnight. May I ask,' he added, with angry humility, 'if you disapprove of the marriage?'

Lady Janet interposed once more. 'Nonsense Horace,' she said. 'Julian congratulates you, of course.'

Julian coldly and absently echoed the words. 'Oh, yes, I congratulate you, of course.'

Lady Janet returned to the main object of the interview.

'Now we thoroughly understand one another,' she said, 'let us speak of a lady who has dropped out of the conversation for the last minute or two. I mean, Julian, the mysterious lady of your letter. We are alone, as you desired. Lift the veil, my reverend nephew, which hides her from mortal eyes! Blush, if you like – and can. Is she the future Mrs Julian Gray?'

'She is a perfect stranger to me,' Julian answered quietly.

'A perfect stranger! You wrote me word you were interested in her.'

'I *am* interested in her. And, what is more, you are interested in her, too.'

Lady Janet's fingers drummed impatiently on the table. 'Have I not warned you, Julian, that I hate mysteries? Will you, or will you not explain yourself?'

Before it was possible to answer, Horace rose from his chair. 'Perhaps I am in the way?' he said.

Julian signed to him to sit down again.

'I have already told Lady Janet that you are not in the way,' he answered. 'I now tell *you* – as Miss Roseberry's future husband – that you too have an interest in hearing what I have to say.'

Horace resumed his seat with an air of suspicious surprise. Julian addressed himself to Lady Janet.

'You have often heard me speak,' he began, 'of an old friend of mine who had an appointment abroad?'

'Yes. The English consul at Mannheim?'

'The same. When I returned from the country, I found, among my other letters, a long letter from the consul. I have brought it with me, and I propose to read certain passages from it, which tell a very strange story more plainly and more credibly than I can tell it in my own words.'

'Will it be very long?' enquired Lady Janet, looking with some alarm at the closely-written sheets of paper which her nephew spread open before him.

Horace followed with a question on his side.

'You are sure I am interested in it?' he asked. 'The consul at Mannheim is a total stranger to me.'

'I answer for it,' replied Julian, gravely, 'neither my aunt's patience nor yours, Horace, will be thrown away if you will favour me by listening attentively to what I am about to read.'

With these words he began his first extract from the consul's letter.

* * * '"My memory is a bad one for dates. But full three months must have passed since information was sent to me of an English patient, received at the hospital here, whose case I, as English consul, might feel an interest in investigating.

"'I went the same day to the hospital, and was taken to the bedside.

"'The patient was a woman – young, and (when in health) I should think, very pretty. When I first saw her she looked, to my uninstructed eye, like a dead woman. I noticed that her head had a bandage over it, and I asked what was the nature of the injury that she had received. The answer informed me that the poor creature had been present, nobody knew why or wherefore, at a skirmish or night attack between the Germans and the French, and that the injury to her head had been inflicted by a fragment of a German shell." '

Horace – thus far leaning back carelessly in his chair – suddenly raised himself and exclaimed, 'Good heavens! can this be the woman I saw laid out for dead in the French cottage?'

'It is impossible for me to say,' replied Julian. 'Listen to the rest of it. The consul's letter may answer your question.'

He went on with his reading:

"'The wounded woman had been reported dead, and had been left by the French in their retreat, at the time when the German forces took possession of the enemy's position. She was found on a bed in a cottage by the director of the German ambulance——"'

'Ignatius Wetzel?' cried Horace.

'Ignatius Wetzel,' repeated Julian, looking at the letter.

'It *is* the same!' said Horace. 'Lady Janet, we are really interested in this. You remember my telling you how I first met with Grace? And you have heard more about it since, no doubt, from Grace herself?'

'She has a horror of referring to that part of her journey home,' replied Lady Janet. 'She mentioned her having been stopped on the frontier, and her finding herself accidentally in the company of another English woman, a perfect stranger to her. I naturally asked questions on my side, and was shocked to hear that she had seen the woman killed by a German shell almost close at her side. Neither she nor I have had a relish for returning to the subject since. You were quite right, Julian, to avoid speaking of it while she was in the room. I understand it all now. Grace, I suppose, mentioned my name and her name to her fellow-traveller. The woman is in want of assistance, and she applies to me through you. I will help her, but she must not come here until I have prepared Grace for seeing her again, a living woman. For the present, there is no reason why they should meet.'

'I am not sure about that,' said Julian in low tones, without looking up at his aunt.

'What do you mean? Is the mystery not at an end yet?'

'The mystery is not even begun yet. Let my friend the consul proceed.'

Julian returned for the second time to his extract from the letter.

'"After a careful examination of the supposed corpse, the German surgeon arrived at the conclusion that a case of suspended animation had (in the hurry of the French retreat) been mistaken for a case of death. Feeling a professional interest in the subject, he decided on putting his opinion to the test. He operated on the patient with complete success. After performing the operation, he kept her for some days under his own care, and then transferred her to the nearest hospital – the hospital at Mannheim. He was obliged to return to his duties as army surgeon, and he left his patient in the condition in which I saw her, insensible on the bed. Neither he nor the hospital authorities knew anything whatever about the woman. No papers were found on her. All the doctors could do, when I asked them for information with a view to communicating with her friends, was to show me her linen marked with her name. I left the hospital after taking down the name in my pocket-book. It was "Mercy Merrick." '

Lady Janet produced *her* pocket-book. 'Let me take the name down too,' she said. 'I never heard it before, and I might otherwise forget it. Go on, Julian.'

Julian advanced to his second extract from the consul's letter :

'"Under these circumstances, I could only wait to hear from the hospital when the patient was sufficiently recovered to be able to speak to me. Some weeks passed without my receiving any communication from the doctors. On calling to make enquiries, I was informed that fever had set in, and that the poor creature's condition now alternated between exhaustion and delirium. In her delirious moments, the name of your aunt, Lady Janet Roy, frequently escaped her. Otherwise, her wanderings were for the most part quite unintelligible to the people at her bedside. I thought once or twice of writing to you and of begging you to speak to Lady Janet. But as the doctors informed me that the chances of life and death were at this time almost equally balanced, I decided to wait until time should determine whether it was necessary to trouble you or not." '

'You know best, Julian,' said Lady Janet. 'But I own I don't quite see in what way I am interested in this part of the story.'

'Just what I was going to say,' added Horace. 'It is very sad, no doubt. But what have *we* to do with it?'

'Let me read my third extract,' Julian answered, 'and you will see.'

He turned to the third extract, and read as follows:

'"At last I received a message from the hospital informing me that Mercy Merrick was out of danger, and that she was capable (though still very weak) of answering any questions which I might think it desirable to put to her. On reaching the hospital, I was requested, rather to my surprise, to pay my first visit to the head physician in his private room. 'I think it right,' said this gentleman, 'to warn you, before you see the patient, to be very careful how you speak to her, and not to irritate her by showing any surprise or expressing any doubts if she talks to you in an extravagant manner. We differ in opinion about her here. Some of us (myself among the number) doubt whether the recovery of her mind has accompanied the recovery of her bodily powers. Without pronouncing her to be mad – she is perfectly gentle and harmless – we are nevertheless of opinion that she is suffering under a species of insane delusion. Bear in mind the caution which I have given you – and now go and judge for yourself.' I obeyed, in some little perplexity and surprise. The sufferer, when I approached her bed, looked sadly weak and worn; but, so far as I could judge, seemed to be in full possession of herself. Her tone and manner were unquestionably the tone and manner of a lady. After briefly introducing myself, I assured her that I should be glad, both

officially and personally, if I could be of any assistance to her. In
saying these trifling words, I happened to address her by the
name I had seen marked on her clothes. The instant the words
'Miss Merrick' passed my lips, a wild, vindictive expression
appeared in her eyes. She exclaimed angrily, 'Don't call me by
that hateful name! It's not my name. All the people here
persecute me by calling me Mercy Merrick. And when I am
angry with them they show me the clothes. Say what I may,
they persist in believing they are *my* clothes. Don't you do the
same if you want to be friends with me.' Remembering what
the physician had said, I made the necessary excuses, and soon
succeeded in soothing her. Without reverting to the irritating
topic of the name, I merely enquired what her plans were, and
assured her that she might command my services if she required
them. 'Why do you want to know what my plans are?' she
asked suspiciously. I reminded her in reply that I held the
position of English consul, and that my object was, if possible,
to be of some assistance to her. 'You can be of the greatest
assistance to me,' she said eagerly. 'Find Mercy Merrick!' I saw
the vindictive look come back into her eyes, and an angry flush
rising on her white cheeks. Abstaining from showing any
surprise, I asked her who Mercy Merrick was? 'A vile woman,
by her own confession,' was the quick reply. 'How am I to find
her?' I enquired next. 'Look for a woman in a black dress, with
the red Geneva Cross on her shoulder; she is a nurse in the
French ambulance.' 'What has she done?' 'I have lost my
papers; I have lost my own clothes; Mercy Merrick has taken
them.' 'How do you know that Mercy Merrick has taken
them?' 'Nobody else could have taken them – that's how I
know it. Do you believe me or not?' She was beginning to
excite herself again; I assured her that I would at once send to
make enquiries after Mercy Merrick. She turned round,
contented, on the pillow. 'There's a good man!' she said.
'Come back and tell me when you have caught her.' Such was
my first interview with the English patient at the hospital at
Mannheim. It is needless to say that I doubted the existence of
the absent person described as a nurse. However, it was possible
to make enquiries, by applying to the surgeon, Ignatius Wetzel,

whose whereabouts was known to his friends in Mannheim. I wrote to him, and received his answer in due time. After the night attack of the Germans had made them masters of the French position, he had entered the cottage occupied by the French ambulance. He had found the wounded Frenchmen left behind, but had seen no such person in attendance on them as the nurse in the black dress, with the red cross on her shoulder. The only living woman in the place was a young English lady, in a grey travelling cloak, who had been stopped on the frontier, and who was forwarded on her way home by the war correspondent of an English journal." '

'That was Grace,' said Lady Janet.

'And I was the war correspondent,' added Horace.

'A few words more,' said Julian, 'and you will understand my object in claiming your attention.'

He returned to the letter for the last time, and concluded his extracts from it as follows:

"'Instead of attending at the hospital myself, I communicated by letter the failure of my attempt to discover the missing nurse. For some little time afterwards I heard no more of the sick woman, whom I shall still call Mercy Merrick. It was only yesterday that I received another summons to visit the patient. She had by this time sufficiently recovered to claim her discharge, and she had announced her intention of returning forthwith to England. The head physician, feeling a sense of responsibility, had sent for me. It was impossible to detain her on the ground that she was not fit to be trusted by herself at large, in consequence of the difference of opinion among the doctors on the case. All that could be done was to give me due notice, and to leave the matter in my hands. On seeing her for the second time, I found her sullen and reserved. She openly attributed my inability to find the nurse to want of zeal for her interests on my part. I had, on my side, no authority whatever to detain her. I could only enquire whether she had enough to pay her travelling expenses. Her reply informed me that the chaplain of the hospital had mentioned her forlorn situation in the town, and that the English residents had subscribed a small sum of money to enable her to return to her own country.

Satisfied on this head, I asked next if she had friends to go to in England. 'I have one friend,' she answered, 'who is a host in herself – Lady Janet Roy.' You can imagine my surprise when I heard this. I found it quite useless to make any further enquiries as to how she came to know your aunt, whether your aunt expected her, and so on. My questions evidently offended her; they were received in sulky silence. Under these circumstances, well knowing that I can trust implicitly to your humane sympathy for misfortune, I have decided (after careful reflection) to ensure the poor creature's safety when she arrives in London, by giving her a letter to you. You will hear what she says; and you will be better able to discover than I am whether she really has any claim on Lady Janet Roy. One last word of information, which it may be necessary to add – and I shall close this inordinately long letter. At my first interview with her I abstained, as I have already told you, from irritating her by any enquiries on the subject of her name. On this second occasion, however, I decided on putting the question." '

As he read those last words, Julian became aware of a sudden movement on the part of his aunt. Lady Janet had risen softly from her chair, and had passed behind him with the purpose of reading the consul's letter for herself over her nephew's shoulder. Julian detected the action just in time to frustrate Lady Janet's intention by placing his hand over the last two lines of the letter.

'What do you do that for?' enquired his aunt sharply.

'You are welcome, Lady Janet, to read the close of the letter for yourself,' Julian replied. 'But before you do so I am anxious to prepare you for a very great surprise. Compose yourself, and let me read on slowly, with your eye on me, until I uncover the last two words which close my friend's letter.'

He read the end of the letter, as he had proposed in these terms:

'"I looked the woman straight in the face, and I said to her, 'You have denied that the name marked on the clothes which you wore when you came here was your name. If you are not Mercy Merrick, who are you?' She answered instantly, 'My name is——'"'

Julian removed his hand from the page. Lady Janet looked at the next two words, and started back with a loud cry of astonishment which brought Horace instantly to his feet.

'Tell me, one of you!' he cried. 'What name did she give?'

Julian told him:

'GRACE ROSEBERRY.'

CHAPTER THE TENTH

A COUNCIL OF THREE

For a moment Horace stood thunderstruck, looking in blank astonishment at Lady Janet. His first words, as soon as he had recovered himself, were addressed to Julian:

'Is this a joke?' he asked sternly. 'If it is, I for one don't see the humour of it.'

Julian pointed to the closely written pages of the consul's letter. 'A man writes in earnest,' he said, ' when he writes at such length as this. The woman seriously gave the name of Grace Roseberry, and when she left Mannheim she travelled to England for the express purpose of presenting herself to Lady Janet Roy.' He turned to his aunt. 'You saw me start,' he went on, ' when you first mentioned Miss Roseberry's name in my hearing. Now you know why.' He addressed himself once more to Horace. 'You heard me say that you, as Miss Roseberry's future husband, had an interest in being present at my interview with Lady Janet. Now *you* know why.'

'The woman is plainly mad,' said Lady Janet. 'But it is certainly a startling form of madness when one first hears of it. Of course we must keep the matter, for the present at least, a secret from Grace.'

'There can be no doubt,' Horace agreed, 'that Grace must be kept in the dark, in her present state of health. The servants had

better be warned beforehand, in case of this adventuress or
madwoman, whichever she may be, attempting to make her
way into the house.'

'It shall be done immediately,' said Lady Janet. 'What
surprises *me*, Julian (ring the bell, if you please), is, that you
should describe yourself in your letter as feeling an interest in
this person.'

Julian answered – without ringing the bell.

'I am more interested than ever,' he said, 'now I find that
Miss Roseberry herself is your guest at Mablethorpe House.'

'You were always perverse, Julian, as a child, in your likings
and dislikings,' Lady Janet rejoined. 'Why don't you ring the
bell?'

'For one good reason, my dear aunt. I don't wish to hear you
tell your servants to close the door on this friendless creature.'

Lady Janet cast a look at her nephew which plainly expressed
that she thought he had taken a liberty with her.

'You don't expect me to see the woman?' she asked, in a
tone of cold surprise.

'I hope you will not refuse to see her,' Julian answered
quietly. 'I was out when she called. I must hear what she has to
say – and I should infinitely prefer hearing it in your presence.
When I got your reply to my letter, permitting me to present
her to you, I wrote to her immediately, appointing a meeting
here.'

Lady Janet lifted her bright black eyes in mute expostulation
to the carved cupids and wreaths on the dining-room ceiling.

'When am I to have the honour of the Lady's visit?' she
enquired, with ironical resignation.

'To-day,' answered her nephew, with impenetrable patience.

'At what hour?'

Julian composedly consulted his watch. 'She is ten minutes
after her time,' he said, and put his watch back in his pocket
again.

At the same moment the servant appeared, and advanced to
Julian, carrying a visiting card on his little silver tray.

'A lady to see you, sir.'

Julian took the card, and bowing, handed it to his aunt.

'Here she is,' he said, just as quietly as ever.

Lady Janet looked at the card, and tossed it indignantly back to her nephew. 'Miss Roseberry!' she exclaimed. 'Printed, actually printed on her card! Julian, even MY patience has its limits. I refuse to see her!'

The servant was still waiting – not like a human being who took an interest in the proceedings – but (as became a perfectly bred footman) like an article of furniture artfully constructed to come and go at the word of command. Julian gave the word of command, addressing the admirably constructed automaton by the name of 'James.'

'Where is the lady now?' he asked.

'In the breakfast-room, sir.'

'Leave her there, if you please; and wait outside within hearing of the bell.'

The legs of the furniture-footman acted, and took him noiselessy out of the room. Julian turned to his aunt.

'Forgive me,' he said, ' for venturing to give the man his orders in your presence. I am very anxious that you should not decide hastily. Surely we ought to hear what this lady has to say?'

Horace dissented widely from his friend's opinion. 'It's an insult to Grace,' he broke out warmly, 'to hear what she has to say!'

Lady Janet nodded her head in high approval. 'I think so, too,' said her ladyship, crossing her handsome old hands resolutely on her lap.

Julian applied himself to answering Horace first.

'Pardon me,' he said, 'I have no intention of presuming to reflect on Miss Roseberry, or of bringing her into the matter at all. The consul's letter,' he went on, speaking to his aunt, 'mentions, if you remember, that the medical authorities of Mannheim were divided in opinion on their patient's case. Some of them – the physician-in-chief being among the number – believe that the recovery of her mind has not accompanied the recovery of her body.'

'In other words,' Lady Janet remarked, 'a madwoman is in my house, and I am expected to receive her!'

'Don't let us exaggerate,' said Julian gently. 'It can serve no good interest, in this serious matter, to exaggerate anything. The consul assures us, on the authority of the doctor, that she is perfectly gentle and harmless. If she is really the victim of a mental delusion, the poor creature is surely an object of compassion, and she ought to be placed under proper care. Ask your own kind heart, my dear aunt, if it would not be downright cruelty to turn this forlorn woman adrift in the world without making some enquiry first?'

Lady Janet's inbred sense of justice admitted — not over-willingly — the reasonableness as well as the humanity of the view expressed in those words. 'There is some truth in that, Julian,' she said, shifting her position uneasily in her chair, and looking at Horace. 'Don't you think so too?' she added.

'I can't say I do,' answered Horace, in the positive tone of a man whose obstinacy is proof against every form of appeal that can be addressed to him.

The patience of Julian was firm enough to be a match for the obstinacy of Horace. 'At any rate,' he resumed, with undiminished good temper, 'we are all three equally interested in setting this matter at rest. I put it to you, Lady Janet, if we are not favoured, at this lucky moment, with the very opportunity that we want? Miss Roseberry is not only out of the room, but out of the house. If we let this chance slip, who can say what awkward accident may not happen in the course of the next few days?'

'Let the woman come in,' cried Lady Janet, deciding headlong with her customary impatience of all delay. 'At once, Julian — before Grace can come back. Will you ring the bell this time?'

This time Julian rang it. 'May I give the man his orders?' he respectfully enquired of his aunt.

'Give him anything you like, and have done with it!' retorted the irritable old lady, getting briskly on her feet, and taking a turn in the room to compose herself.

The servant withdrew, with orders to show the visitor in. Horace crossed the room at the same time — apparently with the intention of leaving it by the door at the opposite end.

'You are not going away?' exclaimed Lady Janet.

'I see no use in my remaining here,' replied Horace, not very graciously.

'In that case,' retorted Lady Janet, 'remain here because I wish it.'

'Certainly – if you wish it. Only remember,' he added, more obstinately than ever, 'that I differ entirely from Julian's view. In my opinion the woman has no claim on us.'

A passing movement of irritation escaped Julian for the first time. 'Don't be hard, Horace,' he said sharply. 'All women have a claim on us.'

They had unconsciously gathered together, in the heat of the little debate, turning their backs on the library door. At the last words of the reproof administered by Julian to Horace, their attention was recalled to passing events by the slight noise produced by the opening and closing of the door. With one accord, the three turned and looked in the direction from which the sound had come.

CHAPTER THE ELEVENTH

THE DEAD ALIVE

Just inside the door there appeared the figure of a small woman dressed in plain and poor black garments. She silently lifted her black net veil, and disclosed a dull, pale, worn weary face. The forehead was low and broad; the eyes were unusually far apart; the lower features were remarkably small and delicate. In health (as the consul at Mannheim had remarked) this woman must have possessed, if not absolute beauty, at least rare attractions peculiarly her own. As it was now, suffering – sullen, silent, self-contained suffering – had marred its beauty. Attention and even curiosity it might still rouse. Admiration or interest it could excite no longer.

The small thin black figure stood immovably inside the door. The dull, worn, white face looked silently at the three persons in the room.

The three persons in the room, on their side, stood for a moment without moving, and looked silently at the stranger on the threshold. There was something, either in the woman herself or in the sudden and stealthy manner of her appearance on the scene, which froze, as if with the touch of an invisible cold hand, the sympathies of all three. Accustomed to the world, habitually at their ease in every social emergency, they were now silenced for the first time in their lives by the first serious sense of embarrassment which they had felt since they were children, in the presence of a stranger.

Had the appearance of the true Grace Roseberry aroused in their minds a suspicion of the woman who had stolen her name, and taken her place in the house?

Not so much as the shadow of a suspicion of Mercy was at the bottom of the strange sense of uneasiness which had now deprived them alike of their habitual courtesy and their habitual presence of mind. It was as practically impossible for any one of the three to doubt the identity of the adopted daughter of the house, as it would be for you who read these lines to doubt the identity of the nearest and dearest relative you have in the world. Circumstances had fortified Mercy behind the strongest of all natural rights — the right of first possession. Circumstances had armed her with the most irresistible of all natural forces — the force of previous association and previous habit. Not by so much as a hair's breadth was the position of the false Grace Roseberry shaken by the first appearance of the true Grace Roseberry within the doors of Mablethorpe House. Lady Janet felt suddenly repelled, without knowing why. Julian and Horace felt suddenly repelled, without knowing why. Asked to describe their own sensations at the moment they would have shaken their heads in despair, and would have answered in those words. The vague presentiment of some misfortune to come had entered the room with the entrance of the woman in black. But it moved invisibly; and it spoke, as all presentiments speak, in the Unknown Tongue.

A moment passed. The crackling of the fire and the ticking of the clock were the only sounds audible in the room.

The voice of the visitor – hard, clear, and quiet – was the first voice that broke the silence.

'Mr Julian Gray?' she said, looking interrogatively from one of the two gentlemen to the other.

Julian advanced a few steps, instantly recovering his self-possession. 'I am sorry I was not at home,' he said, 'when you called with your letter from the consul. Pray take a chair.'

By way of setting the example, Lady Janet seated herself at some little distance, with Horace in attendance standing near. She bowed to the stranger with studious politeness, but without uttering a word, before she settled herself in her chair. 'I am obliged to listen to this person,' thought the old lady. 'But I am *not* obliged to speak to her. That is Julian's business – not mine.' 'Don't stand, Horace! You fidget me. Sit down.' Armed beforehand in her policy of silence, Lady Janet folded her handsome hands as usual, and waited for the proceedings to begin, like a judge on the bench.

'Will you take a chair?' Julian repeated, observing that the visitor appeared neither to heed nor to hear his first words of welcome to her.

At this second appeal she spoke to him. 'Is that Lady Janet Roy?' she asked with her eyes fixed on the mistress of the house.

Julian answered, and drew back to watch the result.

The woman in the poor black garments changed her position for the first time. She moved slowly across the room to the place at which Lady Janet was sitting, and addressed her respectfully with perfect self-possession of manner. Her whole demeanour, from the moment when she had appeared at the door, had expressed – at once plainly and becomingly – confidence in the reception that awaited her.

'Almost the last words my father said to me on his death-bed,' she began, 'were words, madam, which told me to expect protection and kindness from you.'

It was not Lady Janet's business to speak. She listened with the blandest attention. She waited with the most exasperating silence, to hear more.

Grace Roseberry drew back a step – not intimidated – only mortified and surprised. 'Was my father wrong?' she asked, with a simple dignity of tone and manner which forced Lady Janet to abandon her policy of silence, in spite of herself.

'Who was your father?' she asked coldly.

Grace Roseberry answered the question in a tone of stern surprise.

'Has the servant not given you my card?' she said. 'Don't you know my name?'

'Which of your names?' rejoined Lady Janet.

'I don't understand your ladyship.'

'I will make myself understood. You asked me if I knew your name. I ask you, in return, which name it is? The name on your card is "Miss Roseberry." The name marked on your clothes, when you were in the hospital, was "Mercy Merrick."'

The self-possession which Grace had maintained from the moment when she had entered the dining-room seemed now for the first time to be on the point of failing her. She turned and looked appealingly at Julian who had thus far kept his place apart, listening attentively.

'Surely,' she said, 'your friend, the consul, has told you in his letter about the mark on the clothes?'

Something of the girlish hesitation and timidity which had marked her demeanour at her interview with Mercy in the French cottage reappeared in her tone and manner as she spoke those words. The changes – mostly changes for the worse – wrought in her by the suffering through which she had passed since that time, were now (for the moment) effaced. All that was left of the better and simpler side of her character asserted itself in her brief appeal to Julian. She had hitherto repelled him. He began to feel a certain compassionate interest in her now.

'The consul has informed me of what you said to him,' he answered kindly. 'But, if you will take my advice, I recommend you to tell your story to Lady Janet in your own words.'

Grace again addressed herself with submissive reluctance to Lady Janet.

'The clothes your ladyship speaks of,' she said, 'were the clothes of another woman. The rain was pouring when the soldiers detained me on the frontier. I had been exposed for hours to the weather − I was wet to the skin. The clothes marked "Mercy Merrick" were the clothes lent to me by Mercy Merrick herself, while my own things were drying. I was struck by the shell in those clothes. I was carried away insensible in those clothes after the operation had been performed on me.'

Lady Janet listened to perfection − and did no more. She turned confidentially to Horace and said to him, in her gracefully ironical way, 'She is ready with her explanation.'

Horace answered in the same tone, 'A great deal too ready.'

Grace looked from one of them to the other. A faint flush of colour showed itself in her face for the first time.

'Am I to understand,' she asked with proud composure, 'that you don't believe me?'

Lady Janet maintained her policy of silence. She waved one hand courteously towards Julian, as if to say, 'Address your enquiries to the gentleman who introduces you.' Julian, noticing the gesture and observing the rising colour in Grace's cheeks, interfered directly in the interests of peace.

'Lady Janet asked you a question just now,' he said; 'Lady Janet enquired who your father was.'

'My father was the late Colonel Roseberry.'

Lady Janet looked indignantly at Horace. 'Her assurance amazes me!' she exclaimed.

Julian interposed before his aunt could add a word more. 'Pray let us hear her,' he said in a tone of entreaty which had something of the imperative in it this time. He turned to Grace. 'Have you any proof to produce,' he added in his gentler voice, 'which will satisfy us that you are Colonel Roseberry's daughter?'

Grace looked at him indignantly. 'Proof!' she repeated. 'Is my word not enough?'

Julian kept his temper perfectly. 'Pardon me,' he rejoined, 'you forget that you and Lady Janet meet now for the first time. Try to put yourself in my aunt's place. How is she to know that you are the late Colonel Roseberry's daughter?'

Grace's head sank on her breast; she dropped into the nearest chair. The expression of her face changed instantly from anger to discouragement. 'Ah,' she exclaimed bitterly, 'if I only had the letters that have been stolen from me!'

'Letters,' asked Julian, 'introducing you to Lady Janet?'

'Yes.' She turned suddenly to Lady Janet. 'Let me tell you how I lost them,' she said, in the first tones of entreaty which had escaped her yet.

Lady Janet hesitated. It was not in her generous nature to resist the appeal that had just been made to her. The sympathies of Horace were far less easily reached. He lightly launched a new shaft of satire – intended for the private amusement of Lady Janet. 'Another explanation!' he exclaimed, with a sigh of comic resignation.

Julian overheard the words. His large lustrous eyes fixed themselves on Horace with a look of unmeasured contempt.

'The least you can do,' he said, sternly, 'is not to irritate her. It is so easy to irritate her!' He addressed himself again to Grace, endeavouring to help her through her difficulty in a new way. 'Never mind explaining yourself for the moment,' he said. 'In the absence of your letters, have you anyone in London who can speak to your identity?'

Grace shook her head sadly. 'I have no friends in London,' she answered.

It was impossible for Lady Janet – who had never in her life heard of anybody without friends in London – to pass this over without notice. 'No friends in London!' she repeated, turning to Horace.

Horace shot another shaft of light satire. 'Of course not!' he rejoined.

Grace saw them comparing notes. 'My friends are in Canada,' she broke out impetuously. 'Plenty of friends who could speak for me, if I could only bring them here.'

As a place of reference – mentioned in the capital city of England – Canada, there is no denying it, is open to objection on the ground of distance. Horace was ready with another shot. 'Far enough off, certainly,' he said.

'Far enough off, as you say,' Lady Janet agreed.

Once more Julian's inexhaustible kindness strove to obtain a hearing for the stranger who had been confided to his care. 'A little patience, Lady Janet,' he pleaded. ' A little consideration, Horace, for a friendless woman.'

'Thank you, sir,' said Grace. 'It is very kind of you to try and help me; but it is useless. They won't even listen to me.' She attempted to rise from her chair as she pronounced the last words. Julian gently laid his hand on her shoulder and obliged her to resume her seat.

'*I* will listen to you,' he said. 'You referred me just now to the consul's letter. The consul tells me you suspected some one of taking your papers and your clothes.'

'I don't suspect,' was the quick reply, ' I am certain! I tell you positively Mercy Merrick was the thief. She was alone with me when I was struck down by the shell. She was the only person who knew that I had letters of introduction about me. She confessed to my face that she had been a bad woman – she had been in a prison – she had come out of a Refuge——'

Julian stopped her there with one plain question, which threw a doubt on the whole story.

'The consul tells me you asked him to search for Mercy Merrick,' he said. 'Is it not true that he caused enquiries to be made, and that no trace of any such person was to be heard of?'

'The consul took no pains to find her,' Grace answered angrily. 'He was, like everybody else, in a conspiracy to neglect and misjudge me.'

Lady Janet and Horace exchanged looks. This time it was impossible for Julian to blame them. The farther the stranger's narrative advanced, the less worthy of serious attention he felt it to be. The longer she spoke, the more disadvantageously she challenged comparison with the absent woman, whose name she so obstinately and so audaciously persisted in assuming as her own.

'Granting all that you have said,' Julian resumed, with a last effort of patience, 'what use could Mercy Merrick make of your letters and your clothes?'

'What use?' repeated Grace, amazed at his not seeing the position as she saw it. 'My clothes were marked with my name. One of my papers was a letter from my father, introducing me to Lady Janet. A woman out of a Refuge would be quite capable of presenting herself here in my place.'

Spoken entirely at random, spoken without so much as a
fragment of evidence to support them, those last words still had
their effect. They cast a reflection on Lady Janet's adopted
daughter which was too outrageous to be borne. Lady Janet
rose instantly. 'Give me your arm, Horace,' she said, turning to
leave the room. 'I have heard enough.'

Horace respectfully offered his arm. 'Your ladyship is quite
right,' he answered. 'A more monstrous story never was
invented.'

He spoke, in the warmth of his indignation, loud enough for
Grace to hear him. 'What is there monstrous in it?' she asked,
advancing a step towards him defiantly.

Julian checked her. He too – though he had only once seen
Mercy – felt an angry sense of the insult offered to the beautiful
creature who had interested him at his first sight of her.
'Silence!' he said, speaking sternly to Grace for the first time.
'You are offending – justly offending – Lady Janet. You are
talking worse than absurdly – you are talking offensively –
when you speak of another woman presenting herself here in
your place.'

Grace's blood was up. Stung by Julian's reproof, she turned
on him a look which was almost a look of fury.

'Are you a clergyman? Are you an educated man?' she asked.
'Have you never read of cases of false personation, in
newspapers and books? I blindly confided in Mercy Merrick
before I found out what her character really was. She left the
cottage – I know it from the surgeon who brought me to life
again – firmly persuaded that the shell had killed me. My papers
and my clothes disappeared at the same time. Is there nothing
suspicious in these circumstances? There were people at the
hospital who thought them highly suspicious – people who
warned me that I might find an imposter in my place.' She
suddenly paused. The rustling sound of a silk dress had caught
her ear. Lady Janet was leaving the room, with Horace, by way
of the conservatory. With a last desperate effort of resolution,
Grace sprang forward, and placed herself in front of them.

'One word, Lady Janet, before you turn your back on me,'
she said, firmly. 'One word, and I will be content. Has Colonel

Roseberry's letter found its way to this house or not? If it has, did a woman bring it to you?'

Lady Janet looked – as only a great lady *can* look, when a person of inferior rank has presumed to fail in respect towards her.

'You are surely not aware,' she said with icy composure, 'that these questions are an insult to Me?'

'And worse than an insult,' Horace added warmly, 'to Grace!'

The little resolute black figure (still barring the way to the conservatory) was suddenly shaken from head to foot. The woman's eyes travelled backwards and forwards between Lady Janet and Horace with the light of a new suspicion in them.

'Grace!' she exclaimed. 'What Grace? That's my name. Lady Janet, you *have* got the letter! The woman is here!'

Lady Janet dropped Horace's arm, and retraced her steps to the place at which her nephew was standing.

'Julian,' she said. 'You force me for the first time in my life to remind you of the respect that is due to me in my own house. Send that woman away.'

Without waiting to be answered, she turned back again, and once more took Horace's arm.

'Stand back, if you please,' she said quietly to Grace.

Grace held her ground.

'The woman is here!' she repeated. 'Confront me with her – and then send me away, if you like.'

Julian advanced, and firmly took her by the arm. 'You forget what is due to Lady Janet,' he said, drawing her aside. 'You forget what is due to yourself.'

With a desperate effort, Grace broke away from him, and stopped Lady Janet on the threshold of the conservatory door.

'Justice!' she cried, shaking her clenched hand with hysterical frenzy in the air. 'I claim my right to meet that woman face to face! Where is she? Confront me with her!'

While those wild words were pouring from her lips, the rumbling of carriage-wheels became audible on the drive in front of the house. In the all-absorbing agitation of the moment, the sound of the wheels (followed by the opening of the house door) passed unnoticed by the persons in the dining-room. Horace's voice was still raised in angry protest against the

insult offered to Lady Janet; Lady Janet herself (leaving him for
the second time) was vehemently ringing the bell to summon
the servants; Julian had once more taken the infuriated woman
by the arm, and was trying vainly to compose her — when the
library door was opened quietly by a young lady wearing a
mantle and a bonnet. Mercy Merrick (true to the appointment
which she had made with Horace) entered the room.

The first eyes that discovered her presence on the scene were
the eyes of Grace Roseberry. Starting violently in Julian's grasp,
she pointed towards the library door. 'Ah!' she cried, with a
shriek of vindictive delight. 'There she is!'

Mercy turned as the sound of the scream rang through the
room, and met — resting on her in savage triumph — the living
gaze of the woman whose identity she had stolen, whose body
she had left laid out for dead. On the instant of that terrible
discovery — with her eyes fixed helplessly on the fierce eyes that
had found her — she dropped senseless on the floor.

CHAPTER THE TWELFTH

EXIT JULIAN

Julian happened to be standing nearest to Mercy. He was the
first at her side when she fell.

In the cry of alarm which burst from him, as he raised her for
a moment in his arms, in the expression of his eyes when he
looked at her death-like face, there escaped the plain — too plain
— confession of the interest which he felt in her, of the
admiration which she had aroused in him. Horace detected it.
There was the quick suspicion of jealousy in the movement by
which he joined Julian; there was the ready resentment of
jealousy in the tone in which he pronounced the words, 'Leave
her to me.' Julian resigned her in silence. A faint flush appeared
on his pale face as he drew back while Horace carried her to the

sofa. His eyes sank to the ground; he seemed to be meditating self-reproachfully on the tone in which his friend had spoken to him. After having been the first to take an active part in meeting the calamity that had happened, he was now to all appearances insensible to everything that was passing in the room.

A touch on his shoulder roused him.

He turned and looked round. The woman who had done the mischief – the stranger in the poor black garments – was standing behind him. She pointed to the prostrate figure on the sofa, with a merciless smile.

'You wanted a proof just now,' she said. 'There it is!'

Horace heard her. He suddenly left the sofa and joined Julian. His face, naturally ruddy, was pale with suppressed fury.

'Take that wretch away!' he said. 'Instantly! or I won't answer for what I may do.'

Those words recalled Julian to himself. He looked round the room. Lady Janet and the housekeeper were together, in attendance on the swooning woman. The startled servants were congregated in the library doorway. Mercy had endeared herself to them by many little acts of kindness and consideration. One of them offered to run to the nearest doctor. Another asked if he should fetch the police. A third – the servant who had been in attendance on Mercy when the carriage took her to the committee-meeting – superstitiously assured Julian that it was Fate, and nothing less, which had brought his young lady home exactly at the wrong time. 'They all disagreed at the meeting, sir,' the man said; 'and the chairman adjourned the debate. If it hadn't been for that, we might not have got back for another good hour to come.'

With some difficulty Julian quieted the anxiety and confusion among the servants. This done he took Grace by the hand to lead her from the room. She hesitated and tried to release herself. Julian pointed to the group at the sofa, and to the servants going out in a body by the library door. 'You have made an enemy of everyone in this house,' he said, 'and you have not a friend in London. Do you wish to make an enemy of *me*?' Her head drooped; she made no reply; she waited,

dumbly obedient to the firmer will than her own. Julian
withdrew to the library, leading Grace after him by the hand.
Before closing the door he paused, and looked back into the
dining-room.

'Is she recovering?' he asked, after a moment's hesitation.

Lady Janet's voice answered him. 'Not yet.'

'Shall I send for the nearest doctor?'

Horace interposed. He declined to let Julian associate himself,
even in that indirect manner, with Mercy's recovery.

'If the doctor is wanted,' he said, 'I will go for him myself.'

Julian closed the library door. He absently released Grace; he
mechanically pointed to a chair. She sat down in silent surprise,
following him with her eyes as he walked slowly to and fro in
the room.

For the moment his mind was far away from her, and from all
that had happened since her appearance in the house. It was
impossible that a man of his fineness of perception could
mistake the meaning of Horace's conduct towards him. He was
questioning his own heart, on the subject of Mercy, sternly and
unreservedly, as it was his habit to do. 'After only once seeing
her,' he thought, 'has she produced such an impression on me
that Horace can discover it, before I have even suspected it
myself? Can the time have come already, when I owe it to my
friend to see her no more?' He stopped irritably in his walk. As
a man devoted to a serious calling in life, there was something
that wounded his self-respect in the bare suspicion that he could
be guilty of the purely sentimental extravagance called 'love at
first sight.'

He had paused exactly opposite to the chair in which Grace
was seated. Weary of the silence, she seized the opportunity of
speaking to him.

'I have come here with you as you wished,' she said. 'Are
you going to help me? Am I to count on you as my friend?'

He looked at her vacantly. It cost him an effort before he
could give her the attention that she had claimed.

'You have been hard on me,' Grace went on. 'But you
showed me some kindness at first; you tried to make them give
me a fair hearing. I ask you, as a just man, do you doubt now

that the woman on the sofa in the next room is an imposter who has taken my place? Can there be any plainer confession that she is Mercy Merrick than the confession she has made? *You* saw it; *they* saw it. She fainted at the sight of me.'

Julian crossed the room – still without answering her – and rang the bell. When the servant appeared, he told the man to fetch a cab.

Grace rose from her chair. 'What is the cab for?' she asked sharply.

'For you and for me,' Julian replied. 'I am going to take you back to your lodgings.'

'I refuse to go. My place is in the house. Neither Lady Janet nor you can get over the plain facts. All I asked was to be confronted with her. And what did she do when she came into the room? She fainted at the sight of me.'

Reiterating her one triumphant assertion, she fixed her eyes on Julian with a look which said plainly, Answer that if you can. In mercy to *her*, Julian answered it on the spot.

'So far as I understand,' he said, 'you appear to take it for granted that no innocent woman would have fainted on first seeing you. I have something to tell you which will alter your opinion. On her arrival in England this lady informed my aunt that she had met with you accidentally on the French frontier, and that she had seen you (so far as she knew) struck dead at her side by a shell. Remember that, and recall what happened just now. Without a word to warn her of your restoration to life, she finds herself suddenly face to face with you, a living woman – and this at a time when it is easy for anyone who looks at her to see that she is in delicate health. What is there wonderful, what is there unaccountable, in her fainting under such circumstances as these?'

The question was plainly put. Where was the answer to it?

There was no answer to it. Mercy's wisely candid statement of the manner in which she had first met with Grace, and of the accident which had followed, had served Mercy's purpose but too well. It was simply impossible for persons acquainted with that statement to attach a guilty meaning to the swoon. The false Grace Roseberry was still as far beyond the reach of

suspicion as ever; and the true Grace was quick enough to see
it. She sank into the chair from which she had risen; her hands
fell in hopeless despair on her lap.

'Everything is against me,' she said. 'The truth itself turns liar,
and takes *her* side.' She paused and rallied her sinking courage.
'No!' she cried resolutely, 'I won't submit to have my name and
my place taken from me by a vile adventuress! Say what you
like, I insist on exposing her; I won't leave the house!'

The servant entered the room, and announced that the cab
was at the door.

Grace turned to Julian with a defiant wave of her hand.
'Don't let me detain you,' she said. 'I see I have neither advice
nor help to expect from Mr Julian Gray.'

Julian beckoned to the servant to follow him into a corner of
the room.

' Do you know if the doctor has been sent for?' he asked.

'I believe not, sir. It is said in the servants' hall that the doctor
is not wanted.'

Julian was too anxious to be satisfied with a report from the
servants' hall. He hastily wrote on a slip of paper: 'Has she
recovered?' and then gave the note to the man, with directions
to take it to Lady Janet.

'Did you hear what I said?' Grace enquired, while the
messenger was absent in the dining-room.

'I will answer you directly,' said Julian.

The servant appeared again as he spoke, with some lines in
pencil written by Lady Janet on the back of Julian's note.
'Thank God we have revived her. In a few minutes we hope to
be able to take her to her room.'

The nearest way to Mercy's room was through the library.
Grace's immediate removal had now become a necessity which
was not to be trifled with. Julian addressed himself to meeting
the difficulty the instant he was left alone with Grace.

'Listen to me,' he said. 'The cab is waiting, and I have my last
words to say to you. You are now (thanks to the consul's
recommendation) in my care. Decide at once whether you will
remain under my charge, or whether you will transfer yourself
to the charge of the police.'

Grace started. 'What do you mean?' she asked angrily.

'If you wish to remain under my charge,' Julian proceeded, 'you will accompany me at once to the cab. In that case I will undertake to give you an opportunity of telling your story to my own lawyer. He will be a fitter person to advise you than I am. Nothing will induce *me* to believe that the lady whom you have accused has committed, or is capable of committing, such a fraud as you charge her with. You will hear what the lawyer thinks, if you come with me. If you refuse, I shall have no choice but to send into the next room and tell them that you are still here. The result will be that you find yourself in charge of the police. Take which course you like; I will give you a minute to decide in. And remember this, if I appear to express myself harshly, it is your conduct which forces me to speak out, I mean kindly towards you, I am advising you honestly for your good.'

He took out his watch to count the minute.

Grace stole one furtive glance at his steady resolute face. She was perfectly unmoved by the manly consideration for her which Julian's last words had expressed. All she understood was, that he was not a man to be trifled with. Future opportunities would offer themselves of returning secretly to the house. She determined to yield – and deceive him.

'I am ready to go,' she said, rising with dogged submission. 'Your turn now,' she muttered to herself as she turned to the looking glass to arrange her shawl. 'My turn will come.'

Julian advanced towards her, as if to offer her his arm, and checked himself. Firmly persuaded as he was that her mind was deranged – readily as he admitted that she claimed, in virtue of her affliction, every indulgence that he could extend to her – there was something repellant to him at that moment in the bare idea of touching her. The image of the beautiful creature who was the object of her monstrous accusation – the image of Mercy as she lay helpless for a moment in his arms – was vivid in his mind while he opened the door that led into the hall, and drew back to let Grace pass out before him. He left the servant to help her into the cab. The man respectfully addressed him as he took his seat opposite to Grace.

'I am ordered to say that your room is ready, sir; and that her ladyship expects you to dinner.'

Absorbed in the events which had followed his aunt's invitation, Julian had forgotten his engagement to stay at Mablethorpe House. Could he return, knowing his own heart as he now knew it? Could he honourably remain, perhaps for weeks together, in Mercy's society, conscious as he was of the impression which she had produced on him? No. The one honourable course that he could take was to find an excuse for withdrawing from his engagement. 'Beg her ladyship not to wait dinner for me,' he said. 'I will write and make my apologies.' The cab drove off. The wondering servant waited on the doorstep, looking after it. 'I wouldn't stand in Mr Julian's shoes for something,' he thought, with his mind running on the difficulties of the young clergyman's position. 'There she is, along with him in the cab. What is he going to do with her after that?'

Julian himself — if it had been put to him at the moment — could not have answered the question.

Lady Janet's anxiety was far from being relieved when Mercy had been restored to her senses and conducted to her own room.

Her mind remained in a condition of unreasoning alarm which it was impossible to remove. Over and over again she was told that the woman who had terrified her had left the house, and would never be permitted to enter it more. Over and over again she was assured that the stranger's frantic assertions were regarded by everybody about her as unworthy of a moment's serious attention. She persisted in doubting whether they were telling her the truth. A shocking distrust of her friends seemed to possess her. She shrank when Lady Janet approached the bedside. She shuddered when Lady Janet kissed her. She flatly refused to let Horace see her. She asked the strangest questions about Julian Gray, and shook her head suspiciously when they told her that he was absent from the house. At intervals, she hid her face in the bedclothes, and murmured to herself piteously, 'Oh! what shall I do? What shall I do?' At other times, her one petition was to be left alone. 'I want nobody in my room' – that was her sullen cry – 'Nobody in my room!'

The evening advanced, and brought with it no change for the better. Lady Janet, by the advice of Horace, sent for her own medical adviser.

The doctor shook his head. The symptoms, he said, indicated a serious shock to the nervous system. He wrote a sedative prescription; and he gave (with a happy choice of language) some sound and safe advice. It amounted briefly to this: 'Take her away, and try the seaside.' Lady Janet's customary energy acted on the advice without a moment's needless delay. She gave the necessary directions for packing the trucks over night, and decided on leaving Mablethorpe House with Mercy the next morning.

Shortly after the doctor had taken his departure, a letter from Julian, addressed to Lady Janet, was delivered by private messenger.

Beginning with the necessary apologies for the writer's absence, the letter proceeded in these terms:

'Before I permitted my companion to accompany me to the lawyer's office, I felt the necessity of consulting him as to my present position towards her.

'I told him – what I think it only right to repeat to you – that I do not feel justified in acting on my own opinion that her mind is deranged. In the case of this friendless woman, I want medical authority, and more even than that, I want some positive proof, to satisfy my conscience as well as to confirm my view.

'Finding me obstinate on this point, the lawyer undertook to consult a physician accustomed to the treatment of the insane, on my behalf.

'After sending a message and receiving the answer, he said, "Bring the lady here – in half an hour; she shall tell her story to the doctor instead of telling it to me." The proposal rather staggered me; I asked how it was possible to induce her to do that. He laughed, and answered, "I shall present the doctor as my senior partner; my senior partner will be the very man to advise her." You know that I hate all deception – even where the end in view appears to justify it. On this occasion, however, there was no other alternative than to let the lawyer take his own course – or to run the risk of a delay which might be followed by serious results.

'I waited in a room by myself (feeling very uneasy I own) until the doctor joined me after the interview was over.

'His opinion is, briefly, this:

'"After careful examination of the unfortunate creature, he thinks that there are unmistakably symptoms of mental aberration, but how far the mischief has gone, and whether her case is, or is not, sufficiently grave to render actual restraint necessary, he cannot positively say in our present state of ignorance as to facts.

'"Thus far," he observed, "we know nothing of that part of her delusion which relates to Mercy Merrick. The solution of the difficulty, in this case, is to be found there. I entirely agree with the lady that the enquiries of the consul at Mannheim are far from being conclusive. Furnish me with satisfactory evidence either that there is, or is not, such a person really in existence as Mercy Merrick, and I will give you a positive opinion on the case, whenever you choose to ask for it."

'Those words have decided me on starting for the Continent, and renewing the search for the missing nurse.

'My friend the lawyer wonders jocosely whether I am in my right senses. His advice is, that I should apply to the nearest magistrate, and relieve you and myself of all further trouble in that way.

'Perhaps you agree with him? My dear aunt (as you have often said), I do nothing like other people. I am interested in this case. I cannot abandon a forlorn woman who has been confided to me to the tender mercies of strangers, so long as there is any hope of my making discoveries which may be instrumental in restoring her to herself – perhaps, also, in restoring her to her friends.

'I start by the mail train of to-night. My plan is, to go first to Mannheim, and consult with the consul and the hospital doctors; then to find my way to the German surgeon, and to question *him*; and, that done, to make the last and hardest effort of all – the effort to trace the French ambulance and to penetrate the mystery of Mercy Merrick.

'Immediately on my return I will wait on you, and tell you what I have accomplished, or how I have failed.

'In the meanwhile, pray be under no alarm about the reappearance of this unhappy woman at your house. She is fully occupied in writing (at my suggestion) to her friends in Canada; and she is under the care of the landlady at her lodgings – an experienced and trustworthy person, who has satisfied the doctor, as well as myself, of her fitness for the charge that she has undertaken.

'Pray mention this to Miss Roseberry (whenever you think it desirable), with the respectful expression of my sympathy, and of my best wishes for her speedy restoration to health. And once more forgive me for failing, under stress of necessity, to enjoy the hospitality of Mablethorpe House.'

Lady Janet closed Julian's letter, feeling far from satisfied with it. She sat for a while, pondering over what her nephew had written to her.

'One of two things,' thought the quick-witted old lady. 'Either the lawyer is right, and Julian is a fit companion for the madwoman whom he has taken under his charge: or he has some second motive for this absurd journey of his, which he has carefully abstained from mentioning in his letter. What can the motive be?'

At intervals during the night that question recurred to her ladyship again and again. The utmost exercise of her ingenuity failing to answer it, her one resource left was to wait patiently for Julian's return, and, in her own favourite phrase, to 'have it out with him' then.

The next morning, Lady Janet and her adopted daughter left Mablethorpe House for Brighton; Horace (who had begged to be allowed to accompany them) being sentenced to remain in London by Mercy's express desire. Why – nobody could guess; and Mercy refused to say.

CHAPTER THE THIRTEENTH

ENTER JULIAN

A week has passed. The scene opens again in the dining-room
at Mablethorpe House.

The hospitable table bears once more its burden of good
things for lunch. But, on this occasion, Lady Janet sits alone.
Her attention is divided between reading her newspaper and
feeding her cat. The cat is a sleek and splendid creature. He
carries an erect tail. He rolls luxuriously on the soft carpet.
He approaches his mistress in a series of coquettish curves.
He smells with dainty hesitation at the choicest morsels that
can be offered to him. The musical monotony of his purring
falls soothingly on her ladyship's ear. She stops in the
middle of the leading article, and looks with a careworn face
at the happy cat. 'Upon my honour,' cries Lady Janet,
thinking, in her inveterately ironical manner, of the cares
that trouble her, 'all things considered, Tom, I wish I was
You!'

The cat starts — not at his mistress's complimentary
apostrophe, but at a knock at the door which follows close
upon it. Lady Janet says, carelessly enough, 'Come in'; looks
round listlessly to see who it is; and starts, like the cat, when the
door opens and discloses — Julian Gray!

'You — or your ghost?' she exclaims.

She has noticed already that Julian is paler than usual, and
that there is something in his manner at once uneasy and
subdued — highly uncharacteristic of him at other times. He
takes a seat by her side, and kisses her hand. But — for the first
time in his aunt's experience of him — he refuses the good
things on the luncheon-table, and he has nothing to say to the
cat! That neglected animal takes refuge on Lady Janet's lap.
Lady Janet, with her eyes fixed expectantly on her nephew
(determining to 'have it out with him' at the first
opportunity), waits to hear what he has to say for himself.
Julian has no alternative but to break the silence, and tell his
story as he best may.

'I got back from the Continent last night,' he began. 'And I come here, as I promised, to report myself on my return. How does your ladyship do? How is Miss Roseberry?'

Lady Janet laid an indicative finger on the lace pelerine which ornamented the upper part of her dress. 'Here is the old lady, well,' she answered – and pointed next to the room above them. 'And there,' she added, 'is the young lady, ill. Is anything the matter with *you*, Julian?'

'Perhaps I am a little tired after my journey. Never mind me. Is Miss Roseberry still suffering from the shock?'

'What else should she be suffering from? I will never forgive you, Julian, for bringing that crazy impostor into my house.'

'My dear aunt, when I was the innocent means of bringing her here I had no idea that such a person as Miss Roseberry was in existence. Nobody laments what has happened more sincerely than I do. Have you had medical advice?'

'I took her to the seaside a week since, by medical advice.'

'Has the change of air done her no good?'

'None whatever. If anything, the change of air has made her worse. Sometimes she sits for hours together, as pale as death, without looking at anything, and without uttering a word. Sometimes she brightens up, and seems as if she was eager to say something – and then, Heaven only knows why, checks herself suddenly as if she was afraid to speak. I could support that. But what cuts me to the heart, Julian, is that she does not appear to trust me and to love me as she did. She seems to be doubtful of me; she seems to be frightened of me. If I did not know that it was simply impossible that such a thing could be, I should really think she suspected me of believing what that wretch said of her. In one word (and between ourselves), I begin to fear she will never get over the fright which caused that fainting fit. There is serious mischief somewhere – and try as I may to discover it, it is mischief beyond my finding.'

'Can the doctor do nothing?'

Lady Janet's bright black eyes answered, before she replied in words, with a look of supreme contempt.

'The doctor!' she repeated disdainfully. 'I brought Grace back last night in sheer despair, and I sent for the doctor this morning.

He is at the head of his profession; he is said to be making ten thousand a year – and he knows no more about it than I do. I am quite serious. The great physician has just gone away with two guineas in his pocket. One guinea for advising me to keep her quiet; another guinea for telling me to trust to time. Do you wonder how he gets on at this rate? My dear boy, they all get on in the same way. The medical profession thrives on two incurable diseases in these modern days – a He-disease and a She-disease. She-disease – nervous depression; He-disease – suppressed gout. Remedies, one guinea if *you* go to the doctor; two guineas if the doctor goes to *you*. I might have bought a new bonnet,' cried her ladyship indignantly, 'with the money I have given to that man! Let us change the subject. I lose my temper when I think of it. Besides, I want to know something. Why did you go abroad?'

At that plain question Julian looked unaffectedly surprised. 'I wrote to explain,' he said. 'Have you not received my letter?'

'Oh, I got your letter. It was long enough, in all conscience – and, long as it was, it didn't tell me the one thing I wanted to know.'

'What is the "one thing?"'

Lady Janet's reply pointed – not too palpably at first – at that second motive for Julian's journey which she had suspected Julian of concealing from her.

'I want to know,' she said, 'why you troubled yourself to make your enquiries on the Continent *in person?* You know where my old courier is to be found. You have yourself pronounced him to be the most intelligent and trustworthy of men. Answer me honestly – could you not have sent him in your place?'

'I *might* have sent him,' Julian admitted – a little reluctantly.

'You might have sent the courier – and you were under an engagement to stay here as my guest. Answer me honestly once more. Why did you go away?'

Julian hesitated. Lady Janet paused for his reply, with the air of a woman who was prepared to wait (if necessary) for the rest of the afternoon.

'I had a reason of my own for going,' Julian said at last.

'Yes?' rejoined Lady Janet, prepared to wait (if necessary) till the next morning.

'A reason,' Julian resumed, 'which I would rather not mention.'

'Oh!' said Lady Janet. 'Another mystery — eh? And another woman at the bottom of it, no doubt? Thank you — that will do — I am sufficiently answered. No wonder — as a clergyman — that you look a little confused. There is perhaps a certain grace, under the circumstances, in looking confused. We will change the subject again. You stay here, of course, now you have come back?'

Once more the famous pulpit orator seemed to find himself in the inconceivable predicament of not knowing what to say. Once more Lady Janet looked resigned to wait — (if necessary) until the middle of next week.

Julian took refuge in an answer worthy of the most commonplace man on the face of the civilised earth.

'I beg your ladyship to accept my thanks and my excuses,' he said.

Lady Janet's many-ringed fingers, mechanically stroking the cat in her lap, began to stroke him the wrong way. Lady Janet's inexhaustible patience showed signs of failing her at last.

'Mighty civil, I am sure,' she said. 'Make it complete. Say, Mr Julian Gray presents his compliments to Lady Janet Roy, and regrets that a previous engagement — Julian!' exclaimed the old lady, suddenly pushing the cat off her lap, and flinging her last pretence of good temper to the winds — 'Julian, I am not to be trifled with ! There is but one explanation of your conduct — you are evidently avoiding my house. Is there someone you dislike in it? Is it me?'

Julian intimated by a gesture that his aunt's last question was absurd. (The much-injured cat elevated his back, waved his tail slowly, walked to the fireplace, and honoured the rug by taking a seat on it.)

Lady Janet persisted. 'Is it Grace Roseberry?' she asked next.

Even Julian's patience began to show signs of yielding. His manner assumed a sudden decision, his voice rose a tone louder.

'You insist on knowing?' he said. 'It *is* Miss Roseberry.'

'You don't like her?' cried Lady Janet, with a sudden burst of angry surprise.

Julian broke out, on his side. 'If I see any more of her,' he answered, the rare colour mounting suddenly in his cheeks, 'I shall be the unhappiest man living. If I see any more of her, I shall be false to my old friend who is to marry her. Keep us apart. If you have any regard for my peace of mind, keep us apart.'

Unutterable amazement expressed itself in his aunt's lifted hands. Ungovernable curiosity uttered itself in his aunt's next words.

'You don't mean to tell me you are in love with Grace?'

Julian sprang restlessly to his feet, and disturbed the cat at the fireplace. (The cat left the room.)

'I don't know what to tell you,' he said, ' I can't realise it to myself. No other woman has ever roused the feeling in me which *this* woman seems to have called to life in an instant. In the hope of forgetting her I broke my engagement here; I purposely seized the opportunity of making those enquiries abroad. Quite useless. I think of her morning, noon, and night. I see her and hear her, at this moment, as plainly as I see and hear You. She has made *her*-self a part of *my*-self. I don't understand my life without her. My power of will seems to be gone. I said to myself this morning, "I will write to my aunt; I won't go back to Mablethorpe House." Here I am in Mablethorpe House, with a mean subterfuge to justify me to my own conscience. "I owe it to my aunt to call on my aunt." That is what I said to myself on the way here; and I was secretly hoping every step of the way that She would come into the room when I got here. I am hoping it now. And she is engaged to Horace Holmcroft – to my oldest friend, to my best friend! Am I an infernal rascal? or am I a weak fool? God knows – I don't. Keep my secret, aunt. I am heartily ashamed of myself; I used to think I was made of better stuff than this. Don't say a word to Horace. I must, and will, conquer it. Let me go.'

He snatched up his hat. Lady Janet, rising with the activity of a young woman, pursued him across the room, and stopped him at the door.

'No,' answered the resolute old lady, 'I won't let you go. Come back with me.'

As she said those words she noticed with a certain fond pride the brilliant colour mounting in his cheeks – the flashing brightness which lent an added lustre to his eyes. He had never, to her mind, looked so handsome before. She took his arm, and led him to the chairs which they had just left. It was shocking, it was wrong (she mentally admitted), to look on Mercy, under the circumstances, with any other eye than the eye of a brother or a friend. In the clergyman (perhaps) doubly shocking, doubly wrong. But, with all her respect for the vested interests of Horace, Lady Janet could not blame Julian. Worse still, she was privately conscious that he had, somehow or other, risen, rather than fallen, in her estimation within the last minute or two. Who could deny that her adopted daughter was a charming creature? Who could wonder if a man of refined tastes admired her? Upon the whole, her ladyship humanely decided that her nephew was rather to be pitied than blamed. What daughter of Eve (no matter whether she was seventeen or seventy) could have honestly arrived at any other conclusion? Do what a man may – let him commit anything he likes, from an error to a crime – so long as there is a woman at the bottom of it, there is an inexhaustible fund of pardon for him in every other woman's heart. 'Sit down,' said Lady Janet, smiling in spite of herself; 'and don't talk in that horrible way again. A man, Julian – especially a famous man like you – ought to know how to control himself.'

Julian burst out laughing bitterly.

'Send upstairs for my self-control,' he said. 'It's in *her* possession – not in mine. Good morning, aunt.'

He rose from his chair. Lady Janet instantly pushed him back into it.

'I insist on your staying here,' she said, 'if it's only for a few minutes longer. I have something to say to you.'

'Does it refer to Miss Roseberry?"

'It refers to the hateful woman who frightened Miss Roseberry. Now are you satisfied?'

Julian bowed, and settled himself in his chair.

'I don't much like to acknowledge it,' his aunt went on. 'But I want you to understand that I have something really serious to speak about, for once in a way. Julian! that wretch not only frightens Grace – she actually frightens Me.'

'Frightens you? She is quite harmless, poor thing.'

'"Poor thing!' repeated Lady Janet. 'Did you say "poor thing"?'

'Yes.'

'Is it possible that you pity her?'

'From the bottom of my heart.'

The old lady's temper gave way again at that reply. 'I hate a man who can't hate anybody!' she burst out. 'If you had been an ancient Roman, Julian, I believe you would have pitied Nero himself.'

Julian cordially agreed with her. 'I believe I should,' he said quietly. 'All sinners, my dear aunt, are more or less miserable sinners. Nero must have been one of the wretchedest of mankind.'

'Wretched!' exclaimed Lady Janet. 'Nero wretched! A man who committed robbery, arson, and murder, to his own violin accompaniment – *only* wretched! What next, I wonder? When modern philanthropy begins to apologise for Nero, modern philanthropy has arrived at a pretty pass indeed! We shall hear next that Bloody Queen Mary was as playful as a kitten; and if poor dear Henry the Eighth carried anything to an extreme, it was the practice of the domestic virtues. Ah, how I hate cant! What were we talking about just now? You wander from the subject, Julian; you are what I call bird-witted. I protest I forget what I wanted to say to you. No, I won't be reminded of it. I may be an old woman, but I am not in my dotage yet! Why do you sit there staring? Have you nothing to say for yourself? Of all the people in the world, have *you* lost the use of your tongue?'

Julian's excellent temper and accurate knowledge of his aunt's character exactly fitted him to calm the rising storm. He contrived to lead Lady Janet insensibly back to the lost subject, by dexterous reference to a narrative which he had thus far left untold – the narrative of his adventures on the Continent.

'I have a great deal to say, aunt,' he replied. 'I have not yet told you of my discoveries abroad.'

Lady Janet instantly took the bait.

'I knew there was something forgotten,' she said. ' You have been all this time in the house, and you have told me nothing. Begin directly.'

Patient Julian began.

CHAPTER THE FOURTEENTH

COMING EVENTS CAST THEIR SHADOWS BEFORE

'I went first to Mannheim, Lady Janet, as I told you I should in my letter; and I heard all that the consul and the hospital doctors could tell me. No new fact of the slightest importance turned up. I got my directions for finding the German surgeon, and I set forth to try what I could make next of the man who had performed the operation. On the question of the patient's identity he had (as a perfect stranger to her) nothing to tell me. On the question of her mental condition, however, he made a very important statement. He owned to me that he had operated on another person injured by a shell-wound on the head, at the battle of Solferino and that the patient (recovering also in this case) recovered – mad. That is a remarkable admission; don't you think so?'

Lady Janet's temper had hardly been allowed time enough to subside to its customary level.

'Very remarkable, I dare say,' she answered, 'to people who feel any doubt of this pitiable lady of yours being mad. I feel no doubt – and, thus far, I find your account of yourself, Julian, tiresome in the extreme. Get on to the end. Did you lay your hand on Mercy Merrick?'

'No.'

'Did you hear anything of her?'

'Nothing. Difficulties beset me on every side. The French ambulance had shared in the disasters of France – it was broken

up. The wounded Frenchmen were prisoners, somewhere in
Germany, nobody knew where. The French surgeon had been
killed in action. His assistants were scattered — most likely in
hiding. I began to despair of making any discovery, when
accident threw in my way two Prussian soldiers who had been
in the French cottage. They confirmed what the German
surgeon told the consul, and what Horace himself told *me,*
namely, that no nurse in a black dress was to be seen in the
place. If there had been such a person, she would certainly (the
Prussians informed me) have been found in attendance on the
injured Frenchmen. The cross of the Geneva Convention
would have been amply sufficient to protect her: no woman
wearing that badge of honour would have disgraced herself by
abandoning the wounded men before the Germans entered the
place.'

'In short,' interposed Lady Janet, 'there is no such person as
Mercy Merrick?'

'I can draw no other conclusion,' said Julian, unless the
English doctor's idea is the right one. After hearing what I have
just told you, he is satisfied that the woman herself is Mercy
Merrick.'

Lady Janet held up her hand, as a sign that she had an
objection to make here.

'You and the doctor seem to have settled everything to your
entire satisfaction on both sides,' she said. 'But there is one
difficulty that you have neither of you accounted for yet.'

'What is it, aunt?'

'You talk glibly enough, Julian, about this woman's mad
assertion that Grace is the missing nurse, and that she is Grace.
But you have not explained yet how the idea first got into her
head; and, more than that, how it is that she is acquainted with
my name and address, and perfectly familiar with Grace's papers
and Grace's affairs. These things are a puzzle to a person of my
average intelligence. Can your clever friend, the doctor,
account for them?'

'Shall I tell you what he said when I saw him this morning?'

'Will it take long?'

'It will take about a minute.'

'You agreeably surprise me. Go on.'

'You want to know how she gained her knowledge of your name, and of Miss Roseberry's affairs,' Julian resumed. 'The doctor says, in one of two ways. Either Miss Roseberry must have spoken of you, and of her own affairs, while she and the stranger were together in the French cottage; or the stranger must have obtained access privately to Miss Roseberry's papers. Do you agree so far?'

Lady Janet began to feel interested for the first time.

'Perfectly,' she said. 'I have no doubt Grace produced a strong impression on her, in the first place. I dare say all sorts of inquisitive questions followed; and Grace rashly talked of matters which an older and wiser person would have kept to herself.'

'Very good. Do you agree that the last idea in the woman's mind when she was struck by the shell might have been (quite probably) the idea of Miss Roseberry's identity and Miss Roseberry's affairs? You think it likely enough? Well! What happens after that? The wounded woman is brought to life by an operation, and she becomes delirious in the hospital at Mannheim. During her delirium the idea of Miss Roseberry's identity ferments in her brain, and assumes its present perverted form. In that form it still remains. As a necessary consequence, she persists in reversing the two identities. She says she is Miss Roseberry, and declares Miss Roseberry to be Mercy Merrick. There is the doctor's view of the matter. As I think, it not only answers your question – it also explains the woman's angry repudiation of the name marked on her clothes (the name of Mercy Merrick) when she was received at the hospital. Do you agree with me?'

'I hardly know, Julian, whether I agree with you or not. Confusion of their own identity with the identity of others is common enough among mad people, I admit. Still, the doctor doesn't quite satisfy me. I think——'

What Lady Janet thought was not destined to be expressed. She suddenly checked herself, and held up her hand for the second time.

'Another objection?' enquired Julian.

'Hold your tongue!' cried the old lady. 'If you say a word more I shall lose it again.'

'Lose what, aunt?'

'What I wanted to say to you, ages ago. I have got it back again — it begins with a question. (No more of the doctor! I have had enough of him!) Where is she — *your* pitiable lady, *my* crazy wretch — where is she now? Still in London?'

'Yes.'

'And still at large?'

'Still with the landlady, at her lodgings.'

'Very well. Now, answer me this. What is to prevent her from making another attempt to force her way (or steal her way) into my house? How am I to protect Grace, how am I to protect myself, if she comes here again?'

'Is that really what you wished to speak to me about?'

'That, and nothing else.'

They were both too deeply interested in the subject of their conversation to look towards the conservatory, and to notice the appearance at that moment of a distant gentleman among the plants and flowers, who had made his way in from the garden outside. Advancing noiselessly on the soft Indian matting, the gentleman ere long revealed himself under the form and features of Horace Holmcroft. Before entering the dining-room, he paused, fixing his eyes inquisitively on the back of Lady Janet's visitor — the back being all that he could see in the position he then occupied. After a pause of an instant, the visitor spoke, and further uncertainty was at once at an end. Horace, nevertheless, made no movement to enter the room. He had his own jealous distrust of what Julian might be tempted to confess privately to Lady Janet; and he waited a little longer, on the chance that his doubts might be verified.

'Neither you nor Miss Roseberry need any protection from the poor deluded creature,' Julian went on. 'I have gained great influence over her, and I have satisfied her that it is useless to present herself here again.'

'I beg your pardon,' interposed Horace, speaking from the conservatory door. 'You have done nothing of the sort.'

(He had heard enough to satisfy him that the talk was not taking the direction which his suspicions had anticipated. And as an additional incentive to show himself, a happy chance had now offered him the opportunity of putting Julian in the wrong.)

'Good heavens, Horace!' exclaimed Lady Janet, 'where do you come from? And what do you mean?'

'I heard at the lodge that your ladyship and Grace had returned last night. And I came in at once, without troubling the servants, by the shortest way.' He turned to Julian next. 'The woman you were speaking of just now,' he proceeded, 'has been here again already – in Lady Janet's absence.'

Lady Janet immediately looked at her nephew. Julian reassured her by a gesture.

'Impossible,' he said. 'There must be some mistake.'

'There is no mistake,' Horace rejoined. 'I am repeating what I have just heard from the lodge-keeper himself. He hesitated to mention it to Lady Janet for fear of alarming her. Only three days since, this person had the audacity to ask him for her ladyship's address at the seaside. Of course he refused to give it.'

'You hear that, Julian?' said Lady Janet.

No signs of anger or mortification escaped Julian. The expression in his face at that moment was an expression of sincere distress.

'Pray don't alarm yourself,' he said to his aunt, in his quietest tones. 'If she attempts to annoy you or Miss Roseberry again, I have it in my power to stop her instantly.'

'How?' asked Lady Janet.

'How, indeed!' echoed Horace. 'If we give her in charge to the police we shall become the subject of a public scandal.'

'I have managed to avoid all danger of scandal,' Julian answered, the expression of distress in his face becoming more and more marked while he spoke. 'Before I called here to-day I had a private consultation with the magistrate of the district, and I have made certain arrangements at the police-station close by. On receipt of my card, an experienced man, in plain clothes, will present himself at any address that I indicate, and will take her quietly away. The magistrate will hear the charge in his private room, and will examine the evidence which I can produce, showing that she is not accountable for her actions. The proper medical officer will report officially on the case, and the law will place her under the necessary restraint.'

Lady Janet and Horace looked at each other in amazement. Julian was, in their opinion, the last man on earth to take the course – at once sensible and severe – which Julian had actually adopted. Lady Janet insisted on an explanation.

'Why do I hear of this now for the first time?' she asked. 'Why did you not tell you had taken these precautions before?'

Julian answered frankly and sadly.

'Because I hoped, aunt, that there would be no necessity for proceeding to extremities. You now force me to acknowledge that the lawyer and the doctor (both of whom I have seen this morning) think, as you do, that she is not to be trusted. It was at their suggestion entirely that I went to the magistrate. They put it to me whether the result of my enquiries abroad – unsatisfactory as it may have been in other respects – did not strengthen the conclusion that the poor woman's mind is deranged. I felt compelled in common honesty to admit that it was so. Having owned this, I was bound to take such precautions as the lawyer and the doctor thought necessary. I have done my duty – sorely against my own will. It was weak of me, I daresay – but I can *not* bear the thought of treating this afflicted creature harshly. Her delusion is so hopeless! her situation is such a pitiable one!'

His voice faltered. He turned away abruptly and took up his hat. Lady Janet followed him, and spoke to him at the door. Horace smiled satirically, and went to warm himself at the fire.

'Are you going away, Julian?'

'I am only going to the lodge-keeper. I want to give him a word of warning in case of his seeing her again.'

'You will come back here?' (Lady Janet lowered her voice to a whisper.) 'There is really a reason, Julian, for you not leaving the house now.'

'I promise not to go away, aunt, until I have provided for your security. If you, or your adopted daughter, are alarmed by another intrusion, I give you my word of honour my card shall go to the police-station – however painfully I may feel it myself.' (He, too, lowered his voice at the next words.) 'In the meantime, remember what I confessed to you while we were alone! For my sake, let me see as little of Miss Roseberry as possible. Shall I find you in this room when I come back?'

'Yes.'

'Alone?'

He laid a strong emphasis, of look as well as of tone, on that one word. Lady Janet understood what the emphasis meant.

'Are you really,' she whispered, 'as much in love with Grace as that?'

Julian laid one hand on his aunt's arm, and pointed with the other to Horace – standing with his back to them, warming his feet on the fender.

'Well?' said Lady Janet.

'Well,' said Julian, with a smile on his lip and a tear in his eye, 'I never envied any man as I envy *him!*'

With those words he left the room.

CHAPTER THE FIFTEENTH

A WOMAN'S REMORSE

Having warmed his feet to his own entire satisfaction, Horace turned round from the fireplace, and discovered that he and Lady Janet were alone.

'Can I see Grace?' he asked.

The easy tone in which he put the question – a tone, as it were, of proprietorship in 'Grace' – jarred on Lady Janet at the moment. For the first time in her life she found herself comparing Horace with Julian to Horace's disadvantage. He was rich; he was a gentleman of ancient lineage; he bore an unblemished character. But who had the strong brain? who had the great heart? Which was the Man of the two?

'Nobody can see her,' answered Lady Janet. 'Not even you!'

The tone of the reply was sharp – with a dash of irony in it. But where is the modern young man – possessed of health and an independent income – who is capable of understanding that irony can be presumptuous enough to address itself to *him?* Horace (with perfect politeness) declined to consider himself answered.

'Does your ladyship mean that Miss Roseberry is in bed?' he asked.

'I mean that Miss Roseberry is in her room. I mean that I have twice tried to persuade Miss Roseberry to dress and come downstairs – and tried in vain. I mean that what Miss Roseberry refuses to do for Me, she is not likely to do for You——'

How many more meanings of her own Lady Janet might have gone on enumerating, it is not easy to calculate. At her third sentence, a sound in the library caught her ear through the incompletely-closed door, and suspended the next words on her lips. Horace heard it also. It was the rustling sound (travelling nearer and nearer over the library carpet) of a silken dress.

(In the interval while a coming event remains in a state of uncertainty, what is it the inevitable tendency of every Englishman under thirty to do? His inevitable tendency is to ask somebody to bet on the event. He can no more resist it than he can resist lifting his stick or his umbrella, in the absence of a gun, and pretending to shoot if a bird flies by him while he is out for a walk.)

'What will your ladyship bet that this is not Grace?' cried Horace.

Her ladyship took no notice of the proposal; her attention remained fixed on the library door. The rustling sound stopped for a moment. The door was softly pushed open. The false Grace Roseberry entered the room.

Horace advanced to meet her, opened his lips to speak, and stopped – struck dumb by the change in his affianced wife since he had seen her last. Some terrible oppression seemed to have crushed her. It was as if she had actually shrunk in height as well as in substance. She walked more slowly than usual; she spoke more rarely than usual, and in a lower tone. To those who had seen her before the fatal visit of the stranger from Mannheim, it was the wreck of the woman that now appeared, instead of the woman herself. And yet, there was the old charm still surviving through it all; the grandeur of the head and eyes, the delicate symmetry of the features, the unsought grace of every movement – in a word, the unconquerable beauty which suffering cannot destroy, and which time itself is powerless to wear out.

Lady Janet advanced, and took her with hearty kindness by both hands.

'My dear child, welcome among us again! You have come downstairs to please me?'

She bent her head in silent acknowledgement that it was so. Lady Janet pointed to Horace: 'Here is somebody who has been longing to see you, Grace.'

She never looked up; she stood submissive, her eyes fixed on a little basket of coloured wools which hung on her arm. 'Thank you, Lady Janet,' she said, faintly. 'Thank you, Horace.'

Horace placed her arm in his, and led her to the sofa. She shivered as she took her seat, and looked round her. It was the first time she had seen the dining-room since the day when she had found herself face to face with the dead-alive.

'Why do you come here, my love?' asked Lady Janet. 'The drawing-room would have been a warmer and a pleasanter place for you.'

'I saw a carriage at the front door. I was afraid of meeting with visitors in the drawing-room.'

As she made that reply, the servant came in, and announced the visitors' names. Lady Janet sighed wearily. 'I must go and get rid of them,' she said, resigning herself to circumstances. 'What will *you* do, Grace?'

'I will stay here, if you please.'

'I will keep her company,' added Horace.

Lady Janet hesitated. She had promised to see her nephew in the dining-room on his return to the house – and to see him alone. Would there be time enough to get rid of the visitors, and to establish her adopted daughter in the empty drawing-room, before Julian appeared? It was a ten minutes' walk to the lodge, and he had to make the gatekeeper understand his instructions. Lady Janet decided that she had time enough at her disposal. She nodded kindly to Mercy, and left her alone with her lover.

Horace seated himself in the vacant place on the sofa. So far as it was in his nature to devote himself to anyone, he was devoted to Mercy. 'I am grieved to see how you have suffered,' he said, with honest distress in his face as he looked at her. 'Try to forget what has happened.'

'I am trying to forget. Do *you* think of it much?'

'My darling, it is too contemptible to be thought of .'

She placed her work-basket on her lap. Her wasted fingers began absently sorting the wools inside.

'Have you seen Mr Julian Gray?' she asked suddenly.

'Yes.'

'What does *he* say about it?' She looked at Horace for the first time, steadily scrutinising his face. Horace took refuge in prevarication.

'I really haven't asked for Julian's opinion,' he said.

She looked down again, with a sigh, at the basket on her lap – considered a little – and tried him once more.

'Why has Mr Julian Gray not been here for a whole week?' she went on. 'The servants say he has been abroad. Is it true?'

It was useless to deny it. Horace admitted that the servants were right.

Her fingers suddenly stopped at their restless work among the wools: her breath quickened perceptibly. What had Julian Gray been doing abroad? Had he been making enquiries? Did he alone, of all the people who saw that terrible meeting, suspect her? Yes! His was the finer intelligence; his was a clergyman's (a London clergyman's) experience of frauds and deceptions, and of the women who were guilty of them. Not a doubt of it now! Julian suspected her.

'When does he come back?' she asked, in tones so low that Horace could barely hear her.

'He has come back already. He returned last night.'

A faint shade of colour stole slowly over the pallor of her face. She suddenly put her basket away, and clasped her hands together to quiet the trembling of them, before she asked her next question.

'Where is——' She paused to steady her voice. 'Where is the person,' she resumed, 'who came here and frightened me?'

Horace hastened to reassure her. 'The person will not come again,' he said. 'Don't talk of her! Don't think of her!'

She shook her head. 'There is something I want to know,' she persisted. 'How did Mr Julian Gray become acquainted with her?'

This was easily answered. Horace mentioned the consul at Mannheim, and the letter of introduction. She listened eagerly, and said her next words in a louder, firmer tone.

'She was quite a stranger, then, to Mr Julian Gray – before that?'

'Quite a stranger,' Horace replied. 'No more questions – not another word about her, Grace! I forbid the subject. Come, my own love!' he said, taking her hand, and bending over her tenderly, 'rally your spirits! We are young – we love each other – now is our time to be happy!'

Her hand turned suddenly cold, and trembled in his. Her head sank with a helpless weariness on her breast. Horace rose in alarm.

'You are cold – you are faint,' he said. 'Let me get you a glass of wine! – let me mend the fire!'

The decanters were still on the luncheon-table. Horace insisted on her drinking some port wine. She barely took half the contents of the wine-glass. Even that little told on her sensitive organisation; it roused her sinking energies of body and mind. After watching her anxiously, without attracting her notice, Horace left her again to attend to the fire at the other end of the room. Her eyes followed him slowly with a hard and tearless despair. 'Rally your spirits,' she repeated to herself in a whisper. 'My spirits! Oh, God!' She looked round her at the luxury and beauty of the room, as those look who take their leave of familiar scenes. The moment after, her eyes sank, and rested on the rich dress that she wore – a gift from Lady Janet. She thought of the past; she thought of the future. Was the time near when she would be back again in

the Refuge, or back again in the streets? – she who had been
Lady Janet's adopted daughter, and Horace Holmcroft's
betrothed wife! A sudden frenzy of recklessness seized on her
as she thought of the coming end. Horace was right! Why
not rally her spirits? Why not make the most of her time?
The last hours of her life in that house were at hand. Why
not enjoy her stolen position while she could? 'Adventuress!'
whispered the mocking spirit within her, 'be true to your
character. Away with your remorse! Remorse is the luxury of
an honest woman. She caught up her basket of wools,
inspired by a new idea. 'Ring the bell!' she cried out to
Horace at the fireplace.

He looked round in wonder. The sound of her voice was so
completely altered that he almost fancied there must have been
another woman in the room.

'Ring the bell!' she repeated. 'I have left my work upstairs. If
you want me to be in good spirits, I must have my work.'

Still looking at her, Horace put his hand mechanically to the
bell and rang. One of the men-servants came in.

'Go upstairs, and ask my maid for my work,' she said
sharply. Even the man was taken by surprise; it was her habit
to speak to the servants with a gentleness and consideration
which had long since won all their hearts. 'Do you hear me?'
she asked impatiently. The servant bowed, and went out on
his errand. She turned to Horace with flashing eyes and
fevered cheeks.

'What a comfort it is,' she said, 'to belong to the upper
classes! A poor woman has no maid to dress her, and no
footman to send upstairs. Is life worth having, Horace, on less
than five thousand a year?'

The servant returned with a strip of embroidery. She
took it with an insolent grace, and told him to bring her a
footstool. The man obeyed. She tossed the embroidery
away from her on the sofa. 'On second thoughts I don't
care about my work,' she said. 'Take it upstairs again.' The
perfectly-trained servant, marvelling privately, obeyed once
more. Horace, in silent astonishment, advanced to the sofa
to observe her more nearly. 'How grave you look!' she

exclaimed, with an air of flippant unconcern. 'You don't approve of my sitting idle, perhaps? Anything to please you! *I* haven't got to go up and down stairs. Ring the bell again.'

'My dear Grace,' Horace remonstrated gravely, 'you are quite mistaken. I never even thought of your work.'

'Never mind; it's inconsistent to send for my work, and then send it away again. Ring the bell.'

Horace looked at her, without moving. 'Grace!' he said, 'what has come to you?'

'How should I know?' she retorted carelessly. 'Didn't you tell me to rally my spirits? Will you ring the bell? or must I?'

Horace submitted. He frowned as he walked back to the bell. He was one of the many people who instinctively resent anything that is new to them. This strange outbreak was quite new to him. For the first time in his life he felt sympathy for a servant, when the much-enduring man appeared once more.

'Bring my work back; I have changed my mind.' With that brief explanation she reclined luxuriously on the soft sofa cushions; swinging one of her balls of wool to and fro above her head, and looking at it lazily as she lay back. 'I have a remark to make, Horace,' she went on, when the door had closed on her messenger. 'It is only people in our rank of life who get good servants. Did you notice? Nothing upsets that man's temper. A servant in a poor family would have been impudent; a maid-of-all-work would have wondered when I was going to know my own mind.' The man returned with the embroidery. This time she received him graciously; she dismissed him with her thanks. 'Have you seen your mother lately, Horace?' she asked, suddenly sitting up and busying herself with her work.

'I saw her yesterday,' Horace answered.

'She understands, I hope, that I am not well enough to call on her? She is not offended with me?'

Horace recovered his serenity. The deference to his mother implied in Mercy's questions gently flattered his self-esteem. He resumed his place on the sofa.

'Offended with you!' he answered, smiling. 'My dear Grace, she sends you her love. And, more than that, she has a wedding-present for you.'

Mercy became absorbed in her work; she stooped close over the embroidery – so close that Horace could not see her face. 'Do you know what the present is?' she asked in lower tones; speaking absently.

'No. I only know it is waiting for you. Shall I go and get it to-day?'

She neither accepted nor refused the proposal – she went on with her work more industriously than ever.

'There is plenty of time,' Horace persisted. 'I can go before dinner.'

Still she took no notice; still she never looked up. 'Your mother is very kind to me,' she said, abruptly. 'I was afraid at one time that she would think me hardly good enough to be your wife.'

Horace laughed indulgently: his self-esteem was more gently flattered than ever.

'Absurd!' he exclaimed. 'My darling, you are connected with Lady Janet Roy. Your family is almost as good as ours.'

'Almost ?' she repeated. 'Only almost?'

The momentary levity of expression vanished from Horace's face. The family-question was far too serious a question to be lightly treated. A becoming shadow of solemnity stole over his manner. He looked as if it was Sunday, and he was just stepping into church.

'In OUR family,' he said, 'we trace back – by my father, to the Saxons: by my mother, to the Normans. Lady Janet's family is an old family – on her side only.'

Mercy dropped her embroidery, and looked Horace full in the face. She, too, attached no common importance to what she had next to say.

'If I had not been connected with Lady Janet,' she began, 'would you ever have thought of marrying me?'

'My love! what is the use of asking? You *are* connected with Lady Janet.'

She refused to let him escape answering her in that way.

'Suppose I had *not* been connected with Lady Janet,' she persisted, 'suppose I had only been a good girl, with nothing but my own merits to speak for me. What would your mother have said, then?'

Horace still parried the question – only to find the point of it pressed home on him once more.

'Why do you ask?' he said.

'I ask to be answered,' she rejoined. 'Would your mother have liked you to marry a poor girl, of no family – with nothing but her own virtues to speak for her?'

Horace was fairly pressed back to the wall.

'If you must know,' he replied, 'my mother would have refused to sanction such a marriage as that.'

'No matter how good the girl might have been?'

There was something defiant – almost threatening – in her tone. Horace was annoyed, and he showed it when he spoke.

'My mother would have respected the girl, without ceasing to respect herself,' he said. 'My mother would have remembered what was due to the family name.'

'And she would have said, No?'

'She would have said, No.'

'Ah!'

There was an undertone of angry contempt in the exclamation which made Horace start. 'What is the matter?' he asked.

'Nothing,' she answered, and took up her embroidery again. There he sat at her side, anxiously looking at her – his hope in the future centred in his marriage! In a week more, if she chose, she might enter that ancient family of which he had spoken so proudly, as his wife. 'Oh!' she thought, 'if I didn't love him! if I had only his merciless mother to think of!'

Uneasily conscious of some estrangement between them, Horace spoke again. 'Surely I have not offended you?' he said.

She turned towards him once more. The work dropped unheeded on her lap. Her grand eyes softened into tenderness. A smile trembled sadly on her delicate lips. She laid one hand caressingly on his shoulder. All the beauty of her voice lent its charm to the next words that she said to him. The woman's heart hungered in its misery for the comfort that could only come from his lips.

'*You* would have loved me, Horace – without stopping to think of the family name?'

The family name again! How strangely she persisted in coming back to that! Horace looked at her without answering; trying vainly to fathom what was passing in her mind.

She took his hand, and wrung it hard – as if she would wring the answer out of him in that way.

'*You* would have loved me?' she repeated.

The double spell of her voice and her touch was on him. He answered warmly, 'Under any circumstances! under any name!'

She put one arm round his neck, and fixed her eyes on his. 'Is that true?' she asked.

'True as the heaven is above us!'

She drank in those few commonplace words with a greedy delight. She forced him to repeat them in a new form.

'No matter who I might have been? For myself alone?'

'For yourself alone.'

She threw both arms round him, and laid her head passionately on his breast. 'I love you! I love you!! I love you!!!' her voice rose with hysterical vehemence at each repetition of the words – then suddenly sank to a low wailing cry of rage and despair. The sense of her true position towards him revealed itself in all its horror as the confession of her love escaped her lips. Her arms dropped from him; she flung herself back on the sofa cushions, hiding her face in her hands. 'Oh, leave me!' she moaned faintly, 'Go! go!'

Horace tried to wind his arm round her, and raise her. She started to her feet, and waved him back from her with a wild action of her hands, as if she was frightened of him. 'The wedding present!' she cried, seizing the first pretext that occurred to her. 'You offered to bring me your mother's present. I am dying to see what it is. Go, and get it!'

Horace tried to compose her. He might as well have tried to compose the winds and the sea.

'Go!' she repeated, pressing one clenched hand on her

bosom. 'I am not well. Talking excites me – I am hysterical; I shall be better alone. Get me the present. Go!'

'Shall I send Lady Janet? Shall I ring for your maid?'

'Send for nobody! ring for nobody! If you love me – leave me here by myself! leave me instantly!'

'I shall see you when I come back?'

'Yes! yes!'

There was no alternative but to obey her. Unwillingly and forebodingly Horace left the room.

She drew a deep breath of relief, and dropped into the nearest chair. If Horace had stayed a moment longer – she felt it, she knew it – her head would have given way; she would have burst out before him with the terrible truth. 'Oh!' she thought, pressing her cold hands on her burning eyes, 'if I could only cry, now there is nobody to see me!'

The room was empty, she had every reason for concluding that she was alone. And yet, at that very moment, there were ears that listened, there were eyes waiting to see her.

Little by little the door behind her which faced the library and led into the billiard-room was opened noiselessly from without, by an inch at a time. As the opening was enlarged, a hand in a black glove, an arm in a black sleeve, appeared, guiding the movement of the door. An interval of a moment passed, and the worn white face of Grace Roseberry showed itself stealthily, looking into the dining-room.

Her eyes brightened with vindictive pleasure as they discovered Mercy sitting alone at the further end of the room. Inch by inch she opened the door more widely, took one step forward, and checked herself. A sound, just audible at the far end of the conservatory had caught her ear.

She listened – satisfied herself that she was not mistaken – and, drawing back with a frown of displeasure, softly closed the door again, so as to hide herself from view. The sound that had disturbed her was the distant murmur of men's voices (apparently two in number) talking together in lowered tones, at the garden entrance to the conservatory.

Who were the men? and what would they do next? They might do one of two things: they might enter the drawing-room, or they might withdraw again by way of the garden. Kneeling behind the door, with her ear at the keyhole, Grace Roseberry waited the event.

CHAPTER THE SIXTEENTH

THEY MEET AGAIN

Absorbed in herself, Mercy failed to notice the opening door or to hear the murmur of voices in the conservatory.

The one terrible necessity which had been present to her mind at intervals for a week past was confronting her at that moment. She owed to Grace Roseberry the tardy justice of owning the truth. The longer her confession was delayed, the more cruelly she was injuring the woman whom she had robbed of her identity – the friendless woman who had neither witnesses nor papers to produce, who was powerless to right her own wrong. Keenly as she felt this, Mercy failed nevertheless to conquer the horror that shook her when she thought of the impending avowal. Day followed day, and still she shrank from the unendurable ordeal of confession – as she was shrinking from it now!

Was it fear for herself that closed her lips?

She trembled – as any human being in her place must have trembled – at the bare idea of finding herself thrown back again on the world, which had no place in it and no hope in it for *her*. But she could have overcome that terror – she could have resigned herself to that doom.

No! it was not the fear of the confession itself, or the fear of the consequences which must follow it, that still held her silent. The horror that daunted her was the horror of owning to Horace and to Lady Janet that she had cheated them out of their love.

Every day, Lady Janet was kinder and kinder. Every day, Horace was fonder and fonder of her. How could she confess to

Lady Janet? how could she own to Horace that she had imposed upon him? 'I can't do it. They are so good to me – I can't do it!' In that hopeless way it had ended during the seven days that had gone by. In that hopeless way it ended again now.

The murmur of the two voices at the further end of the conservatory ceased. The billiard-room door opened again slowly by an inch at a time.

Mercy still kept her place, unconscious of the events that were passing round her. Sinking under the hard stress laid on it, her mind had drifted little by little into a new train of thought. For the first time, she found the courage to question the future in a new way. Supposing her confession to have been made, or supposing the woman she had personated to have discovered the means of exposing the fraud, what advantage, she now asked herself, would Miss Roseberry derive from Mercy Merrick's disgrace?

Could Lady Janet transfer to the woman who was really her relative by marriage the affection which she had given to the woman who had pretended to be her relative? No! All the right in the world would not put the true Grace into the false Grace's vacant place. The qualities by which Mercy had won Lady Janet's love were the qualities which were Mercy's own. Lady Janet could do rigid justice – but hers was not the heart to give itself to a stranger (and to give itself unreservedly) a second time. Grace Roseberry would be formally acknowledged – and there it would end.

Was there hope in this new view?

Yes! There was the false hope of making the inevitable atonement by some other means than by the confession of the fraud.

What had Grace Roseberry actually lost by the wrong done to her? She had lost the salary of Lady Janet's 'companion and reader.' Say that she wanted money, Mercy had her savings from the generous allowance made her by Lady Janet; Mercy could offer money. Or say that she wanted employment, Mercy's interest with Lady Janet could offer employment, could offer anything Grace might ask for, if she would only come to terms.

Invigorated by the new hope, Mercy rose excitedly, weary of inaction in the empty room. She, who but a few minutes since had shuddered at the thought of their meeting again, was now eager to devise a means of finding her way privately to an interview with Grace. It should be done without loss of time – on that very day, if possible; by the next day at the latest. She looked round her mechanically, pondering how to reach the end in view. Her eyes rested by chance on the door of the billiard-room.

Was it fancy? or did she really see the door first open a little – then suddenly and softly close again?

Was it fancy? or did she really hear, at the same moment, a sound behind her as of persons speaking in the conservatory?

She paused, and, looking back in that direction, listened intently. The sound – if she had really heard it – was no longer audible. She advanced towards the billiard-room, to set her first doubt at rest. She stretched out her hand to open the door – when the voices (recognisable now as the voices of two men) caught her ear once more.

This time she was able to distinguish the words that were spoken.

'Any further orders, sir?' enquired one of the men.

'Nothing more,' replied the other.

Mercy started, and faintly flushed, as the second voice answered the first. She stood irresolute, close to the billiard-room, hesitating what to do next.

After an interval, the second voice made itself heard again, advancing nearer to the dining-room: 'Are you there aunt?' it asked, cautiously. There was a moment's pause. Then the voice spoke for the third time, sounding louder and nearer. 'Are you there?' it reiterated; 'I have something to tell you.' Mercy summoned her resolution, and answered, 'Lady Janet is not here.' She turned, as she spoke, towards the conservatory door, and confronted on the threshold Julian Gray.

They looked at one another without exchanging a word on either side. The situation – for widely different reasons – was equally embarrassing to both of them.

There – as Julian saw *her* – was the woman forbidden to him, the woman whom he loved.

There — as Mercy saw *him* — was the man whom she dreaded; the man whose actions (as she interpreted them) proved that he suspected her.

On the surface of it, the incidents which had marked their first meeting were now exactly repeated, with the one difference, that the impulse to withdraw this time appeared to be on the man's side, and not on the woman's. It was Mercy who spoke first.

'Did you expect to find Lady Janet here?' she asked, constrainedly.

He answered, on his part, more constrainedly still.

'It doesn't matter,' he said. 'Another time will do.'

He drew back as he made the reply. She advanced desperately, with the deliberate intention of detaining him by speaking again.

The attempt which he had made to withdraw, the constraint in his manner when he had answered, had instantly confirmed her in the false conviction that he, and he alone, had guessed the truth! If she was right — if he had secretly made discoveries abroad which placed her entirely at his mercy — the attempt to induce Grace to consent to a compromise with her would be manifestly useless. Her first and foremost interest now was to find out how she really stood in the estimation of Julian Gray. In a terror of suspense that turned her cold from head to foot, she stopped him on his way out, and spoke to him with the piteous counterfeit of a smile.

'Lady Janet is receiving some visitors,' she said. 'If you will wait here, she will be back directly.'

The effort of hiding her agitation from him had brought a passing colour into her cheeks. Worn and wasted as she was, the spell of her beauty was strong enough to hold him against his own will. All he had to tell Lady Janet was that he had met one of the gardeners in the conservatory, and had cautioned him as well as the lodge-keeper. It would have been easy to write this, and to send the note to his aunt on quitting the house. For the sake of his own peace of mind, for the sake of his duty to Horace, he was doubly bound to make the first polite excuse that occurred to him, and to leave Mercy as he had found her, alone in the room. He made the attempt, and hesitated. Despising himself for doing it, he allowed himself to look at her. Their eyes met. Julian stepped into the dining-room.

'If I am not in the way,' he said, confusedly, 'I will wait, as you kindly propose.'

She noticed his embarrassment; she saw that he was strongly restraining himself from looking at her again. Her own eyes dropped to the ground as she made the discovery. Her speech failed her; her heart throbbed faster and faster.

'If I look at him again' (was the thought in *her* mind) 'I shall fall at his feet and tell him all I have done!'

'If I look at her again' (was the thought in *his* mind) 'I shall fall at her feet and own that I am in love with her!'

With downcast eyes he placed a chair for her. With downcast eyes she bowed to him and took it. A dead silence followed. Never was any human misunderstanding more intricately complete than the misunderstanding which had now established itself between these two!

Mercy's work-basket was near her. She took it, and gained time for composing herself by pretending to arrange the coloured wools. He stood behind her chair, looking at the graceful turn of her head, looking at the rich masses of her hair. He reviled himself as the weakest of men, as the falsest of friends, for still remaining near her – and yet he remained.

The silence continued. The billiard-room door opened again noiselessly. The face of the listening woman appeared stealthily behind it.

At the same moment Mercy roused herself and spoke: 'Won't you sit down?' she said, softly; still not looking round at him; still busy with her basket of wools.

He turned to get a chair – turned so quickly that he saw the billiard-room door move, as Grace Roseberry closed it again.

'Is there anyone in that room?' he asked, addressing Mercy.

'I don't know,' she answered. 'I thought I saw the door open and shut again a little while ago.'

He advanced at once to look into the room. As he did so, Mercy dropped one of her balls of wool. He stopped to pick it up for her – then threw open the door and looked into the billiard-room. It was empty.

Had some person been listening, and had that person retreated in time to escape discovery? The open door of the smoking-room showed that room also to be empty. A third door was open – the door of the side-hall, leading into the grounds. After a moment's consideration, Julian closed it, and returned to the dining-room.

'I can only suppose,' he said to Mercy, 'that the billiard-room door was not properly shut, and that the draught of air from the hall must have moved it.'

She accepted the explanation in silence. He was, to all appearance, not quite satisfied with it himself. For a moment or two he looked about him uneasily. Then the old fascination fastened its hold on him again. Once more he looked at the graceful turn of her head, at the rich masses of her hair. The courage to put the critical question to him, now that she had lured him into remaining in the room, was still a courage that failed her. She remained as busy as ever with her work – too busy to look at him; too busy to speak to him. The silence became unendurable. He broke it by making a commonplace enquiry after her health.

'I am well enough to be ashamed of the anxiety I have caused and the trouble I have given,' she answered. 'To-day I have got downstairs for the first time. I am trying to do a little work.' She looked into the basket. The various specimens of wool in it were partly in balls and partly in loose skeins. The skeins were mixed and tangled. 'Here is sad confusion!' she exclaimed timidly, with a faint smile. 'How am I to set it right again?'

'Let me help you,' said Julian.

'You!'

'Why not?' he asked, with a momentary return of quaint humour which she remembered so well. 'You forget that I am a curate. Curates are privileged to make themselves useful to young ladies. Let me try.'

He took a stool at her feet, and set himself to unravel one of the tangled skeins. In a minute the wool was stretched on his hands, and the loose end was ready for Mercy to wind. There

was something in the trivial action, and in the homely attention
that it implied, which in some degree quieted her fear of him.
She began to roll the wool off his hands into a ball. Thus
occupied, she said the daring words which were to lead him
little by little into betraying his suspicions, if he did indeed
suspect the truth.

CHAPTER THE SEVENTEENTH

THE GUARDIAN ANGEL

'You were here when I fainted, were you not?' Mercy began.
'You must think me a sad coward, even for a woman.'

He shook his head. 'I am far from thinking that,' he replied.
'No courage could have sustained the shock which fell on you.
I don't wonder that you fainted. I don't wonder that you have
been ill.'

She paused in rolling up the ball of wool. What did those
words of unexpected sympathy mean? Was he laying a trap for
her? Urged by that serious doubt, she questioned him more
boldly.

'Horace tells me you have been abroad,' she said. 'Did you
enjoy your holiday?'

'It was no holiday. I went abroad because I thought it right to
make certain enquiries——' He stopped there, unwilling to
return to a subject that was painful to her.

Her voice sank, her fingers trembled round the ball of wool —
but she managed to go on.

'Did you arrive at any results?' she asked.

'At no results worth mentioning.'

The caution of that reply renewed her worst suspicions of
him. In sheer despair, she spoke out plainly.

'I want to know your opinion——' she began.

'Gently!' said Julian. 'You are entangling the wool again.'

'I want to know your opinion of the person who so terribly frightened me. Do you think her——'

'Do I think her – what?'

'Do you think her an adventuress?'

(As she said those words the branches of a shrub in the conservatory were noiselessly parted by a hand in a black glove. The face of Grace Roseberry appeared dimly behind the leaves. Undiscovered, she had escaped from the billiard-room, and had stolen her way into the conservatory as the safer hiding-place of the two. Behind the shrub she could see as well as listen. Behind the shrub she waited as patiently as ever.)

'I take a more merciful view,' Julian answered. 'I believe she is acting under a delusion. I don't blame her: I pity her.'

'You pity her?' as Mercy repeated the words, she took from Julian's hands the last lengths of wool left, and threw the imperfectly-wound skein back into the basket. 'Does that mean,' she resumed abruptly, 'that you believe her?'

Julian rose from his seat and looked at Mercy in astonishment.

'Good heavens, Miss Roseberry! what put such an idea as that into your head?'

'I am little better than a stranger to you,' she rejoined, with an effort to assume a jesting tone. 'You met that person before you met with me. It is not so very far from pitying her to believing her. How could I feel sure that you might not suspect me?'

'Suspect *you!*' he exclaimed. 'You don't know how you distress, how you shock me. Suspect *you!* The bare idea of it never entered my mind. The man doesn't live who trusts you more implicitly, who believes in you more devotedly than I do.'

His eyes, his voice, his manner, all told her that those words came from the heart. She contrasted his generous confidence in her (the confidence of which she was unworthy) with her ungracious distrust of him. Not only had she wronged Grace Roseberry – she had wronged Julian Gray. Could she deceive *him* as she had deceived the others? Could she meanly accept that implicit trust, that devoted belief? Never had she felt the base submissions which her own imposture condemned her to undergo, with a loathing of them so overwhelming as the loathing that she felt now. In horror of herself, she turned her head aside in silence, and shrank from meeting his eye. He noticed the movement, placing his own interpretation on it. Advancing closer, he asked anxiously if he had offended her?

'You don't know how your confidence touches me,' she said, without looking up. 'You little think how keenly I feel your kindness.'

She checked herself abruptly. Her fine tact warned her that she was speaking too warmly – that the expression of her gratitude might strike him as being strangely exaggerated. She handed him her work-basket, before he could speak again.

'Will you put it away for me?' she asked in her quieter tones. 'I don't feel able to work just now.'

His back was turned on her for a moment, while he placed the basket on a side table. In that moment her mind advanced at a bound from present to future. Accident might one day put the true Grace in possession of the proofs that she needed, and might reveal the false Grace to him in the identity that was her own. What would he think of her then? Could she make him tell her, without betraying herself? She determined to try.

'Children are notoriously insatiable if you once answer their questions, and women are nearly as bad,' she said, when Julian returned to her. 'Will your patience hold out if I go back for the third time to the person whom we have been speaking of?'

'Try me,' he answered with a smile.

'Suppose you had *not* taken your merciful view of her?'

'Yes?'

'Suppose you believed that she was wickedly bent on deceiving others for a purpose of her own – would you not shrink from such a woman in horror and disgust?'

'God forbid that I should shrink from any human creature!' he answered earnestly. 'Who among us has a right to do that?'

She hardly dared trust herself to believe him. 'You would still pity her?' she persisted, 'and still feel for her?'

'With all my heart.'

'Oh, how good you are!'

He held up his hand in warning. The tones of his voice deepened; the lustre of his eyes brightened. She had stirred in the depths of that great heart the faith in which the man lived – the steady principle which guided his modest and noble life.

'No!' he cried. 'Don't say that! Say that I try to love my neighbour as myself. Who but a Pharisee can believe he is better than another? The best among us to-day may, but for the mercy of God, be the worst among us to-morrow. The true Christian virtue is the virtue which never despairs of a fellow-creature. The true Christian faith believes in Man as well as in God. Frail and fallen as we are, we can rise on the wings of repentance from earth to heaven. Humanity is sacred. Humanity has its immortal destiny. Who shall dare say to man or woman, "There is no hope in you?" Who shall dare say the work is all vile, when that work bears on it the stamp of the Creator's hand?'

He turned away for a moment, struggling with the emotion which she had roused in him.

Her eyes, as they followed him, lighted with a momentary enthusiasm – then sank wearily in the vain regret which comes too late. Ah! if he could have been her friend and her adviser on the fatal day when she first turned her steps towards Mablethorpe House! She sighed bitterly as the hopeless aspiration wrung her heart. He heard the sigh; and, turning again, looked at her with a new interest in his face.

'Miss Roseberry,' he said.

She was still absorbed in the bitter memories of the past: she failed to hear him.

'Miss Roseberry,' he repeated, approaching her.

She looked up at him with a start.

'May I venture to ask you something?' he said gently.

She shrank at the question.

'Don't suppose I am speaking out of mere curiosity,' he went on. 'And pray don't answer me, unless you can answer without betraying any confidence which may have been placed in you.'

'Confidence!' she repeated. 'What confidence do you mean?'

'It has just struck me that you might have felt more than a common interest in the questions which you put to me a

moment since,' he answered. 'Were you by any chance speaking
of some unhappy woman – not the person who frightened you,
of course – but of some other woman whom you know?'

Her head sank slowly on her bosom. He had plainly no
suspicion that she had been speaking of herself: his tone and
manner both answered for it that his belief in her was as strong
as ever. Still, those last words made her tremble; she could not
trust herself to reply to them.

He accepted the bending of her head as a reply.

'Are you interested in her?' he asked next.

She faintly answered this time. 'Yes.'

'Have you encouraged her?'

'I have not dared to encourage her.'

His face lit up suddenly with enthusiasm. 'Go to her,' he said,
'and let me go with you and help you!'

The answer came faintly and mournfully. 'She has sunk too
low for that!'

He interrupted her with a gesture of impatience.

'What has she done?' he asked.

'She has deceived – basely deceived – innocent people who
trusted her. She has wronged – cruelly wronged – another
woman.'

For the first time, Julian seated himself at her side. The
interest that was now roused in him was an interest above
reproach. He could speak to Mercy without restraint; he could
look at Mercy with a pure heart.

'You judge her very harshly,' he said. 'Do *you* know how she
may have been tried and tempted?'

There was no answer.

'Tell me,' he went on, 'is the person whom she has injured
still living?'

'Yes.'

'If the person is still living, she may atone for the wrong. The
time may come when this sinner, too, may win our pardon and
deserve our respect.'

'Could *you* respect her?' Mercy asked, sadly. 'Can such a
mind as yours understand what she has gone through?'

A smile, kind and momentary, brightened his attentive face.

'You forget my melancholy experience,' he answered. 'Young as I am, I have seen more than most men of women who have sinned and suffered. Even after the little that you have told me, I think I can put myself in her place. I can well understand, for instance, that she may have been tempted beyond human resistance. Am I right?'

'You are right.'

'She may have had nobody near at the time to advise her, to warn her, to save her. Is it true?'

'It is true.'

'Tempted and friendless, self-abandoned to the evil impulse of the moment, this woman may have committed herself headlong to the act which she now vainly repents. She may long to make atonement, and may not know how to begin. All her energies may be crushed under the despair and horror of herself, out of which the truest repentance grows. Is such a woman as this all wicked, all vile? I deny it! She may have a noble nature; and she may show it nobly yet. Give her the opportunity she needs – and our poor fallen fellow-creature may take her place again among the best of us; honoured, blameless, happy once more!'

Mercy's eyes, resting eagerly on him while he was speaking, dropped again despondingly when he had done.

'There is no such future as that,' she answered, 'for the woman whom I am thinking of. She has lost her opportunity. She has done with hope.'

Julian gravely considered with himself for a moment.

'Let us understand each other,' he said. 'She has committed an act of deception to the injury of another woman. Was that what you told me?'

'Yes.'

'And she has gained something to her own advantage by the act?'

'Yes.'

'Is she threatened with discovery?'

'She is safe from discovery – for the present, at least.'

'Safe as long as she closes her lips?'

'As long as she closes her lips.'

'There is her opportunity!' cried Julian. 'Her future is before her. She has *not* done with hope.'

With clasped hands, in breathless suspense, Mercy looked at that inspiriting face, and listened to those golden words.

'Explain yourself,' she said. 'Tell her, through me, what she must do.'

'Let her own the truth,' answered Julian, 'without the base fear of discovery to drive her to it. Let her do justice to the woman whom she has wronged, while that woman is still powerless to expose her. Let her sacrifice everything that she has gained by the fraud to the sacred duty of atonement. If she can do that – for conscience' sake and for pity's sake – to her own prejudice, to her own shame, to her own loss – then her repentance has nobly revealed the noble nature that is in her; then she is a woman to be trusted, respected, beloved! If I saw the Pharisees and Fanatics of this lower earth passing her by in contempt, I would hold out my hand to her before them all. I would say to her in her solitude and her affliction, "Rise, poor wounded heart! Beautiful, purified soul, God's angels rejoice over you! Take your place among the noblest of God's creatures!"'

In those last sentences he unconsciously repeated the language in which he had spoken to his outcast congregation in the chapel of the Refuge. With tenfold power and tenfold persuasion they now found their way again to Mercy's heart. Softly, suddenly, mysteriously, a change passed over her. Her troubled face grew beautifully still. The shifting light of terror and suspense vanished from her grand grey eyes, and left in them the steady inner glow of a high and pure resolve.

There was a moment of silence between them. They both had need of silence. Julian was the first to speak again.

'Have I satisfied you that her opportunity is still before her?' he asked. 'Do you feel as I feel, that she has *not* done with hope?'

'You have satisfied me that the world holds no truer friend to her than you,' Mercy answered gently and gratefully. 'She shall prove herself worthy of your generous confidence in her. She shall show you yet that you have not spoken in vain.'

Still inevitably failing to understand her, he led the way to the door.

'Don't waste the precious time,' he said. 'Don't leave her cruelly to herself. If you can't go to her, let me go as your messenger, in your place.'

She stopped him by a gesture. He took a step back into the room, and paused; observing with surprise that she made no attempt to move from the chair that she occupied.

'Stay here,' she said to him in slightly-altered tones.

'Pardon me,' he rejoined, 'I don't understand you.'

'You will understand me directly. Give me a little time.'

He still lingered near the door, with his eyes fixed enquiringly on her. A man of a lower nature than his, or a man believing in Mercy less devotedly than he believed, would now have felt his first suspicion of her. Julian was as far as ever from suspecting her, even yet.

'Do you wish to be alone?' he asked considerately. 'Shall I leave you for awhile and return again?'

She looked up with a start of terror. 'Leave me?' she repeated, and suddenly checked herself on the point of saying more. Nearly half the length of the room divided them from each other. The words which she was longing to say were words that would never pass her lips unless she could see some encouragement in his face. 'No!' she cried out to him on a sudden, in her sore need, 'don't leave me! Come back to me!'

He obeyed her in silence. In silence on her side, she pointed to the chair near her. He took it. She looked at him, and checked herself again; resolute to make her terrible confession, yet still hesitating how to begin. Her woman's instinct whispered to her, 'Find courage in his touch!' She said to him, simply and artlessly said to him, 'Give me encouragement. Give me strength. Let me take your hand.' He neither answered nor moved. His mind seemed to have become suddenly preoccupied; his eyes rested on her vacantly; he was on the brink of discovering her secret; in another instant he would have found his way to the truth. In that instant, innocently as a sister might have taken it, she took his hand. The soft clasp of her fingers, clinging round his, roused his senses, fired his passion for her, swept out of his mind the pure aspirations which had filled it but the moment before, paralysed his perception when it was just penetrating the mystery of her disturbed manner and her strange words. All the man in him trembled under the rapture of her touch. But the thought of Horace was still present to him: his hand lay passive in hers; his eyes looked uneasily away from her.

She innocently strengthened her clasp of his hand. She innocently said to him, 'Don't look away from me. Your eyes give me courage.'

His hand returned the pressure of hers. He tasted to the full the delicious joy of looking at her. She had broken down his last reserves of self-control. The thought of Horace, the sense of honour, became obscured in him. In a moment more he might have said the words which he would have deplored for the rest of his life, if she had not stopped him by speaking first. 'I have more to say to you,' she resumed abruptly; feeling the animating resolution to lay her heart bare before him at last; 'more, far more, than I have said yet. Generous, merciful friend, let me say it *here!*'

She attempted to throw herself on her knees at his feet. He sprang from his seat and checked her, holding her with both his hands, raising her as he rose himself. In the words which had just escaped her, in the startling action which had accompanied them, the truth burst on him.

The guilty woman she had spoken of was herself!

CHAPTER THE EIGHTEENTH

THE SEARCH IN THE GROUNDS

While Mercy was almost in Julian's arms, while her bosom was just touching his – before a word more had passed his lips or hers – the library door opened.

Lady Janet Roy entered the room.

Grace Roseberry, still listening in the conservatory, saw the door open, and recognised the mistress of the house. She softly drew back and placed herself in safer hiding, beyond the range of view from the dining-room.

Lady Janet advanced no further than the threshold. She stood there and looked at her nephew and her adopted daughter in stern silence.

Mercy dropped into the chair at her side. Julian kept his place by her. His mind was still stunned by the discovery that had burst on it; his eyes still rested on her in a mute terror of enquiry. He was as completely absorbed in the one act of looking at her as if they had been still alone together in the room.

Lady Janet was the first of the three who spoke. She addressed herself to her nephew.

'You were right, Mr Julian Gray,' she said, with her bitterest emphasis of tone and manner. 'You ought to have found nobody in this room on your return but *me*. I detain you no longer. You are free to leave my house.'

Julian looked round at his aunt. She was pointing to the door. In the excited state of his sensibilities at that moment the action stung him to the quick. He answered without his customary consideration for his aunt's age and his aunt's position towards him:

'You apparently forget, Lady Janet, that you are not speaking to one of your footmen,' he said. 'There are serious reasons (of which you know nothing) for my remaining in your house a little longer. You may rely upon my trespassing on your hospitality as short a time as possible.'

He turned again to Mercy as he said those words, and surprised her timidly looking up at him. In the instant when their eyes met, the tumult of emotions struggling in him became suddenly stilled. Sorrow for her – compassionating sorrow – rose in the new calm and filled his heart. Now, and now only, he could read in the wasted and noble face how she had suffered. The pity which he had felt for the unnamed woman grew to a tenfold pity for *her*. The faith which he had professed – honestly professed – in the better nature of the unnamed woman strengthened into a tenfold faith in *her*. He addressed himself again to his aunt in a gentler tone. 'This lady,' he resumed, 'has something to say to me in private which she has not said yet. That is my reason and my apology for not immediately leaving the house.'

Still under the impression of what she had seen on entering the room, Lady Janet looked at him in angry amazement. Was Julian actually ignoring Horace Holmcroft's claims in the presence of Horace Holmcroft's betrothed wife? She appealed to her adopted daughter. 'Grace!' she exclaimed, 'have you heard him? Have you nothing to say? Must I remind you ——'

She stopped. For the first time in Lady Janet's experience of her young companion, she found herself speaking to ears that were deaf to her. Mercy was incapable of listening. Julian's eyes had told her that Julian had understood her at last.

Lady Janet turned to her nephew once more, and addressed him in the hardest words that she had ever spoken to her sister's son:

'If you have any sense of decency,' she said – 'I say nothing of a sense of honour – you will leave my house, and your acquaintance with that lady will end here. Spare me your protests and excuses; I can place but one interpretation on what I saw when I opened that door.'

'You entirely misunderstand what you saw when you opened that door,' Julian answered quietly.

'Perhaps I misunderstood the confession which you made to me not an hour ago?' retorted Lady Janet.

Julian cast a look of alarm at Mercy. 'Don't speak of it!' he said, in a whisper. 'She might hear you.'

'Do you mean to say she doesn't know you are in love with her?'

'Thank God, she has not the faintest suspicion of it!'

There was no mistaking the earnestness with which he made that reply. It proved his innocence as nothing else could have proved it. Lady Janet drew back a step – utterly bewildered; completely at a loss what to say or what to do next.

The silence that followed was broken by a knock at the library door. The man-servant – with news, and bad news, legibly written in his disturbed face and manner – entered the room.

In the nervous irritability of the moment, Lady Janet resented the servant's appearance as a positive offence on the part of the harmless man. 'Who sent for you?' she asked sharply. 'What do you mean by interrupting us?'

The servant made his excuses in an oddly bewildered manner.

'I beg your ladyship's pardon. I wished to take the liberty – I wanted to speak to Mr Julian Gray.'

'What is it?' asked Julian.

The man looked uneasily at Lady Janet, hesitated, and glanced at the door as if he wished himself well out of the room again.

'I hardly know if I can tell you, sir, before her ladyship,' he answered.

Lady Janet instantly penetrated the secret of her servant's hesitation.

'I know what has happened!' she said. 'That abominable woman has found her way here again. Am I right?'

The man's eyes helplessly consulted Julian.

'Yes? or no?' cried Lady Janet, imperatively.

'Yes, my lady.'

Julian at once assumed the duty of asking the necessary questions.

'Where is she?' he began.

'Somewhere in the grounds, as we suppose, sir.'

'Did *you* see her?'

'No, sir.'

'Who saw her?'

'The lodge-keeper's wife.'

This looked serious. The lodge-keeper's wife had been present while Julian had given his instructions to her husband. She was not likely to have mistaken the identity of the person whom she had discovered.

'How long since?' Julian asked next.

'Not very long, sir.'

'Be more particular. *How* long?'

'I didn't hear, sir.'

'Did the lodge-keeper's wife speak to the person when she saw her?'

'No, sir: she didn't get the chance, as I understand it. She is a stout woman, if you remember. The other was too quick for her – discovered her, sir; and (as the saying is) gave her the slip.'

'In what part of the grounds did this happen?'

The servant pointed in the direction of the side hall. 'In that part, sir. Either in the Dutch garden or the shrubbery. I am not sure which.'

It was plain, by this time, that the man's information was too imperfect to be practically of any use. Julian asked if the lodge-keeper's wife was in the house.

'No, sir. Her husband has gone out to search the grounds in her place, and she is minding the gate. They sent their boy with the message. From what I can make out from the lad, they would be thankful if they could get a word more of advice from you, sir.'

Julian reflected for a moment.

So far as he could estimate them, the probabilities were that the stranger from Mannheim had already made her way into the house; that she had been listening in the billiard-room; that she had found time enough to escape him on his approaching to open the door; and that she was now (in the servant's phrase) 'somewhere in the grounds,' after eluding the pursuit of the lodge-keeper's wife.

The matter was serious. Any mistake in dealing with it might lead to very painful results.

If Julian had correctly anticipated the nature of the confession which Mercy had been on the point of addressing to him, the person whom he had been the means of introducing into the house, was – what she had vainly asserted herself to be – no other than the true Grace Roseberry.

Taking this for granted, it was of the utmost importance that he should speak to Grace privately, before she committed herself to any rashly-renewed assertion of her claims, and before she could gain access to Lady Janet's adopted daughter. The landlady at her lodgings had already warned him that the object which she held steadily in view was to find her way to 'Miss Roseberry' when Lady Janet was not present to take her part, and when no gentlemen were at hand to protect her. 'Only let me meet her face to face' (she had said), 'and I will make her confess herself the imposter that she is!' As matters now stood, it was impossible to estimate too seriously the mischief which might ensue from such a meeting as this. Everything now depended on Julian's skilful management of an exasperated woman; and nobody, at that moment, knew where the woman was.

In this position of affairs, as Julian understood it, there seemed to be no other alternative than to make his enquiries instantly at the lodge, and then to direct the search in person.

He looked towards Mercy's chair as he arrived at this resolution. It was at a cruel sacrifice of his own anxieties and his own wishes that he deferred continuing the conversation with her, from the critical point at which Lady Janet's appearance had interrupted it.

Mercy had risen while he had been questioning the servant. The attention which she had failed to accord to what had passed between his aunt and himself she had given to the imperfect statement which he had extracted from the man. Her face plainly showed that she had listened as eagerly as Lady Janet had listened; with this remarkable difference between them, that Lady Janet looked frightened, and that Lady Janet's companion showed no signs of alarm. She appeared to be interested; perhaps anxious – nothing more.

Julian spoke a parting word to his aunt.

'Pray compose yourself,' he said. 'I have little doubt, when I can learn the particulars, that we shall easily find this person in the grounds. There is no reason to be uneasy. I am going to superintend the search myself. I will return to you as soon as possible.'

Lady Janet listened absently. There was a certain expression in her eyes which suggested to Julian that her mind was busy with some project of its own. He stopped as he passed Mercy, on his way out by the billiard-room door. It cost him a hard effort to control the contending emotions which the mere act of looking at her now awakened in him. His heart beat fast, his voice sank low, as he spoke to her:

'You shall see me again,' he said. 'I never was more in earnest in promising you my truest help and sympathy than I am now.'

She understood him. Her bosom heaved painfully; her eyes fell to the ground – she made no reply. The tears rose in Julian's eyes as he looked at her. He hurriedly left the room.

When he turned to close the billiard-room door, he heard Lady Janet say, 'I will be with you again in a moment, Grace; don't go away.'

Interpreting these words as meaning that his aunt had some business of her own to attend to in the library, he shut the door.

He had just advanced into the smoking-room beyond, when he thought he heard the door opened again. He turned round. Lady Janet had followed him.

'Do you wish to speak to me?' he asked.

'I want something of you,' Lady Janet answered, 'before you go.'

'What is it?'

'Your card.'

'My card?'

'You have just told me not to be uneasy,' said the old lady. 'I *am* uneasy, for all that. I don't feel as sure as you do that this woman really is in the grounds. She may be lurking somewhere in the house, and she may appear when your back is turned. Remember what you told me.'

Julian understood the allusion. He made no reply.

'The people at the police-station close by,' pursued Lady Janet, 'have instructions to send an experienced man, in plain clothes, to any address indicated on your card the moment they receive it. That is what you told me. For Grace's protection, I want your card before you leave us.'

It was impossible for Julian to mention the reasons which now forbade him to make use of his own precautions – in the very face of the emergency which they had been especially designed to meet. How could he declare the true Grace Roseberry to be mad? How could he give the true Grace Roseberry in to custody? On the other hand, he had personally pledged himself (when the circumstances appeared to require it) to place the means of legal protection from insult and annoyance at his aunt's disposal. And now, there stood Lady

Janet, unaccustomed to have her wishes disregarded by anybody, with her hand extended, waiting for the card!

What was to be done? The one way out of the difficulty appeared to be to submit for the moment. If he succeeded in discovering the missing woman, he could easily take care that she should be subjected to no needless indignity. If she contrived to slip into the house in his absence, he could provide against that contingency by sending a second card privately to the police-station, forbidding the officer to stir in the affair until he had received further orders. Julian made one stipulation only before he handed his card to his aunt.

'You will not use this, I am sure, without positive and pressing necessity,' he said. 'But I must make one condition. Promise me to keep my plan for communicating with the police a strict secret——'

'A strict secret from Grace?' interposed Lady Janet. (Julian bowed.) 'Do you suppose I want to frighten her? Do you think I have not had anxiety enough about her already? Of course I shall keep it a secret from Grace!'

Reassured on this point, Julian hastened out into the grounds. As soon as his back was turned Lady Janet lifted the gold pencil-case that hung at her watch-chain, and wrote on her nephew's card (for the information of the officer in plain clothes): '*You are wanted at Mablethorpe House.*' This done, she put the card into the old-fashioned pocket of her dress, and returned to the dining-room.

Grace was waiting, in obedience to the instructions which she had received.

For the first moment or two not a word was spoken on either side. Now that she was alone with her adopted daughter, a certain coldness and hardness began to show itself in Lady Janet's manner. The discovery that she had made, on opening the drawing-room door, still hung on her mind. Julian had certainly convinced her that she had misinterpreted what she had seen; but he had convinced her against her will. 'There is some secret understanding between them,' thought the old lady, 'and She is to blame; the women always are!'

Mercy still waited to be spoken to; pale and quiet, silent and submissive. Lady Janet – in a highly uncertain state of temper – was obliged to begin.

'My dear!' she called out sharply.

'Yes, Lady Janet.'

'How much longer are you going to sit there, with your mouth shut up and your eyes on the carpet? Have you no opinion to offer on this alarming state of things? You heard what the man said to Julian – I saw you listening. Are you horribly frightened?'

'No, Lady Janet.'

'Not even nervous?'

'No, Lady Janet.'

'Ha! I should hardly have given you credit for so much courage after my experience of you a week ago. I congratulate you on your recovery. Do you hear? I congratulate you on your recovery.'

'Thank you, Lady Janet.'

'I am not so composed as you are. We were an excitable set in *my* youth – and I haven't got the better of it yet. I feel nervous. Do you hear? I feel nervous.'

'I am sorry, Lady Janet.'

'You are very good. Do you know what I am going to do?'

'No, Lady Janet.'

'I am going to summon the household. When I say the household I mean the men; the women are of no use. I am afraid I fail to attract your attention?'

'You have my best attention, Lady Janet.'

'You are very good again. I said the women were of no use.'

'Yes, Lady Janet?'

'I mean to place a man-servant on guard at every entrance to the house. I am going to do it at once. Will you come with me?'

'Can I be of any use if I go with your ladyship?'

'You can't be of the slightest use. I give the orders in this house – not you. I had quite another motive in asking you to come with me. I am more considerate of you than you seem to think – I don't like leaving you here by yourself. Do you understand?'

'I am much obliged to your ladyship. I don't mind being left here by myself.'

'You don't mind? I never heard of such heroism in my life – out of a novel! Suppose that crazy wretch should find her way in here?'

'She would not frighten me this time, as she frightened me before.'

'Not too fast, my young lady! Suppose – Good Heavens! now I think of it, there is the conservatory. Suppose she should be hidden in there? Julian is searching the grounds. Who is to search the conservatory?'

'With your ladyship's permission, *I* will search the conservatory.'

'You!!!'

'With your ladyship's permission.'

'I can hardly believe my own ears! Well, "Live and learn" is an old proverb. I thought I knew your character. This *is* a change!'

'You forget, Lady Janet (if I may venture to say so), that the circumstances are changed. She took me by surprise on the last occasion; I am prepared for her now.'

'Do you really feel as coolly as you speak?'

'Yes, Lady Janet.'

'Have your own way, then. I shall do one thing, however, in case of your having over-estimated your own courage. I shall place one of the men in the library. You will only have to ring for him, if anything happens. He will give the alarm – and I shall act accordingly. I have my plan,' said her ladyship, comfortably conscious of the card in her pocket. 'Don't look as if you wanted to know what it is. I have no intention of saying anything about it – except that it will do. Once more, and for the last time – do you stay here? or do you go with me?'

'I stay here.'

She respectfully opened the library door for Lady Janet's departure as she made that reply. Throughout the interview she had been carefully and coldly deferential; she had not once lifted her eyes to Lady Janet's face. The conviction in her that a few hours more would, in all probability, see her dismissed from the house, had of necessity fettered every word that she spoke – had morally separated her already from the injured mistress whose love she had won in disguise. Utterly incapable of attributing the change in her young companion to the true motive, Lady Janet left the room to summon her domestic garrison, thoroughly puzzled, and (as a necessary consequence of that condition) thoroughly displeased.

Still holding the library door in her hand, Mercy stood watching with a heavy heart the progress of her benefactress down the length of the room, on the way to the front hall beyond. She had honestly loved and respected the warm-hearted, quick-tempered old lady. A sharp pang of pain wrung her as she thought of the time when even the chance utterance of her name would become an unpardonable offence in Lady Janet's house.

But there was no shrinking in her now from the ordeal of the confession. She was not only anxious, she was impatient for Julian's return. Before she slept that night, Julian's confidence in her should be a confidence that she had deserved.

'Let her own the truth, without the base fear of discovery to drive her to it. Let her do justice to the woman whom she has wronged, while that woman is still powerless to expose her. Let her sacrifice everything that she has gained by the fraud to the sacred duty of atonement. If she can do that, then her repentance has nobly revealed the noble nature that is in her; then, she is a woman to be trusted, respected, beloved.' Those words were as vividly present to her as if she still heard them falling from his lips. Those other words which followed them rang as grandly as ever in her ears: 'Rise, poor wounded heart! Beautiful, purified soul, God's angels rejoice over you! Take your place among the noblest of God's creatures!' Did the woman live who could hear Julian Gray say that, and who could hesitate, at any sacrifice, at any loss, to justify his belief in her? 'Oh!' she thought, longingly, while her eyes followed Lady Janet to the end of the library, 'if your worst fears could only be realised! If I could only see Grace Roseberry in this room, how fearlessly I could meet her now!'

She closed the library door, while Lady Janet opened the other door which led into the hall.

As she turned and looked back into the dining-room, a cry of astonishment escaped her.

There – as if in answer to the aspiration which was still in her mind; there, established in triumph on the chair that she just left – sat Grace Roseberry, in sinister silence, waiting for her.

CHAPTER THE NINETEENTH

THE EVIL GENIUS

Recovering from the first overpowering sensation of surprise, Mercy rapidly advanced, eager to say her first penitent words. Grace stopped her by a warning gesture of the hand. 'No nearer to me,' she said, with a look of contemptuous command. 'Stay where you are.'

Mercy paused. Grace's reception had startled her. She instinctively took the chair nearest to her to support herself. Grace raised a warning hand for the second time, and issued another command:

'I forbid you to be seated in my presence. You have no right to be in this house at all. Remember, if you please, who you are, and who I am.'

The tone in which those words were spoken was an insult in itself. Mercy suddenly lifted her head; the angry answer was on her lips. She checked it, and submitted in silence. 'I will be worthy of Julian Gray's confidence in me,' she thought, as she stood patiently by the chair. 'I will bear anything from the woman whom I have wronged.'

In silence the two faced each other: alone together, for the first time since they had met in the French cottage. The contrast between them was strange to see. Grace Roseberry, seated in her chair, little and lean, with her dull white complexion, with her

hard threatening face, with her shrunken figure clad in its plain
and poor black garments, looked like a being of a lower sphere
compared with Mercy Merrick, standing erect in her rich silken
dress; her tall, shapely figure towering over the little creature
before her, her grand head bent in graceful submission; gentle,
patient, beautiful; a woman whom it was a privilege to look at
and a distinction to admire. If a stranger had been told that those
two had played their parts in a romance of real life – that one of
them was really connected by the ties of relationship with Lady
Janet Roy, and that the other had audaciously ventured to
personate her – he would inevitably, if it had been left to him to
guess which was which, have picked out Grace as the
counterfeit, and Mercy as the true woman.

Grace broke the silence. She had waited to open her lips until
she had eyed her conquered victim all over, with disdainfully
minute attention, from head to foot.

'Stand there. I like to look at you,' she said, speaking with a
spiteful relish of her own cruel words. 'It's no use fainting this
time. You have not got Lady Janet Roy to bring you to. There
are no gentlemen here to-day to pity you and pick you up.
Mercy Merrick, I have got you at last. Thank God, my turn has
come! You can't escape me now!'

All the littleness of heart and mind which had first shown
itself in Grace at the meeting in the cottage, when Mercy told
the sad story of her life, now revealed itself once more. The
woman who, in those past times, had felt no impulse to take a
suffering and a penitent fellow-creature by the hand, was the
same woman who could feel no pity, who could spare no
insolence of triumph, now. Mercy's sweet voice answered her
patiently, in low pleading tones.

'I have not avoided you,' she said. 'I would have gone to you
of my own accord if I had known that you were here. It is my
heartfelt wish to own that I have sinned against you, and to
make all the atonement that I can. I am too anxious to deserve
your forgiveness to have any fear of seeing you.'

Conciliatory as the reply was, it was spoken with a simple and
modest dignity of manner which roused Grace Roseberry to
fury.

'How dare you speak to me as if you were my equal?' she burst out. 'You stand there and answer me as if you had your right and your place in this house. You audacious woman! *I* have my right and my place here – and what am I obliged to do? I am obliged to hang about in the grounds, and fly from the sight of the servants, and hide like a thief, and wait like a beggar: and all for what? For the chance of having a word with *you*. Yes! you, madam, with the air of the Refuge and the dirt of the streets on you!'

Mercy's head sank lower; her hand trembled as it held the back of the chair.

It was hard to bear the reiterated insults heaped on her, but Julian's influence still made itself felt. She answered as patiently as ever:

'If it is your pleasure to use hard words to me,' she said, 'I have no right to resent them.'

'You have no right to anything!' Grace retorted. 'You have no right to the gown on your back. Look at Yourself, and look at Me!' Her eyes travelled with a tigerish stare over Mercy's costly silk dress. 'Who gave you that dress? who gave you those jewels? I know! Lady Janet gave them to Grace Roseberry. Are *you* Grace Roseberry? That dress is mine. Take off your bracelets and your brooch. They were meant for me.'

'You may soon have them, Miss Roseberry. They will not be in my possession many hours longer.'

'What do you mean?'

'However badly you may use me, it is my duty to undo the harm that I have done. I am bound to do you justice – I am determined to confess the truth.'

Grace smiled scornfully.

'You confess!' she said. 'Do you think I am fool enough to believe that? You are one shameful brazen lie from head to foot! Are *you* the woman to give up your silks and your jewels and your position in this house, and to go back to the Refuge of your own accord! Not you! not you!'

A first faint flush of colour showed itself stealing slowly over Mercy's face; but she still held resolutely by the good influence which Julian had left behind him. She could still say to herself, 'Anything rather than disappoint Julian Gray!' Sustained by the courage which *he* had called to life in her, she submitted to her martyrdom as bravely as ever. But there was an ominous change in her now: she could only submit in silence; she could no longer trust herself to answer.

The mute endurance in her face additionally exasperated Grace Roseberry.

'*You* won't confess,' she went on. 'You have had a week to confess in, and you have not done it yet. No, no! you are of the sort that cheat and lie to the last. I am glad of it; I shall have the joy of exposing you myself before the whole house. I shall be the blessed means of casting you back on the streets. Oh! it will be almost worth all I have gone through, to see you with a policeman's hand on your arm, and the mob pointing at you and mocking you on your way to gaol!'

This time the sting struck deep; the outrage was beyond endurance. Mercy gave the woman who had again and again deliberately insulted her a first warning.

'Miss Roseberry,' she said, 'I have borne without a murmur the bitterest words you could say to me. Spare me any more insults. Indeed, indeed, I am eager to restore you to your just rights. With my whole heart I say it to you – I am resolved to confess everything!'

She spoke with trembling earnestness of tone. Grace listened with a hard smile of incredulity and a hard look of contempt.

'You are not far from the bell,' she said; 'ring it.'

Mercy looked at her in speechless surprise.

'You are a perfect picture of repentance – you are dying to own the truth,' pursued the other satirically. 'Own it before everybody, and own it at once. Call in Lady Janet – call in Mr Gray and Mr Holmcroft – call in the servants. Go down on your knees and acknowledge yourself an impostor before them all. Then I will believe you – not before.'

'Don't, don't turn me against you!' cried Mercy entreatingly.

'What do I care whether you are against me or not?'

'Don't – for your own sake don't go on provoking me much longer!'

'For my own sake? You insolent creature! Do you mean to threaten me?'

With a last desperate effort – her heart beating faster and faster, the blood burning hotter and hotter in her cheeks – Mercy still controlled herself.

'Have some compassion on me!' she pleaded. 'Badly as I have behaved to you, I am still a woman like yourself. I can't face the shame of acknowledging what I have done before the whole house. Lady Janet treats me like a daughter; Mr Holmcroft has engaged himself to marry me. I can't tell Lady Janet and Mr Holmcroft to their faces that I have cheated them out of their love. But they shall know it for all that. I can, and will, before I rest to-night, tell the whole truth to Mr Julian Gray.'

Grace burst out laughing. 'Aha!' she exclaimed, with a cynical outburst of gaiety. 'Now we have come to it at last!'

'Take care!' said Mercy. 'Take care!'

'Mr Julian Gray! I was behind the billiard-room door – I saw you coax Mr Julian Gray to come in. Confession loses all its horrors, and becomes quite a luxury, with Mr Julian Gray!'

'No more, Miss Roseberry! no more! For God's sake don't put me beside myself! You have tortured me enough already.'

'You haven't been on the streets for nothing. You are a woman with resources; you know the value of having two strings to your bow. If Mr Holmcroft fails you, you have got Mr Julian Gray. Ah! you sicken me. *I'll* see that Mr Holmcroft's eyes are opened; he shall know what a woman he might have married, but for Me——'

She checked herself; the next refinement of insult remained suspended on her lips.

The woman whom she had outraged suddenly advanced on her. Her eyes, staring helplessly upward, saw Mercy Merrick's face, white with the terrible anger which drives the blood back on the heart, bending threateningly over her.

'"You will see that Mr Holmcroft's eyes are opened,"' Mercy slowly repeated; '"he shall know what a woman he might have married, but for You!"'

She paused, and followed those words by a question which struck a creeping terror through Grace Roseberry, from the hair of her head to the soles of her feet:

'*Who are you?*'

The suppressed fury of look and tone which accompanied
that question told, as no violence could have told it, that the
limits of Mercy's endurance had been found at last. In the
guardian angel's absence, the evil genius had done its evil work.
The better nature which Julian Gray had brought to life sank,
poisoned by the vile venom of a woman's spiteful tongue. An
easy and a terrible means of avenging the outrages heaped on
her was within Mercy's reach if she chose to take it. In the
frenzy of her indignation she never hesitated — she took it.

'Who are you?' she asked for the second time.

Grace roused herself and attempted to speak. Mercy stopped
her with a scornful gesture of her hand.

'I remember!' she went on, with the same fiercely suppressed
rage. 'You are the madwoman from the German hospital who
came here a week ago. I'm not afraid of you this time. Sit down
and rest yourself — Mercy Merrick.'

Deliberately giving her that name to her face, Mercy turned
from her and took the chair which Grace had forbidden her to
occupy when the interview began.

Grace started to her feet.

'What does this mean?' she asked.

'It means,' answered Mercy contemptuously, 'that I recall
every word I said to you just now. It means that I am resolved
to keep my place in this house.'

'Are you out of your senses?'

'You are not far from the bell. Ring it. Do what you told *me*
to do. Call in the whole household, and ask them which of us is
mad — you or I?'

'Mercy Merrick! you shall repent this to the last hour of your
life!'

Mercy rose again and fixed her flashing eyes on the woman
who still defied her.

'I have had enough of you!' she said. 'Leave the house while
you *can* leave it. Stay here, and I will send for Lady Janet Roy.'

'You can't send for her! You daren't send for her!'

'I can and I dare. You have not a shadow of a proof against
me. I have got the papers; I am in possession of the place; I
have established myself in Lady Janet's confidence. I mean to

deserve your opinion of me – I will keep my dresses and my jewels, and my position in the house. I deny that I have done wrong. Society has used me cruelly; I owe nothing to Society. I have a right to take any advantage of it if I can. I deny that I have injured you. How was I to know that you would come to life again? Have I degraded your name and your character? I have done honour to both. I have won everybody's liking and respect. Do you think Lady Janet would have loved you as she loves me? Not she! I tell you to your face, I have filled the false position more creditably than you could have filled the true one, and I mean to keep it. I won't give up your name; I won't restore your character! Do your worst, I defy you!'

She poured out those reckless words in one headlong flow which defied interruption. There was no answering her until she was too breathless to say more. Grace seized the opportunity the moment it was within her reach.

'You defy me?' she returned resolutely. 'You won't defy me long. I have written to Canada. My friends will speak for me.'

'What of it, if they do? Your friends are strangers here. I am Lady Janet's adopted daughter. Do you think she will believe your friends? She will believe me. She will burn their letters, if they write. She will forbid the house to them if they come. I shall be Mrs Horace Holmcroft in a week's time. Who can shake *my* position? Who can injure Me?'

'Wait a little. You forget the matron at the Refuge?'

'Find her if you can. I never told you her name. I never told you where the Refuge was.'

'I will advertise your name, and find the matron in that way.'

'Advertise in every newspaper in London. Do you think I gave a stranger like you the name I really bore in the Refuge? I gave you the name I assumed when I left England. No such person as Mercy Merrick is known to the matron. No such person is known to Mr Holmcroft. He saw me at the French cottage while you were senseless on the bed. I had my grey cloak on; neither he nor any of them saw me in my nurse's dress. Enquiries have been made about me on the Continent – and (I happen to know, from the person who made them) with no result. I am safe in your place; I am known by your name. I am Grace Roseberry; and you are Mercy Merrick. Disprove it if you can!'

Summing up the unassailable security of her false position in those closing words, Mercy pointed significantly to the billiard-room door.

'You were hiding there, by your own confession,' she said. 'You know your way out by that door. Will you leave the room?'

'I won't stir a step!'

Mercy walked to a side-table, and struck the bell placed on it.

At the same moment, the billiard-room door opened. Julian Gray appeared – returning from his unsuccessful search in the grounds.

He had barely crossed the threshold before the library-door was thrown open by the servant posted in the room. The man drew back respectfully, and gave admission to Lady Janet Roy. She was followed by Horace Holmcroft, with his mother's wedding-present to Mercy in his hand.

CHAPTER THE TWENTIETH

THE POLICEMAN IN PLAIN CLOTHES

Julian looked round the room, and stopped at the door which he had just opened.

His eyes rested – first on Mercy, next on Grace.

The disturbed faces of both the women told him but too plainly that the disaster which he had dreaded had actually happened. They had met without any third person to interfere between them. To what extremities the hostile interview might have led, it was impossible for him to guess. In his aunt's presence, he could only wait his opportunity of speaking to Mercy, and be ready to interpose if anything was ignorantly done which might give just cause of offence to Grace.

Lady Janet's course of action, on entering the dining-room, was in perfect harmony with Lady Janet's character.

Instantly discovering the intruder, she looked sharply at Mercy. 'What did I tell you?' she asked. 'Are you frightened? No! not in the least frightened! Well done, my dear!' She had recovered her temper: she took Mercy's hand as kindly as ever, and gave it a little friendly squeeze – then turned to the servant. 'Wait in the library; I may want you again.' She looked next at Julian. 'Leave it all to me; I can manage it.' She made a sign to Horace: 'Stay where you are, and hold your tongue.' Having now said all that was necessary to everyone else, she advanced to the part of the room in which Grace was standing, with lowering brows and firmly-shut lips, defiant of everybody.

'I have no desire to offend you, or to act harshly towards you,' her ladyship began, very quietly. 'I only suggest that your visits to my house cannot possibly lead to any satisfactory result. I hope you will not oblige me to make use of harder words than these – I hope you will understand that I wish you to withdraw.'

The order of dismissal could hardly have been issued with more humane consideration for the supposed mental infirmity of the person to whom it was addressed. Grace instantly resisted it in the plainest possible terms.

'In justice to my father's memory, and in justice to myself,' she answered, 'I insist on a hearing. I refuse to withdraw.' She deliberately took a chair and seated herself in the presence of the mistress of the house.

Lady Janet waited a moment – steadily controlling herself. In the interval of silence, Julian seized the opportunity of remonstrating with Grace.

'Is this what you promised me?' he asked gently. 'You gave me your word that you would not return to Mablethorpe House.'

Before he could say more, Lady Janet spoke again. She began her answer to Grace by pointing with a peremptory forefinger to the library door.

'If you have not made up your mind to take my advice by the time I have walked back to that door,' she said, 'I will put it out of your power to set me at defiance. I am used to be obeyed, and I will be obeyed. You force me to use hard words. I warn you, before it is too late. Go.'

She returned slowly towards the library. Julian attempted to interfere with another word of remonstrance. His aunt stopped him by a gesture which said plainly, 'I insist on acting for. myself.' He looked next at Mercy. Would she remain passive? Yes. She never lifted her head; she never moved from the place in which she was standing, apart from the rest. Horace himself tried to attract her attention, and tried in vain.

Arrived at the library door, Lady Janet looked over her shoulder at the little immovable black figure in the chair.

'Will you go?' she asked for the last time.

Grace started up angrily from her seat, and fixed her viperish eyes on Mercy.

'I won't be turned out of your ladyship's house in the presence of that imposter,' she said. 'I may yield to force – but I will yield to nothing else. I insist on my right to the place that she has stolen from me. It's no use scolding me,' she added, turning doggedly to Julian. 'As long as that woman is here under my name, I can't and won't keep away from the house. I warn her, in your presence, that I have written to my friends in Canada! I dare her before you all to deny that she is the outcast and adventuress, Mercy Merrick!'

The challenge forced Mercy to take part in the proceedings in her own defence. She had pledged herself to meet and defy Grace Roseberry on her own ground. She attempted to speak – Horace stopped her.

'You degrade yourself if you answer her,' he said. 'Take my arm, and let us leave the room.'

'Yes! Take her out!' cried Grace. 'She may well be ashamed to face an honest woman. It's her place to leave the room – not mine!'

Mercy drew her hand out of Horace's arm. 'I decline to leave the room,' she said quietly.

Horace still tried to persuade her to withdraw. 'I can't bear to hear you insulted,' he rejoined. 'The woman offends me, though I know she is not responsible for what she says.'

'Nobody's endurance will be tried much longer,' said Lady Janet. She glanced at Julian, and, taking from her pocket the card which he had given to her, opened the library door.

'Go to the police-station,' she said to the servant in an undertone, 'and give that card to the inspector on duty. Tell him there is not a moment to lose.'

'Stop!' said Julian, before his aunt could close the door again.

'Stop?' repeated Lady Janet, sharply. 'I have given the man his orders. What do you mean?'

'Before you send the card, I wish to say a word in private to this lady,' replied Julian, indicating Grace. 'When that is done,' he continued, approaching Mercy, and pointedly addressing himself to her, 'I shall have a request to make – I shall ask you to give me an opportunity of speaking to you without interruption.'

His tone pointed the allusion. Mercy shrank from looking at him. The signs of painful agitation began to show themselves in her shifting colour and her uneasy silence. Roused by Julian's significantly distant reference to what had passed between them, her better impulses were struggling already to recover their influence over her. She might, at that critical moment, have yielded to the promptings of her own nobler nature – she might have risen superior to the galling remembrance of the insults that had been heaped upon her – if Grace's malice had not seen in her hesitation a means of referring offensively once again to her interview with Julian Gray.

'Pray don't think twice about trusting him alone with me,' she said, with a sardonic affectation of politeness. '*I* am not interested in making a conquest of Mr Julian Gray.'

The jealous distrust in Horace (already awakened by Julian's request) now attempted to assert itself openly. Before he could speak, Mercy's indignation had dictated Mercy's answer.

'I am much obliged to you, Mr Gray,' she said, addressing Julian (but still not raising her eyes to his). 'I have nothing more to say to you. There is no need for any further conversation between us.'

In those rash words she recalled the confession to which she stood pledged. In those rash words she committed herself to keeping the position that she had usurped, in the face of the woman whom she had deprived of it!

Horace was silenced, but not satisfied. He saw Julian's eyes fixed in sad and searching attention on Mercy's face while she was speaking. He heard Julian sigh to himself when she had done. He observed Julian – after a moment's serious consideration, and a moment's glance backward at the stranger in the poor black clothes – lift his head with the air of a man who had taken a sudden resolution.

'Bring me that card directly,' he said to the servant. His tone announced that he was not to be trifled with. The man obeyed.

Without answering Lady Janet – who still peremptorily insisted on her right to act for herself – Julian took the pencil from his pocket-book, and added his signature to the writing already inscribed on the card. When he had handed it back to the servant he made his apologies to his aunt.

'Pardon me for venturing to interfere,' he said. 'There is a serious reason for what I have done, which I will explain to you at a fitter time. In the meanwhile I offer no further obstruction to the course which you propose taking. On the contrary, I have just assisted you in gaining the end that you have in view.'

As he said that, he held up the pencil with which he had signed his name.

Lady Janet, naturally perplexed, and (with some reason perhaps) offended as well, made no answer. She waved her hand to the servant, and sent him away with the card.

There was silence in the room. The eyes of all the persons present turned more or less anxiously on Julian. Mercy was vaguely surprised and alarmed. Horace, like Lady Janet, felt offended, without clearly knowing why. Even Grace Roseberry herself was subdued by her own presentiment of some coming interference for which she was completely unprepared. Julian's words and actions, from the moment when he had written on the card, were involved in a mystery to which not one of the persons round him held the clue.

The motive which had animated his conduct may, nevertheless, be described in two words: Julian still held to his faith in the inbred nobility of Mercy's nature.

He had inferred, with little difficulty, from the language which Grace had used towards Mercy in his presence, that the injured woman must have taken pitiless advantage of her position at the interview which he had interrupted. Instead of appealing to Mercy's sympathies and Mercy's sense of right – instead of accepting the expression of her sincere contrition, and encouraging her to make the completest and the speediest atonement – Grace had evidently outraged and insulted her. As a necessary result, her endurance had given way – under her own sense of intolerable severity and intolerable wrong.

The remedy for the mischief thus done was (as Julian had first seen it) to speak privately with Grace – to soothe her by owning that his opinion of the justice of her claims had undergone a change in her favour – and then to persuade her, in her own interests, to let him carry to Mercy such expressions of apology and regret as might lead to a friendly understanding between them.

With those motives, he had made his request to be permitted to speak separately to the one and the other. The scene that had followed, the new insult offered by Grace, and the answer which it had wrung from Mercy, had convinced him that no such interference as he had contemplated would have the slightest prospect of success.

The one remedy now left to try was the desperate remedy of letting things take their course, and trusting implicitly to Mercy's better nature for the result.

Let her see the police-officer in plain clothes enter the room. Let her understand clearly what the result of his interference would be. Let her confront the alternative of consigning Grace Roseberry to a madhouse, or of confessing the truth – and what would happen? If Julian's confidence in her was a confidence soundly placed, she would nobly pardon the outrages that had been heaped upon her, and she would do justice to the woman whom she had wronged.

If, on the other hand, his belief in her was nothing better than the blind belief of an infatuated man – if she faced the alternative, and persisted in asserting her assumed identity, what then?

Julian's faith in Mercy refused to let that darker side of the question find a place in his thoughts. It rested entirely with him to bring the officer into the house. He had prevented Lady Janet from making any mischievous use of his card, by sending to the police-station, and warning them to attend to no message which they might receive unless the card produced bore his signature. Knowing the responsibility that he was taking on himself — knowing that Mercy had made no confession to him to which it was possible to appeal — he had signed his name without an instant's hesitation: and there he stood now, looking at the woman whose better nature he was determined to vindicate, the only calm person in the room.

Horace's jealousy saw something suspiciously suggestive of a private understanding in Julian's earnest attention and in Mercy's downcast face. Having no excuse for open interference, he made an effort to part them.

'You spoke just now,' he said to Julian, 'of wishing to say a word in private to that person.' (He pointed to Grace.) 'Shall we retire, or will you take her into the library?'

'I refuse to have anything to say to him,' Grace burst out, before Julian could answer. 'I happen to know that he is the last person to do me justice. *He* has been effectually hoodwinked. If I speak to anybody privately, it ought to be to you. *You* have the greatest interest of any of them in finding out the truth.'

'What do you mean?'

'Do you want to marry an outcast from the streets?'

Horace took one step forward towards her. There was a look in his face which plainly betrayed that he was capable of turning her out of the house with his own hands. Lady Janet stopped him.

'You were right in suggesting just now that Grace had better leave the room,' she said. 'Let us all three go. Julian will remain here and give the man his directions when he arrives. Come.'

No. By a strange contradiction, it was Horace himself who now interfered to prevent Mercy from leaving the room. In the heat of his indignation he lost all sense of his own dignity; he descended to the level of a woman whose intellect he believed to be deranged. To the surprise of everyone present, he stepped back, and took from the table a jewel-case which he had placed there when he came into the room. It was the wedding present from his mother which he had brought to his betrothed wife. His outraged self-esteem seized the opportunity of vindicating Mercy by a public bestowal of the gift.

'Wait!' he called out sternly. 'That wretch shall have her answer. She has sense enough to see, and sense enough to hear. Let her see and hear!'

He opened the jewel-case, and took from it a magnificent pearl necklace in an antique setting.

'Grace,' he said, with his highest distinction of manner, 'my mother sends you her love, and her congratulations on our approaching marriage. She begs you to accept, as part of your bridal dress, these pearls. She was married in them herself. They have been in our family for centuries. As one of the family, honoured and beloved, my mother offers them to my wife.'

He lifted the necklace to clasp it round Mercy's neck.

Julian watched her in breathless suspense. Would she sustain the ordeal through which Horace had innocently condemned her to pass?

Yes! In the insolent presence of Grace Roseberry, what was there now that she could not sustain? Her pride was in arms. Her lovely eyes lighted up as only a woman's eyes can light up when they see jewellery. Her grand head bent gracefully to receive the necklace. Her face warmed into colour; her beauty rallied its charms. Her triumph over Grace Roseberry was complete! Julian's head sank. For one sad moment he secretly asked himself the question: 'Have I been mistaken in her?'

Horace arrayed her in the pearls.

'Your husband puts these pearls on your neck, love,' he said proudly, and paused to look at her.

'Now,' he added with a contemptuous backward glance at Grace, 'we may go into the library. She has seen, and she has heard.'

He believed that he had silenced her. He had simply furnished her sharp tongue with a new sting.

'*You* will hear, and *you* will see, when my proofs come from Canada,' she retorted. 'You will hear that your wife has stolen my name and my character! You will see your wife dismissed from this house!'

Mercy turned on her with an uncontrollable outburst of passion.

'You are mad!' she cried.

Lady Janet caught the electric infection of anger in the air of the room. She too turned on Grace. She too said it:

'You are mad!'

Horace followed Lady Janet. *He* was beside himself. *He* fixed his pitiless eyes on Grace, and echoed the contagious words:

'You are mad!'

She was silenced, she was daunted at last. The treble accusation revealed to her, for the first time, the frightful suspicion to which she had exposed herself. She shrank back, with a low cry of horror, and struck against a chair. She would have fallen if Julian had not sprung forward and caught her.

Lady Janet led the way to the library. She opened the door – started – and suddenly stepped aside, so as to leave the entrance free.

A man appeared in the open doorway.

He was not a gentleman; he was not a workman; he was not a servant. He was vilely dressed, in glossy black broadcloth. His frock coat hung on him instead of fitting him. His waistcoat was too short and too tight over the chest. His trousers were a pair of shapeless black bags. His gloves were too large for him. His highly-polished boots creaked detestably whenever he moved. He had odiously watchful eyes – eyes that looked skilled in peeping through keyholes. His large ears, set forward like the ears of a monkey, pleaded guilty to meanly listening behind other people's doors. His manner was quietly confidential, when he spoke: impenetrably self-possessed when he was silent. A lurking air of secret-service enveloped the fellow, like an atmosphere of his own, from head to foot. He looked all round the magnificent room, without betraying either surprise or admiration. He closely investigated every person in it with one glance of his cunningly-watchful eyes. Making his bow to Lady

Janet, he silently showed her, as his introduction, the card that had summoned him. And then he stood at ease, self-revealed in his own sinister identity – a police-officer in plain clothes.

Nobody spoke to him. Everybody shrank inwardly, as if a reptile had crawled into the room.

He looked backwards and forwards, perfectly unembarrassed, between Julian and Horace.

'Is Mr Julian Gray here?' he asked.

Julian led Grace to a seat. Her eyes were fixed on the man. She trembled – she whispered, 'Who is he?' Julian spoke to the police-officer without answering her.

'Wait there,' he said, pointing to a chair in the most distant corner of the room. 'I will speak to you directly.'

The man advanced to the chair, marching to the discord of his creaking boots. He privately valued the carpet, at so much a yard, as he walked over it. He privately valued the chair, at so much the dozen, as he sat down on it. He was quite at his ease: it was no matter to him, whether he waited and did nothing, or whether he pried into the private character of every one in the room, as long as he was paid for it.

Even Lady Janet's resolution to act for herself was not proof against the appearance of the policeman in plain clothes. She left it to her nephew to take the lead. Julian glanced at Mercy before he stirred further in the matter. He knew that the end rested now, not with him, but with her.

She felt his eye on her, while her own eyes were looking at the man. She turned her head – hesitated – and suddenly approached Julian. Like Grace Roseberry, she was trembling. Like Grace Roseberry, she whispered, 'Who is he?'

Julian told her plainly who he was.

'Why is he here?'

'Can't you guess?'

'No!'

Horace left Lady Janet, and joined Mercy and Julian – impatient of the private colloquy between them.

'Am I in the way?' he enquired.

Julian drew back a little, understanding Horace perfectly. He looked round at Grace. Nearly the whole length of the spacious room divided them from the place in which she was sitting. She had never moved since he placed her in the chair. The direst of all terrors was in possession of her – terror of the unknown. There was no fear of her interfering, and no fear of her hearing what they said, so long as they were careful to speak in guarded tones. Julian set the example by lowering his voice.

'Ask Horace why the police-officer is here,' he said to Mercy.

She put the question directly. 'Why is he here?'

Horace looked across the room at Grace, and answered, 'He is here to relieve us of that woman.'

'Do you mean that he will take her away?'

'Yes.'

'Where will he take her to?'

'To the police-station.'

Mercy started and looked at Julian. He was still watching the slightest changes in her face. She looked back again at Horace.

'To the police-station!' she repeated. 'What for?'

'How can you ask the question?' said Horace irritably. 'To be placed under restraint, of course.'

'Do you mean a prison?'

'I mean an asylum.'

Again Mercy turned to Julian. There was horror now, as well as surprise, in her face. 'Oh!' she said to him, 'Horace is surely wrong? It can't be?'

Julian left it to Horace to answer. Every faculty in him seemed to be still absorbed in watching Mercy's face. She was compelled to address herself to Horace once more.

'What sort of asylum?' she asked. 'You don't surely mean a mad-house?'

'I do,' he rejoined. 'The workhouse first, perhaps – and then the mad-house. What is there to surprise you in that? You yourself told her to her face she was mad. Good heavens! how pale you are! What is the matter?'

She turned to Julian for the third time. The terrible alternative that was offered to her had showed itself at last, without reserve or disguise. Restore the identity that you have stolen, or shut her up in a mad-house – it rests with you to choose! In that form the situation shaped itself in her mind. She chose on the instant.

Before she opened her lips, the higher nature in her spoke to Julian in her eyes. The steady inner light that he had seen in them once already shone in them again, brighter and purer than before. The conscience that he had fortified, the soul that he had saved, looked at him and said, Doubt us no more!

'Send that man out of the house.'

Those were her first words. She spoke (pointing to the police-officer) in clear, ringing, resolute tones, audible in the remotest corner of the room.

Julian's hand stole unobserved to hers, and told her, in its momentary pressure, to count on his brotherly sympathy and help. All the other persons in the room looked at her in speechless surprise. Grace rose from her chair. Even the man in plain clothes started to his feet. Lady Janet (hurriedly joining Horace, and fully sharing his perplexity and alarm,) took Mercy impulsively by the arm, and shook it, as if to rouse her to a sense of what she was doing. Mercy held firm; Mercy resolutely repeated what she had said: 'Send that man out of the house.'

Lady Janet lost all patience with her. 'What has come to you?' she asked sternly. 'Do you know what you are saying? The man is here to spare you, as well as me, further annoyance and insult. And you insist — insist, in my presence — on his being sent away! What does it mean?'

'You shall know what it means, Lady Janet, in half an hour. I don't insist — I only reiterate my entreaty. Let the man be sent away!'

Julian stepped aside (with his aunt's eyes angrily following him) and spoke to the police-officer. 'Go back to the station,' he said, 'and wait there till you hear from me.'

The meanly-vigilant eyes of the man in plain clothes travelled sidelong from Julian to Mercy, and valued her beauty as they had valued the carpet and the chairs. 'The old story,' he thought. 'The nice-looking woman is always at the bottom of it; and, sooner or later, the nice-looking woman has her way.' He marched back across the room, to the discord of his own creaking boots; bowed, with a villainous smile which put the worst construction upon everything; and vanished through the library door.

Lady Janet's high breeding restrained her from saying anything until the police-officer was out of hearing. Then, and not till then, she appealed to Julian.

'I presume you are in the secret of this?' she said. 'I suppose you have some reason for setting my authority at defiance in my own house?'

'I have never yet failed to respect your ladyship,' Julian answered. 'Before long you will know that I am not failing in respect towards you now.'

Lady Janet looked across the room. Grace was listening eagerly, conscious that events had taken some mysterious turn in her favour within the last minute.

'Is it part of your new arrangement of my affairs,' her ladyship continued, 'that this person is to remain in the house?'

The terror that had daunted Grace had not lost all hold of her yet. She left it to Julian to reply. Before he could speak, Mercy crossed the room and whispered to her, 'Give me time to confess it in writing. I can't own it before them – with this round my neck.' She pointed to the necklace. Grace cast a threatening glance at her, and suddenly looked away again in silence.

Mercy answered Lady Janet's question. 'I beg your ladyship to permit her to remain until the half hour is over,' she said. 'My request will have explained itself by that time.'

Lady Janet raised no further obstacles. Something in Mercy's face, or in Mercy's tone, seemed to have silenced her, as it had silenced Grace. Horace was the next who spoke. In tones of suppressed rage and suspicion, he addressed himself to Mercy, standing fronting him by Julian's side.

'Am I included,' he asked, 'in the arrangement which engages you to explain your extraordinary conduct in half an hour?'

His hand had placed his mother's wedding-present round Mercy's neck. A sharp pang wrung her as she looked at Horace, and saw how deeply she had already distressed and offended him. The tears rose in her eyes: she humbly and faintly answered him.

'If you please,' was all she could say, before the cruel swelling at her heart rose and silenced her.

Horace's sense of injury refused to be soothed by such simple submission as this.

'I dislike mysteries and innuendoes,' he went on harshly. 'In my family circle we are accustomed to meet each other frankly. Why am I to wait half an hour for an explanation which might be given now? What am I to wait for?'

Lady Janet recovered herself as Horace spoke.

'I entirely agree with you,' she said. 'I ask, too, what are we to wait for?'

Even Julian's self-possession failed him when his aunt repeated that cruelly plain question. How would Mercy answer it? Would her courage still hold out?

'You have asked me what you have to wait for,' she said to Horace, quietly and firmly. 'Wait to hear something more of Mercy Merrick.'

Lady Janet listened with a look of weary disgust.

'Don't return to *that*!' she said. 'We know enough about Mercy Merrick already.'

'Pardon me – your ladyship does *not* know. I am the only person who can inform you.'

'You?'

She bent her head respectfully.

'I have begged you, Lady Janet, to give me half an hour,' she went on. 'In half an hour I solemnly engage myself to produce Mercy Merrick in this room. Lady Janet Roy, Mr Horace Holmcroft, you are to wait for that.'

Steadily pledging herself in those terms to make her confession, she unclasped the pearls from her neck, put them away in their case, and placed it in Horace's hand. 'Keep it,' she said, with a momentary faltering in her voice, 'until we meet again.'

Horace took the case in silence; he looked and acted like a man whose mind was paralysed by surprise. His hand moved mechanically. His eyes followed Mercy with a vacant questioning look. Lady Janet seemed, in her different way, to share the strange oppression that had fallen on him. A marked change had appeared in her since Mercy had spoken last.

'Have I your ladyship's leave,' said Mercy, respectfully, 'to go to my room?'

Lady Janet mutely granted the request. Mercy's last look, before she went out, was a look at Grace. 'Are you satisfied now?' the grand grey eyes seemed to say mournfully. Grace turned her head aside, with a quick petulant action. Even her narrow nature opened for a moment unwillingly, and let pity in a little way, in spite of herself.

Mercy's parting words recommended Grace to Julian's care:

'You will see that she is allowed a room to wait in? You will warn her yourself when the half hour has expired?'

Julian opened the library door for her.

'Well done! Nobly done!' he whispered. 'All my sympathy is with you — all my help is yours.'

Her eyes looked at him, and thanked him, through her gathering tears. His own eyes were dimmed. She passed quietly down the room, and was lost to him before he had shut the door again.

CHAPTER THE TWENTY-FIRST

THE FOOTSTEP IN THE CORRIDOR

Mercy was alone.

She had secured one half-hour of retirement in her own room; designing to devote that interval to the writing of her confession in the form of a letter addressed to Julian Gray.

No recent change in her position had, as yet, mitigated her horror of acknowledging to Horace and to Lady Janet that she had won her way to their hearts in disguise. Through Julian only could she say the words which were to establish Grace Roseberry in her right position in the house.

How was her confession to be addressed to him? In writing? or by word of mouth?

After all that had happened, from the time when Lady Janet's appearance had interrupted them, she would have felt relief rather than embarrassment in personally opening her heart to the man who had so delicately understood her, who had so faithfully befriended her in her sorest need. But the repeated betrayals of Horace's jealous suspicion of Julian warned her that she would only be surrounding herself with new difficulties, and be placing Julian in a position of painful embarrassment, if she admitted him to a private interview while Horace was in the house.

The one course left to take was the course that she had adopted. Determining to address the narrative of the Fraud to Julian in the form of a letter, she arranged to add, at the close, certain instructions, pointing out to him the line of conduct which she wished him to pursue.

These instructions contemplated the communication of her letter to Lady Janet and to Horace, in the library, while Mercy − self-confessed as the missing woman whom she had pledged herself to produce − awaited in the adjoining room whatever sentence it pleased them to pronounce on her. Her resolution not to screen herself behind Julian from any consequences which might follow the confession, had taken root in her mind from the moment when Horace had harshly asked her (and when Lady Janet had joined him asking) why she delayed her explanation, and what she was keeping them waiting for. Out of the very pain which those questions inflicted, the idea of waiting her sentence in her own person, in one room, while her letter to Julian was speaking for her in another, had sprung to life. 'Let them break my heart if they like,' she had thought to herself in the self-abasement of that bitter moment; 'it will be no more than I have deserved.'

She locked her door and opened her writing-desk. Knowing what she had to do, she tried to collect herself and do it.

The effort was in vain. Those persons who study writing as an art are probably the only persons who can measure the vast distance which separates a conception as it exists in the mind from the reduction of that conception to form and shape in words. The heavy stress of agitation that had been laid on Mercy for hours together had utterly unfitted her for the delicate and

difficult process of arranging the events of a narrative in their
due sequence and their due proportion towards each other.
Again and again she was baffled by the same hopeless confusion
of ideas. She gave up the struggle in despair.

A sense of sinking at her heart, a weight of hysterical
oppression on her bosom, warned her not to leave herself
unoccupied — a prey to morbid self-investigation and
imaginary alarms.

She turned instinctively, for a temporary employment of
some kind, to the consideration of her own future. Here there
were no intricacies or entanglements. The prospect began and
ended with her return to the Refuge, if the matron would
receive her. She did no injustice to Julian Gray; that great heart
would feel for her, that kind hand would be held out to her,
she knew. But what would happen if she thoughtlessly accepted
all that his sympathy might offer? Scandal would point to her
beauty and to his youth, and would place its own vile
interpretation on the purest friendship that could exist between
them. And *he* would be the sufferer, for *he* had a character — a
clergyman's character — to lose. No! for his sake, out of
gratitude to him, the farewell to Mablethorpe House must be
also the farewell to Julian Gray.

The precious minutes were passing. She resolved to write to
the matron, and ask if she might hope to be forgiven and
employed at the Refuge again. Occupation over the letter that
was easy to write might have its fortifying effect on her mind,
and might pave the way for resuming the letter that was hard to
write. She waited a moment at the window, thinking of the
past life to which she was soon to return, before she took up
the pen again.

Her window looked eastward. The dusky glare of lighted
London met her as her eyes rested on the sky. It seemed to
beckon her back to the horror of the cruel streets — to point
her way mockingly to the bridges over the black river — to
lure her to the top of the parapet, and the dreadful leap into
God's arms, or into annihilation — who knew which?

She turned, shuddering, from the window. 'Will it end in
that way,' she asked herself, 'if the matron says No?'

She began her letter.

'DEAR MADAM, – So long a time has passed since you heard from me, that I almost shrink from writing to you. I am afraid you have already given me up in your own mind as a hard-hearted, ungrateful woman.

'I have been leading a false life; I have not been fit to write to you before today. Now, when I am doing what I can to atone to those whom I have injured – now, when I repent with my whole heart – may I ask leave to return to the friend who has borne with me and helped me through many miserable years? Oh, madam, do not cast me off! I have no one to turn to but you.

'Will you let me own everything to you? Will you forgive me when you know what I have done? Will you take me back into the Refuge, if you have any employment for me by which I may earn my shelter and my bread?

'Before the night comes I must leave the house from which I am now writing. I have nowhere to go to. The little money, the few valuable possessions I have, must be left behind me: they have been obtained under false pretences; they are not mine. No more forlorn creature than I am lives at this moment. You are a Christian woman. Not for my sake – for Christ's sake, pity me and take me back.

'I am a good nurse, as you know, and I am a quick worker with my needle. In one way or the other, can you not find occupation for me?

'I could also teach, in a very unpretending way. But that is useless. Who would trust their children to a woman without a character? There is no hope for me in this direction. And yet I am so fond of children! I think I could be – not happy again, perhaps, but content with my lot, if I could be associated with them in some way. Are there not charitable societies which are trying to help and protect destitute children wandering about the streets? I think of my own wretched childhood – and oh! I should so like to be employed in saving other children from ending as I have ended. I could work, for such an object as that, from morning to night, and never feel weary. All my heart would be in it; and I should have this advantage over happy and prosperous women — I should have nothing else to think of. Surely they might trust me with the poor little starving wanderers of the streets — if you said a word for me? If I am asking too much, please forgive me. I am so wretched, madam — so lonely and so weary of my life.

'There is only one thing more. My time here is very short. Will you please reply to this letter (to say yes or no) by telegram?

'The name by which you know me is not the name by which I have been known here. I must beg you to address the telegram to 'The Revd Julian Gray, Mablethorpe House, Kensington.' He is here, and will show it to me. No words of mine can describe what I owe to him. He has never despaired of me — he has saved me from myself. God bless and reward the kindest, truest, best man I have ever known!

'I have no more to say, except to ask you to excuse this long letter, and to believe me your grateful servant,

————'

She signed and enclosed the letter and wrote the address. Then, for the first time, an obstacle which she ought to have seen before showed itself, standing straight in her way.

There was no time to forward her letter in the ordinary manner by post. It must be taken to its destination by a private messenger. Lady Janet's servants had hitherto been, one and all, at her disposal. Could she presume to employ them on her own affairs when she might be dismissed from the house, a disgraced woman, in half an hour's time? Of the two alternatives, it seemed better to take her chance, and present herself at the Refuge, without asking leave first.

While she was still considering the question, she was startled by a knock at her door. On opening it, she admitted Lady Janet's maid with a morsel of folded note paper in her hand.

'From my lady, miss,' said the woman, giving her the note. 'There is no answer.'

Mercy stopped her, as she was about to leave the room. The appearance of the maid suggested an enquiry to her. She asked if any of the servants were likely to be going into town that afternoon?

'Yes, miss. One of the grooms is going on horseback, with a message to her ladyship's coachmaker.'

The Refuge was close by the coachmaker's place of business. Under the circumstances, Mercy was emboldened to make use of the man. It was a pardonable liberty to employ his services now.

'Will you kindly give the groom that letter for me?' she said. 'It will not take him out of his way. He has only to deliver it — nothing more.'

The woman willingly complied with the request. Left once more by herself, Mercy looked at the little note which had been placed in her hands.

It was the first time that her benefactress had employed this formal method of communicating with her when they were both in the house. What did such a departure from established habits mean? Had she received her notice of dismissal? Had Lady Janet's quick intelligence found its way already to a suspicion of the truth? Mercy's nerves were unstrung. She trembled pitiably as she opened the folded note.

It began without a form of address, and it ended without a signature. Thus it ran:

'I must request you to delay for a little while the explanation which you have promised me. At my age, painful surprises are very trying things. I must have time to compose myself, before I can hear what you have to say. You shall not be kept waiting longer than I can help. In the meanwhile, everything will go on as usual. My nephew, Julian, and Horace Holmcroft, and the lady whom I found in the dining-room, will, by my desire, remain in the house until I am able to meet them, and to meet you, again.'

There the note ended. To what conclusion did it point?

Had Lady Janet really guessed the truth? or had she only surmised that her adopted daughter was connected in some discreditable manner with the mystery of 'Mercy Merrick'? The line in which she referred to the intruder in the dining-room as 'the lady,' showed very remarkably that her opinions had undergone a change in that quarter. But was the phrase enough of itself to justify the inference that she actually

anticipated the nature of Mercy's confession? It was not easy to
decide that doubt at the moment — and it proved to be equally
difficult to throw any light on it at an after time. To the end of
her life, Lady Janet resolutely refused to communicate to
anyone the conclusions which she might have privately formed,
the griefs which she might have secretly stifled, on that
memorable day.

Amid much, however, which was beset with uncertainty, one
thing at least was clear. The time at Mercy's disposal in her own
room had been indefinitely prolonged by Mercy's benefactress.
Hours might pass before the disclosure to which she stood
committed would be expected of her. In those hours she might
surely compose her mind sufficiently to be able to write her
letter of confession to Julian Gray.

Standing near her glass, as these thoughts occurred to her, she
noticed the reflection of herself still arrayed in the rich dress,
still wearing the jewels which Lady Janet had given to her.

She shuddered as the remembrance of what Grace Roseberry
had said recurred to her mind. The plain dress in which she had
entered Mablethorpe House still hung in a dark corner of her
wardrobe. She put her jewels back in the casket, and dressed
herself in the plain black gown. 'I shall take nothing away with
me,' she thought, as she looked her last at the wardrobe and the
jewels. 'Miss Roseberry will find all her presents here when she
takes possession of this room.'

She seated herself again at the table — bent on making
another attempt to write her letter to Julian. Resting her head
on her hand, she tried to trace her way through the labyrinth of
the past, beginning with the day when she had met Grace
Roseberry in the French cottage, and ending with the day
which had brought them face to face, for the second time, in
the dining-room at Mablethorpe House.

The chain of events began to unroll itself in her mind clearly,
link by link.

She remarked, as she pursued the retrospect, how strangely
Chance or Fate had paved the way for the act of personation, in
the first place. She had met with Grace Roseberry under those
extraordinary circumstances of common trial and common

peril, in a strange country, which would especially predispose two women of the same nation to open their hearts to each other. In no other way could she have obtained at a first interview, that fatal knowledge of Grace's position and Grace's affairs which had placed temptation before her, as the necessary consequence that followed the bursting of the German shell.

Advancing from this point, through the succeeding series of events which had so naturally, and yet so strangely, favoured the perpetration of the fraud, Mercy reached the later period when Grace had followed her to England. Here again, she remarked, in the second place, how Chance or Fate had once more paved the way for that second meeting which had confronted them with one another at Mablethorpe House.

She had, as she well remembered, attended at a certain assembly (convened by a charitable society) in the character of Lady Janet's representative, at Lady Janet's own request. For that reason, she had been absent from the house when Grace had entered it. If her return had been delayed by a few minutes only, Julian would have had time to remove Grace from the room; and the terrible meeting which had stretched Mercy senseless on the floor would never have taken place. As the event had happened, the persons assembled at the society's rooms had disagreed so seriously on the business which had brought them together as to render it necessary to take the ordinary course of adjourning the proceedings to a future day. And Chance, or Fate, had so timed that adjournment as to bring Mercy back into the dining-room exactly at the moment when Grace Roseberry insisted on being confronted with the woman who had taken her place!

She had never yet seen the circumstances in this sinister light. She was alone, at a crisis in her life. She was worn and weakened by contending emotions which had shaken her to the soul.

Little by little, she felt the enervating influences let loose on her, in her lonely position, by her new train of thought. Little by little, her heart began to sink under the stealthy chill of superstitious dread. Vaguely horrible presentiments throbbed in her with her pulses, flowed through her with her blood. Mystic oppressions of hidden disaster hovered over her in the atmosphere of the room. The cheerful candlelight turned traitor to her and grew dim. Supernatural murmurs trembled round the house in the moaning of the winter wind. She was afraid to look behind her. On a sudden, she felt her own cold hands covering her face, without knowing when she had lifted them to it, or why.

Still helpless under the horror that held her, she suddenly heard footsteps − a man's footsteps − in the corridor outside. At other times the sound would have startled her: now it broke the spell. The footsteps suggested life, companionship, human interposition − no matter of what sort. She mechanically took up her pen; she found herself beginning to remember her letter to Julian Gray.

At the same moment the footsteps stopped outside her door. The man knocked.

She still felt shaken. She was hardly mistress of herself yet. A faint cry of alarm escaped her at the sound of the knock. Before it could be repeated she had rallied her courage, and had opened the door.

The man in the corridor was Horace Holmcroft.

His ruddy complexion had turned pale. His hair (of which he was especially careful at other times) was in disorder. The superficial polish of his manner was gone; the undisguised man, sullen, distrustful, irritated to the last degree of endurance, showed through. He looked at her with a watchfully-suspicious eye; he spoke to her without preface or apology, in a coldly angry voice:

'Are you aware,' he asked, 'of what is going on downstairs?'

'I have not left my room,' she answered. 'I know that Lady Janet has deferred the explanation which I had promised to give her, and I know no more.'

'Has nobody told you what Lady Janet did after you left us? Has nobody told you that she politely placed her own boudoir at the disposal of the very woman whom she had ordered half an hour before to leave the house? Do you really not know that Mr Julian Gray has himself conducted this suddenly honoured guest to her place of retirement? and that I am left alone in the midst of these changes, contradictions, and mysteries − the only person who is kept out in the dark?'

'It is surely needless to ask me these questions,' said Mercy gently. 'Who could possibly have told me what was going on below stairs, before you knocked at my door?'

He looked at her with an ironical affectation of surprise.

'You are strangely forgetful today,' he said. 'Surely your friend Mr Julian Gray might have told you? I am astonished to hear that he has not had his private interview yet.'

'I don't understand you, Horace.'

'I don't want you to understand me,' he retorted irritably. 'The proper person to understand me is Julian Gray. I look to *him* to account to me for the confidential relations which seem to have been established between you behind my back. He has avoided me thus far, but I shall find my way to him yet.'

His manner threatened more than his words expressed. In Mercy's nervous condition at the moment, it suggested to her that he might attempt to fasten a quarrel on Julian Gray.

'You are entirely mistaken,' she said warmly. 'You are ungratefully doubting your best and truest friend. I say nothing of myself. You will soon discover why I patiently submit to suspicions which other women would resent as an insult.'

'Let me discover it at once. Now! Without wasting a moment more!'

There had hitherto been some little distance between them. Mercy had listened, waiting on the threshold of her door; Horace had spoken, standing against the opposite wall of the corridor. When he said his last words, he suddenly stepped forward, and (with something imperative in the gesture) laid his hand on her arm. The strong grasp of it almost hurt her. She struggled to release herself.

'Let me go!' she said. 'What do you mean?'

He dropped her arm as suddenly as he had taken it.

'You shall know what I mean,' he replied. 'A woman who has grossly outraged and insulted you — whose only excuse is that she is mad — is detained in the house at your desire, I might almost say at your command, when the police-officer is waiting to take her away. I have a right to know what this means. I am engaged to marry you. If you won't trust other people, you are bound to explain yourself to me. I refuse to wait

for Lady Janet's convenience. I insist (if you force me to say so)
– I insist on knowing the real nature of your connection with
this affair. You have obliged me to follow you here; it is my
only opportunity of speaking to you. You avoid me; you shut
yourself up from me in your own room. I am not your husband
yet – I have no right to follow you in. But there are other
rooms open to us. The library is at our disposal, and I will take
care that we are not interrupted. I am now going there, and I
have a last question to ask. You are to be my wife in a week's
time; will you take me into your confidence or not?'

To hesitate, was, in this case, literally to be lost. Mercy's sense
of justice told her that Horace had claimed no more than his
due. She answered instantly.

'I will follow you to the library, Horace, in five minutes.'

Her prompt and frank compliance with his wishes surprised
and touched him. He took her hand.

She had endured all that his angry sense of injury could say. His
gratitude wounded her to the quick. The bitterest moment she
had felt yet was the moment in which he raised her hand to his
lips, and murmured tenderly, 'My own true Grace!' She could
only sign to him to leave her, and hurry back into her own room.

Her first feeling, when she found herself alone again, was
wonder – wonder that it should never have occurred to her,
until he had himself suggested it, that her betrothed husband
had the foremost right to her confession. Her horror of owning
to either of them that she had cheated them out of their love
had hitherto placed Horace and Lady Janet on the same level.
She now saw for the first time that there was no comparison
between the claims which they respectively had on her. She
owed an allegiance to Horace to which Lady Janet could assert
no right. Cost her what it might to avow the truth to him with
her own lips, the cruel sacrifice must be made.

Without a moment's hesitation, she put away her writing
materials. It amazed her that she should ever have thought of using
Julian Gray as an interpreter between the man to whom she was
betrothed and herself. Julian's sympathy (she thought) must have
made a strong impression on her indeed, to blind her to a duty
which was beyond all compromise, which admitted of no dispute!

She had asked for five minutes of delay before she followed Horace. It was too long a time.

Her one chance of finding courage to crush him with the dreadful revelation of what she had really done was to plunge headlong into the disclosure without giving herself time to think. The shame of it would inevitably overpower her if she gave herself time to think.

She turned to the door to follow him at once.

Even at that trying moment, the most ineradicable of all a woman's instincts — the instinct of personal self-respect — brought her to a pause. She had passed through more than one terrible trial since she had dressed to go downstairs. Remembering this, she stopped mechanically, retraced her steps, and looked at herself in the glass.

There was no motive of vanity in what she now did. The action was as unconscious as if she had buttoned an unfastened glove, or shaken out a crumpled dress. Not the faintest idea crossed her mind of looking to see if her beauty might still plead for her, and of trying to set it off at its best.

A momentary smile, the most weary, the most hopeless that ever saddened a woman's face, appeared in the reflection which her mirror gave her back. 'Haggard, ghastly, old before my time!' she said to herself. 'Well! better so. He will feel it less — he will not regret me.'

With that thought she went downstairs to meet him in the library.

CHAPTER THE TWENTY- SECOND

THE MAN IN THE DINING-ROOM

In the great emergencies of life we feel, or we act, as our dispositions incline us. But we never think. Mercy's mind was a blank as she descended the stairs. On her way down, she was conscious of nothing but the one headlong impulse to get to the library in the shortest possible space of time. Arrived at the door, the impulse capriciously left her. She stopped on the mat, wondering why she had hurried herself, with time to spare. Her heart sank; the fever of her excitement changed suddenly to a chill, as she faced the closed door, and asked herself the question, Dare I go in?

Her own hand answered her. She lifted it to turn the handle of the lock. It dropped again helplessly at her side.

The sense of her own irresolution wrung from her a low exclamation of despair. Faint as it was, it had apparently not passed unheard. The door was opened from within – and Horace stood before her.

He drew aside to let her pass into the room. But he never followed her in. He stood in the doorway, and spoke to her, keeping the door open with his hand.

'Do you mind waiting here for me?' he asked.

She looked at him, in vacant surprise, doubting whether she had heard him right.

'It will not be for long,' he went on. 'I am far too anxious to hear what you have to tell me to submit to any needless delays. The truth is, I have had a message from Lady Janet.'

(From Lady Janet! What could Lady Janet want with him, at a time when she was bent on composing herself in the retirement of her own room?)

'I ought to have said two messages,' Horace proceeded. 'The first was given to me on my way downstairs. Lady Janet wished to see me immediately. I sent an excuse. A second message followed. Lady Janet would accept no excuse. If I refused to go to her I should be merely obliging her to come to me. It is impossible to risk being interrupted in that way, my only alternative is to get the thing over as soon as possible. Do you mind waiting?'

'Certainly not. Have you any idea of what Lady Janet wants with you?'

'No. Whatever it is, she shall not keep me long away from you. You will be quite alone here; I have warned the servants not to show anyone in.' With those words, he left her.

Mercy's first sensation was a sensation of relief — soon lost in a feeling of shame at the weakness which could welcome any temporary relief in such a position as hers. The emotion thus roused merged in its turn into a sense of impatient regret. 'But for Lady Janet's message,' she thought to herself, 'I might have known my fate by this time!'

The slow minutes followed each other drearily. She paced to and fro in the library, faster and faster, under the intolerable irritation, the maddening uncertainty of her own suspense. Ere long, even the spacious room seemed to be too small for her. The sober monotony of the long book-lined shelves oppressed and offended her. She threw open the door which led into the dining-room, and dashed in, eager for a change of objects, a thirst for more space and more air.

At the first step, she checked herself; rooted to the spot, under a sudden revulsion of feeling which quieted her in an instant.

The room was only illuminated by the waning firelight. A man was obscurely visible seated on the sofa, with his elbows on his knees and his head resting on his hands. He looked up, as the open door let in the light from the library lamps. The mellow glow reached his face, and revealed Julian Gray.

Mercy was standing with her back to the light; her face being necessarily hidden in deep shadow. He recognised her by her figure, and by the attitude into which it unconsciously fell. That unsought grace, that lithe long beauty of line, belonged to but one woman in the house. He rose, and approached her.

'I have been wishing to see you,' he said, 'and hoping that accident might bring about some such meeting as this.'

He offered her a chair. Mercy hesitated before she took her seat. This was their first meeting alone since Lady Janet had interrupted her at the moment when she was about to confide to Julian the melancholy story of the past. Was he anxious to seize the opportunity of returning to her confession? The terms in which he had addressed her seemed to imply it. She put the question to him in plain words.

'I feel the deepest interest in hearing all that you have still to confide to me,' he answered. 'But anxious as I may be, I will not hurry you. I will wait, if you wish it.'

'I am afraid I must own that I do wish it,' Mercy rejoined. 'Not on my own account — but because my time is at the disposal of Horace Holmcroft. I expect to see him in a few minutes.'

'Could you give me those few minutes?' Julian asked. 'I have something, on my side, to say to you, which I think you ought to know, before you see anyone — Horace himself included.'

He spoke with a certain depression of tone which was not associated with her previous experience of him. His face looked prematurely old and care-worn, in the red light of the fire. Something had plainly happened to sadden and to disappoint him since they had last met.

'I willingly offer you all the time that I have at my own command,' Mercy replied. 'Does what you have to tell me relate to Lady Janet?'

He gave her no direct reply. 'What I have to tell you of Lady Janet,' he said gravely, 'is soon told. So far as she is concerned, you have nothing more to dread. Lady Janet knows all.'

Even the heavy weight of oppression caused by the impending interview with Horace failed to hold its place in Mercy's mind when Julian answered her in those words.

'Come into the lighted room,' she said faintly. 'It is too terrible to hear you say that in the dark.'

Julian followed her into the library. Her limbs trembled under her. She dropped into a chair, and shrank under his great bright eyes, as he stood by her side, looking sadly down on her.

'Lady Janet knows all!' she repeated, with her head on her breast, and the tears falling slowly over her cheeks. 'Have you told her?'

'I have said nothing to Lady Janet or to anyone. Your confidence is a sacred confidence to me, until you have spoken first.'

'Has Lady Janet said anything to you?'

'Not a word. She has looked at you with the vigilant eyes of love; she has listened to you with the quick hearing of love — and she has found her own way to the truth. She will not speak of it to any living creature. I only know now how dearly she loved you. In spite of herself she clings to you still. Her life, poor soul, has been a barren one; unworthy, miserably unworthy, of such a nature as hers. Her marriage was loveless and childless. She has had admirers, but never, in the higher sense of the word, a friend. All the best years of her life have been wasted in the unsatisfied longing for something to love. At the end of her life You have filled the void. Her heart has found its youth again, through You. At her age − at any age − is such a tie as this to be rudely broken at the mere bidding of circumstances? No! She will suffer anything, risk anything, forgive anything, rather than own, even to herself, that she has been deceived in you. There is more than her happiness at stake; there is pride, a noble pride, in such love as hers, which will ignore the plainest discovery and deny the most unanswerable truth. I am firmly convinced − from my own knowledge of her character, and from what I have observed in her today − that she will find some excuse for refusing to hear your confession. And more than that, I believe (if the exertion of her influence can do it), that she will leave no means untried of preventing you from acknowledging your true position here to any living creature. I take a serious responsibility on myself in telling you this − and I don't shrink from it. You ought to know, and you shall, what trials and what temptations may yet lie before you.'

He paused − leaving Mercy time to compose herself, if she wished to speak to him.

She felt that there was a necessity for her speaking to him. He was plainly not aware that Lady Janet had already written to her to defer her promised explanation. This circumstance was in itself a confirmation of the opinion which he had expressed. She ought to mention it to him. She tried to mention it to him. But she was not equal to the effort. The few simple words in which he had touched on the tie that bound Lady Janet to her had wrung her heart. Her tears choked her. She could only sign to him to go on.

'You may wonder at my speaking so positively,' he continued, 'with nothing better than my own conviction to justify me. I can only say that I have watched Lady Janet too closely to feel any doubt. I saw the moment in which the truth flashed on her as plainly as I now see you. It did not disclose itself gradually — it burst on her, as it burst on me. She suspected nothing — she was frankly indignant at your sudden interference and your strange language — until the time came when you pledged yourself to produce Mercy Merrick. Then (and then only) the truth broke on her mind; trebly revealed to her in your words, your voice, and your look. Then (and then only) I saw a marked change come over her, and remain in her while she remained in the room. I dread to think of what she may do in the first reckless despair of the discovery that she has made. I distrust — though God knows I am not naturally a suspicious man — the most apparently trifling events that are now taking place about us. You have held nobly to your resolution to own the truth. Prepare yourself, before the evening is over, to be tried and tempted again.'

Mercy lifted her head. Fear took the place of grief in her eyes as they rested in startled enquiry on Julian's face.

'How is it possible that temptation can come to me now?' she asked.

'I will leave it to events to answer that question,' he said. 'You will not have long to wait. In the meantime I have put you on your guard.' He stooped, and spoke his next words earnestly close at her ear. 'Hold fast by the admirable courage which you have shown thus far,' he went on. 'Suffer anything, rather than suffer the degradation of yourself. Be the woman whom I once spoke of — the woman I still have in my mind — who can nobly reveal the noble nature that is in her. And never forget this — my faith in you is as firm as ever!'

She looked at him proudly and gratefully.

'I am pledged to justify your faith in me,' she said. 'I have put it out of my own power to yield. Horace has my promise that I will explain everything to him in this room.'

Julian started.

'Has Horace himself asked it of you?' he enquired. '*He*, at least, has no suspicion of the truth.'

'Horace has appealed to my duty to him as his betrothed wife,' she answered. 'He has the first claim to my confidence — he resents my silence, and he has a right to resent it. Terrible as it will be to open *his* eyes to the truth, I must do it if he asks me.'

She was looking at Julian while she spoke. The old longing to associate with the hard trial of the confession the one man who had felt for her and believed in her revived under another form. If she could only know, while she was saying the fatal words to Horace, that Julian was listening too, she would be encouraged to meet the worst that could happen! As the idea crossed her mind she observed that Julian was looking towards the door through which they had lately passed. In an instant she saw the means to her end. Hardly waiting to hear the few kind expressions of sympathy and approval which he addressed to her, she hinted timidly at the proposal which she had now to make to him.

'Are you going back into the next room?' she asked.

'Not if you object to it,' he replied.

'I don't object. I want you to be there.'

'After Horace has joined you?'

'Yes. After Horace has joined me.'

'Do you wish to see me when it is over?'

She summoned her resolution, and told him frankly what she had in her mind.

'I want you to be near me while I am speaking to Horace,' she said. 'It will give me courage if I can feel that I am speaking to you as well as to him. I can count on *your* sympathy — and sympathy is so precious to me now! Am I asking too much if I ask you to leave the door unclosed when you go back to the dining-room? Think of the dreadful trial — to him as well as to me! I am only a woman. I am afraid I may sink under it if I have no friend near me. And I have no friend but you.'

In those simple words she tried her powers of persuasion on him for the first time.

Between perplexity and distress, Julian was, for the moment, at a loss how to answer her. The love for Mercy which he dared not acknowledge was as vital a feeling in him as the faith in her which he had been free to avow. To refuse anything that she asked of him in her sore need — and, more even than that, to refuse to hear the confession which it had been her first impulse to make to *him* — these were cruel sacrifices to his sense of what was due to Horace and of what was due to himself. But shrink as he might, even from the appearance of deserting her, it was impossible for him (except under a reserve which was almost equivalent to a denial) to grant her request.

'All that I can do I will do,' he said. 'The door shall be left unclosed, and I will remain in the next room, on this condition — that Horace knows of it as well as you. I should be unworthy of your confidence in me if I consented to be a listener on any other terms. You understand that, I am sure, as well as I do.'

She had never thought of her proposal to him in this light. Womanlike, she had thought of nothing but the comfort of having him near her. She understood him now. A faint flush of shame rose on her pale cheeks as she thanked him. He delicately relieved her from her embarrassment by putting a question which naturally occurred under the circumstances.

'Where is Horace all this time?' he asked. 'Why is he not here?'

'He has been called away,' she answered, 'by a message from Lady Janet.'

The reply more than astonished Julian; it seemed almost to alarm him. He returned to Mercy's chair; he said to her eagerly, 'Are you sure?'

'Horace himself told me that Lady Janet had insisted on seeing him.'

'When?'

'Not long ago. He asked me to wait for him here, while he went upstairs.'

Julian's face darkened ominously.

'This confirms my worst fears,' he said. 'Have *you* had any communication with Lady Janet?'

Mercy replied by showing him his aunt's note. He read it carefully through.

'Did I not tell you,' he said, 'that she would find some excuse for refusing to hear your confession? She begins by delaying it, simply to gain time for something else which she has it in her mind to do. When did you receive this note? Soon after you went upstairs?'

'About a quarter of an hour after, as well as I can guess.'

'Do you know what happened down here, after you left us?'

'Horace told me that Lady Janet had offered Miss Roseberry the use of her boudoir.'

'Any more?'

'He said that you had shown her the way to the room.'

'Did he tell you what happened after that?'

'No.'

'Then I must tell you. If I can do nothing more in this serious state of things, I can at least prevent your being taken by surprise. In the first place, it is right you should know that I had a motive for accompanying Miss Roseberry to the boudoir. I was anxious (for your sake) to make some appeal to her better self — if she had any better self to address. I own I had doubts of my success — judging by what I had already seen of her. My doubts were confirmed. In the ordinary intercourse of life, I should merely have thought her a commonplace uninteresting woman. Seeing her as I saw her while we were alone — in other words, penetrating below the surface — I have never, in all my sad experience, met with such a hopelessly narrow, mean, and low nature as hers. Understanding, as she could not fail to do, what the sudden change in Lady Janet's behaviour towards her really meant, her one idea was to take the cruellest possible advantage of it. So far from feeling any consideration for *you*, she protested against your being permitted to claim the merit of placing her in her right position here, by your own voluntary avowal of the truth. She insisted on publicly denouncing you, and on forcing Lady Janet to dismiss you, unheard, before the whole household. "Now I can have my revenge! At last Lady Janet is afraid of me!" Those were her own words — I am almost ashamed to repeat them — those, on my honour, were her own words! Every possible humiliation to be heaped on you; no consideration to be shown for Lady Janet's age and Lady Janet's position; nothing, absolutely nothing, to be allowed to interfere with Miss Roseberry's vengeance and Miss Roseberry's triumph! There is this woman's shameless view of what is due to her, as stated by herself in the plainest terms. I kept my temper; I did all I could to bring to her a better frame of mind. I might as well have pleaded — I won't say with a savage; savages are sometimes accessible to remonstrance, if you know how to reach them – I might as well have pleaded with a hungry animal to abstain from eating while food was within its reach. I had just given up the hopeless effort in disgust, when Lady Janet's maid appeared with a message for Miss Roseberry from her mistress: "My lady's compliments, ma'am, and she would be glad to see you at your earliest convenience, in her room."'

(Another surprise! Grace Roseberry invited to an interview with Lady Janet! It would have been impossible to believe it if Julian had not heard the invitation with his own ears.)

'She instantly rose,' Julian proceeded. '"I won't keep her ladyship waiting a moment," she said; "show me the way." She signed to the maid to go out of the room first, and then turned round and spoke to me from the door. I despair of describing the insolent exultation of her manner – I can only repeat her words: – "This is exactly what I wanted! I had intended to insist on seeing Lady Janet: she saves me the trouble; I am infinitely obliged to her." With that, she nodded to me, and closed the door. I have not seen her, I have not heard of her, since. For all I know, she may be still with my aunt, and Horace may have found her there when he entered the room.'

'What can Lady Janet have to say to her?' Mercy asked eagerly.

'It is impossible even to guess. When you found me in the dining-room I was considering that very question. I cannot imagine that any neutral ground can exist on which it is possible for Lady Janet and this woman to meet. In her present frame of mind, she will in all probability insult Lady Janet before they have been five minutes together. I own I am completely puzzled. The one conclusion I can arrive at is, that the note which my aunt sent to you, the private interview with Miss Roseberry which has followed, and the summons to Horace which has succeeded in its turn, are all links in the same chain of events, and are all tending to that renewed temptation against which I have already warned you.'

Mercy held up her hand for silence. She looked towards the door that opened on the hall; had she heard a footstep outside? No. All was still. Not a sign yet of Horace's return.

'Oh!' she exclaimed, 'what would I not give to know what is going on upstairs!'

'You will soon know it now,' said Julian. 'It is impossible that our present uncertainty can last much longer.'

He turned away, intending to go back to the room in which she had found him. Looking at her situation from a man's point of view, he naturally assumed that the best service he could now render to Mercy would be to leave her to prepare herself for the interview with Horace. Before he had taken three steps away from her, she showed him the difference between the woman's point of view and the man's. The idea of considering beforehand what she should say never entered her mind. In her horror of being left by herself at that critical moment, she forgot every other consideration. Even the warning remembrance of Horace's jealous distrust of Julian passed away from her as completely as if it had never had a place in her memory. 'Don't leave me!' she cried. 'I can't wait here alone. Come back — come back!'

She rose impulsively, while she spoke, as if to follow him into the dining-room, if he persisted in leaving her.

A momentary expression of doubt crossed Julian's face as he retraced his steps and signed to her to be seated again. Could she be depended on (he asked himself) to sustain the coming test of her resolution, when she had not courage enough to wait for events in a room by herself? Julian had yet to learn that a woman's courage rises with the greatness of the emergency. Ask her to accompany you through a field in which some harmless cattle happen to be grazing, and it is doubtful, in nine cases out of ten, if she will do it. Ask her, as one of the passengers in a ship on fire, to help in setting an example of composure to the rest, and it is certain, in nine cases out of ten, that she will do it. As soon as Julian had taken a chair near her, Mercy was calm again.

'Are you sure of your resolution?' he asked.

'I am certain of it,' she answered, 'as long as you don't leave me by myself.'

The talk between them dropped there. They sat together, in silence, with their eyes fixed on the door, waiting for Horace to come in.

After the lapse of a few minutes, their attention was attracted by a sound outside in the grounds. A carriage of some sort was plainly audible, approaching the house.

The carriage stopped; the bell rang; the front door was opened. Had a visitor arrived? No voice could be heard making enquiries. No footsteps but the servant's footsteps crossed the hall. A long pause followed; the carriage remaining at the door. Instead of bringing some one to the house, it had apparently arrived to take some one away.

The next event was the return of the servant to the front door. They listened again. Again, no second footstep was audible. The door was closed; the servant recrossed the hall; the carriage was driven away. Judging by the sounds alone, no one had arrived at the house, and no one had left the house.

Julian looked at Mercy. 'Do you understand this?' he asked.

She silently shook her head.

'If any person has gone away in the carriage, Julian went on, 'that person can hardly have been a man, or we must have heard him in the hall.'

The conclusion which her companion had just drawn from the noiseless departure of the supposed visitor raised a sudden doubt in Mercy's mind.

'Go, and enquire!' she said eagerly.

Julian left the room; and returned again, after a brief absence, with signs of grave anxiety in his face and manner.

'I told you I dreaded the most trifling events that were passing about us,' he said. 'An event, which is far from being trifling, has just happened. The carriage which we heard approaching along the drive, turns out to have been a cab sent for from the house. The person who has gone away in it——'

'Is a woman, as you supposed?'

'Yes.'

Mercy rose excitedly from her chair.

'It can't be Grace Roseberry?' she exclaimed.

'It *is* Grace Roseberry.'

'Has she gone away alone?'

'Alone — after an interview with Lady Janet.'

'Did she go willingly?'

'She herself sent the servant for the cab.'

'What does it mean?'

'It is useless to enquire. We shall soon know.'

They resumed their seats; waiting, as they had waited already, with their eyes on the library door.

CHAPTER THE TWENTY-THIRD

LADY JANET AT BAY

The narrative leaves Julian and Mercy for awhile, and, ascending to the upper regions of the house, follows the march of events in Lady Janet's room.

The maid had delivered her mistress's note to Mercy, and had gone away again on her second errand to Grace Roseberry in the boudoir. Lady Janet was seated at her writing-table, waiting for the appearance of the woman whom she had summoned to her presence. A single lamp diffused its mild light over the books, pictures, and busts round her, leaving the farther end of the room, in which the bed was placed, almost lost in obscurity. The works of art were all portraits; the books were all presentation copies from the authors. It was Lady Janet's fancy to associate her bedroom with memorials of the various persons whom she had known in the long course of her life − all of them more or less distinguished; most of them, by this time, gathered with the dead.

She sat near her writing-table, lying back in her easy-chair − the living realisation of the picture which Julian's description had drawn. Her eyes were fixed on a photographic likeness of Mercy, which was so raised upon a little gilt easel as to enable her to contemplate it under the full light of the lamp. The bright mobile old face was strangely and sadly changed. The brow was fixed; the mouth was rigid; the whole face would have been like a mask, moulded in the hardest forms of passive resistance and suppressed rage, but for the light and life still thrown over it by the eyes. There was something unutterably touching in the keen hungering tenderness of the look which they fixed on the portrait, intensified by an underlying expression of fond and patient reproach. The danger which Julian so wisely dreaded was in the rest of the face; the love which he had so truly described was in the eyes alone. *They* still spoke of the cruelly-profaned affection which had been the one immeasurable joy, the one inexhaustible hope, of Lady Janet's closing life. The brow expressed nothing but her obstinate determination to stand by the wreck of that joy, to rekindle the dead ashes of that hope. The lips were only eloquent of her unflinching resolution to ignore the hateful present and to save the sacred past. 'My idol may be shattered, but none of you shall know it. I stop the march of discovery; I extinguish the light of truth. I am deaf to your words, I am blind to your proofs. At seventy years old, my idol is my life. It shall be my idol still.'

The silence in the bedroom was broken by a murmuring of women's voices outside the door.

Lady Janet instantly raised herself in the chair, and snatched the photograph off the easel. She laid the portrait face downwards among some papers on the table – then abruptly changed her mind, and hid it among the thick folds of lace which clothed her neck and bosom. There was a world of love in the action itself, and in the sudden softening of the eyes which accompanied it. The next moment Lady Janet's mask was on. Any superficial observer who had seen her now would have said, 'This is a hard woman!'

The door was opened by the maid. Grace Roseberry entered the room.

She advanced rapidly, with a defiant assurance in her manner, and a lofty carriage of her head. She sat down in the chair to which Lady Janet silently pointed, with a thump; she returned Lady Janet's grave bow with a nod and a smile. Every movement and every look of the little worn, white-faced, shabbily-dressed woman expressed insolent triumph, and said, as if in words, 'My turn has come!'

'I am glad to wait on your ladyship,' she began, without giving Lady Janet an opportunity of speaking first. 'Indeed, I should have felt it my duty to request an interview if you had not sent your maid to invite me up here.'

'You would have felt it your duty to request an interview?' Lady Janet repeated very quietly. 'Why?'

The tone in which that one last word was spoken embarrassed Grace at the outset. It established as great a distance between Lady Janet and herself as if she had been lifted in her chair and conveyed bodily to the other end of the room.

'I am surprised that your ladyship should not understand me,' she said, struggling to conceal her confusion. 'Especially after your kind offer of your own boudoir.'

Lady Janet remained perfectly unmoved. 'I do *not* understand you,' she answered, just as quietly as ever. Grace's temper came to her assistance. She recovered the assurance which had marked her first appearance on the scene.

'In that case,' she resumed, ' I must enter into particulars, in justice to myself. I can place but one interpretation on the extraordinary change in your ladyship's behaviour to me downstairs. The conduct of that abominable woman has, at last, opened your eyes to the deception that has been practised on you. For some reason of your own, however, you have not yet chosen to recognise me openly. In this painful position something is due to my own self-respect. I cannot, and will not, permit Mercy Merrick to claim the merit of restoring me to my proper place in this house. After what I have suffered, it is quite impossible for me to endure that. I should have requested an interview (if you had not sent for me) for the express purpose of claiming this person's immediate expulsion from the house. I claim it now as a proper concession to me. Whatever you or Mr Julian Gray may do, *I* will not tamely permit her to exhibit herself as an interesting penitent. It is really a little too much to hear this brazen adventuress appoint her own time for explaining herself. It is too deliberately insulting to see her sail out of the room — with a clergyman of the Church of England opening the door for her — as if she was laying me under an obligation! I can forgive much, Lady Janet, including the terms

in which you thought it decent to order me out of your house.
I am quite willing to accept the offer of your boudoir as the
expression on your part of a better frame of mind. But even
Christian charity has its limits. The continued presence of that
wretch under your roof is, you will permit me to remark, not
only a monument of your own weakness, but a perfectly
insufferable insult to me.'

There she stopped abruptly – not for want of words, but for
want of a listener.

Lady Janet was not even pretending to attend to her. Lady
Janet, with a deliberate rudeness entirely foreign to her usual
habits, was composedly busying herself in arranging the various
papers scattered about the table. Some she tied together with
little morsels of string; some she placed under paper-weights;
some she deposited in the fantastic pigeon-holes of a little
Japanese cabinet – working with a placid enjoyment of her
own orderly occupation, and perfectly unaware, to all outward
appearance, that any second person was in the room. She
looked up with her papers in both hands when Grace stopped
and said quietly,

'Have you done?'

'Is your ladyship's purpose in sending for me to treat me with
studied rudeness?' Grace retorted angrily.

'My purpose in sending for you is to say something, as soon
as you will allow me the opportunity.'

The impenetrable composure of that reply took Grace
completely by surprise. She had no retort ready. In sheer
astonishment she waited silently, with her eyes riveted on the
mistress of the house.

Lady Janet put down her papers, and settled herself
comfortably in the easy chair, preparatory to opening the
interview on her side.

'The little that I have to say to you,' she began, 'may be said
in a question. Am I right in supposing that you have no present
employment, and that a little advance in money (delicately
offered) would be very acceptable to you?'

'Do you mean to insult me, Lady Janet?'

'Certainly not. I mean to ask you a question.'

'Your question is an insult.'

'My question is a kindness if you will only understand it as it is intended. I don't complain of your not understanding it. I don't even hold you responsible for any one of the many breaches of good manners which you have committed since you have been in this room. I was honestly anxious to be of some service to you, and you have repelled my advances. I am sorry. Let us drop the subject.'

Expressing herself with the most perfect temper in those terms, Lady Janet resumed the arrangement of her papers, and became unconscious once more of the presence of any second person in the room.

Grace opened her lips to reply with the utmost intemperance of an angry woman, and, thinking better of it, controlled herself. It was plainly useless to take the violent way with Lady Janet Roy. Her age and her social position were enough of themselves to repel any violence. She evidently knew that, and trusted to it. Grace resolved to meet the enemy on the neutral ground of politeness, as the most promising ground that she could occupy under present circumstances.

'If I have said anything hasty, I beg to apologise to your ladyship,' she began. 'May I ask if your only object in sending for me was to enquire into my pecuniary affairs, with a view to assisting me?'

'That,' said Lady Janet, 'was my only object.'

'You had nothing to say to me on the subject of Mercy Merrick?'

'Nothing whatever. I am weary of hearing of Mercy Merrick. Have you any more questions to ask me?'

'I have one more.'

'Yes?'

'I wish to ask your ladyship whether you propose to recognise me in the presence of your household as the late Colonel Roseberry's daughter?'

'I have already recognised you as a lady in embarrassed circumstances, who has peculiar claims on my consideration and forbearance. If you wish me to repeat those words in the presence of the servants (absurd as it is) I am ready to comply with your request.'

Grace's temper began to get the better of her prudent resolutions.

'Lady Janet!' she said, 'this won't do. I must request you to express yourself plainly. You talk of my peculiar claims on your forbearance. What claims do you mean?'

'It will be painful to both of us if we enter into details,' replied Lady Janet. 'Pray don't let us enter into details.'

'I insist on it, madam.'

'Pray don't insist on it.'

Grace was deaf to remonstrance.

'I ask you in plain words,' she went on, 'do you acknowledge that you have been deceived by an adventuress who has personated me? Do you mean to restore me to my proper place in this house?'

Lady Janet returned to the arrangement of her papers.

'Does your ladyship refuse to listen to me?'

Lady Janet looked up from her papers as blandly as ever.

'If *you* persist in returning to your delusion,' she said, 'you will oblige *me* to persist in returning to my papers.'

'What is my delusion, if you please?'

'Your delusion is expressed in the questions you have just put to me. Your delusion constitutes your peculiar claim on my forbearance. Nothing you can say or do will shake my forbearance. When I first found you in the dining-room, I acted most improperly; I lost my temper. I was foolish enough and imprudent enough to send for a police-officer. I owe you every possible atonement (afflicted as you are) for treating you in that cruel manner. I offered you the use of my boudoir, as part of my atonement. I sent for you, in the hope that you would allow me to assist you, as part of my atonement. You may behave rudely to me, you may speak in the most abusive terms of my adopted daughter; I will submit to anything, as part of my atonement. So long as you abstain from speaking on one painful subject, I will listen to you with the greatest pleasure. Whenever you return to that subject I shall return to my papers.'

Grace looked at Lady Janet with an evil smile.

'I begin to understand your ladyship,' she said. 'You are ashamed to acknowledge that you have been grossly imposed upon. Your only alternative, of course, is to ignore everything that has happened. Pray count on *my* forbearance. I am not at all offended — I am merely amused. It is not every day that a lady of high rank exhibits herself in such a position as yours to an obscure woman like me. Your humane consideration for me dates, I presume, from the time when your adopted daughter set you the example, by ordering the police-officer out of the room?'

Lady Janet's composure was proof even against this assault on it. She gravely accepted Grace's enquiry as a question addressed to her in perfect good faith.

'I am not at all surprised,' she replied, 'to find that my adopted daughter's interference has exposed her to misrepresentation. She ought to have remonstrated with me privately before she interfered. But she has one fault — she is too impulsive. I have never, in all my experience, met with such a warm-hearted person as she is. Always too considerate of others; always too forgetful of herself ! The mere appearance of the police-officer placed you in a situation to appeal to her compassion, and her impulses carried her away as usual. My fault! All my fault!'

Grace changed her tone once more. She was quick enough to discern that Lady Janet was a match for her with her own weapons.

'We have had enough of this,' she said. 'It is time to be serious. Your adopted daughter (as you call her) is Mercy Merrick — and you know it.'

Lady Janet returned to her papers.

'I am Grace Roseberry, whose name she has stolen — and you know *that*.'

Lady Janet went on with her papers.

Grace got up from her chair.

'I accept your silence, Lady Janet,' she said, 'as an acknowledgment of your deliberate resolution to suppress the truth. You are evidently determined to receive the adventuress as the true woman; and you don't scruple to face the consequences of that proceeding, by pretending to my face to believe that I am mad. I will not allow myself to be impudently cheated out of my rights in this way. You will hear from me again, madam, when the Canadian mail arrives in England.'

She walked towards the door. This time Lady Janet answered, as readily and as explicity as it was possible to desire.

'I shall refuse to receive your letters,' she said.

Grace returned a few steps, threateningly.

'My letters will be followed by my witnesses,' she proceeded.

'I shall refuse to receive your witnesses.'

'Refuse at your peril. I will appeal to the law!'

Lady Janet smiled.

'I don't pretend to much knowledge of the subject,' she said; 'but I should be surprised indeed if I discovered that you had any claim on me which the law could enforce. However, let us suppose that you *can* set the law in action. You know as well as I do that the only motive power which can do that is — money. I am rich; fees, costs, and all the rest of it are matters of no sort of consquence to me. May I ask if you are in the same position?'

The question silenced Grace. So far as money was concerned, she was literally at the end of her resources. Her only friends were friends in Canada. After what she had said to him in the boudoir, it would be quite useless to appeal to the sympathies of Julian Gray. In the pecuniary sense, and in one word, she was absolutely incapable of gratifying her own vindictive longings. And there sat the mistress of Mablethorpe House, perfectly well aware of it.

Lady Janet pointed to the empty chair.

'Suppose you sit down again?' she suggested. 'The course of our interview seems to have brought us back to the question that I asked you when you came into my room. Instead of threatening me with the law, suppose you consider the propriety of permitting me to be of some use to you? I am in the habit of assisting ladies in embarrassed circumstances, and nobody knows of it but my steward — who keeps the accounts — and myself. Once more, let me enquire if a little advance of the pecuniary sort (delicately offered) would be acceptable to you?'

Grace returned slowly to the chair that she had left. She stood by it, with one hand grasping the top rail, and with her eyes fixed in mocking scrutiny on Lady Janet's face.

'At last your ladyship shows your hand,' she said. 'Hush-money!'

'You *will* send me back to my papers,' rejoined Lady Janet. 'How obstinate you are!'

Grace's hand closed tighter and tighter round the rail of the chair. Without witnesses, without means, without so much as a refuge — thanks to her own coarse cruelties of language and conduct — in the sympathies of others, the sense of her isolation and her helplessness was almost maddening at that final moment. A woman of finer sensibilities would have instantly left the room. Grace's impenetrably hard and narrow mind impelled her to meet the emergency in a very different way. A last base vengeance, to which Lady Janet had voluntarily exposed herself, was still within her reach. 'For the present,' she thought, 'there is but one way of being even with your ladyship. I can cost you as much as possible.'

'Pray make some allowances for me,' she said. 'I am not obstinate — I am only a little awkward at matching the audacity of a lady of high rank. I shall improve with practice. My own language is, as I am painfully aware, only plain English. Permit me to withdraw it, and to substitute yours. What advance is your ladyship (delicately) prepared to offer me?'

Lady Janet opened a drawer and took out a cheque-book.

The moment of relief had come at last! The only question now left to discuss was evidently the question of amount. Lady Janet considered a little. The question of amount was (to her mind) in some sort a question of conscience as well. Her love for Mercy and her loathing for Grace, her horror of seeing her darling degraded and her affection profaned by a public exposure, had hurried her — there was no disputing it — into treating an injured woman harshly. Hateful as Grace Roseberry might be, her father had left her, in his last moments, with Lady

Janet's full concurrence, to Lady Janet's care. But for Mercy, she
would have been received at Mablethorpe House as Lady Janet's
companion, with a salary of one hundred pounds a year. On the
other hand, how long (with such a temper as she had revealed)
would Grace have remained in the service of her protectress?
She would, probably, have been dismissed in a few weeks, with
a year's salary to compensate her, and with a recommendation to
some suitable employment. What would be a fair compensation
now? Lady Janet decided that five years' salary immediately
given, and future assistance rendered if necessary, would
represent a fit remembrance of the late Colonel Roseberry's
claims, and a liberal pecuniary acknowledgment of any harshness
of treatment which Grace might have sustained at her hands. At
the same time, and for the further satisfying of her own
conscience, she determined to discover the sum which Grace
herself would consider sufficient, by the simple process of
making Grace herself propose the terms.

'It is impossible for me to make you an offer,' she said, 'for
this reason, – your need of money will depend greatly on your
future plans. I am quite ignorant of your plans.'

'Perhaps your ladyship will kindly advise me?' said Grace
satirically.

'I cannot altogether undertake to advise you,' Lady Janet
replied. 'I can only suppose that you will scarcely remain in
England, where you have no friends. Whether you go to law
with me or not, you will surely feel the necessity of
communicating personally with your friends in Canada. Am I
right?'

Grace was quite quick enough to understand this as it was
meant. Properly interpreted the answer signified – 'If you take
your compensation in money, it is understood, as part of the
bargain, that you don't remain in England to annoy me.'

'Your ladyship is quite right,' she said. 'I shall certainly not
remain in England. I shall consult my friends – and,' she added
mentally, 'go to law with you afterwards, if I possibly can, with
your own money!'

'You will return to Canada,' Lady Janet proceeded; 'and your
prospects there will be, probably, a little uncertain at first.

Taking this into consideration, at what amount do you estimate, in your own mind, the pecuniary assistance which you will require?'

'May I count on your ladyship's kindness to correct me if my own ignorant calculations turn out to be wrong?' Grace asked innocently.

Here again the words, properly interpreted, had a special signification of their own: 'It is stipulated, on my part, that I put myself up to auction, and that my estimate shall be regulated by your ladyship's highest bid.' Thoroughly understanding the stipulation, Lady Janet bowed, and waited gravely.

Gravely, on her side, Grace began.

'I am afraid I should want more than a hundred pounds,' she said.

Lady Janet made her first bid. 'I think so too.'

'More, perhaps, than two hundred?'

'Lady Janet made her second bid. 'Probably.'

'More than three hundred? Four hundred? Five hundred?'

Lady Janet made her highest bid. 'Five hundred pounds will do,' she said.

In spite of herself, Grace's rising colour betrayed her ungovernable excitement. From her earliest childhood she had been accustomed to see shillings and sixpences carefully considered before they were parted with. She had never known her father to possess so much as five golden sovereigns at his own disposal (unencumbered by debt) in all her experience of him. The atmosphere in which she had lived and breathed was the all-stifling atmosphere of genteel poverty. There was something horrible in the greedy eagerness of her eyes as they watched Lady Janet, to see if she was really sufficiently in earnest to give away five hundred pounds sterling with a stroke of her pen.

Lady Janet wrote the cheque in a few seconds, and pushed it across the table.

Grace's hungry eyes devoured the golden line, 'Pay to myself or bearer five hundred pounds,' and verified the signature beneath, 'Janet Roy.' Once sure of the money whenever she chose to take it, the native meanness of her nature instantly asserted itself. She tossed her head, and let the cheque lie on the

table, with an over-acted appearance of caring very little
whether she took it or not.

'Your ladyship is not to suppose that I snap at your cheque,'
she said.

Lady Janet leaned back in her chair and closed her eyes. The
very sight of Grace Roseberry sickened her. Her mind filled
suddenly with the image of Mercy. She longed to feast her eyes
again on that grand beauty, to fill her eyes again with the
melody of that gentle voice.

'I require time to consider — in justice to my own self-
respect,' Grace went to.

Lady Janet wearily made a sign, granting time to consider.

'Your ladyship's boudoir is, I presume, still at my disposal?'

Lady Janet silently granted the boudoir.

'And your ladyship's servants are at my orders, if I have
occasion to employ them?'

Lady Janet suddenly opened her eyes. 'The whole household
is at your orders!' she cried furiously. 'Leave me!'

Grace was far from being offended. If anything, she was
gratified — there was a certain triumph in having stung Lady
Janet into an open outbreak of temper. She insisted forthwith
on another condition.

'In the event of my deciding to receive the cheque,' she said,
'I cannot, consistently with my own self-respect, permit it to be
delivered to me otherwise than enclosed. Your ladyship will (if
necessary) be so kind as to enclose it. Good evening.'

She sauntered to the door; looking from side to side, with an
air of supreme disparagement, at the priceless treasures of art
which adorned the walls. Her eyes dropped superciliously on
the carpet (the design of a famous French painter) as if her feet
condescended in walking over it. The audacity with which she
had entered the room had been marked enough; it shrank to
nothing before the infinitely superior proportions of the
insolence with which she left it.

The instant the door was closed, Lady Janet rose from her
chair. Reckless of the wintry chill in the outer air, she threw
open one of the windows. 'Pah!' she exclaimed with a shudder
of disgust, 'the very air of the room is tainted by her!'

She returned to her chair. Her mood changed as she sat down
again – her heart was with Mercy once more. 'Oh, my love!'
she murmured, 'how low I have stooped, how miserably I have
degraded myself – and all for You!' The bitterness of the
retrospect was unendurable. The inbred force of the woman's
nature took refuge from it in an outburst of defiance and despair.
'Whatever she has done, that wretch deserves it! Not a living
creature in this house shall say she has deceived me. She has *not*
deceived me – she loves me! What do I care whether she has
given me her true name or not? She has given me her true heart.
What right had Julian to play upon her feelings and pry into her
secrets? My poor tempted, tortured child! I won't hear her
confession. Not another word shall she say to any living
creature. I am mistress – I will forbid it at once!' She snatched a
piece of note-paper from the case; hesitated; and threw it from
her on the table. 'Why not send for my darling?' she thought.
'Why write?' She hesitated once more, and resigned the idea.
'No! I can't trust myself! I daren't see her yet!'

She took up the sheet of paper again, and wrote her second
message to Mercy. This time the note began fondly with a
familiar form of address.

'MY DEAR CHILD, – I have had time to think, and compose
myself a little, since I last wrote, requesting you to defer the
explanation which you had promised me. I already understand
(and appreciate) the motives which led you to interfere as you
did downstairs, and I now ask you to entirely abandon the
explanation. It will, I am sure, be painful to you (from reasons of
your own into which I have no wish to enquire) to produce the
person of whom you spoke, and as you know already, I myself
am weary of hearing of her. Besides, there is really no need now
for you to explain anything. The stranger whose visits here have
caused us so much pain and anxiety will trouble us no more. She
leaves England of her own free will, after a conversation with
me which has perfectly succeeded in composing and satisfying
her. Not a word more, my dear, to me, or to my nephew, or to
any other human creature, of what has happened in the dining-
room to-day. When we next meet, let it be understood between

us that the past is henceforth and for ever *buried in oblivion*. This is not only the earnest request — it is, if necessary, the positive command of your mother and friend,

JANET ROY

'P.S. — I shall find opportunities (before you leave your room) of speaking separately to my nephew and to Horace Holmcroft. You need dread no embarrassment, when you next meet them. I will not ask you to answer my note in writing. Say "Yes" to the maid who will bring it to you, and I shall know we understand each other.'

After sealing the envelope which enclosed these lines, Lady Janet addressed it, as usual, to 'Miss Grace Roseberry.' She was just rising to ring the bell, when the maid appeared with a message from the boudoir. The woman's tones and looks showed plainly that she had been made the object of Grace's insolent self-assertion as well as her mistress.

'If you please, my lady, the person downstairs wishes—— '

Lady Janet, frowning contemptuously, interrupted the message at the outset. 'I know what the person downstairs wishes. She has sent you for a letter from me?'

'Yes, my lady.'

'Anything more?'

'She has sent one of the men-servants, my lady, for a cab. If your ladyship had only heard how she spoke to him!—— '

Lady Janet intimated by a sign that she would rather not hear. She at once inclosed the cheque in an undirected envelope.

'Take that to her,' she said, 'and then come back to me.'

Dismissing Grace Roseberry from all further consideration, Lady Janet sat, with her letter to Mercy in her hand, reflecting on her position, and on the efforts which it might still demand from her. Pursuing this train of thought, it now occurred to her that accident might bring Horace and Mercy together at any moment, and that, in Horace's present frame of mind, he would certainly insist on the explanation which it was the foremost interest of her life to suppress. The dread of this disaster was in full possession of her when the maid returned.

'Where is Mr Holmcroft?' she asked, the moment the woman entered the room.

'I saw him open the library door, my lady, just now, on my way upstairs.'

'Was he alone?'

'Yes, my lady.'

'Go to him, and say I want to see him here immediately.'

The maid withdrew on her second errand. Lady Janet rose restlessly, and closed the open window. Her impatient desire to make sure of Horace so completely mastered her, that she left her room, and met the woman in the corridor on her return. Receiving Horace's message of excuse, she instantly sent back the peremptory rejoinder. 'Say that he will oblige me to go to him, if he persists in refusing to come to me. And, stay!' she added, remembering the undelivered letter. 'Send Miss Roseberry's maid here; I want her.'

Left alone again, Lady Janet paced once or twice up and down the corridor — then grew suddenly weary of the sight of it, and went back to her room. The two maids returned together. One of them, having announced Horace's submission, was dismissed. The other was sent to Mercy's room, with Lady Janet's letter. In a minute or two, the messenger appeared again, with the news that she had found the room empty.

'Have you any idea where Miss Roseberry is?'

'No, my lady.'

Lady Janet reflected for a moment. If Horace presented himself without any needless delay, the plain inference would be that she had succeeded in separating him from Mercy. If his appearance was suspiciously deferred, she decided on personally searching for Mercy in the reception-rooms on the lower floor of the house.

'What have you done with the letter?' she asked.

'I left it on Miss Roseberry's table, my lady.'

'Very well. Keep within hearing of the bell, in case I want you again.'

Another minute brought Lady Janet's suspense to an end. She heard the welcome sound of a knock at her door from a man's hand. Horace hurriedly entered the room.

'What is it you want with me, Lady Janet?' he enquired, not very graciously.

'Sit down, Horace, and you shall hear.'

Horace did not accept the invitation.

'Excuse me,' he said, 'if I mention that I am rather in a hurry.'

'Why are you in a hurry?'

'I have reasons for wishing to see Grace as soon as possible.'

'And *I* have reasons,' Lady Janet rejoined, 'for wishing to speak to you about Grace before you see her; serious reasons. Sit down.'

Horace started. 'Serious reasons!' he repeated. 'You surprise me.'

'I shall surprise you still more before I have done.'

Their eyes met, as Lady Janet answered in those terms. Horace observed signs of agitation in her, which he now noticed for the first time. His face darkened with an expression of sullen distrust − and he took the chair in silence.

CHAPTER THE TWENTY-FOURTH

LADY JANET'S LETTER

The narrative leaves Lady Janet and Horace Holmcroft together, and returns to Julian and Mercy in the library.

An interval passed − a long interval, measured by the impatient reckoning of suspense − after the cab which had taken Grace Roseberry away had left the house. The minutes followed each other; and still the warning sound of Horace's footstep was not heard on the marble pavement of the hall. By common (though unexpressed) consent, Julian and Mercy avoided touching upon the one subject on which they were now both interested alike. With their thoughts fixed secretly in vain speculation on the

nature of the interview which was then taking place in Lady
Janet's room, they tried to speak on topics indifferent to both of
them – tried, and failed, and tried again. In a last, and longest
pause of silence between them, the next event happened. The
door from the hall was softly and suddenly opened.

Was it Horace? No – not even yet! The person who had
opened the door was only Mercy's maid.

'My lady's love, miss; and you will please to read this
directly?'

Giving her message in those terms, the woman produced
from the pocket of her apron Lady Janet's second letter to
Mercy, with a strip of paper oddly pinned round the envelope.
Mercy detached the paper, and found on the inner side some
lines in pencil, hurriedly written in Lady Janet's hand. They ran
thus:

'Don't lose a moment in reading my letter. And mind this,
when H. returns to you – meet him firmly: say nothing.'

Enlightened by the warning words which Julian had spoken
to her, Mercy was at no loss to place the right interpretation on
those strange lines. Instead of immediately opening the letter,
she stopped the maid at the library door. Julian's suspicion of
the most trifling events that were taking place in the house had
found its way from his mind to hers. 'Wait!' she said. 'I don't
understand what is going on upstairs; I want to ask you
something.'

The woman came back – not very willingly.

'How did you know I was here?' Mercy enquired.

'If you please, miss, her ladyship ordered me to take the letter
to you some little time since. You were not in your room, and
I left it on your table——'

'I understand that. But how came you to bring the letter
here?'

'My lady rang for me, miss. Before I could knock at her door,
she came out into the corridor, with that morsel of paper in her
hand——'

'So as to keep you from entering her room?'

'Yes, miss. Her ladyship wrote on the paper in a great hurry,
and told me to pin it round the letter that I had left in your

room. I was to take them both together to you and to let nobody see me. "You will find Miss Roseberry in the library" (her ladyship says), "and run, run, run! there isn't a moment to lose!" Those were her own words, miss.'

'Did you hear anything in the room before Lady Janet came out, and met you?'

The woman hesitated, and looked at Julian.

'I hardly know whether I ought to tell you, miss.'

Julian turned away to leave the library. Mercy stopped him by a motion of her hand.

'You know that I shall not get you into any trouble,' she said to the maid. 'And you may speak quite safely before Mr Julian Gray.'

Thus reassured, the maid spoke.

'To own the truth, miss, I heard Mr Holmcroft in my lady's room. His voice sounded as if he was angry. I may say they were both angry – Mr Holmcroft and my lady.' (She turned to Julian.) 'And just before her ladyship came out, sir, I heard your name – as if it was you they were having words about. I can't say exactly what it was; I hadn't time to hear. And I didn't listen, miss. The door was ajar; and the voices were so loud, nobody could help hearing them.'

It was useless to detain the woman any longer. Having given her leave to withdraw, Mercy turned to Julian.

'Why were they quarrelling about you?' she asked.

Julian pointed to the unopened letter in her hand.

'The answer to your question may be there,' he said. 'Read the letter while you have the chance. And if I can advise you, say so at once.'

With a strange reluctance she opened the envelope. With a sinking heart she read the lines in which Lady Janet, as 'mother and friend,' commanded her absolutely to suppress the confession which she had pledged herself to make in the sacred interests of justice and truth. A low cry of despair escaped her, as the cruel complication in her position revealed itself in all its unmerited hardship. 'Oh, Lady Janet, Lady Janet!' she thought, 'there was but one trial more left in my hard lot – and it comes to me from *you!*'

She handed the letter to Julian. He took it from her in silence; turning paler and paler as he read it. His eyes rested on her compassionately as he handed it back.

'To my mind,' he said, 'Lady Janet herself sets all further doubt at rest. Her letter tells me what she wanted when she sent for Horace, and why my name was mentioned between them.'

'Tell me!' cried Mercy, eagerly.

He did not immediately answer her. He sat down again in the chair by her side, and pointed to the letter.

'Has Lady Janet shaken your resolution?' he asked.

'She has strengthened my resolution,' Mercy answered. 'She has added a new bitterness to my remorse.'

She did not mean it harshly; but the reply sounded harshly in Julian's ear. It stirred the generous impulses which were the strongest impulses in his nature. He who had once pleaded with Mercy for compassionate consideration for herself, now pleaded with her for compassionate consideration for Lady Janet. With persuasive gentleness, he drew a little nearer, and laid his hand on her arm.

'Don't judge her harshly,' he said. 'She is wrong, miserably wrong. She has recklessly degraded herelf; she has recklessly tempted you. Still, is it generous – is it even just – to hold her responsible for deliberate sin? She is at the close of her days; she can feel no new affection; she can never replace you. View her position in that light, and you will see (as I see) that it is no base motive that has led her astray. Think of her wounded heart and her wasted life – and say to yourself forgivingly, She loves me!'

Mercy's eyes filled with tears.

'I do say it!' she answered. 'Not forgivingly – it is *I* who have need of forgiveness. I say it gratefully when I think of her – I say it with shame and sorrow when I think of myself.'

He took her hand for the first time. He looked, guiltlessly looked, at her downcast face. He spoke as he had spoken at the memorable interview between them which had made a new woman of her.

'I can imagine no crueller trial,' he said, 'than the trial that is now before you. The benefactress to whom you owe everything, asks nothing from you but your silence. The person whom you have wronged is no longer present to stimulate your resolution to speak. Horace himself (unless I am entirely mistaken) will not hold you to the explanation that you have promised. The temptation to keep your false position in this house is, I do not scruple to say, all but irresistible. Sister and friend! Can you still justify my faith in you? Will you still own the truth, without the base fear of discovery to drive you to it?'

She lifted her head, with the steady light of resolution shining again in her grand grey eyes. Her low sweet voice answered him, without a faltering note in it.

'I will!'

'You will do justice to the woman whom you have wronged – unworthy as she is; powerless as she is to expose you?'

'I will!'

'You will sacrifice everything you have gained by the fraud to the sacred duty of atonement? You will suffer anything – even though you offend the second mother who has loved you and sinned for you – rather than suffer the degradation of yourself?'

Her hand closed firmly on his. Again, and for the last time, she answered.

'I will!'

His voice had not trembled yet. It failed him now. His next words were spoken in faint whispering tones – to himself; not to her.

'Thank God for this day!' he said. 'I have been of some service to one of the noblest of God's creatures!'

Some subtle influence, as he spoke, passed from his hand to hers. It trembled through her nerves; it entwined itself mysteriously with the finest sensibilities in her nature; it softly opened her heart to a first vague surmising of the devotion that she had inspired in him. A faint glow of colour, lovely in its faintness, stole over her face and neck. Her breathing quickened tremblingly. She drew her hand away from him, and sighed when she had released it.

He rose suddenly to his feet and left her without a word or a look, walking slowly down the length of the room. When he turned and came back to her, his face was composed; he was master of himself again.

Mercy was the first to speak. She turned the conversation from herself by reverting to the proceedings in Lady Janet's room.

'You spoke of Horace just now,' she said, 'in terms which surprised me. You appeared to think that he would not hold me to my explanation. Is that one of the conclusions which you draw from Lady Janet's letter?'

'Most assuredly,' Julian answered. 'You will see the conclusion as I see it, if we return for a moment to Grace Roseberry's departure from the house.'

Mercy interrupted him there. 'Can you guess,' she asked, 'how Lady Janet prevailed upon her to go?'

'I hardly like to own it,' said Julian. 'There is an expression in the letter which suggests to me that Lady Janet has offered her money, and that she has taken the bribe.'

'Oh, I can't think that!'

'Let us return to Horace. Miss Roseberry once out of the house, but one serious obstacle is left in Lady Janet's way. That obstacle is Horace Holmcroft.'

'How is Horace an obstacle?'

'He is an obstacle in this sense. He is under an engagement to marry you in a week's time; and Lady Janet is determined to keep him (as she is determined to keep everyone else) in ignorance of the truth. She will do that without scruple. But the inbred sense of honour in her is not utterly silenced yet. She cannot, she dare not, let Horace make you his wife, under the false impression that you are Colonel Roseberry's daughter. You see the situation? On the one hand she won't enlighten him. On the other hand, she cannot allow him to marry you blindfold. In this emergency, what is she to do? There is but one alternative that I can discover. She must persuade Horace (or she must irritate Horace) into acting for himself, and breaking off the engagement on his own responsibility.'

Mercy stopped him. 'Impossible!' she cried warmly. 'Impossible!'

'Look again at her letter,' Julian rejoined. 'It tells you plainly that you need fear no embarrassment when you next meet Horace. If words mean anything, those words mean that he will not claim from you the confidence which you have promised to repose in him. On what condition is it possible for him to abstain from doing that? On the one condition that you have ceased to represent the first and foremost interest of his life.'

Mercy still held firm. 'You are wronging Lady Janet,' she said.

Julian smiled sadly.

'Try to look at it,' he answered, 'from Lady Janet's point of view. Do you suppose *she* sees anything derogatory to her in attempting to break off the marriage? I will answer for it she believes she is doing you a kindness. In one sense, it *would* be a kindness to spare you the shame of a humiliating confession, and to save you (possibly) from being rejected to your face by the man you love. In my opinion, the thing is done already. I have reasons of my own for believing that my aunt will succeed far more easily than she could anticipate. Horace's temper will help her.'

Mercy's mind began to yield to him in spite of herself.

'What do you mean by Horace's temper?' she enquired.

'Must you ask me that?' he said, drawing back a little from her.

'I must.'

'I mean by Horace's temper, Horace's unworthy distrust of the interest that I feel in you.'

She instantly understood him. And more than that, she secretly admired him for the scrupulous delicacy with which he had expressed himself. Another man would not have thought of sparing her in that way. Another man would have said plainly, 'Horace is jealous of me.'

Julian did not wait for her to answer him. He considerately went on.

'For the reason that I have just mentioned,' he said, 'Horace will be easily irritated into taking a course which, in his calmer moments, nothing would induce him to adopt. Until I heard what your maid said to you, I had thought (for your sake) of retiring before he joined you here. Now I know that my name has been introduced, and has made mischief upstairs, I feel the necessity (for your sake again) of meeting Horace and his temper face to face before you see him. Let me, if I can, prepare him to hear you, without any angry feeling in his mind towards *me*. Do you object to retire to the next room for a few minutes, in the event of his coming back to the library?'

Mercy's courage instantly rose with the emergency. She refused to leave the two men together.

'Don't think me insensible to your kindness,' she said. 'If I leave you with Horace I may expose you to insult. I refuse to do that. What makes you doubt his coming back?'

'His prolonged absence makes me doubt it,' Julian replied. 'In my belief the marriage is broken off. He may go as Grace Roseberry has gone. You may never see him again.'

The instant the opinion was uttered, it was practically contradicted by the man himself. Horace opened the library door.

CHAPTER THE TWENTY-FIFTH

THE CONFESSION

He stopped just inside the door. His first look was for Mercy; his second look was for Julian.

'I knew it!' he said, with an assumption of sardonic composure. 'If I could only have persuaded Lady Janet to bet, I should have won a hundred pounds.' He advanced to Julian, with a sudden change from irony to anger. 'Would you like to hear what the bet was?' he asked.

'I should prefer seeing you able to control yourself, in the presence of this lady,' Julian answered quietly.

'I offered to lay Lady Janet two hundred pounds to one,' Horace proceeded, 'that I should find you here, making love to Miss Roseberry behind my back.'

Mercy interfered before Julian could reply.

'If you cannot speak without insulting one of us,' she said, 'permit me to request that you will *not* address yourself to Mr Julian Gray.'

Horace bowed to her, with a mockery of respect.

'Pray don't alarm yourself – I am pledged to be scrupulously civil to both of you,' he replied. 'Lady Janet only allowed me to leave her, on condition of my promising to behave with perfect politeness. What else can I do? I have two privileged people to deal with – a parson and a woman. The parson's profession protects him, and the woman's sex protects her. You have got me at a disadvantage, and you both of you know it. I beg to apologise if I have forgotten the clergyman's profession and the lady's sex.'

'You have forgotten more than that,' said Julian. 'You have forgotten that you were born a gentleman and bred a man of honour. So far as I am concerned I don't ask you to remember that I am a clergyman – I obtrude my profession on nobody – I only ask you to remember your birth and your breeding. It is quite bad enough to cruelly and unjustly suspect an old friend who has never forgotten what he owes to you and to himself. But it is still more unworthy of you to acknowledge those suspicions in the hearing of a woman whom your own choice has doubly bound you to respect.'

He stopped. The two eyed each other for a moment in silence.

It was impossible for Mercy to look at them, as she was looking now, without drawing the inevitable comparison between the manly force and dignity of Julian and the womanish malice and irritability of Horace. A last faithful impulse of loyalty towards the man to whom she had been betrothed impelled her to part them before Horace had hopelessly degraded himself in her estimation by contrast with Julian.

'You had better wait to speak to me,' she said to him, 'until we are alone.'

'Certainly,' Horace answered with a sneer, 'if Mr Julian Gray will permit it.'

Mercy turned to Julian, with a look which said plainly, 'Pity us both, and leave us!'

'Do you wish me to go?' he asked.

'Add to all your other kindnesses to me,' she answered. 'Wait for me in that room.'

She pointed to the door that led into the dining-room. Julian hesitated.

'You promise to let me know it, if I can be of the smallest service to you?' he said.

'Yes, yes!' She followed him as he withdrew, and added rapidly in a whisper, 'Leave the door ajar!'

He made no answer. As she returned to Horace, he entered the dining-room. The one concession he could make to her he did make. He closed the door so noiselessly that not even her quick hearing could detect that he had shut it.

Mercy spoke to Horace, without waiting to let him speak first.

'I have promised you an explanation of my conduct,' she said, in accents that trembled a little in spite of herself. 'I am ready to perform my promise.'

'I have a question to ask you before you do that,' he rejoined. 'Can you speak the truth?'

'I am waiting to speak the truth.'

'I will give you an opportunity. Are you, or are you not, in love with Julian Gray?'

'You ought to be ashamed to ask the question!'

'Is that your only answer?'

'I have never been unfaithful to you, Horace, even in thought. If I had *not* been true to you, should I feel my position as you see I feel it now?'

He smiled bitterly. 'I have my own opinion of your fidelity and of his honour,' he said. 'You couldn't even send him into the next room, without whispering to him first. Never mind that now. At least you know that Julian Gray is in love with you.'

'Mr Julian Gray has never breathed a word of it to me.'

'A man can show a woman that he loves her, without saying it in words.'

Mercy's power of endurance began to fail her. Not even Grace Roseberry had spoken more insultingly to her of Julian than Horace was speaking now. 'Whoever says that of Mr Julian Gray, lies!' she answered warmly.

'Then Lady Janet lies,' Horace retorted.

'Lady Janet never said it! Lady Janet is incapable of saying it!'

'She may not have said it in so many words; but she never denied it when *I* said it. I reminded her of the time when Julian Gray first heard from me that I was going to marry you: he was so overwhelmed that he was barely capable of being civil to me. Lady Janet was present and could not deny it. I asked her if she had observed, since then, signs of a confidential understanding between you two. She could not deny the signs. I asked her if she had ever found you two together. She could not deny that she had found you together, this very day, under circumstances which justified suspicion. Yes! yes! Look as angry as you like! You don't know what has been going on upstairs. Lady Janet is bent on breaking off our engagement – and Julian Gray is at the bottom of it.'

As to Julian, Horace was utterly wrong. But as to Lady Janet, he echoed the warning words which Julian himself had spoken to Mercy. She was staggered, but she still held to her own opinion. 'I don't believe it!' she said, firmly.

He advanced a step, and fixed his angry eyes on her searchingly.

'Do you know why Lady Janet sent for me?' he asked.

'No.'

'Then I will tell you. Lady Janet is a staunch friend of yours, there is no denying that. She wished to inform me that she had altered her mind about your promised explanation of your conduct. She said, "Reflection has convinced me that no explanation is required; I have laid my positive commands on my adopted daughter that no explanation shall take place." Has she done that?'

'Yes.'

'Now observe! I waited till she had finished, and then I said, "What have I to do with this?" Lady Janet has one merit – she speaks out. "You are to do as I do," she answered. "You are to consider that no explanation is required, and you are to consign the whole matter to oblivion, from this time forth." "Are you serious?" I asked. "Quite serious." "In that case I have to inform your ladyship that you insist on more than you may suppose – you insist on my breaking my engagement to Miss

Roseberry. Either I am to have the explanation that she has promised me, or I refuse to marry her." How do you think Lady Janet took that? She shut up her lips, and she spread out her hands, and she looked at me as much as to say, "Just as you please! Refuse if you like; it's nothing to me!"'

He paused for a moment. Mercy remained silent, on her side: she foresaw what was coming. Mistaken in supposing that Horace had left the house Julian had, beyond all doubt, been equally in error in concluding that he had been entrapped into breaking off the engagement upstairs.

'Do you understand me, so far?' Horace asked.

'I understand you perfectly.'

'I will not trouble you much longer,' he resumed. 'I said to Lady Janet, "Be so good as to answer me in plain words. Do you still insist on closing Miss Roseberry's lips?" "I still insist," she answered. "No explanation is required. If you are base enough to suspect your betrothed wife, I am just enough to believe in my adopted daughter." I replied – and I beg you will give your best attention to what I am now going to say – I replied to that, "It is not fair to charge me with suspecting her. I don't understand her confidential relations with Julian Gray, and I don't understand her language and conduct in the presence of the police-officer. I claim it as my right to be satisfied on both those points – in the character of the man who is to marry her." There was my answer. I spare you all that followed. I only repeat what I said to Lady Janet. She has commanded you to be silent. If you obey her commands, I owe it to myself and I owe it to my family to release you from your engagement. Choose between your duty to Lady Janet and your duty to Me.'

He had mastered his temper at last: he spoke with dignity, and he spoke to the point. His position was unassailable; he claimed nothing but his right.

'My choice was made,' Mercy answered, 'when I gave you my promise upstairs.'

She waited a little, struggling to control herself on the brink of the terrible revelation that was coming. Her eyes dropped before his; her heart beat faster and faster – but she rallied bravely. With a desperate courage she faced the position. 'If you are ready to listen,' she went on, 'I am ready to tell you why I insisted on having the police-officer sent out of the house.'

Horace held up his hand warningly.

'Stop!' he said, 'that is not all.'

His infatuated jealousy of Julian (fatally misinterpreting her agitation) distrusted her at the very outset. She had limited herself to clearing up the one question of her interference with the officer of justice. The other question of her relations with Julian she had deliberately passed over. Horace instantly drew his own ungenerous conclusion.

'Let us not misunderstand one another,' he said. 'The explanation of your conduct in the other room is only one of the explanations which you owe me. You have something else to account for. Let us begin with *that*, if you please.'

She looked at him in unaffected surprise.

'What else have I to account for?' she asked.

He again repeated his reply to Lady Janet.

'I have told you already,' he said. 'I don't understand your confidential relations with Julian Gray.'

Mercy's colour rose; Mercy's eyes began to brighten.

'Don't return to that!' she cried, with an irrepressible outbreak of disgust. 'Don't, for God's sake, make me despise you at such a moment as this!'

His obstinacy only gathered fresh encouragement from that appeal to his better sense.

'I insist on returning to it.'

She had resolved to bear anything from him – as her fit punishment for the deception of which she had been guilty. But it was not in womanhood (at the moment when the first words of her confession were trembling on her lips) to endure Horace's unworthy suspicion of her. She rose from her seat and met his eye firmly.

'I refuse to degrade myself, and to degrade Mr Julian Gray, by answering you,' she said.

'Consider what you are doing,' he rejoined. 'Change your mind before it is too late!'

'You have had my reply.'

Those resolute words, that steady resistance, seemed to infuriate him. He caught her roughly by the arm.

'You are as false as hell!' he cried. 'It's all over between you and me!'

The loud threatening tone in which he had spoken penetrated through the closed door of the dining-room. The door instantly opened. Julian returned to the library.

He had just set foot in the room, when there was a knock at the other door – the door that opened on the hall. One of the men-servants appeared, with a telegraphic message in his hand. Mercy was the first to see it. It was the Matron's answer to the letter which she had sent to the Refuge.

'For Mr Julian Gray?' she asked.

'Yes, miss.'

'Give it to me.'

She signed to the man to withdraw, and herself gave the telegram to Julian. 'It is addressed to you, at my request,' she said. 'You will recognise the name of the person who sends it, and you will find a message in it for me.'

Horace interfered before Julian could open the telegram.

'Another private understanding between you!' he said. 'Give me that telegram.'

Julian looked at him with quiet contempt.

'It is directed to Me!' he answered – and opened the envelope.

The message inside was expressed in these terms; 'I am as deeply interested in her as you are. Say that I have received her letter, and that I welcome her back to the Refuge with all my heart. I have business this evening in the neighbourhood. I will call for her myself at Mablethorpe House.'

The message explained itself. Of her own free will, she had made the expiation complete! Of her own free will, she was going back to the martyrdom of her old life! Bound as he knew himself to be to let no compromising word or action escape him in the presence of Horace, the irrepressible expression of Julian's admiration glowed in his eyes as they rested on Mercy. Horace detected the look. He sprang forward and tried to snatch the telegram out of Julian's hand.

'Give it to me!' he said. 'I will have it!'

Julian silently put him back at arm's length.

Maddened with rage, he lifted his hand threateningly. 'Give it to me,' he repeated between his set teeth, 'or it will be the worse for you!'

'Give it to *me*!' said Mercy, suddenly placing herself between them.

Julian gave it. She turned, and offered it to Horace, looking at him with a steady eye, holding it out to him with a steady hand.

'Read it,' she said.

Julian's generous nature pitied the man who had insulted him. Julian's great heart only remembered the friend of former times.

'Spare him!' he said to Mercy. 'Spare him, if he is not yet prepared!'

She neither answered nor moved. Nothing stirred the horrible torpor of her resignation to her fate. She knew that the time had come.

Julian looked at Horace.

'Don't read it!' he cried. 'Hear what she has to say to you first!'

Horace's hand answered him with a contemptuous gesture. Horace's eyes devoured, word by word, the Matron's message.

He looked up when he had read it through. There was a ghastly change in his face as he turned it on Mercy.

She stood between the two men like a statue. The life in her seemed to have died out except in her eyes. Her eyes rested on Horace with a steady, glittering calmness.

The silence was only broken by the low murmuring of Julian's voice. His face was hidden in his hands – he was praying for them.

Horace spoke – laying his finger on the telegram. His voice had changed with the change in his face. The tone was low and trembling: no one would have recognised it as the tone of Horace's voice.

'What does this mean?' he said to Mercy. 'It can't be for you?'

'It *is* for me.'

'What have You to do with a Refuge?'

Without a change in her face, without a movement in her limbs, she spoke the fatal words.

'I have come from a Refuge, and I am going back to a Refuge. Mr Horace Holmcroft, I am Mercy Merrick.'

CHAPTER THE TWENTY-SIXTH

GREAT HEART AND LITTLE HEART

There was a pause.

The moments passed – and not one of the three moved. The moments passed – and not one of the three spoke. Insensibly the words of supplication died away on Julian's lips. Even his energy failed to sustain him, tried as it now was by the crushing oppression of suspense. The first trifling movement which suggested the idea of change, and which so brought with it the first vague sense of relief, came from Mercy. Incapable of sustaining the prolonged effort of standing, she drew back a little, and took a chair. No outward manifestation of emotion escaped her. There she sat – with the death-like torpor of resignation in her face – waiting her sentence in silence from the man at whom she had hurled the whole terrible confession of the truth in one sentence.

Julian lifted his head as she moved. He looked once more at Horace, and drew back a few steps. There was fear in his face, as he suddenly turned it towards Mercy.

'Speak to him!' he said in a whisper. 'Rouse him, before it's too late!'

She moved mechanically in her chair; she looked mechanically at Julian.

'What more have I to say to him?' she asked in faint, weary tones. 'Did I not tell him everything when I told him my name?'

The natural sound of her voice might have failed to affect Horace. The altered sound of it roused him. He approached Mercy's chair, with a dull surprise in his face, and put his hand in a weak, wavering way on her shoulder. In that position he stood for a while, looking down at her in silence.

The one idea in him that found its way outwards to expression was the idea of Julian. Without moving his hand, without looking up from Mercy, he spoke for the first time since the shock had fallen on him.

'Where is Julian?' he asked, very quietly.

'I am here, Horace – close by you.'

'Will you do me a service?'

'Certainly. How can I help you?'

He considered a little before he replied. His hand left Mercy's shoulder, and went up to his head – then dropped at his side. His next words were spoken in a sadly helpless, bewildered way.

'I have an idea, Julian, that I have been somehow to blame. I said some hard words to you. It was a little while since. I don't clearly remember what it was all about. My temper has been a good deal tried in this house; I have never been used to the sort of thing that goes on here – secrets and mysteries, and hateful, low-lived quarrels. We have no secrets and mysteries at home. And as for quarrels – ridiculous! My mother and my sisters are highly-bred women (you know them); gentlewomen, in the best sense of the word. When I am with *them* I have no anxieties. I am not harassed at home by doubts of who people are, and confusion about names, and so on. I suspect the contrast weighs a little on my mind, and upsets it. They make me over-suspicious among them here – and it ends in my feeling doubts and fears that I can't get over; doubts about you, and fears about myself. I have got a fear about myself now. I want you to help me. Shall I make an apology first?'

'Don't say a word. Tell me what I can do.'

He turned his face towards Julian for the first time.

'Just look at me,' he said. 'Does it strike you that I am at all wrong in my mind? Tell me the truth, old fellow.'

'Your nerves are a little shaken, Horace. Nothing more.'

He considered again, after that reply; his eyes remaining anxiously fixed on Julian's face.

'My nerves are a little shaken,' he repeated. 'That is true; I feel they are shaken. I should like, if you don't mind, to make sure that it's no worse. Will you help me to try if my memory is all right?'

'I will do anything you like.'

'Ah! you are a good fellow, Julian – and a clear-headed fellow, too, which is very important just now. Look here! I say it's about a week since the troubles began in this house. Do you say so too?'

'Yes.'

'The troubles came in with the coming of a woman from Germany, a stranger to us, who behaved very violently in the dining-room there. Am I right, so far?'

'Quite right.'

'The woman carried matters with a high hand. She claimed Colonel Roseberry – no, I wish to be strictly accurate – she claimed the *late* Colonel Roseberry as her father. She told a tiresome story about her having been robbed of her papers and her name by an impostor who had personated her. She said the name of the impostor was Mercy Merrick. And she afterwards put the climax to it all: she pointed to the lady who is engaged to be my wife, and declared that *she* was Mercy Merrick. Tell me again, is that right or wrong?'

Julian answered him as before. He went on, speaking more confidently and more excitedly than he had spoken yet.

'Now attend to this, Julian. I am going to pass from my memory of what happened a week ago to my memory of what happened five minutes since. You were present; I want to know if you heard it too.' He paused, and, without taking his eyes off Julian, pointed backwards to Mercy. 'There is the lady who is engaged to marry me,' he resumed. 'Did I, or did I not, hear her say that she had come out of a Refuge, and that she was going back to a Refuge? Did I, or did I not, hear her own to my face that her name was Mercy Merrick? Answer me, Julian. My good friend, answer me for the sake of old times.'

His voice faltered as he spoke these imploring words. Under the dull blank of his face there appeared the first signs of emotion slowly forcing its way outwards. The stunned mind was reviving faintly. Julian saw his opportunity of aiding the recovery, and seized it. He took Horace gently by the arm and pointed to Mercy.

'There is your answer!' he said. 'Look! – and pity her.'

She had not once interrupted them while they had been speaking: she had changed her position again, and that was all. There was a writing-table at the side of her chair; her outstretched arms rested on it. Her head had dropped on her arms, and her face was hidden. Julian's judgment had not misled him; the utter self-abandonment of her attitude answered Horace as no human language could have answered him. He looked at her. A quick spasm of pain passed across his face. He turned once more to the faithful friend who had forgiven him. His head fell on Julian's shoulder, and he burst into tears.

Mercy started wildly to her feet and looked at the two men.

'O God!' she cried, 'what have I done!'

Julian quieted her by a motion of the hand.

'You have helped me to save him,' he said. 'Let his tears have their way. Wait.'

He put one arm round Horace to support him. The manly tenderness of the action, the complete and noble pardon of past injuries which it implied, touched Mercy to the heart. She went back to her chair. Again shame and sorrow overpowered her, and again she hid her face from view.

Julian led Horace to a seat, and silently waited by him until he had recovered his self-control. He gratefully took the kind hand that had sustained him; he said simply, almost boyishly, 'Thank you, Julian. I am better now.'

'Are you composed enough to listen to what is said to you?' Julian asked.

'Yes. Do *you* wish to speak to me?'

Julian left him without immediately replying, and returned to Mercy.

'The time has come,' he said. 'Tell him all – truly, unreservedly, as you would tell it to me.'

She shuddered as he spoke. 'Have I not told him enough?' she asked. 'Do you want me to break his heart? Look at him! See what I have done already!'

Horace shrank from the ordeal as Mercy shrank from it.

'No! no! I can't listen to it! I daren't listen to it!' he cried, and rose to leave the room.

Julian had taken the good work in hand: he never faltered over it for an instant. Horace had loved her – how dearly, Julian now knew for the first time. The bare possibility that she might earn her pardon if she was allowed to plead her own cause, was a possibility still left. To let her win on Horace to forgive her, was death to the love that still filled his heart in secret. But he never hesitated. With a resolution which the weaker man was powerless to resist, he took him by the arm and led him back to his place.

'For her sake, and for your sake, you shall not condemn her unheard,' he said to Horace firmly. 'One temptation to deceive you after another has tried her, and she has resisted them all. With no discovery to fear; with a letter from the benefactress who loves her, commanding her to be silent; with everything that a woman values in this world to lose, if she owns what she had done – *this* woman, for the truth's sake, has spoken the truth. Does she deserve nothing at your hands in return for that? Respect her, Horace, and hear her.'

Horace yielded. Julian turned to Mercy.

'You have allowed me to guide you so far,' he said. 'Will you allow me to guide you still?'

Her eyes sank before his; her bosom rose and fell rapidly. His influence over her maintained its sway. She bowed her head in speechless submission.

'Tell him,' Julian proceeded, in accents of entreaty, not of command, 'tell him what your life has been. Tell him how you were tried and tempted, with no friend near to speak the words which might have saved you. And then,' he added, raising her from the chair, 'let him judge you – if he can!'

He attempted to lead her across the room to the place which Horace occupied. But her submission had its limits. Half way to the place she stopped, and refused to go further. Julian offered her a chair. She declined to take it. Standing, with one hand on the back of the chair, she waited for the word from Horace which would permit her to speak. She was resigned to the ordeal. Her face was calm; her mind was clear. The hardest of all humiliations to endure – the humiliation of acknowledging her name – she had passed through. Nothing remained but to show her gratitude to Julian by acceding to his wishes, and to ask pardon of Horace before they parted for ever. In a little while the Matron would arrive at the house – and then it would be over.

Unwillingly Horace looked at her. Their eyes met. He broke out suddenly wih something of his former violence.

'I can't realise it, even now!' he cried. '*Is* it true that you are not Grace Roseberry? Don't look at me! Say in one word – Yes or No.'

She answered him humbly and sadly, 'Yes.'

'You have done what that woman accused you of doing? Am I to believe that?'

'You are to believe it, sir.'

All the weakness of Horace's character disclosed itself when she made her reply.

'Infamous!' he exclaimed. 'What excuse can you make for the cruel deception you have practised on me? Too bad! too bad! There can be no excuse for you!'

She accepted his reproaches with unshaken resignation. 'I have deserved it!' was all she said to herself, 'I have deserved it!'

Julian interposed once more in Mercy's defence.

'Wait till you are sure there is no excuse for her, Horace,' he said quietly. 'Grant her justice, if you can grant no more. I leave you together.'

He advanced towards the door of the dining-room. Horace's weakness disclosed itself once more.

'Don't leave me alone with her!' he burst out. 'The misery of it is more than I can bear!'

Julian looked at Mercy. Her face brightened faintly. That momentary expression of relief told him how truly he would be befriending her if he consented to remain in the room. A position of retirement was offered to him by a recess formed by the central bay window of the library. If he occupied this place they could see or not see that he was present, as their own inclinations might decide them.

'I will stay with you, Horace, as long as you wish me to be here.' Having answered in those terms, he stopped as he passed Mercy on his way to the window. His quick and kindly insight told him that he might still be of some service to her. A hint from him might show her the shortest and the easiest way of making her confession. Delicately and briefly he gave her the hint. 'The first time I met you,' he said, 'I saw that your life had had its troubles. Let us hear how those troubles began.'

He withdrew to his place in the recess. For the first time since the fatal evening when she and Grace Roseberry had met in the French cottage, Mercy Merrick looked back into the purgatory on earth of her past life, and told her sad story simply and truly in these words.

CHAPTER THE TWENTY-SEVENTH

MAGDALEN'S APPRENTICESHIP

'Mr Julian Gray has asked me to tell him, and to tell you, Mr Holmcroft, how my troubles began. They began before my recollection. They began with my birth.

'My mother (as I have heard her say) ruined her prospects, when she was quite a young girl, by a marriage with one of her father's servants – the groom who rode out with her. She suffered the usual penalty of such conduct as hers. After a short time she and her husband were separated – on the condition of her sacrificing to the man whom she had married the whole of the little fortune that she possessed in her own right.

'Gaining her freedom, my mother had to gain her daily bread next. Her family refused to take her back. She attached herself to a company of strolling players.

'She was earning a bare living in this way, when my father accidentally met with her. He was a man of high rank; proud of his position, and well known in the society of that time for his many accomplishments and his refined tastes. My mother's beauty fascinated him. He took her from the strolling players, and surrounded her with every luxury that a woman could desire in a house of her own.

'I don't know how long they lived together. I only know that my father, at the time of my first recollections, had abandoned her. She had excited his suspicions of her fidelity – suspicions which cruelly wronged her, as she declared to her dying day. I believed her, because she was my mother. But I cannot expect others to do as I did – I can only repeat what she said. My father left her absolutely penniless. He never saw her again; and he refused to go to her, when she sent to him in her last moments on earth.

'She was back again among the strolling players when I first remember her. It was not an unhappy time for me. I was the favourite pet and plaything of the poor actors. They taught me to sing and to dance, at an age when other children are just beginning to learn to read. At five years old I was in what is called "the profession," and had made my poor little reputation in booths at country fairs. As early as that, Mr Holmcroft, I had begun to live under an assumed name – the prettiest name they could invent for me, "to look well in the bills." It was sometimes a hard struggle for us, in bad seasons, to keep body and soul together. Learning to sing and dance in public often meant learning to bear hunger and cold in private, when I was apprenticed to the stage – and yet I have lived to look back on my days with the strolling players as the happiest days of my life!

'I was ten years old when the first serious misfortune that I can remember fell upon me. My mother died, worn out in the prime of her life. And not long afterwards the strolling company, brought to the end of its resources by a succession of bad seasons, was broken up.

'I was left on the world, a nameless, penniless outcast, with one fatal inheritance – God knows I can speak of it without vanity, after what I have gone through; — the inheritance of my mother's beauty.

'My only friends were the poor starved-out players. Two of them (husband and wife) obtained engagements in another company, and I was included in the bargain. The new manager by whom I was employed was a drunkard and a brute. One night, I made a trifling mistake in the course of the performances — and I was savagely beaten for it. Perhaps I had inherited some of my father's spirit – without, I hope, also inheriting my father's pitiless nature. However that may be, I resolved (no matter what became of me) never again to serve the man who had beaten me. I unlocked the door of our miserable lodging at daybreak the next morning; and, at ten years old, with my little bundle in my hand, I faced the world alone.

'My mother had confided to me, in her last moments, my father's name, and the address of his house in London. "He may feel some compassion for you" (she said) "though he feels none for me: try him." I had a few shillings, the last pitiful remains of my wages, in my pocket, and I was not far from London. But I never went near my father: child as I was, I would have starved and died rather than go to him. I had loved my mother dearly; and I hated the man who had turned his back on her when she lay on her deathbed. It made no difference to Me that he happened to be my father.

'Does this confession revolt you? You look at me, Mr Holmcroft, as if it did.

'Think a little, sir. Does what I have just said condemn me as a heartless creature, even in my earliest years? What is a father to a child, when the child has never sat on his knee and never had a kiss or a present from him? If we had met in the street, we should not have known each other. Perhaps, in afterdays, when I was starving in London, I may have begged of my father without-knowing it, and he may have thrown his daughter a penny without knowing it either! What is there sacred in the relations between father and child, when they are such relations as these? Even the flowers of the field cannot grow without light and air to help them. How is a child's love to grow, with nothing to help it?

'My small savings would have been soon exhausted, even if I
had been old enough and strong enough to protect them
myself. As things were, my few shillings were taken from me by
gipsies. I had no reason to complain. They gave me food and
the shelter of their tents; and they made me of use to them in
various ways. After a while, hard times came to the gipsies, as
they had come to the strolling players. Some of them were
imprisoned, the rest were dispersed. It was the season for hop-
gathering at the time. I got employment among the hop-pickers
next; and that done, I went to London with my new friends.

'I have no wish to weary and pain you by dwelling on this
part of my childhood in detail. It will be enough if I tell you
that I ended in begging, under the pretence of selling matches
in the street. My mother's legacy got me many a sixpence
which my matches would never have charmed out of the
pockets of strangers if I had been an ugly child. My face, which
was destined to be my greatest misfortune in after years, was my
best friend in those days.

'Is there anything, Mr Holmcroft, in the life I am now trying
to describe which reminds you of a day when we were out
walking together, not long since?

'I surprised and offended you, I remember; and it was not
possible for me to explain my conduct at the time. Do you
recollect the little wandering girl, with the miserable faded
nosegay in her hand, who ran after us and begged for a
halfpenny? I shocked you by bursting out crying when the child
asked us to buy her a bit of bread. Now you know why I was
so sorry for her. Now you know why I offended you the next
day, by breaking an engagement with your mother, trying
(vainly) to trace that child to her home. After what I have
confessed, you will admit that my poor little sister in adversity
had the first claim on me.

'Let me go on, I am sorry if I have distressed you. Let me go
on.

'The forlorn wanderers of the streets have (as I found it) one
way, always open to them, of presenting their sufferings to the
notice of their rich and charitable fellow-creatures. They have
only to break the law – and they make a public appearance in a

court of justice. If the circumstances connected with their offence are of an interesting kind, they gain a second advantage; they are advertised all over England by a report in the newspapers.

'Yes; even *I* have my knowledge of the law. I know that it completely overlooked me so long as I respected it; but on two different occasions it became by best friend when I set it at defiance. My first fortunate offence was committed when I was just twelve years old.

'It was evening time. I was half dead with starvation; the rain was falling; the night was coming on. I begged – openly, loudly, as only a hungry child *can* beg. An old lady in a carriage at a shop-door complained of my importunity. The policeman did his duty. The law gave me a supper and a shelter at the station-house that night. I appeared at the police-court, and, questioned by the magistrate, I told my story truly. It was the everyday story of thousands of children like me; but it had one element of interest in it. I confessed to having had a father (he was then dead) who had been a man of rank; and I owned (just as openly as I owned everything else), that I had never applied to him for help, in resentment of his treatment of my mother. This incident was new, I suppose: it led to the appearance of my "case" in the newspapers. The reporters further served my interests by describing me as "pretty and interesting." Subscriptions were sent to the court. A benevolent married couple, in a respectable sphere of life, visited the workhouse to see me. I produced a favourable impression on them – especially on the wife. I was literally friendless – I had no unwelcome relatives to follow me and claim me. The wife was childless; the husband was a good-natured man. It ended in their taking me away with them to try me in service.

'I have always felt the aspiration, no matter how low I may have fallen, to struggle upwards to a position above me; to rise, in spite of fortune, superior to my lot in life. Perhaps some of my father's pride may be at the root of this restless feeling in me. It seems to be a part of my nature. It brought me into this house, and it will go with me out of this house. Is it my curse, or my blessing? I am not able to decide.

'On the first night when I slept in my new home, I said to myself: "They have taken me to be their servant; I will be something more than that; they shall end in taking me for their child." Before I had been a week in the house I was my mistress's favourite companion, while my master was at his place of business. She was a highly-accomplished woman; greatly her husband's superior in cultivation, and, unfortunately for herself, also his superior in years. The love was all on her side. Excepting certain occasions on which he roused her jealousy, they lived together on sufficiently friendly terms. She was one of the many wives who resign themselves to be disappointed in their husbands, and he was one of the many husbands who never know what their wives really think of them. Her one great happiness was in teaching me. I was eager to learn; I made rapid progress. At my pliant age I soon acquired the refinements of language and manner which characterised my mistress. It is only the truth to say, that the cultivation which has made me capable of personating a lady was her work.

'For three happy years I lived under that friendly roof. I was between fifteen and sixteen years of age when the fatal inheritance from my mother cast its first shadow on my life. One miserable day the wife's maternal love for me changed, in an instant, to the jealous hatred that never forgives. Can you guess the reason? The husband fell in love with me.

'I was innocent; I was blameless. He owned it himself to the clergyman who was with him at his death. By that time years had passed – it was too late to justify me.

'He was at an age (while I was under his care) when men are usually supposed to regard women with tranquillity, if not with indifference. It had been the habit of years with me to look upon him as my second father. In my innocent ignorance of the feeling which really inspired him, I permitted him to indulge in little paternal familiarities with me, which inflamed his guilty passion. His wife discovered him – not I. No words can describe my astonishment and my horror when the first outbreak of her indignation forced on me the knowledge of the truth. On my knees I declared myself guiltless. On my knees I implored her to do justice to my purity and my youth. At other times the sweetest and the most considerate of women, jealousy had now transformed her to a perfect fury. She accused me of deliberately encouraging him; she declared she would turn me out of the house with her own hands. Like other easy-tempered men, her husband had reserves of anger in him which it was dangerous to provoke. When his wife lifted her hand against me he lost all self-control on his side. He openly told her that life was worth nothing to him, without me; he openly avowed his resolution to go with me when I left the house. The maddened woman seized him by the arm – I saw that, and saw no more. I ran out into the street, panic-stricken. A cab was passing. I got into it, before he could open the house-door, and drove to the only place of refuge I could think of – a small shop, kept by the widowed sister of one of our servants. Here I obtained shelter for the night. The next day he discovered me. He made his vile proposals; he offered me the whole of his fortune; he declared his resolution, say what I might, to return the next day. That night, by help of the good woman who had taken care of me – under cover of the darkness, as if *I* had been to blame! – I was secretly removed to the East End of London, and placed under the charge of a trustworthy person who lived, in a very humble way, by letting lodgings.

'Here, in a little back garret at the top of the house, I was thrown again on the world – at an age when it was doubly perilous for me to be left to my own resources to gain the bread I eat, and the roof that covered me.

'I claim no credit to myself – young as I was; placed as I was between the easy life of Vice and the hard life of Virtue – for acting as I did. The man simply horrified me: my natural impulse was to escape from him. But let it be remembered, before I approach the saddest part of my sad story, that I was an innocent girl, and that I was at least not to blame.

'Forgive me for dwelling as I have done on my early years. I shrink from speaking of the events that are still to come.

'In losing the esteem of my first benefactress, I had, in my friendless position, lost all hold on an honest life – except the one frail hold of needlework. The only reference of which I could now dispose, was the recommendation of me by my landlady to a place of business which largely employed expert needlewomen. It is needless for me to tell you how miserably work of that sort is remunerated – you have read about it in the newspapers. As long as my health lasted, I contrived to live and to keep out of debt. Few girls could have resisted as long as I did the slow-poisoning influences of crowded workrooms, insufficient nourishment, and almost total privation of exercise. My life as a child had been a life in the open air – it had helped to strengthen a constitution naturally hardy, naturally free from all taint of hereditary disease. But my time came at last. Under the cruel stress laid on it, my health gave way. I was struck down by low fever, and sentence was pronounced on me by my fellow-lodgers: "Ah poor thing, *her* troubles will soon be at an end!"

'The prediction might have proved true – I might never have committed the errors and endured the sufferings of after-years – if I had fallen ill in another house.

'But it was my good, or my evil fortune – I dare not say which – to have interested in myself and my sorrows an actress at a suburban theatre, who occupied the room under mine. Except when her stage-duties took her away for two or three hours in the evening, this noble creature never left my bedside. Ill as she could afford it, her purse paid my inevitable expenses while I lay helpless. The landlady, moved by her example, accepted half the weekly rent of my room. The doctor, with the Christian kindness of his profession, would take no fees. All that the tenderest care could accomplish was lavished on me; my youth and my constitution did the rest. I struggled back to life – and then I took up my needle again.

'It may surprise you that I should have failed (having an actress for my dearest friend) to use the means of introduction thus offered to me to try the stage – especially as my childish training had given me, in some small degree, a familiarity with the art.

'I had only one motive for shrinking from an appearance at the theatre; but it was strong enough to induce me to submit to any alternative that remained, no matter how hopeless it might be. If I showed myself on the public stage, my discovery by the man from whom I had escaped would be only a question of time. I knew him to be habitually a playgoer, and a subscriber to a theatrical newspaper. I had even heard him speak of the theatre to which my friend was attached, and compare it advantageously with places of amusement of far higher pretensions. Sooner or later, if I joined the company, he would be certain to go and see "the new actress." The bare thought of it reconciled me to returning to my needle. Before I was strong enough to endure the atmosphere of the crowded workroom, I obtained permission, as a favour, to resume my occupation at home.

'Surely my choice was the choice of a virtuous girl? And yet, the day when I returned to my needle was the fatal day of my life.

'I had now not only to provide for the wants of the passing hour – I had my debts to pay. It was only to be done by toiling harder than ever, and by living more poorly than ever. I soon paid the penalty, in my weakened state, of leading such a life as this. One evening my head turned suddenly giddy; my heart throbbed frightfully. I managed to open the window, and to let the fresh air into the room; and I felt better. But I was not sufficiently recovered to be able to thread my needle. I thought to myself, "If I go out for half an hour, a little exercise may put me right again." I had not, as I suppose, been out more than ten minutes, when the attack from which I had suffered in my room was renewed. There was no shop near in which I could take refuge. I tried to ring the bell of the nearest house-door. Before I could reach it, I fainted in the street.

'How long hunger and weakness left me at the mercy of the first stranger who might pass by, it is impossible for me to say.

'When I partially recovered my senses I was conscious of being under shelter somewhere, and of having a wine glass containing some cordial drink held to my lips by a man. I managed to swallow – I don't know how little, or how much. The stimulant had a very strange effect on me. Reviving me at first, it ended in stupefying me. I lost my senses once more.

'When I next recovered myself, the day was breaking. I was in a bed, in a strange room. A nameless terror seized me. I

called out. Three or four women came in, whose faces betrayed
even to my inexperienced eyes the shameless infamy of their
lives. I started up in the bed; I implored them to tell me where
I was and what had happened——

'Spare me! I can say no more. Not long since, you heard Miss
Roseberry call me an outcast from the streets. Now you know
– as God is my judge I am speaking the truth! – now you know
what made me an outcast, and in what measure I deserved my
disgrace.'

Her voice faltered, her resolution failed her, for the first time.

'Give me a few minutes,' she said, in low, pleading tones. 'If
I try to go on now, I am afraid I shall cry.'

She took the chair which Julian had placed for her, turning
her face aside so that neither of the men could see it. One of
her hands was pressed over her bosom, the other hung listlessly
at her side.

Julian rose from the place that he had occupied. Horace
neither moved nor spoke. His head was on his breast; the traces
of tears on his cheeks suggested that she had not quite failed to
touch his heart. Would he forgive her? Julian passed on, and
approached Mercy's chair.

In silence he took the hand which hung at her side. In silence
he lifted it to his lips and kissed it, as her brother might have
kissed it. She started, but she never looked up. Some strange
fear of discovery seemed to possess her. 'Horace?' she whispered
timidly. Julian made no reply. He went back to his place, and
allowed her to think it was Horace.

The sacrifice was immense enough – feeling towards her as
he felt – to be worthy of the man who made it.

A few minutes had been all she asked for. In a few minutes
she turned towards them again. Her sweet voice was steady
once more; her eyes rested softly on Horace as she went on.

'What was it possible for a friendless girl in my position to do,
when the full knowledge of the outrage had been revealed to me?

'If I had possessed near and dear relatives to protect and advise
me, the wretches into whose hands I had fallen might have felt

the penalty of the law. I knew no more of the formalities which set the law in motion than a child. But I had another alternative (you will say). Charitable societies would have received me and helped me, if I had stated my case to them. I knew no more of the charitable societies than I knew of the law. At least, then, I might have gone back to the honest people among whom I had lived? When I recovered my freedom, after an interval of some days, I was ashamed to go back to the honest people. Helplessly and hopelessly, without sin or choice of mine, I drifted, as thousands of other women have drifted, into the life which set a mark on me for the rest of my days.

'Are you surprised at the ignorance which this confession reveals?

'You, who have your solicitors to inform you of legal remedies, and your newspapers, circulars, and active friends, to sound the praises of charitable institutions continually in your ears – you, who possess these advantages, have no idea of the outer world of ignorance in which your lost fellow-creatures live. They know nothing (unless they are rogues accustomed to prey on society) of your benevolent schemes to help them. The purpose of public charities, and the way to discover and apply to them, ought to be posted at the corner of every street. What do *we* know of public dinners, and eloquent sermons, and neatly-printed circulars? Every now and then the case of some forlorn creature (generally of a woman), who has committed suicide, within five minutes' walk perhaps of an institution which would have opened its doors to her, appears in the newspapers, shocks you dreadfully, and is then forgotten again. Take as much pains to make charities and asylums known among the people *without* money, as are taken to make a new play, a new journal, or a new medicine known among the people *with* money, and you will save many a lost creature who is perishing now.

'You will forgive and understand me if I say no more of this period of my life. Let me pass to the new incident in my career which brought me for the second time before the public notice in a court of law.

'Sad as my experience has been, it has not taught me to think ill of human nature. I had found kind hearts to feel for me in my former troubles; and I had friends – faithful, self-denying, generous friends – among my sisters in adversity now. One of these poor women (she has gone, I am glad to think, from the world that used her so hardly!) especially attracted my sympathies. She was the gentlest, the most unselfish creature I have ever met with. We lived together like sisters. More than once, in the dark hours when the thought of self-destruction comes to a desperate woman, the image of my poor devoted friend, left to suffer alone, rose in my mind and restrained me. You will hardly understand it, but even *we* had our happy days. When she or I had a few shillings to spare, we used to offer one another little presents. And, stranger still, we enjoyed our simple pleasure in giving and receiving as keenly as if we had been the most reputable women living!

'One day I took my friend into a shop to buy her a ribbon – only a bow for her dress. She was to choose it, and I was to pay for it, and it was to be the prettiest ribbon that money could buy.

'The shop was full; we had to wait a little before we could be served.

'Next to me, as I stood at the counter with my companion, was a gaudily-dressed woman, looking at some handkerchiefs. The handkerchiefs were finely embroidered, but the smart lady was hard to please. She tumbled them up disdainfully in a heap, and asked for other specimens from the stock in the shop. The man, in clearing the handkerchiefs out of the way, suddenly missed one. He was quite sure of it, from a peculiarity in the embroidery which made the handkerchief especially noticeable. I was poorly dressed, and I was close to the handkerchiefs. After one look at me, he shouted to the superintendent, "Shut the door! There is a thief in the shop!"

'The door was closed; the lost handkerchief was vainly sought for on the counter and on the floor. A robbery had been committed; and I was accused of being the thief.

'I will say nothing of what I felt – I will only tell you what happened.

'I was searched, and the handkerchief was discovered on me. The woman who had stood next to me, on finding herself threatened with discovery, had no doubt contrived to slip the stolen handkerchief into my pocket. Only an accomplished thief could have escaped detection in that way, without my knowledge. It was useless, in the face of the facts, to declare my innocence. I had no character to appeal to. My friend tried to speak for me; but what was she? Only a lost woman like myself. My landlady's evidence in favour of my honesty produced no effect; it was against her that she let lodgings to people in my position. I was prosecuted, and found guilty. The tale of my disgrace is now complete, Mr Holmcroft. No matter whether I was innocent or not; the shame of it remains − I have been imprisoned for theft.

'The matron of the prison was the next person who took an interest in me. She reported favourably of my behaviour to the authorities; and when I had served my time (as the phrase was among us) she gave me a letter to the kind friend and guardian of my later years − to the lady who is coming here to take me back with her to the Refuge.

'From this time the story of my life is little more than the story of a woman's vain efforts to recover her lost place in the world.

'The matron, on receiving me into the Refuge, frankly acknowledged that there were terrible obstacles in my way. But she saw that I was sincere, and she felt a good woman's sympathy and compassion for me. On my side, I did not shrink from beginning the slow and weary journey back again to a reputable life, from the humblest starting-point − from domestic service. After first earning my new character in the Refuge, I obtained a trial in a respectable house. I worked hard, and worked uncomplainingly; but my mother's fatal legacy was against me from the first. My personal appearance excited remark; my manners and habits were not the manners and habits of the women among whom my lot was cast. I tried one place after another − always with the same results. Suspicion and jealousy I could endure: but I was defenceless when curiosity assailed me in its turn. Sooner or later enquiry led to discovery. Sometimes the servants threatened to give warning in a body − and I was obliged to go. Sometimes, when there was a young man in the family, scandal pointed at me and at him – and again I was obliged to go. If you care to know it, Miss Roseberry can tell you the story of those sad days. I confided it to her on the memorable night when we met in the French cottage; I have no heart to repeat it now. After a while I wearied of the hopeless struggle. Despair laid its hold on me – I lost all hope in the mercy of God. More than once I walked to one or other of the bridges, and looked over the parapet at the river, and said to myself, "Other women have done it: why shouldn't I?"

'You saved me at that time, Mr Gray – as you have saved me since. I was one of your congregation when you preached in the chapel of the Refuge. You reconciled others besides me to our hard pilgrimage. In their name, and in mine, sir, I thank you.

'I forget how long it was after the bright day when you comforted and sustained us that the war broke out between France and Germany. But I can never forget the evening when the matron sent for me into her own room, and said, "My dear, your life here is a wasted life. If you have courage enough left to try it, I can give you another chance."

'I passed through a month of probation in a London hospital. A week after that, I wore the red cross of the Geneva Convention – I was appointed nurse in a French ambulance. When you first saw me, Mr Holmcroft, I still had my nurse's dress on, hidden from you and from everybody under a grey cloak.

'You know what the next event was; you know how I entered this house.

'I have not tried to make the worst of my trials and troubles in telling you what my life has been. I have honestly described it for what it was when I met with Miss Roseberry – a life without hope. May you never know the temptation that tried me when the shell struck its victim in the French cottage. There she lay – dead! *Her* name was untainted. *Her* future promised me the reward which had been denied to the honest efforts of a penitent woman. My lost place in the world was offered back to me on the one condition, that I stooped to win it by a fraud. I had no prospect to look forward to; I had no friend near to advise me and to save me; the fairest years of my womanhood had been wasted in the vain struggle to recover my good name. Such was my position when the possibility of personating Miss Roseberry first forced itself on my mind. Impulsively, recklessly – wickedly, if you like – I seized the opportunity, and let you pass me through the German lines under Miss Roseberry's name. Arrived in England, having had time to reflect, I made my first and last effort to draw back before it was too late. I went to the Refuge, and stopped on the opposite side of the street looking at it. The old hopeless life of irretrievable disgrace confronted me as I fixed my eyes on the familiar door; the horror of returning to that life was more than I could force myself to endure. An empty cab passed me at the moment. The driver held up his hand. In sheer despair I stopped him; and when he said "Where to?" – in sheer despair again, I answered, "Mablethorpe House."

'Of what I have suffered in secret since my own successful deception established me under Lady Janet's care I shall say nothing. Many things which must have surprised you in my conduct are made plain to you by this time. You must have noticed long since that I was not a happy woman. Now you know why.

'My confession is made; my conscience has spoken at last. You are released from your promise to me – you are free. Thank Mr Julian Gray if I stand here, self-accused of the offence that I have committed, before the man whom I have wronged.'

CHAPTER THE TWENTY-EIGHTH

SENTENCE IS PRONOUNCED ON HER

It was done. The last tones of her voice died away in silence.

Her eyes still rested on Horace. After hearing what he had heard, could he resist that gentle, pleading look? Would he forgive her? Awhile since, Julian had seen tears on his cheeks, and had believed that he felt for her. Why was he now silent? Was it possible that he only felt for himself?

For the last time — at the crisis of her life — Julian spoke for her. He had never loved her as he loved her at that moment; it tried even his generous nature to plead her cause with Horace against himself. But he had promised her, without reserve, all the help that her truest friend could offer. Faithfully and manfully he redeemed his promise.

'Horace!' he said.

Horace slowly looked up. Julian rose and approached him.

'She has told you to thank *me*, if her conscience has spoken. Thank the noble nature which answered when I called upon it! Own the priceless value of a woman who can speak the truth. Her heartfelt repentance is a joy in Heaven. Shall it not plead for her on earth? Honour her, if you are a Christian. Feel for her, if you are a man!'

He waited. Horace never answered him.

Mercy's eyes turned tearfully on Julian. *His* heart was the heart that felt for her! *His* words were the words which comforted and pardoned her! When she looked back again at Horace, it was with an effort. His last hold on her was lost. In her inmost mind a thought rose unbidden — a thought which was not to be repressed. 'Can I ever have loved this man?'

She advanced a step toward him; it was not possible, even yet, to completely forget the past. She held out her hand.

He rose, on his side — without looking at her.

'Before we part for ever,' she said to him, 'will you take my hand as a token that you forgive me?'

He hesitated. He half lifted his hand. The next moment the generous impulse died away in him. In its place came the mean fear of what might happen if he trusted himself to the dangerous fascination of her touch. His hand dropped again at his side; he turned away quickly.

'I can't forgive her!' he said.

With that horrible confession — without even a last look at her — he left the room.

At the moment when he opened the door, Julian's contempt for him burst its way through all restraints.

'Horace,' he said, 'I pity you!'

As the words escaped him, he looked back at Mercy. She had turned aside from both of them – she had retired to a distant part of the library. The first bitter foretaste of what was in store for her when she faced the world again had come to her from Horace! The energy which had sustained her thus far, quailed before the dreadful prospect – doubly dreadful to a woman – of obloquy and contempt. Hopeless and helpless, she sank on her knees before a little couch in the darkest corner of the room. 'Oh, Christ, have mercy on me!' That was her prayer – no more.

Julian followed her. He waited little. Then his kind hand touched her; his friendly voice fell consolingly on her ear.

'Rise, poor wounded heart! Beautiful, purified soul, God's angels rejoice over you! Take your place among the noblest of Gods creatures!'

He raised her as he spoke. All her heart went out to him. She caught his hand – she pressed it to her bosom; she pressed it to her lips – then dropped it suddenly, and stood before him trembling like a frightened child.

'Forgive me!' was all she could say. 'I was so lost and lonely – and you are so good to me!'

She tried to leave him. It was useless – her strength was gone; she caught at the head of the couch to support herself. He looked at her. The confession of his love was just rising to his lips – he looked again, and checked it. No; not at that moment; not when she was helpless and ashamed; not when her weakness might make her yield, only to regret it at a later time. The great heart which had spared her and felt for her from the first, spared her and felt for her now.

He, too, left her – but not without a word at parting.

'Don't think of your future life just yet,' he said, gently. 'I have something to propose when rest and quiet have restored you.' He opened the nearest door – the door of the dining-room – and went out.

The servants engaged in completing the decoration of the dinner-table noticed, when 'Mr Julian' entered the room, that his eyes were 'brighter than ever.' He looked (they remarked) like a man who 'expected good news.' They were inclined to suspect – though he was certainly rather young for it – that her ladyship's nephew was in a fair way of preferment in the church.

* * *

Mercy seated herself on the couch.

There are limits, in the physical organisation of man, to the action of pain. When suffering has reached a given point of intensity, the nervous sensibility becomes incapable of feeling more. The rule of Nature in this respect, applies not only to sufferers in the body, but to sufferers in the mind as well. Grief, rage, terror, have also their appointed limits. The moral sensibility, like the nervous sensibility, reaches its period of absolute exhaustion, and feels no more.

The capacity for suffering in Mercy had attained its term. Alone in the library, she could feel the physical relief of repose; she could vaguely recall Julian's parting words to her, and sadly wonder what they meant – and she could do no more.

An interval passed: a brief interval of perfect rest.

She recovered herself sufficiently to be able to look at her watch and to estimate the lapse of time that might yet pass before Julian returned to her as he had promised. While her mind was still languidly following this train of thought, she was disturbed by the ringing of a bell in the hall, used to summon the servant whose duties were connected with that part of the house. In leaving the library, Horace had gone out by the door which led into the hall, and had failed to close it. She plainly heard the bell – and a moment later (more plainly still) she heard Lady Janet's voice!

She started to her feet. Lady Janet's letter was still in the pocket of her apron – the letter which imperatively commanded her to abstain from making the very confession that had just passed her lips! It was near the dinner hour; and the library was the favourite place in which the mistress of the house and her guests assembled at that time. It was no matter of doubt; it was an absolute certainty that Lady Janet had only stopped in the hall on her way into the room.

The alternative for Mercy lay between instantly leaving the library by the dining-room door – or remaining where she was, at the risk of being sooner or later compelled to own that she had deliberately disobeyed her benefactress. Exhausted by what she had already suffered, she stood trembling and irresolute, incapable of deciding which alternative she should choose.

Lady Janet's voice, clear and resolute, penetrated into the room. She was reprimanding the servant who had answered the bell.

'Is it your duty in my house to look after the lamps?'

'Yes, my lady.'

'And is it my duty to pay you your wages?'

'If you please, my lady.'

'Why do I find the light in the hall dim, and the wick of that lamp smoking? I have not failed in my duty to You. Don't let me find you failing again in your duty to Me.'

(Never had Lady Janet's voice sounded so sternly in Mercy's ear as it sounded now. If she spoke with that tone of severity to a servant who had neglected a lamp, what had her adopted daughter to expect, when she discovered that her entreaties and her commands had been alike set at defiance?)

Having administered her reprimand, Lady Janet had not done with the servant yet. She had a question to put to him next.

'Where is Miss Roseberry?'

'In the library, my lady.'

Mercy returned to the couch. She could stand no longer; she had no resolution enough left to lift her eyes to the door.

Lady Janet came in more rapidly than usual. She advanced to the couch, and tapped Mercy playfully on the cheek with two of her fingers.

'You lazy child! Not dressed for dinner? Oh, fie, fie!'

Her tone was as playfully affectionate as the action which had accompanied her words. In speechless astonishment Mercy looked up at her.

Always remarkable for the taste and splendour of her dress, Lady Janet had, on this occasion, surpassed herself. There she stood revealed in her grandest velvet, her richest jewellery, her finest lace — with no one to entertain at the dinner-table but the ordinary members of the circle of Mablethorpe House. Noticing this as strange to begin with, Mercy further observed, for the first time in her experience, that Lady Janet's eyes avoided meeting hers. The old lady took her place companionably on the couch; she ridiculed her 'lazy child's' plain dress, without an ornament of any sort on it, with her best grace; she affectionately put her arm round Mercy's waist, and re-arranged with her own hand the disordered locks of Mercy's hair — but the instant Mercy herself looked at her, Lady Janet's eyes discovered something supremely interesting in the familiar objects that surrounded her on the library walls.

How were these changes to be interpreted? To what possible conclusion did they point?

Julian's profounder knowledge of human nature, if Julian had been present, might have found the clue to the mystery. *He* might have surmised (incredible as it was) that Mercy's timidity before Lady Janet was fully reciprocated by Lady Janet's timidity before Mercy. It was even so. The woman whose immovable composure had conquered Grace Roseberry's utmost insolence in the hour of her triumph — the woman who, without once flinching, had faced every other consequence of her resolution to ignore Mercy's true position in the house — quailed for the first time, when she found herself face to face with the very person for whom she had suffered and sacrificed so much. She had shrunk from the meeting with Mercy, as Mercy had shrunk from the meeting with *her*. The splendour of her dress meant simply that, when other excuses for delaying the meeting downstairs had all been exhausted, the excuse of a long and elaborate toilet had been tried next. Even the moments occupied in reprimanding the servant had been moments seized on as the pretext for another delay. The hasty entrance into the room, the nervous assumption of playfulness in language and manner, the evasive and wandering eyes, were all referable to the same cause. In the presence of others, Lady Janet had successfully silenced the protest of her own inbred delicacy and inbred sense of honour. In the presence of Mercy, whom she loved with a mother's love – in the presence of Mercy, for whom she had stooped to deliberate concealment of the truth – all that was high and noble in the woman's nature rose in her and rebuked her. 'What will the daughter of my adoption, the child of my first and last experience of maternal love, think of me, now that I have made myself an accomplice in the fraud of which she is ashamed? How can I look her in the face, when I have not hesitated, out of selfish consideration for my own tranquillity, to forbid that frank avowal of the truth which her finer sense of duty had spontaneously bound her to make?' Those were the torturing questions in Lady Janet's mind, while her arm was wound affectionately round Mercy's waist, while her fingers were busying themselves familiarly with the arrangement of Mercy's hair. Thence, and thence only, sprang the impulse which set her talking, with an uneasy affectation of frivolity, of any topic within the range of conversation – so long as it related to the future, and completely ignored the present and the past.

'The winter here is unendurable,' Lady Janet began. 'I have been thinking, Grace, about what we had better do next.'

Mercy started. Lady Janet had called her 'Grace.' Lady Janet was still deliberately assuming to be innocent of the faintest suspicion of the truth.

'No!' resumed her ladyship, affecting to misunderstand Mercy's movement, 'you are not to go up now and dress. There is no time, and I am quite ready to excuse you. You are a foil to me, my dear. You have reached the perfection of shabbiness. Ah! I remember when I had my whims and fancies too, and when I looked well in anything I wore, just

as you do. No more of that. As I was saying, I have been
thinking and planning what we are to do. We really can't
stay here. Cold one day, and hot the next – what a climate!
As for society, what do we lose if we go away? There is no
such thing as society now. Assemblies of well-dressed mobs
meet at each other's houses, tear each other's clothes, tread
on each other's toes. If you are particularly lucky you sit on
the staircase, you get a tepid ice, and you hear vapid talk in
slang phrases all round you. There is modern society. If we
had a good opera it would be something to stay in London
for. Look at the programme for the season on that table –
promising as much as possible on paper, and performing as
little as possible on the stage. The same works, sung by the
same singers year after year, to the same stupid people – in
short, the dullest musical evenings in Europe. No! The more
I think of it, the more plainly I perceive that there is but one
sensible choice before us: we must go abroad. Set that pretty
head to work; choose north or south, east or west; it's all the
same to me. Where shall we go?'

Mercy looked at her quickly as she put the question.

Lady Janet, more quickly yet, looked away at the
programme of the opera-house. Still the same melancholy
false pretences! Still the same useless and cruel delay!
Incapable of enduring the position now forced upon her,
Mercy put her hand into the pocket of her apron, and drew
from it Lady Janet's letter.

'Will your ladyship forgive me,' she began, in faint
faltering tones, 'if I venture on a painful subject? I hardly
dare acknowledge——' In spite of her resolution to speak
out plainly, the memory of past love and past kindness
prevailed with her; the next words died away on her lips.
She could only hold up the letter.

Lady Janet declined to see the letter. Lady Janet suddenly
became absorbed in the arrangement of her bracelets.

'I know what you daren't acknowledge, you foolish
child!' she exclaimed. 'You daren't acknowledge that you
are tired of this dull house. My dear! I am entirely of your
opinion – I am weary of my own magnificence; I long to

be living in one snug little room, with one servant to wait on me. I'll tell you what we will do. We will go to Paris in the first place. My excellent Migliore, prince of couriers, shall be the only person in attendance. He shall take a lodging for us in one of the unfashionable quarters of Paris. We will rough it, Grace (to use the slang phrase), merely for a change. We will lead what they call a "Bohemian life." I know plenty of writers and painters and actors in Paris – the liveliest society in the world, my dear, until one gets tired of them. We will dine at the restaurant, and go to the play, and drive about in shabby little hired carriages. And when it begins to get monotonous (which it is only too sure to do) we will spread our wings and fly to Italy, and cheat the winter in that way. There is a plan for you! Migliore is in town. I will send to him this evening, and we will start to-morrow.'

Mercy made another effort.

'I entreat your ladyship to pardon me,' she resumed. 'I have something serious to say. I am afraid——'

'I understand! You are afraid of crossing the Channel, and you don't like to say so plainly. Pooh! The passage barely lasts two hours; we will shut ourselves up in a private cabin. I will send at once – the courier may be engaged. Ring the bell.'

'Lady Janet, I must submit to my hard lot. I cannot hope to associate myself again with any future plans of yours——'

'What! you are afraid of our "Bohemian life" in Paris? Observe this, Grace! If there is one thing I hate more than another, it is "an old head on young shoulders." I say no more. Ring the bell.'

'This cannot go on, Lady Janet! No words can say how unworthy I feel of your kindness, how ashamed I am——'

'Upon my honour, my dear, I agree with you. You *ought* to be ashamed, at your age, of making me get up to ring the bell.'

Her obstinacy was immovable; she attempted to rise from the couch. But one choice was left to Mercy. She anticipated Lady Janet, and rang the bell.

The man-servant came in. He had his little letter tray in his hand, with a card on it, and a sheet of paper beside the card, which looked like an open letter.

'You know where my courier lives when he is in London?' asked Lady Janet.

'Yes, my lady.'

'Send one of the grooms to him on horseback; I am in a hurry. The courier is to come here without fail to-morrow morning – in time for the tidal train to Paris. You understand?'

'Yes, my lady.'

'What have you got there? Anything for me?'

'For Miss Roseberry, my lady.'

As he answered, the man handed the card and the open letter to Mercy.

'The lady is waiting in the morning-room, miss. She wished me to say she has time to spare, and she will wait for you if you are not ready yet.'

Having delivered his message in those terms, he withdrew.

Mercy read the name on the card. The Matron had arrived! She looked at the letter next. It appeared to be a printed circular, with some lines in pencil added on the empty page. Printed lines and written lines swam before her eyes. She felt, rather than saw, Lady Janet's attention steadily and suspiciously fixed on her. With the Matron's arrival, the foredoomed end of the flimsy false pretences and the cruel delays had come.

'A friend of yours, my dear?'

'Yes, Lady Janet.'

'Am I acquainted with her?'

'I think not, Lady Janet.'

'You appear to be agitated. Does your visitor bring bad news? Is there anything that I can do for you?'

'You can add – immeasurably add, madam – to all your past kindness, if you will only bear with me and forgive me.'

'Bear with you, and forgive you? I don't understand.'

'I will try to explain. Whatever else you may think of me, Lady Janet, for God's sake don't think me ungrateful.'

Lady Janet held up her hand for silence.

'I dislike explanations,' she said, sharply. 'Nobody ought to know that better than you. Perhaps the lady's letter will explain for you. Why have you not looked at it yet?'

'I am in great trouble, madam, as you noticed just now——'

'Have you any objection to my knowing who your visitor is?'

'No, Lady Janet.'

'Let me look at her card, then.'

Mercy gave the Matron's card to Lady Janet, as she had given the Matron's telegram to Horace.

Lady Janet read the name on the card – considered – decided that it was a name quite unknown to her – and looked next at the address: 'Western District Refuge, Milburn Road.'

'A lady connected with a Refuge?' she said, speaking to herself; 'and calling here by appointment – if I remember the servant's message? A strange time to choose, if she has come for a subscription!'

She paused. Her brow contracted; her face hardened. A word from her would now have brought the interview to its inevitable end, and she refused to speak the word. To the last moment she persisted in ignoring the truth! Placing the card on the couch at her side, she pointed with her long yellow-white forefinger to the printed letter lying side by side with her own letter on Mercy's lap.

'Do you mean to read it, or not?' she asked.

Mercy lifted her eyes, fast filling with tears, to Lady Janet's face.

'May I beg that your ladyship will read it for me?' she said – and placed the Matron's letter in Lady Janet's hand.

It was a printed circular announcing a new development in the charitable work of the Refuge. Subscribers were informed that it had been decided to extend the shelter and the training of the institution (thus far devoted to fallen women alone) so as to include destitute and helpless children found wandering in the streets. The question of the number of children to be thus rescued and protected was left dependent, as a matter of course, on the bounty of the friends of the Refuge; the cost of the maintenance of each one child being stated at the lowest possible rate. A list of influential persons who had increased their subscriptions so as to cover the cost, and a brief statement of the progress already made with the new work, completed the appeal, and brought the circular to its end.

The lines traced in pencil (in the Matron's hand-writing) followed on the blank page.

'Your letter tells me, my dear, that you would like — remembering your own childhood — to be employed when you return among us in saving other poor children left helpless on the world. Our circular will inform you that I am able to meet your wishes. My first errand this evening in your neighbourhood was to take charge of a poor child — a little girl — who stands sadly in need of our care. I have ventured to bring her with me, thinking she might help to reconcile you to the coming change in your life. You will find us both waiting to go back with you to the old house. I write this instead of saying it, hearing from the servant that you are not alone, and being unwilling to intrude myself, as a stranger, on the lady of the house.'

Lady Janet read the pencilled lines, as she had read the printed sentences, aloud. Without a word of comment, she laid the letter where she had laid the card; and, rising from her seat, stood for a moment in silence, looking at Mercy. The sudden change in her which the letter had produced — quietly as it had taken place — was terrible to see. On the frowning brow, in the flashing eyes, on the hardened lips, outraged love and outraged pride looked down on the lost woman, and said, as if in words, 'You have roused us at last.'

'If that letter means anything,' she began, 'it means you are about to leave my house. There can be but one reason for your taking such a step as that.'

'It is the only atonement I can make, madam——'

'I see another letter on your lap. Is it *my* letter?'

'Yes.'

'Have you read it?'

'I have read it.'

'Have you seen Horace Holmcroft?'

'Yes.'

'Have you told Horace Holmcroft——'

'Oh, Lady Janet——'

'Don't interrupt me. Have you told Horace Holmcroft what my letter positively forbade you to communicate, either to him or to any living creature? I want no protestations and excuses. Answer me instantly; and answer in one word – Yes, or No.'

Not even that haughty language, not even those pitiless tones, could extinguish in Mercy's heart the sacred memories of past kindness and past love. She fell on her knees – her outstretched hands touched Lady Janet's dress. Lady Janet sharply drew her dress away, and sternly repeated her last words.

'Yes, or No?'

'Yes.'

She had owned it at last! To this end Lady Janet had submitted to Grace Roseberry; had offended Horace Holmcroft; had stooped for the first time in her life to concealments and compromises that degraded her. After all that she had sacrificed and suffered – there Mercy knelt at her feet, self-convicted of violating her commands, trampling on her feelings, deserting her house! And who was the woman who had done this? The same woman who had perpetrated the fraud, and who had persisted in the fraud, until her benefactress had descended to become her accomplice. Then, and then only, she had suddenly discovered that it was her sacred duty to tell the truth!

In proud silence the great lady met the blow that had fallen on her. In proud silence she turned her back on her adopted daughter, and walked to the door.

Mercy made her last appeal to the generous friend whom she had offended – to the second mother whom she had loved.

'Lady Janet! Lady Janet! Don't leave me without a word. Oh, madam, try to feel for me a little! I am returning to a life of humiliation – the shadow of my old disgrace is falling on me once more. We shall never meet again. Even though

I have not deserved it, let my repentance plead with you! Say you forgive me!'

Lady Janet turned round on the threshold of the door.

'I never forgive ingratitude,' she said. 'Go back to the Refuge.'

The door opened, and closed on her. Mercy was alone again in the room.

Unforgiven by Horace, unforgiven by Lady Janet! She put her hands to her burning head – and tried to think. Oh, for the cool air of the night! Oh, for the friendly shelter of the Refuge! She could feel those sad longings in her; it was impossible to think.

She rang the bell – and shrank back the instant she had done it. Had *she* any right to take that liberty? She ought to have thought of it before she rang. Habit – all habit. How many hundreds of times she had rung the bell at Mablethorpe House!

The servant came in. She amazed the man – she spoke to him so timidly: she even apologised for troubling him!

'I am sorry to disturb you. Will you be so kind as to say to the lady that I am ready for her?'

'Wait to give that message,' said a voice behind them, 'until you hear the bell rung again.'

Mercy looked round in amazement. Julian had returned to the library by the dining-room door.

CHAPTER THE TWENTY-NINTH

THE LAST TRIAL

The servant left them together. Mercy spoke first.

'Mr Gray!' she exclaimed, 'why have you delayed my message? If you knew all, you would know that it is far from being a kindness to me to keep me in this house.'

He advanced closer to her — surprised by her words, alarmed by her looks.

'Has anyone been here in my absence?' he asked.

'Lady Janet has been here in your absence. I can't speak of it — my heart feels crushed — I can bear no more. Let me go!'

Briefly as she had replied, she had said enough. Julian's knowledge of Lady Janet's character told him what had happened. His face showed plainly that he was disappointed as well as distressed.

'I had hoped to have been with you when you and my aunt met, and to have prevented this,' he said. 'Believe me, she will atone for all that she may have harshly and hastily done, when she has had time to think. Try not to regret it, if she has made your hard sacrifice harder still. She has only raised you the higher — she has additionally ennobled you and endeared you in my estimation. Forgive me, if I own this in plain words. I cannot control myself, I feel too strongly.'

At other times Mercy might have heard the coming avowal in his tones, might have discovered it in his eyes. As it was, her delicate insight was dulled, her fine perception was blunted. She held out her hand to him, feeling a vague conviction that he was kinder to her than ever — and feeling no more.

'I must thank you for the last time,' she said. 'As long as life is left, my gratitude will be a part of my life. Let me go. While I have some strength left, let me go!'

She tried to leave him, and ring the bell. He held her hand firmly, and drew her closer to him.

'To the Refuge?' he asked.

'Yes!' she said. 'Home again!'

'Don't say that!' he exclaimed. 'I can't bear to hear it. Don't call the Refuge your home!'

'What else is it? Where else can I go?'

'I have come here to tell you. I said, if you remember, I had something to propose.'

She felt the fervent pressure of his hand; she saw the mounting enthusiasm flashing in his eyes. Her weary mind roused itself a little. She began to tremble under the electric influence of his touch.

'Something to propose?' she repeated. 'What is there to propose?'

'Let me ask you a question on my side. What have you done to-day?'

'You know what I have done – it is your work,' she answered humbly. 'Why return to it now?'

'I return to it for the last time; I return to it, with a purpose which you will soon understand. You have abandoned your marriage engagement; you have forfeited Lady Janet's love; you have ruined all your worldly prospects – you are now returning, self-devoted, to a life which you have yourself described as a life without hope. And all this you have done of your own free will – at a time when you are absolutely secure of your position in the house – for the sake of speaking the truth. Now tell me. Is a woman who can make that sacrifice a woman who will prove unworthy of the trust, if a man places in her keeping his honour and his name?'

She understood him at last. She broke away from him with a cry. She stood with her hands clasped, trembling and looking at him.

He gave her no time to think. The words poured from his lips, without conscious will or conscious effort of his own.

'Mercy, from the first moment when I saw you I loved you! You are free; I may own it; I may ask you to be my wife!'

She drew back from him farther and farther, with a wild, imploring gesture of her hand.

'No! no!' she cried. 'Think of what you are saying! Think of what you would sacrifice! It cannot, must not, be.'

His face darkened with a sudden dread. His head fell on his breast. His voice sank so low that she could barely hear it.

'I had forgotten something,' he said. 'You have reminded me of it.'

She ventured back a little nearer to him. 'Have I offended you?'

He smiled sadly. 'You have enlightened me. I had forgotten that it doesn't follow, because I love you, that you should love me in return. Say that it is so, Mercy — and I leave you.'

A faint tinge of colour rose on her face — then left it again paler than ever. Her eyes looked downward timidly under the eager gaze that he fastened on her.

'How *can* I say so?' she answered simply. 'Where is the woman in my place whose heart could resist you?'

He eagerly advanced; he held out his arms to her in breathless, speechless joy. She drew back from him once more with a look that horrified him — a look of blank despair.

'Am *I* fit to be your wife?' she asked. 'Must *I* remind you of what you owe to your high position, your spotless integrity, your famous name? Think of all you have done for me, and then think of the black ingratitude of it if I ruin you for life by consenting to our marriage — if I selfishly, cruelly, wickedly, drag you down to the level of a woman like me?'

'I raise you to *my* level when I make you my wife,' he answered. 'For heaven's sake do me justice! Don't refer me to the world and its opinions. It rests with you, and you alone, to make the misery or the happiness of my life. The world! Good God! What can the world give me in exchange for You?'

She clasped her hands imploringly; the tears flowed fast over her cheeks.

'Oh, have pity on my weakness!' she cried. 'Kindest, best of men, help me to do my hard duty towards you, it is *so* hard, after all that I have suffered — when my heart is yearning for peace and happiness and love!' She checked herself, shuddering at the words that had escaped her. 'Remember how Mr Holmcroft has used me! Remember how Lady Janet has left me! Remember what I have told you of my life! The scorn of every creature you know would strike at you through me. No! no! no! Not a word more. Spare me! pity me! leave me!'

Her voice failed her; sobs choked her utterance. He sprang to her and took her in his arms. She was incapable of resisting him; but there was no yielding in her. Her head lay on his bosom, passive – horribly passive, like the head of a corpse.

'Mercy! My darling! We will go away – we will leave England – we will take refuge among new people, in a new world – I will change my name – I will break with relatives, friends, everybody. Anything, anything, rather than lose you!'

She lifted her head slowly and looked at him.

He suddenly released her; he reeled back like a man staggered by a blow, and dropped into a chair. Before she had uttered a word he saw the terrible resolution in her face – Death, rather than yield to her own weakness and disgrace him.

She stood with her hands lightly clasped in front of her. Her grand head was raised; her soft grey eyes shone again undimmed by tears. The storm of emotion had swept over her and had passed away. A sad tranquillity was in her face; a gentle resignation was in her voice. The calm of a martyr was the calm that confronted him as she spoke her last words.

'A woman who has lived my life, a woman who has suffered what I have suffered, may love you – as *I* love you – but she must not be your wife. *That* place is too high above her. Any other place is too far below her and below you.' She paused, and advancing to the bell gave the signal for her departure. That done, she slowly retraced her steps until she stood at Julian's side.

Tenderly she lifted his head, and laid it for a moment on her bosom. Silently she stooped, and touched his forehead with her lips. All the gratitude that filled her heart and all the sacrifice that rent it, were in those two actions – so modestly, so tenderly performed! As the last lingering pressure of her fingers left him, Julian burst into tears.

The servant answered the bell. At the moment when he opened the door a woman's voice was audible, in the hall, speaking to him.

'Let the child go in,' the voice said. 'I will wait here.'

The child appeared – the same forlorn little creature who had reminded Mercy of her own early years, on the day

when she and Horace Holmcroft had been out for their
walk.

There was no beauty in *this* child; no halo of romance
brightened the commonplace horror of her story. She came
cringing into the room, staring stupidly at the magnificence
all round her – the daughter of the London streets! The pet
creation of the laws of political economy! the savage and
terrible product of a worn-out system of government and of
a civilisation rotten to its core! Cleaned for the first time in
her life; fed sufficiently for the first time in her life; dressed
in clothes instead of rags for the first time in her life, Mercy's
sister in adversity crept fearfully over the beautiful carpet,
and stopped wonderstruck before the marbles of an inlaid
table – a blot of mud on the splendour of the room.

Mercy turned from Julian to meet the child. The woman's
heart, hungering in its horrible isolation for something that it
might harmlessly love, welcomed the rescued waif of the
streets as a consolation sent from God. She caught the
stupefied little creature up in her arms. 'Kiss me!' she
whispered in the reckless agony of the moment. 'Call me
sister!' The child stared vacantly. Sister meant nothing to her
mind but an older girl who was strong enough to beat her.

She put the child down again, and turned for a last look at
the man whose happiness she had wrecked – in pity to *him*.

He had never moved. His head was down; his face was
hidden. She went back to him a few steps.

'The others have gone from me without one kind word.
Can *you* forgive me?'

He held out his hand to her without looking up. Sorely as
she had wounded him, his generous nature understood her.
True to her from the first, *he* was true to her still.

'God bless, and comfort you,' he said in broken tones.
'The earth holds no nobler woman than you.'

She knelt and kissed the kind hand that pressed hers for
the last time. 'It doesn't end with this world,' she whispered,
'there is a better world to come!' Then she rose, and went
back to the child. Hand-in-hand, the two citizens of the
Government of God – outcasts of the Government of Man –

passed slowly down the length of the room. Then, out into the hall. Then, out into the night. The heavy clang of the closing door tolled the knell of their departure. They were gone.

But the orderly routine of the house — inexorable as death — pursued its appointed course. As the clock struck the hour the dinner-bell rang. An interval of a minute passed, and marked the limit of delay. The butler appeared at the dining-room door.

'Dinner is served, sir.'

Julian looked up. The empty room met his eyes. Something white lay on the carpet close by him. It was her handkerchief — wet with her tears. He took it up, and pressed it to his lips. Was that to be the last of her? Had she left him for ever?

The native energy of the man, arming itself with all the might of his love, kindled in him again. No! While life was in him, while time was before him, there was the hope of winning her yet!

He turned to the servant, reckless of what his face might betray.

'Where is Lady Janet?'

'In the dining-room, sir.'

He reflected for a moment. His own influence had failed. Through what other influence could he now hope to reach her? As the question crossed his mind, the light broke on him. He saw the way back to her — through the influence of Lady Janet.

'Her ladyship is waiting, sir.'

Julian entered the dining-room.

THE END OF THE SECOND SCENE

EPILOGUE:

Containing

SELECTIONS FROM THE CORRESPONDENCE OF
MISS GRACE ROSEBERRY AND MR HORACE
HOLMCROFT

to which are added

EXTRACTS FROM THE DIARY OF THE
REVEREND JULIAN GRAY

I

FROM MR. HORACE HOLMCROFT TO MISS GRACE ROSEBERRY

'I hasten to thank you, dear Miss Roseberry, for your very kind letter, received by yesterday's mail from Canada. Believe me, I appreciate your generous readiness to pardon and forget what I so rudely said to you at a time when the arts of an adventuress had blinded me to the truth. In the grace which has forgiven me I recognise the inbred sense of justice of a true lady. Birth and breeding can never fail to assert themselves; I believe in them, thank God, more firmly than ever.

'You ask me to keep you informed of the progress of Julian Gray's infatuation, and of the course of conduct pursued towards him by Mercy Merrick.

'If you had not favoured me by explaining your object, I might have felt some surprise at receiving, from a lady in your position, such a request as this. But the motives by which you describe yourself as being actuated are beyond dispute. The existence of Society, as you truly say, is threatened by the present lamentable prevalence of Liberal ideas throughout the length and breadth of the land. We can only hope to protect ourselves against impostors interested in gaining a position among persons of our rank, by becoming in some sort (unpleasant as it may be) familiar with the arts by which imposture too frequently succeeds. If we wish to know to what daring lengths cunning can go, to what pitiable self-delusion credulity can consent, we must watch the proceedings – even while we shrink from them – of a Mercy Merrick and a Julian Gray.

'In taking up my narrative again, where my last letter left off, I must venture to set you right on one point.

'Certain expressions which have escaped your pen suggest to me that you blame Julian Gray as the cause of Lady Janet's regrettable visit to the Refuge, the day after Mercy Merrick had left her house. This is not quite correct. Julian, as you will presently see, has enough to answer for, without being held responsible for errors of judgment in which he has had no share. Lady Janet (as she herself told me) went to the Refuge of her own free-will, to ask Mercy Merrick's pardon for the language which she had used on the previous day. "I passed a night of such misery as no words can describe" – this, I assure you, is what her ladyship really said to me – "thinking over what my vile pride and selfishness and obstinacy had made me say and do. I would have gone down on my knees to beg her pardon if she would have let me. My first happy moment was when I won her consent to come and visit me sometimes at Mablethorpe House."

'You will, I am sure, agree with me that such extravagance as this is to be pitied rather than blamed. How sad to see the decay of the faculties with advancing age! It is a matter of grave anxiety to consider how much longer poor Lady Janet can be trusted to manage her own affairs. I shall take an opportunity of touching on the matter delicately when I next see her lawyer.

'I am straying from my subject. And – is it not strange? – I am writing to you as confidentially as if we were old friends.

'To return to Julian Gray. Innocent of instigating his aunt's first visit to the Refuge, he is guilty of having induced her to go there for the second time, the day after I had despatched my last letter to you. Lady Janet's object on this occasion was neither more nor less than to plead her nephew's cause as humble suitor for the hand of Mercy Merrick. Imagine the descendant of one of the oldest families in England inviting an adventuress in a Refuge to honour a clergyman of the Church of England by becoming his wife! In what times do we live! My dear mother shed tears of shame when she heard of it. How you would love and admire my mother!

'I dined at Mablethorpe House by previous appointment, on the day when Lady Janet returned from her degrading errand.

'"Well!" I said, waiting of course until the servant was out of the room.

'"Well," Lady Janet answered, "Julian was quite right."

'"Quite right in what?"

'"In saying that the earth holds no nobler woman than Mercy Merrick."

'"Has she refused him again?"

'"She has refused him again."

'"Thank God!" I felt it fervently, and I said so fervently. Lady Janet laid down her knife and fork, and fixed one of her fierce looks on me.

'"It may not be your fault, Horace," she said, "if your nature is incapable of comprehending what is great and generous in other natures higher than yours. But the least you can do is to distrust your own capacity of appreciation. For the future keep your opinions (on questions which you don't understand) modestly to yourself. I have a tenderness for you for your father's sake; and I take the most favourable view of your conduct towards Mercy Merrick. I humanely consider it the conduct of a fool." (Her own words, Miss Roseberry. I assure you once more, her own words.) "But don't trespass too far on my indulgence – don't insinuate again that a woman who is good enough (if she died this night) to go to Heaven, is *not* good enough to be my nephew's wife."

'I expressed to you my conviction a little way back, that it was doubtful whether poor Lady Janet would be much longer competent to manage her own affairs. Perhaps you thought me hasty, then? What do you think, now?

'It was of course useless to reply seriously to the extraordinary reprimand that I had received. Besides, I was really shocked by a decay of principle which proceeded but too plainly from decay of the mental powers. I made a soothing and respectful reply; and I was favoured in return with some account of what had really happened at the

Refuge. My mother and my sisters were disgusted when I repeated the particulars to them. You will be disgusted too.

'The interesting penitent (expecting Lady Janet's visit) was, of course, discovered in a touching domestic position! She had a foundling baby asleep on her lap and she was teaching the alphabet to an ugly little vagabond girl whose acquaintance she had first made in the street. Just the sort of artful *tableau vivant* to impose on an old lady – was it not?

'You will understand what followed, when Lady Janet opened her matrimonial negotiation. Having perfected herself in her part, Mercy Merrick, to do her justice, was not the woman to play it badly. The most magnanimous sentiments flowed from her lips. She declared that her future life was devoted to acts of charity, typified of course by the foundling infant and the ugly little girl. However she might personally suffer, whatever might be the sacrifice of her own feelings – observe how artfully this was put, to insinuate that she was herself in love with him! – she could not accept from Mr Julian Gray an honour of which she was unworthy. Her gratitude to him and her interest in him alike forbade her to compromise his brilliant future, by consenting to a marriage which would degrade him in the estimation of all his friends. She thanked him (with tears); she thanked Lady Janet (with more tears); but she dare not, in the interests of *his* honour and *his* happiness, accept the hand that he offered to her. God bless and comfort him; and God help her to bear with her hard lot.

'The object of this contemptible comedy is plain enough to my mind. She is simply holding off (Julian, as you know, is a poor man), until the influence of Lady Janet's persuasion is backed by the opening of Lady Janet's purse. In one word – Settlements! But for the profanity of the woman's language, and the really lamentable credulity of the poor old lady, the whole thing would make a fit subject for a burlesque.

'But the saddest part of the story is still to come.

'In due course of time, the lady's decision was communicated to Julian Gray. He took leave of his senses on the spot. Can you believe it? — he has resigned his curacy! At a time when the church is thronged every Sunday to hear him preach, this madman shuts the door and walks out of the pulpit. Even Lady Janet was not far enough gone in folly to abet him in this. She remonstrated, like the rest of his friends. Perfectly useless! He had but one answer to everything they could say: "My career is closed." What stuff!

'You will ask, naturally enough, what this perverse man is going to do next. I don't scruple to say that he is bent on committing suicide. Pray do not be alarmed! There is no fear of the pistol, the rope, or the river. Julian is simply courting death — within the limits of the law.

'This is strong language, I know. You shall hear what the facts are, and judge for yourself.

'Having resigned his curacy, his next proceeding was to offer his services, as volunteer, to a new missionary enterprise on the West Coast of Africa. The persons at the head of the Mission proved, most fortunately, to have a proper sense of their duty. Expressing their conviction of the value of Julian's assistance in the most handsome terms, they made it nevertheless a condition of entertaining his proposal that he should submit to examination by a competent medical man. After some hesitation he consented to this. The doctor's report was conclusive. In Julian's present state of health the climate of West Africa would in all probability kill him in three months' time.

'Foiled in his first attempt, he addressed himself next to a London Mission. Here, it was impossible to raise the question of climate; and here, I grieve to say, he has succeeded.

'He is now working — in other words, he is now deliberately risking his life — in the Mission to Green Anchor Fields. The district known by this name is situated in a remote part of London, near the Thames. It is notoriously infested by the most desperate and degraded set of wretches in the whole metropolitan population; and it is so thickly inhabited that it is hardly ever completely free from epidemic disease. In this horrible place, and among these dangerous people, Julian is now employing himself from morning to night. None of his old friends ever see him. Since he joined the Mission he has not even called on Lady Janet Roy.

'My pledge is redeemed – the facts are before you. Am I wrong in taking my gloomy view of the prospect? I cannot forget that this unhappy man was once my friend; and I really see no hope for him in the future. Deliberately self-exposed to the violence of ruffians and the outbreak of disease, who is to extricate him from his shocking position? The one person who can do it is the person whose association with him would be his ruin – Mercy Merrick. Heaven only knows what disasters it may be my painful duty to communicate to you in my next letter!

'You are so kind as to ask me to tell you something about myself and my plans.

'I have very little to say on either head. After what I have suffered – my feelings trampled on, my confidence betrayed – I am as yet hardly capable of deciding what I shall do. Returning to my old profession – to the army – is out of the question, in these levelling days, when any obscure person who can pass an examination may call himself my brother officer, and may one day perhaps command me as my superior in rank. If I think of any career, it is the career of diplomacy. Birth and breeding have not quite disappeared as essential qualifications in *that* branch of the public service. But I have decided nothing as yet.

'My mother and sisters, in the event of your returning to England, desire me to say that it will afford them the greatest pleasure to make your acquaintance. Sympathising with me, they do not forget what you too have suffered. A warm welcome awaits you when you pay your first visit at our house.

'Most truly yours,

'HORACE HOLMCROFT'

II

FROM MISS GRACE ROSEBERRY TO
MR HORACE HOLMCROFT

'DEAR MR HOLMCROFT,

'I snatch a few moments from my other avocations to thank you for your most interesting and delightful letter. How well you describe, how accurately you judge! If Literature stood a little higher as a profession, I should almost advise you – but no! if you entered Literature, how could *you* associate with the people whom you would be likely to meet?

'Between ourselves, I always thought Mr Julian Gray an over-rated man. I will not say he has justified my opinion. I will only say I pity him. But, dear Mr Holmcroft, how can you, with your sound judgment, place the sad alternatives now before him on the same level? To die in Green Anchor Fields, or to fall into the clutches of that vile wretch – is there any comparison between the two? Better a thousand times die at the post of duty than marry Mercy Merrick.

'As I have written the creature's name, I may add – so as to have all the sooner done with the subject – that I shall look with anxiety for your next letter. Do not suppose that I feel the smallest curiosity about this degraded and designing woman. My interest in her is purely religious. To persons of my devout turn of mind, she is an awful warning. When I feel Satan near me – it will be *such* a means of grace to think of Mercy Merrick!

'Poor Lady Janet! I noticed those signs of mental decay to which you so feelingly allude, at the last interview I had with her in Mablethorpe House. If you can find an opportunity, will you say that I wish her well, here and hereafter? and will you please add, that I do not omit to remember her in my prayers?

'There is just a chance of my visiting England towards the close of the autumn. My fortunes have changed since I wrote last. I have been received as reader and companion by a lady who is the wife of one of our high judicial functionaries in this part of the world. I do not take much interest in *him*; he is what they call a "self-made man." His wife is charming. Besides being a person of highly intellectual tastes, she is greatly her husband's superior — as you will understand when I tell you that she is related to the Gommerys of Pommery; *not* the Pommerys of Gommery, who (as your knowledge of our old families will inform you) only claim kindred with the younger branch of that ancient race.

'In the elegant and improving companionship which I now enjoy, I should feel quite happy but for one drawback. The climate of Canada is not favourable to my kind patroness; and her medical advisers recommend her to winter in London. In this event, I am to have the privilege of accompanying her. Is it necessary to add that my first visit will be paid at your house? I feel already united by sympathy to your mother and your sisters. There is a sort of freemasonry among gentlewomen, is there not? With best thanks and remembrances, and many delightful anticipations of your next letter, believe me, dear Mr Holmcroft,

'Truly yours,

'GRACE ROSEBERRY'

III

FROM MR HORACE HOLMCROFT TO MISS GRACE ROSEBERRY

'MY DEAR MISS ROSEBERRY,

'Pray excuse my long silence. I have waited for mail after mail, in the hope of being able to send you some good news at last. It is useless to wait longer. My worst forebodings have been realised: my painful duty compels me to write a letter which will surprise and shock you.

'Let me describe events in their order as they happened. In this way I may hope to gradually prepare your mind for what is to come.

'About three weeks after I wrote to you last, Julian Gray paid the penalty of his headlong rashness. I do not mean that he suffered any actual violence at the hands of the people among whom he had cast his lot. On the contrary, he succeeded, incredible as it may appear, in producing a favourable impression on the ruffians about him. As I understand it, they began by respecting his courage in venturing among them alone; and they ended in discovering that he was really interested in promoting their welfare. It is to the other peril, indicated in my last letter, that he has fallen a victim – the peril of disease. Not long after he began his labours in the district fever broke out. We only heard that Julian had been struck down by the epidemic when it was too late to remove him from the lodging that he occupied in the neighbourhood. I made enquiries personally the moment the news reached us. The doctor in attendance refused to answer for his life.

'In this alarming state of things, poor Lady Janet, impulsive and unreasonable as usual, insisted on leaving Mablethorpe House and taking up her residence near her nephew.

'Finding it impossible to persuade her of the folly of removing from home and its comforts at her age, I felt it my duty to accompany her. We found accommodation (such as it was) in a riverside inn, used by ship-captains and commercial travellers. I took it on myself to provide the best medical assistance; Lady Janet's insane prejudices against doctors impelling her to leave this important part of the arrangements entirely in my hands.

'It is needless to weary you by entering into details on the subject of Julian's illness.

'The fever pursued the ordinary course, and was characterised by the usual intervals of delirium and exhaustion succeeding each other. Subsequent events, which

it is, unfortunately, necessary to relate to you, leave me no
choice but to dwell (as briefly as possible) on the painful
subject of the delirium. In other cases, the wanderings of
fever-stricken people present, I am told, a certain variety of
range. In Julian's case they were limited to one topic. He
talked incessantly of Mercy Merrick. His invariable petition
to his medical attendants entreated them to send for her to
nurse him. Day and night that one idea was in his mind, and
that one name on his lips.

'The doctors naturally made enquiries as to this absent
person. I was obliged (in confidence) to state the
circumstances to them plainly.

'The eminent physician whom I had called in to
superintend the treatment behaved admirably. Though he
has risen from the lower order of the people, he has strange
to say, the instincts of a gentleman. He thoroughly
understood our trying position, and felt all the importance of
preventing such a person as Mercy Merrick from seizing the
opportunity of intruding herself at the bedside. A soothing
prescription (I have his own authority for saying it) was all
that was required to meet the patient's case. The local
doctor, on the other hand, a young man (and evidently a
red-hot Radical), proved to be obstinate, and, considering
his position, insolent as well. "I have nothing to do with the
lady's character and with your opinion of it," he said to me.
"I have only, to the best of my judgment, to point out to
you the likeliest means of saving the patient's life. Our art is
at the end of its resources. Send for Mercy Merrick, no
matter who she is or what she is. There is just a chance –
especially if she proves to be a sensible person and a good
nurse – that he may astonish you all by recognising her. In
that case only his recovery is probable. If you persist in
disregarding his entreaties, if you let the delirium go on for
four and twenty hours more, he is a dead man."

'Lady Janet was, most unluckily, present when this
impudent opinion was delivered at the bedside.

'Need I tell you the sequel? Called upon to choose
between the course indicated by a physician who is making

his five thousand a year, and who is certain of the next medical baronetcy, and the advice volunteered by an obscure general practitioner at the East End of London, who is not making his five hundred a year — need I stop to inform you of her ladyship's decision? You know her; and you will only too well understand that her next proceeding was to pay a third visit to the Refuge.

'Two hours later — I give you my word of honour I am not exaggerating — Mercy Merrick was established at Julian's bedside.

'The excuse, of course, was that it was her duty not to let any private scruples of her own stand in the way, when a medical authority had declared that she might save the patient's life. You will not be surprised to hear that I withdrew from the scene. The physician followed my example — after having written his soothing prescription, and having been grossly insulted by the local practitioner's refusal to make use of it. I went back in the doctor's carriage. He spoke most feelingly and properly. Without giving any positive opinion, I could see that he had abandoned all hope of Julian's recovery. "We are in the hands of Providence, Mr Holmcroft" — those were his last words as he set me down at my mother's door.

'I have hardly the heart to go on. If I studied my own wishes, I should feel inclined to stop here.

'Let me at least hasten to the end. In two or three days' time, I received my first intelligence of the patient and his nurse. Lady Janet informed me that he had recognised her. When I heard this I felt prepared for what was to come. The next report announced that he was gaining strength, and the next that he was out of danger. Upon this, Lady Janet returned to Mablethorpe House. I called there a week ago — and heard that he had been removed to the seaside. I called yesterday — and received the latest information from her ladyship's own lips. My pen almost refuses to write it. Mercy Merrick has consented to marry him!

'An Outrage on Society — that is how my mother and my sisters view it; that is how *you* will view it too. My mother has herself struck Julian's name off her invitation list. The servants have their orders if he presumes to call: "Not at home."

'I am unhappily only too certain that I am correct in writing to you of this disgraceful marriage as of a settled thing. Lady Janet went the length of showing me the letters – one from Julian; the other from the woman herself. Fancy Mercy Merrick in correspondence with Lady Janet Roy! – addressing her as "My dear Lady Janet," and signing, "Yours affectionately"!

'I had not the patience to read either of the letters through. Julian's tone is the tone of a Socialist; in my opinion his bishop ought to be informed of it. As for *her*, she plays her part just as cleverly with her pen as she played it with her tongue. "I cannot disguise from myself that I am wrong in yielding." . . . "Sad forebodings fill my mind when I think of the future." . . . "I feel as if the first contemptuous look that is cast at my husband will destroy *my* happiness though it may not disturb *him*." . . . "As long as I was parted from him I could control my own weakness; I could accept my hard lot. But how can I resist him, after having watched for weeks at his bedside; after having seen his first smile, and heard his first grateful words to me while I was slowly helping him back to life?"

'There is the tone which she takes through four closely written pages of nauseous humility and claptrap sentiment! It is enough to make one despise women. Thank God, there is the contrast at hand, to remind me of what is due to the better few among the sex. I feel that my mother and my sisters are doubly precious to me now. May I add, on the side of consolation, that I prize with hardly inferior gratitude, the privilege of corresponding with *you*?

'Farewell, for the present. I am too rudely shaken in my most cherished convictions, I am too depressed and disheartened, to write more. All good wishes go with you, dear Miss Roseberry, until we meet.

'Most truly yours,

'HORACE HOLMCROFT'

IV

EXTRACTS FROM THE DIARY OF THE REVEREND JULIAN GRAY

FIRST EXTRACT

. . . 'A month to-day since we were married! I have only one thing to say: I would cheerfully go through all that I have suffered, to live this one month over again. I never knew what happiness was until now. And better still, I have persuaded Mercy that it is all her doing. I have scattered her misgivings to the winds; she is obliged to submit to evidence, and to own that she *can* make the happiness of my life.

'We go back to London to-morrow. She regrets leaving the tranquil retirement of this remote seaside place − she dreads change. I care nothing for it. It is all one to me where I go so long as my wife is with me.'

SECOND EXTRACT

'The first cloud has risen. I entered the room unexpectedly just now, and found her in tears.

'With considerable difficulty I persuaded her to tell me what had happened. Are there any limits to the mischief that can be done by the tongue of a foolish woman? The landlady at my lodgings is the woman, in this case. Having no decided plans for the future as yet, we returned (most unfortunately as the event has proved) to the rooms in London which I inhabited in my bachelor days. They are still mine for six weeks to come, and Mercy was unwilling to let me incur the expense of taking her to an hotel. At breakfast this morning, I rashly congratulated myself (in my wife's hearing) on finding that a much smaller collection than usual of letters and cards had accumulated in my absence. Breakfast over, I was obliged to go out. Painfully sensitive, poor thing, to any change in my experience of the little world around me which it is possible to connect with the event of my marriage, Mercy questioned the landlady in my absence about the diminished number of my visitors and my correspondents. The woman seized the opportunity of gossiping about me and my affairs, and my wife's quick perception drew the right conclusion unerringly. My marriage has decided certain wise heads of families on discontinuing their social relations with me. The facts, unfortunately, speak for themselves. People who in former years habitually called upon me and invited me – or who, in the event of my absence, habitually wrote to me at this season – have abstained with a remarkable unanimity from calling, inviting, or writing now.

'It would have been sheer waste of time – to say nothing of its also implying a want of confidence in my wife – if I had attempted to set things right by disputing Mercy's conclusion. I could only satisfy her that not so much as the shadow of disappointment or mortification rested on *my* mind. In this way I have, to some extent, succeeded in composing my poor darling. But the wound has been inflicted, and the wound is felt. There is no disguising *that* result. I must face it boldly.

'Trifling as this incident is in my estimation, it has decided me on one point already. In shaping my future course, I am now resolved to act on my own convictions – in preference to taking the well-meant advice of such friends as are still left to me.

'Most of my success in life has been gained in the pulpit. I am what is termed a popular preacher – but I have never, in my secret self, felt any exultation in my own notoriety, or any extraordinary respect for the means by which it has been won. In the first place, I have a very low idea of the importance of oratory as an intellectual accomplishment. There is no other art in which the conditions of success are so easy of attainment; there is no other art in the practice of which so much that is purely superficial passes itself off habitually for something that claims to be profound. Then again, how poor it is in the results which it achieves! Take my own case. How often (for example) have I thundered with all my heart and soul against the wicked extravagance of dress amongst women – against their filthy false hair, and their nauseous powders and paints! How often (to take another example) have I denounced the mercenary and material spirit of the age, the habitual corruptions and dishonesties of commerce, in high places and in low! What good have I done? I have delighted the very people whom it was my object to rebuke. "What a charming sermon!" "More eloquent than ever!" "I used to dread the sermon at the other church – do you know I quite look forward to it now?" That is the effect I produce on Sunday. On Monday the women are off to the milliners to spend more money than ever; the City men are off to business to make more money than ever – while my grocer, loud in my praises in his Sunday coat, turns up his weekday sleeves and adulterates his favourite preacher's sugar as cheerfully as usual!

'I have often, in past years, felt the objections to pursuing my career which are here indicated. They were bitterly present to my mind when I resigned my curacy, and they strongly influence me now.

'I am weary of my cheaply-won success in the pulpit. I am weary of society as I find it in my time. I felt some respect for myself, and some heart and hope in my work, among the miserable wretches in Green Anchor Fields. But I cannot, and must not, return among them: I have no right, *now*, to trifle with my health and my life. I must go back to my preaching, or I must leave England. Among a primitive people; away from the cities – in the far and fertile West of the great American continent – I might live happily with my wife, and do good among my neighbours; secure of providing for our wants out of the modest little income which is almost useless to me here. In the life which I thus picture to myself I see love, peace, health, and duties and occupations that are worthy of a Christian man. What prospect is before me, if I take the advice of my friends and stay here? Work of which I am weary, because I have long

since ceased to respect it; petty malice that strikes at me
through my wife, and mortifies and humiliates her, turn
where she may. If I had only myself to think of, I might defy
the worst that malice can do. But I have Mercy to think of —
Mercy, whom I love better than my own life! Women live,
poor things, in the opinions of others. I have had one
warning already of what my wife is likely to suffer at the
hands of my "friends" — heaven forgive me for misusing the
word! Shall I deliberately expose her to fresh mortifications?
— and this for the sake of returning to a career the rewards of
which I no longer prize? No! We will both be happy — we
will both be free! God is merciful; Nature is kind; Love is
true, in the New World as well as the Old. To the New
World we will go!'

THIRD EXTRACT

'I hardly know whether I have done right or wrong. I
mentioned yesterday to Lady Janet the cold reception of me
on my return to London, and the painful sense of it felt by
my wife.

'My aunt looks at the matter from her own peculiar point
of view, and makes light of it accordingly. "You never did,
and never will, understand Society, Julian," said her ladyship.
"These poor stupid people simply don't know what to do.
They are waiting to be told by a person of distinction
whether they are, or are not, to recognise your marriage. In
plain English, they are waiting to be led by Me. Consider it
done. I will lead them."

'I thought my aunt was joking. The event of today has
shown me that she is terribly in earnest. Lady Janet has issued
invitations for one of her grand balls at Mablethorpe House;
and she has caused the report to be circulated everywhere
that the object of the festival is "to celebrate the marriage of
Mr and Mrs Julian Gray!"

'I at first refused to be present. To my amazement,
however, Mercy sides with my aunt. She reminds me of all

that we both owe to Lady Janet; and she has persuaded me to alter my mind. We are to go to the ball – at my wife's express request!

'The meaning of this, as I interpret it, is that my poor love is still pursued in secret by the idea that my marriage has injured me in the general estimation. She will suffer anything, risk anything, believe anything, to be freed from that one haunting thought. Lady Janet predicts a social triumph; and my wife's despair – not my wife's conviction – accepts the prophecy. As for me, I am prepared for the result. It will end in our going to the New World, and trying Society in its infancy, among the forests and the plains. I shall quietly prepare for our departure, and own what I have done at the right time – that is to say, when the ball is over.'

FOURTH EXTRACT

'I have met with the man for my purpose – an old college friend of mine, now partner in a firm of ship-owners, largely concerned in emigration.

'One of their vessels sails for America, from the port of London, in a fortnight; touching at Plymouth. By a fortunate coincidence, Lady Janet's ball takes place in a fortnight. I see my way.

'Helped by the kindness of my friend, I have arranged to have a cabin kept in reserve, on payment of a small deposit. If the ball ends (as I believe it will) in new mortifications for Mercy – do what they may, I defy them to mortify *me* – I have only to say the word by telegraph, and we shall catch the ship at Plymouth.

'I know the effect it will have when I break the news to her; but I am prepared with my remedy. The pages of my diary, written in past years, will show plainly enough that it is not *she* who is driving me away from England. She will see the longing in me for other work and other scenes, expressing itself over and over again, long before the time when we first met.'

FIFTH EXTRACT

'Mercy's ball-dress — a present from kind Lady Janet — is finished. I was allowed to see the first trial, or preliminary rehearsal, of this work of art. I don't in the least understand the merits of silk and lace; but one thing I know — my wife will be the most beautiful woman at the ball.

'The same day I called on Lady Janet to thank her, and encountered a new revelation of the wayward and original character of my dear old aunt.

'She was on the point of tearing up a letter when I went into her room. Seeing me, she suspended her purpose and handed me the letter. It was in Mercy's handwriting. Lady Janet pointed to a passage on the last page. "Tell your wife, with my love," she said, "that I am the most obstinate woman of the two. I positively refuse to read her, as I positively refuse to listen to her, whenever she attempts to return to that one subject. Now give me the letter back." I gave it back, and saw it torn up before my face. The one topic prohibited to Mercy as sternly as ever is still the personation of Grace Roseberry! Nothing could have been more naturally introduced, or more delicately managed, than my wife's brief reference to the subject. No matter. The reading of the first line was enough. Lady Janet shut her eyes and destroyed the letter — Lady Janet will live and die absolutely ignorant of the true story of "Mercy Merrick." What unanswerable riddles we are! Is it wonderful if we perpetually fail to understand one another?'

LAST EXTRACT

'The morning after the ball.

'It is done and over. Society has beaten Lady Janet. I have neither patience nor time to write at any length of it. We leave for Plymouth by the afternoon express.

'We were rather late in arriving at the ball. The magnificent rooms were filling fast. Walking through them with my wife, she drew my attention to a circumstance which I had not noticed at the time. "Julian," she said, "look round among the ladies, and tell me if you see anything strange." As I looked round the band began playing a waltz. I observed that a few people only passed by us to the dancing-room. I noticed next that of those few, fewer still were young. At last it burst upon me. With certain exceptions (so rare as to prove the rule), there were no young girls at Lady Janet's ball. I took Mercy at once back to the reception-room. Lady Janet's face showed that she too was aware of what had happened. The guests were still arriving. We received the men and their wives, the men and their mothers, the men and their grand-mothers – but, in place of their unmarried daughters, elaborate excuses offered with a shameless politeness wonderful to see. Yes! This was how the matrons in high life had got over the difficulty of meeting Mrs Julian Gray at Lady Janet's house!

'Let me do strict justice to everyone. The ladies who *were* present showed the needful respect for their hostess. They did their duty – no, overdid it, is perhaps the better phrase.

'I really had no adequate idea of the coarseness and rudeness which have filtered their way through society in these later times until I saw the reception accorded to my wife. The days of prudery and prejudice are days gone by. Excessive amiability and excessive liberality are the two favourite assumptions of the modern generation. To see the women expressing their liberal forgetfulness of my wife's misfortunes, and the men their amiable anxiety to encourage her husband – to hear the same set phrases repeated in every room: "So charmed to make your acquaintance, Mrs Gray; so *much* obliged to dear Lady Janet for giving us this opportunity! Julian, old man, what a beautiful creature! I envy you; upon my honour, I envy you!" – to receive this sort of welcome, emphasised by obtrusive hand-shakings, sometimes actually by downright kissings of my wife, and then to look round and see that not one in thirty of these very people had brought their unmarried daughters to the ball, was, I honestly believe, to see civilised human nature in its basest conceivable aspect. The New World may have its disappointments in store for us – but it cannot possibly show us any spectacle so abject as the spectacle which we witnessed last night at my aunt's ball.

'Lady Janet marked her sense of the proceeding adopted by her guests, by leaving them to themselves. Her guests remained and supped heartily notwithstanding. They all knew by experience that there were no stale dishes and no cheap wines at Mablethorpe House. They drank to the end of the bottle, and they ate to the last truffle in the pie.

'Mercy and I had an interview with my aunt upstairs before we left. I felt it necessary to state plainly my resolution to leave England. The scene that followed was so painful, that I cannot prevail on myself to return to it in these pages. My wife is reconciled to our departure; and Lady Janet accompanies us as far as Plymouth – these are the results. No words can express my sense of relief now that it is all settled. The one sorrow I shall carry away with me from the shores of England will be the sorrow of parting with dear warm-hearted Lady Janet. At her age it is a parting for life.

'So closes my connection with my own country. While I have Mercy by my side, I face the unknown future, certain of carrying my happiness with me, go where I may. We shall find five hundred adventurers like ourselves, when we join the emigrant ship, for whom their native land has no occupation and no home. Gentlemen of the Statistical Department, add two more to the number of social failures produced by England in the year of our Lord eighteen hundred and seventy-one – Julian Gray and Mercy Merrick.'